Green Stone Ring

Book One from the series Forever Friends

Novel by

Karleen Staible

www.kssnovels.com

www.facebook.com/KSSNovels

kssnovels@gmail.com

ISBN-13: 978-1546357858
ISBN-10: 1546357858

Acknowledgments

I would like to thank my friends and family who have encouraged me to pursue a writing career. Especially my mother and sister, who faithfully read the first draft to the end, even though it needed some work. And a big thanks to my two friends Jeanne and Claire. They both pushed me, back in 2010, to start writing, encouraged me to finish my first book, and then took the time to read it, critique it, and congratulate me for my efforts.

Then I found Margaret Diehl. She not only made corrections, but mentored me to open my mind to make the book much stronger and easier to read.

And a grateful thank you to Nancy for her hands-on lobbyist information, and what part these people play in our country's politics.

Of course, I couldn't have accomplished my mission without the understanding of my husband and his tolerance when I go into "project mode." He lovingly supports all that I do.

Prelude

Franco was going away again for at least three more months, and probably more, just like the last time. Oh, sure, he was very attentive at first, calling nearly every night, then once a week, but before he came back, nothing. Gini wasn't certain how long it would be this time from the way he talked. He said he had missed her as much as she missed him, but if that were true, how could he leave her again?

Her new job was exciting and keeping her busy—filling some of the lonely hours. And it had been great the last two weeks with him there to do the cooking, cleaning, and laundry, while she set up all her contact spreadsheets. She loved being wrapped in his arms when she was so tired she could hardly move. Waking in the morning with him by her side was what she always wanted to feel—that happy feeling of being in love.

Two days, that's all she had with him before he left again. Back to *that* loneliness, that awful, awful quiet in the house. The endless decision on what to fix for dinner—dinner for one. How could he leave her again? Didn't he long to be with her all the time as she did him?

She could go to China with him, but she really didn't see much more of him when they were there together. He was dedicated to his work. Determined to make life better for so many deprived people out in the middle of nowhere. How could she fault him for that? Oh… what should she do?

"What is it, babe?" Franco wrapped his arms around her from the back. "You look deep in thought."

"I'm just thinking about being here alone again." She turned around and squeezed him tight. "Except for the three weeks you went to China in college, we hadn't been apart for more than a few hours, let alone a few months, since we were in grade school, and now you're leaving once more."

"Just three for sure this time, maybe not even that long. I just need to get the project started now that I have everything in place, then I'll go to Shijiazhuang and find us an apartment so you can come over when you want to."

She pulled away from him and went to the breakfast bar, not sure how to say she didn't want to go to China. "I'm getting pretty busy with Catherine. She wants me in Washington, DC, next week. I think my life is in for a really fun ride with her."

"See." He reached over and took her hand, pulling her back to him. "We'd be apart anyway."

She giggled when he tickled her in that spot below her ribs on her right side he knew would get her going. "Oh, Franco, stop," she pleaded, laughing, and pushed at his hands. "I'm not going to miss that."

He loved her deep dimples and the way her big blue eyes lit up when she laughed. He wrapped her tight in his arms.

"And now, you're going to squeeze me to death? You don't know your own strength." She groaned, pushing back.

He stood back abruptly and flexed his arms. The bicep muscles hardened and rose up. "Strong to protect my woman."

"Hahaha, you are aware, you're not so scary."

"Excuse me, I'm the great Franco Legotti, feared by all."

"You're not." Her voice rose at the end. She turned away from him again. "It's just I have to take care of everything now."

"Well, not completely. I have an accountant to take care of our finances."

"I know, I have a meeting with him on Monday, remember?"

"And I now have a lawyer. If you need anything and can't contact me, you call him for help."

"Help? Really?" She could certainly take care of herself; she knew that now after the last four months of being by herself. But she hadn't gotten married to be a *single wife*.

"Okay… never mind." He gave her a quick peck on her cheek. "If you want me to set up the monthly bills to be automatically paid by credit card, I can do that." He grabbed her into his arms again.

"I've already taken care of that."

"Such a brilliant, lovable woman. Before you know it, Virginia Anderson will be known in the world of politics."

"Not just in politics, but the country when I'm president of the United States. It's okay with you that I didn't take your name for my professional stuff?" She giggled again. "Mr. Franco Legotti, First Man of the United States."

"I'd take the position proudly, and yes, I'm okay with you not taking my name. It's not my lineage name, anyway. Legotti was one of my mom's husbands. Never met the man or knew my father."

She gave him that mischievous look of hers and went to her knees, squeezing tight around his legs. "Don't leave me!" Her statement was part in fun and part for real.

He went down to her and lifted her face with his hand—their eyes locked.

She didn't want to think about the loneliness without him and the constant worry about their marriage. She knew of others who couldn't handle long-distance relationships. Was her lack of interest in what he was doing over there making him have questions? He had to know how much she loved him. Would they survive as a family?

Her fears lessened when his big hands encircled her face.

She needed to push away her uncertainty. He loved her.

Her eyes had that heavy-lidded look and her breaths deepened as he surrounded her lips with his, and then he slowly laid both of them down on the floor.

Chapter 1 – Friends

Backstory

Virginia (Gini) Elizabeth Anderson was the youngest of five children in the blended family of Thomas John and Elizabeth Rossi Anderson. She was petite, lovable, and the apple of her mother's eye.

Elizabeth Rossi had lived in the Italian neighborhood on the east side of Sacramento all her life. When she was young, the neighborhood had been full of life and children. But the years had taken their toll on the community, and it had turned into an area of older houses and elderly people. There were a few nice homes that had been kept up, but most of it could have been easily made into a tear-down area.

Elizabeth had learned from her mother how to make delicious pastries and was known for her friendliness and good cooking. The once-vibrant stores in the neighborhood shopping area where she worked at the bakery and a couple of the restaurants had been boarded up one by one, leaving only two or three to survive.

She had lived in the family home her whole life. Unmarried, she had stayed to take care of her parents until they died, when she inherited the house. An older gentleman, Tom, started frequenting the restaurant where she worked. He was pleasant, and they talked a lot, mostly about his family. He had married young and had two sons, Thomas and Larry. That marriage hadn't worked out, and the boys left to be raised by their mother. He had little contact with them until they were older, when he began to teach them his trade, cabinetmaking. He had thought he would be alone the rest of his life and was surprised to meet a woman with whom he immediately fell in love. They married and had a daughter named Cindy. When Cindy was ten, her mother died. Both she and her dad were devastated. Tom had tried his best to raise Cindy, but he had to work long hours to make a living. Cindy became rebellious and started running with the wrong crowd in high school. He had been troubled about the situation.

Elizabeth—in her forties at the time—had told him about her love for children and how she had wanted a big family, but she knew that wouldn't happen. After a few weeks, she had invited him to bring Cindy with him for dinner at her house. Although Cindy had no interest in going on a date with her dad, he told her she could leave when she wanted; he just wanted her to go eat the delicious meal he knew Elizabeth would prepare.

That night, to Cindy, the house was warm and comforting, and as much as she had not wanted to like Elizabeth, she did. There was a gentle easiness about her that made Cindy want to hear Elizabeth's stories about the old neighborhood and all the kids. Cindy had been moody all night but ended up staying and left with her father.

A few months later, Tom and Elizabeth married, and Cindy moved into her new home. It was a struggle the first year. Cindy had refused to accept a new mother, and Tom and Elizabeth spent many hours at the high school trying to get Cindy on the right track. By her junior year, Cindy had turned her life around, and she was thrilled to find out she was going to be a big sister.

At the age of forty-three, Elizabeth had been blessed with a son, Dwayne. He was a cute little boy, always wanting to be in his mother's arms. But he had a rude awakening when his mom and dad brought home a baby girl when he was only twenty months. Now, she got the love and affection that was once only for him, and he didn't want to share.

Gini was an adorable child, born with a full head of dark curls, big blue eyes, and dimples that swallowed her cheeks when she smiled. Elizabeth, Tom, and Cindy always wanted to hold her. Cindy immediately took to the new baby, becoming almost like her second mother.

Thomas and Larry started coming around on Sundays for dinner. Elizabeth had the family she had dreamed of all those years.

The two older brothers were strange and somewhat mean, especially to Dwayne, constantly picking on him. They had shown little respect to Elizabeth or Cindy. But Elizabeth had been happy to have them visit because she saw the happiness on Tom's face when he showed them new tools or techniques.

Gini would cuddle close to her dad every chance she had and look up at him with those eyes—her skin was so fair and soft it looked like china. Tom had been powerless to say no to any of her requests. Although Elizabeth had given the same love and guidance to both of her children, Dwayne always felt somehow slighted.

More and more of the older people died, and a few younger families moved into the homes. Gini was the dimpled darling of the neighborhood, always bringing other children to their house. Elizabeth had welcomed them all, giving them homemade goodies and playing games with them.

Dwayne was able to get his needed attention if he acted out, picking on Gini or getting in fights with other boys. Tom had found it much easier to parent Gini but spent as much time with Dwayne as he could, trying to teach him to work with his hands so he could make a living when he was grown.

The elementary school had small classes and few students. Gini's birthday was the end of October, but the school had allowed her to start kindergarten when she was four. It had taken no time for everyone to recognize how intelligent she was. The second and third grades were a combined class. After going in as a second-grader, she had skipped right over third grade straight to the fourth, making her the youngest in her class by far. With that, she had jumped to only one grade behind Dwayne, which further troubled him. Needless to say, he and his sister had never been close; in fact, he cared little for any of his siblings, whole or half.

Gini's mother would take in kids like other families took in stray animals. If they had followed Gini or Dwayne home, she would invite them in, feed them, entertain them, make sure they did their homework, and send them home before dark. Everyone in the neighborhood—kids and adults—loved Elizabeth Anderson.

The same year Gini entered the fourth grade, Cindy married and had a child of her own.

Franco Raul Legotti's mother had never been able to control him. He had been a colicky baby, and she never got any sleep. Once he was mobile, she just let him do as he pleased. She hadn't had the energy to keep up with him.

They lived on the edge of the neighborhood, on one of the busy main streets through the area. Because of his darker skin, many thought he was Mexican. Maybe he was, partly; his mother had never talked about his father, and he had never known him, but he knew his mom and grandmother were full-blood Italian.

By the age of six, he was a street kid, and he skipped school often and was constantly getting into fights.

Mama Elizabeth had been walking home from church one evening when she found him sitting on the curb. His clothes were torn and dirty, and blood streamed out of his nose.

She knelt next to him. "What's your name?"

He looked up at her. His face was streaked with dirty tears. "Leave me alone!"

"I have some freshly baked goods at my house. You look like you could use a good cookie."

"Lady, I said leave me alone!"

Mama took his hand, pulled him up, and they went to the Anderson house.

6

She fed him and cleaned him up. Dwayne's clothes were way too big for Franco, but they had cinched up the waist with his belt. She took him home and talked to his mom and grandma. Although they had both said the right things, Mama could tell that neither of them cared what he did. It became her mission to get him straightened out, although it wasn't an easy or quick task. She knew it would take time for her to gain his trust.

One day she had been late leaving to walk to the grade school to get Gini. When she saw her walking and talking with Franco, her first instinct had been fear. He was a tough kid. What was he doing with her daughter? But Gini was her usual girly self and had jumped and then twirled around, challenging him to do the same. Elizabeth stopped and watched. He stood looking at the funny little girl with his arms folded across his body.

"Come on, it will make you feel free. Just jump and twirl." She made the movements again.

Much to Elizabeth's surprise, Franco also jumped, twirled, and fell to the ground, rolling down the small hill. Gini laughed and giggled, and then she did the same, landing next to him in a sitting position.

Elizabeth smiled when she met up with the two children. She took hold of both of their hands and walked them to her house. On the way, the two talked about the book they had read that day and the tough spelling words.

Gini suddenly jumped in front, facing her mom and Franco, halting the walk. "Consequences," she said.

Franco quickly rattled off the correct spelling.

"Yes, yes," Gini said with glee, twirling around before taking her mother's hand again.

Elizabeth realized there was no need for fear—Franco was looking for a friend, and she believed he had found one—a good one.

Franco had only been to the Andersons' a couple of times since that night Mama found him bloodied: once after following Dwayne home and promptly getting into a fistfight in the front yard, and then another time when Elizabeth had seen him when she was walking Gini home from school.

He and Gini were in the same class, and he watched her play with all her friends, with some envy. He only went to school on the days he chose but started wanting to go more and more. Okay, maybe he liked learning, but he didn't want anyone to know that; it would make him look like a sissy to the older boys. Still, he wanted to go to see the cute little girl, and hopefully go to her house again.

When he started going to the Anderson house on a regular basis, there was a rivalry between him and Dwayne. Dwayne had been the tough guy on the block, and later the star athlete. Franco had encroached on his territory. They were always fighting. Mama and Pop would only step in if they thought the two were going to seriously hurt one another. There had been several bloody noses and blackened eyes over the first few years.

Pop tried to be involved with the children and teach Franco and Dwayne to wrestle rather than fistfight. But he was twenty years Elizabeth's senior, and he had less energy as each year passed.

The bond between Gini and Franco had become genuine. She was fun to be with, and they could whip right through their homework together. But he still had had the restlessness within him. He had to somehow prove he was his own man, and the only way to do that was to be tough and show the world he was the best and not someone to mess with. The only time he hadn't felt that way was when he was with Gini. Then he wanted to protect her.

Gini, always a girl, loved to challenge Franco. They each tried to outdo the other in math and spelling. But he made her angry—or sad—when he acted macho, trying to compete with the gang of boys that roamed the streets near where he lived. She had never been allowed to go to his house unless Elizabeth was with them. It was a tough neighborhood, and Gini knew it, but she knew even without Mama, she would always be safe there with him.

It was pretty clear to everyone by the time Gini and Franco had entered high school—they were a couple. You almost never saw one without the other. He absolutely adored her and her family. She admired his strength—not only the strength of his body but his success in overcoming the desire to be in a gang.

"Hahaha, look at the nerd!" someone shouted across the high school room where the political science club met after school.

Riccardo (Ric) Anthony Santini put his head down, a bit abashed, not sure if he wanted to enter or not. He was new to the community, didn't know anyone, and all the emotions churning inside him had taken any confidence he had ever had. His dad had suddenly passed away in an airplane accident in the Colorado Rockies a few months earlier. It was hard for him to grasp. He and his dad had been so close. Each day he woke hoping it was all a bad dream and his father would walk through the door. Not only had he lost his dad, but his mother insisted they move in with her great aunt. Ric had never met the woman—she seemed unwilling to acknowledge him, rather hovering over his mother who was tearful most of the time. The move from Walnut Creek, California, to

Sacramento—(a new house, new people, and not one person he could talk to)—was overwhelming.

Something inside Ric said he must step up now and be the man of the family, but he honestly did not have any idea how to do that. His dental braces, the flopping of his big feet, and his pants that were always too short because he grew tall so fast made him seem awkward and clumsy. How could he take care of his mother when he didn't know what to do to take care of himself? Thank goodness, he could get lost in a book and not have to deal with his grief, his choking desolation. His world seemed blurred, with no conclusions or clear course to follow. He'd always been a good student and loved school; now, that was the only thing that seemed right to him—it was getting him through the crushing times.

His counselor had recommended he join a sports team or club to meet new people. She knew of his family tragedy and tried to help him any way she could. She could see he was wandering down an aimless path, not knowing where to turn. Ric had never been interested in sports. He and his dad played chess constantly when his father wasn't traveling. Ric had just started to win the matches, which made him feel proud and accomplished. It gave his dad great joy to see his son strive for success. And Ric read as many books as he could squeeze in between school and homework. His dad had told him the only way to make it in life was to work hard and get a good education. From a young age, Ric had decided he wanted to be a lawyer, and he wanted to go to Harvard. As he got older, and still had the commitment, his father encouraged him to realize his dream.

Being an only child wasn't a problem for Ric. He loved his time with his parents. The three of them would go on outings often: to museums, plays, movies, or on road trips. He didn't need many friends. Now that he had none of that loving parental attention, he was more determined than ever to keep on track to become a Harvard lawyer by working hard in school and making good grades.

"What's the matter, nerd, are you lost?"

He started to turn and walk away, then a gritty feeling grabbed him. No, he was not going to leave; he was going to get involved.

"Aw, that's not nice," Gini said to Franco when she heard the guys laughing at the new student in their freshman class. She could see his hesitation and shyness.

Franco walked from her to Ric. She followed.

"Don't pay any attention to those half-wits. Hi, my name is Franco."

Ric put out his hand to shake hands. "Ric Santini." His lips were bulging out over his braces. "Nice to meet you, Frank."

Franco laughed. "No nicknames for me. I am the amazing and wonderful Franco Legotti. Friend and foe, all call me Franco, with respect." He leaned forward and gave an exaggerated wink.

Franco put his arm around Gini standing next to him. "Oh, I'm sorry, this is my girl, Gini, and I mean MY GIRL. No one messes with her!"

She smiled sweetly. "Hi, don't pay any attention to him. Franco is way too full of himself. I guess you are new to the neighborhood?"

"Dah," Franco said, making a silly face at her. "Where'd you get that news flash?"

After the meeting, Gini invited Ric to come to her house. Franco informed him that Gini's mother was everyone's mama. Ric immediately felt comfortable when he walked in the door. There were other kids there, and Mama Elizabeth was handing out homemade treats.

"Mama, this is Ric," Gini introduced. "He's a new student in our class."

"Welcome, Ric. Here, have a brownie."

Mama hugged both Gini and Franco.

As the weeks went on, Ric's life began to change for the better. He was almost constantly with Franco and Gini, and they went to the Anderson house every day after school.

Mama had made it a point to get Ric to talk to her. She could see he was troubled and wanted to help him. One afternoon, she asked if he would help her carry some potting soil to her garden in the backyard. After he had stacked the bags, they sat down at the old weathered redwood table. He poured out his life story to her. He kept control of his emotions but told her about his mother going into a deep depression and how helpless he felt. He longed for his dad to come home, but he knew that would never happen. She listened to him with her heart breaking. For the first time since the accident, Ric felt relief. Someone cared to hear his story; someone cared about his feelings. That was all he needed. He could go on with his life knowing someone was there for him.

The afternoons Franco had sports practice, Gini and Ric either stayed after school and did homework together or walked to her house. When they both had practice, he'd stay and watch Gini cheerleading. He loved her perkiness, her joy for life. She seemed to not have a care in the world. Why would she? There were people all around her who loved her, and she gave affection and kindness back in return. He could easily fall for her, but he would never mess with his best friend's girl; he had too much respect for Franco to ever do that. The feeling in his heart for both of them became that of sister and brother. He had a new family—a family full of love.

As the friendship between Ric and Franco deepened, Ric found Franco's home life wasn't too different than his own, as he lived with his mother and grandmother. He didn't know if Legotti was Franco's mother's maiden or married name; he had never asked.

All through high school, the three friends hung with the popular crowd. But Gini was really the one everyone wanted to be with. Her petite five-foot stature, bouncy, dark, long curls, and deep dimples just added to her magnetism. With her vibrant personality, she always drew a crowd. Everyone knew if they wanted her at their party, they'd have to invite Franco and Ric, or she wouldn't go.

By their senior year, Ric had stretched to just under six foot two. Mama helped him pick a wardrobe that flattered his physique. She could see his maturity developing after his freshman year. He was older than most of the kids in his class due to a late birthday, September eighth. Without his braces, he had a gleaming white smile set off by his light, tan skin tone and dark, wavy hair. His light chocolate-brown eyes told of his sensitivity. He could be a lady killer; many of the girls at school would swoon for him, but he continued to be guarded and closed, only opening up in private around his two best friends.

Although Franco always wanted everyone to see him as tough—and had a chip on his shoulder because he wasn't a taller, bigger man—his facade had become invisible to most. He was intelligent and talented, two of his greatest attributes, but his big heart was especially hard to hide, particularly when it came to children. He played ball with them, teaching the proper way to bat or throw, or wrestled with them on the ground. When they went to the playground, he was like a magnet for kids. It warmed Gini's heart to see his compassion for the young ones. They had often talked about having a big family someday. And his devotion to Gini was undeniable. He had loved her, it seemed, all his life. There was no one in the world he trusted and admired more than her. He had never had eyes for any other girl, and he never would. She was his soul mate.

Franco was a private person—no public affection was ever allowed. At her house, he put his arm loosely around her. She longed for him to hug her so she could melt into his body like butter. But the hugs were stiff. Maybe the hardness of his well-toned body had something to do with it. But when he kissed her… once their lips met, a wonderful sensation filled her head and surrounded her body. He had never kissed another, not even on the cheek. She knew those were his special Gini kisses, meant just for her.

Many envied her for having such a strong man with bulging muscles and rugged good looks to always be there to protect and love her.

Franco was accepted to MIT with a full scholarship. And, strangely enough, Ric received the same from Harvard. Ric had other university offers, but there was not even a remote chance of him going anywhere other than the Massachusetts Ivy League school. He was so excited when he got the letter. Ric never knew if his mother was drunk or high on pills. When she saw the letter, she said, "Good for you, Ricci," and walked away. He took the letter to school, and that afternoon at the Anderson house he showed it to Gini, Franco, and Mama Elizabeth.

Elizabeth cried and threw her arms around him. "I'm so proud of you boys, both of you going to such prestigious schools. We must have a big celebration before you leave."

Mama wanted Gini to stay home for a year before she went to college so she could grow up a little. But when Gini was accepted at Emerson College in Boston, she told her mother she had to go with Franco. Reluctantly, Elizabeth let her go.

The three packed all their things for school into Ric's big SUV. The boys took turns driving. They all slept in the same motel room to save money and ate the cheapest meals they could find. Mama Elizabeth sent them off with homemade cookies and other goodies, and a big cooler with soft drinks and water. She never thought once about her little girl's safety. Elizabeth completely trusted both the boys and knew they would protect Gini both on the road and when she got to college.

There were two things everyone knew for sure: Franco and Gini would eventually marry and live happily ever after, and the trio would be forever friends.

The three got settled in their schools. Ric was the only one with a vehicle, but it sat parked on the Harvard campus most of the time because the mass transit in Boston was so easy to use.

Gini's roommate's name was Margarita. She came from Santa Clara, California, but her parents were Hawaiian. The two of them hit it off immediately. Soon the threesome turned into a foursome.

Perhaps not surprising, Ric fell for Margarita, as she was nearly a clone of Gini. She was born to loving parents in their forties, and her body type and personality were similar to Gini's: both girls were petite, with dark, long hair and bubbly personalities.

The roommates were together all the time except when they were in class. They met up with the boys as often as their study loads allowed. In their second semester, Ric and Margarita became a couple, and by summer they were lovers.

Ric, Gini, and Franco decided to go to school during the summer semester since none of them could afford to go home; that way they could graduate early. Each got a job besides taking classes. Ric went to work at a law firm helping with filing and research. Gini worked at the State Department as a file clerk, and Franco was on the staff of one of the professors at MIT working on publishing a paper. Margarita went home for the summer.

The first semester of year two, during finals week, Gini received a call from Cindy telling her their pop had passed away. The family had all put in money so Gini could fly home. She had one college final remaining, and then she left to spend the rest of the winter break in Sacramento.

Ric remembered Tom (Pop) as always being old. He wasn't very mobile and sat in his overstuffed leather chair in a small room off the kitchen. The chair was taped in several places where the leather had split. The TV was directly in front of him, and there were always stacks of magazines, catalogs, and newspapers on either side of his chair. He was friendly and warm; Gini's friends thought he was funny with his comments about life.

At the reception after the funeral, everyone who knew the Andersons came to give respect. Gini quickly found she had outgrown her old neighborhood. Several of her friends were either pregnant or already mothers. Some of them were married; some were not. When Gini talked about her life in New England and college, no one seemed interested after a few minutes, not even her family. She thought it would be wonderful to be home for Christmas, but it wasn't at all like when she was little. She counted the days until she returned to school.

November the following year, Margarita told Gini she was pregnant. She was sobbing and didn't know what to do. She knew Ric would be upset because he thought they were protected. She wanted Gini to help her find a place to get an abortion.

"Wait a minute, Margs, have you told Ric?"

"No, he'll be furious with me." Margarita was sobbing so hard she could hardly talk. "What would Franco do if you told him you were pregnant?"

"Franco and I made a pledge to save ourselves until we were married. And we wouldn't get married until we had our degrees. But this isn't about Franco and me. This is about Ric and you! This is Ric's baby, too. He needs to know, Margs, he needs to know. And you have to decide what is best for both of you and the baby."

"Oh, Gini, I don't think I can do this. I just don't know what to do."

Margarita fell on her bed, crying hard into her pillow. Gini sat next to her and rubbed her back.

"Ric loves you; I know he does, and he's a super guy. You have to tell him, you do."

"I'll tell him tonight." Her voice cracked. "Can I tell him here so we can be alone?"

"Yes, of course."

She tucked Margarita's dampened hair back behind her ear. Then she leaned over and held her friend until she finally stopped crying.

Margarita called Ric and asked him if he could come to her dorm room that night.

"Are you okay?"

"Umm, yes, I just want to see you." She fought back the tears.

After the call, Margarita fell onto her bed in tears again.

Gini hopped on the T and headed to see Franco. They had already planned to get a coffee at Kendall Square before he went to work. She felt so bad for her friends and hoped everything would turn out well because she loved them both so much. At the coffee shop, she told Franco what Margarita had told her.

Franco put his head in his hands and shook his head. "Wow, a kid. That's a tough one. I'm glad we don't have to decide about a family right now."

Gini agreed and wrapped her arms around his arm as she laid her head on his shoulder.

When Ric arrived, Margarita fell into his arms crying.

"Hey, hey, what's going on?"

She pulled back from him. "I'm just going to say it, Ric. I'm pregnant."

"What!" He was sharp in his tone. "How can you be pregnant? I thought we were protected."

"I haven't been very responsible. I forgot to get my prescription refilled so haven't been taking the pills."

"How long?" he bit off.

"Three months."

"Margarita!"

There was a long pause. Ric paced the floor—rubbing his mouth with his fingers.

"I'll get an abortion. I don't have a problem with that. I'm sorry, I certainly didn't want to complicate your life."

"My life! We're talking about three lives here, aren't we?"

She hung her head still weeping with no answer.

There was a long silence. "I need to think; we need to think," Ric said, still walking the room. "Let's not do anything until we decide what's best for us all, okay?"

14

She agreed.

He grabbed her by the shoulders, pulled her toward him, and kissed her on the top of her head.

"It will all work out. I have to go and… and, I just have to go."

Later that night walking home from work, Franco received a call from Ric asking if he could come to his room and talk.

Ric had never had a friend like Franco, not just a friend, but a brother. He felt he was just getting a good handle on his life. Only another year and a half and he would be a lawyer—a good one, capable of making good money. But now this… taking on the responsibility of a family. How was he going to do that? He knew Franco, with his intelligence and wisdom, would know what to do.

Franco took the Red Line at Kendall to Harvard Square, knowing exactly what Ric wanted to talk about.

"Come on in." Ric held up his bottle. "There's beer in the fridge if you want one. I guess you heard Margarita is pregnant."

"Gini told me earlier."

"I don't know what to do. What should I do?" Ric sighed.

"Marry Margarita, take care of and raise your family."

Ric led Franco into the room. He stopped, turned around, and looked at him. "You make it sound so easy."

"I didn't say it was going to be easy." Franco grabbed a beer. "I said that's what you need to do. You did ask?"

Ric dragged his hand from his forehead, over the top of his head to the back of his neck. "I hardly have my head above water just taking care of myself. How can I support a wife and a baby? Sure, I wanted to have a family someday. I was thinking more like in my thirties after I finished school and worked for a few years."

"We all have a master plan, but life happens. Do you think your dad had it in his master plan to die in the prime of his life? Or your mom to have her life destroyed, or even you? You started your plan as a young boy wanting to go to Harvard. Did you have the page in your plan where your dad dies and you have to find a way to pay for school on your own? No, I think not."

"Riti said she's okay to get an abortion."

Franco turned quickly. "You're talking about a life. This is a baby, your child. Can you do that?"

The room went eerily quiet.

"Sorry," Franco said. "I know that's a personal opinion, my Catholic upbringing coming out. If my mother had decided to have an abortion, I wouldn't be here today. Listen, I know you will do what is best for you, best for Margarita, and best for... the whole situation."

"I guess I didn't know how young and immature Riti is. Who doesn't get birth control pills when they are sexually active? Did I need to call her every day to make sure she had taken her pill? I know she lived a sheltered life. She was given whatever she needed and probably whatever she wanted. I mean, really, she's the only one of us four who isn't struggling moneywise. Oh, geez!" Ric took the last drink of his beer and tossed the bottle in the trash.

"She isn't that much younger than you, and okay, we all make mistakes. But you can't say 'what if' at this point. 'Now that' is the issue."

"You're right... you're right. Thanks, buddy. You are a true friend, and now I know what I have to do."

"I can spend the night and sleep on the floor if you want me to."

"No, no, I'm good. You've been a great sounding board, and you're the best. Thanks." Ric gave a man hug to Franco.

The next day, between classes, Ric went to the university housing and talked to the clerk. He explained he needed family housing. Was that possible? She looked at his scholarship, checked lists, and made calls. Then she told him there was an efficiency apartment available starting the second semester, and he could put the housing money from his scholarship toward the rent. He said he would take it.

After his next class, he called the law firm and made an appointment to meet with the office manager late that afternoon when he was finished with classes for the day.

"Come in, Mr. Santini," Nancy said. "What can I do for you?"

Ric wasn't sure how to approach the subject. "It appears I'm going to be a family man, and I need to know if I can get more hours of work."

She assured him the firm was satisfied with his skills and there were probably more hours available than he could possibly work. A schedule was put together that worked around his classes.

She walked around from her desk and hugged him. "It'll be okay."

It had been two days, and Margarita hadn't heard from Ric since she told him. She just lay on her bed and slept and cried, not going to classes and eating very little.

"Come on, Margs, let's go to the cafeteria."

"I'm not hungry. I know he hates me now. I just know he hates me."

16

"Margarita, Ric loves you. You just need to stop thinking the worst. You'll have to admit you kind of blindsided him. He's just figuring everything out. Give him time; it'll be okay."

Margarita loved Ric, and she hated that she had disappointed him with her lack of responsibility. She deserved to lose his love.

Gini finally convinced her to go get some lunch.

While they were eating, Ric called Margarita and made plans for them to meet at Gary's Bar and Grill for dinner. They needed to talk.

Before they met up, he went straight to the big bin full of plastic rings at the South Boston dollar store they had all been to many times, picking two bands with no decoration on them—light gold in color. One was his left ring finger size, and one he guessed was Margarita's size. He also got a gift bag and picked up a heart-shaped chocolate wrapped in gold foil. The total cost was four dollars.

At six o'clock Margarita walked into Gary's. Ric walked to her and hugged her. As they sat across from each other at the table, he picked up her left hand.

"Margarita, will you be my wife?" His eyes were full of passion.

She gasped and put her right hand over her mouth. "Oh, Ric, you don't have to marry me. How can we get married? You're still in school. I'm still in school. I don't think that can work."

Still holding her hand, he said, "I have reserved an apartment for us starting in December. It's just an efficiency, but it's big enough for the two of us for now, and there's room for a crib when the baby comes. We would only be there for about a year after the baby's born. When I graduate from law school, I'll get a good job, and we can get a proper place. I talked to the law firm, and they can give me as many hours as I can work, so we'll have some money."

As he talked, her eyes filled with tears. She couldn't believe he had done all that in two days. He truly loved her, and he wanted them to be a family.

He took the bag out of his coat pocket and placed the chocolate heart in front of her.

"Riti, I love you, and I love our baby. You haven't answered me; will you marry me?"

She put her hand back over her mouth. The tears were raining down her cheeks. She picked up the chocolate on her way to sit on his lap, then wrapped her arms around his neck.

"Yes, I will be your wife. I love you… I love you so much." She hugged him.

He put his hand on the back of her head and drew her tightly to him, taking the two rings out of the bag.

"I know these are pretty cheap, but this is all I can afford for now. I promise someday I'll buy a gorgeous wedding ring for you."

Margarita gave a small laugh as she looked at the rings. "They're perfect. All I'll ever want."

She grinned with happiness. He had made the right decision to marry her and become a father—this was the right thing to do.

"Gini, it's Margarita… Guess what? Ric asked me to marry him… of course I said yes… I know; can you believe it? Listen, we want you and Franco to go to dinner with us."

They agreed to meet at the girls' dorm room.

Gini quickly ran to the corner store to get some items for a celebration.

She ran back to the room and cleared off her desk, sprinkled small hearts around, cut the curly ribbon off a bow, and dropped the curls over the hearts; four plastic flutes were set around in the decorations on the desk. She wrote, "We love you…" on the card envelope. As she was writing, Franco walked in the room. He hugged her from behind and kissed her as she turned her head to him.

"What's going on?"

"Margs called." Gini was still writing. "She and Ric are engaged. They're on the way over, so I put together a little something to celebrate. Here, sign the engagement card."

A few minutes later, Ric and Margarita walked in the door. They had their arms around each other, laughing about something. Gini ran over and hugged Margarita. Franco grabbed Ric and shook his hand, then gave him a quick hug.

"Congratulations, you two," Franco said as he side-hugged Margarita.

They each filled a flute full of Sprite and toasted.

"Here's to two of the greatest people on this earth," Gini said raising her glass. "May you always be happy and in love."

"Here, here," Franco said. "This is just the first of many celebrations we'll all drink to in the years to come."

"Happiness to us all," Margarita said. They clicked their flutes and took a drink.

The four of them went to the courthouse together for the marriage ceremony. Margarita looked beautiful in the off-white dress they bought on sale at Downtown Crossing. It looked good on her—setting off her dark complexion—and went perfectly with the flower bouquet Gini had brought. Ric was handsome, wearing his new black interview suit. Everyone on the subway wished the bride and groom good luck. Gini and Franco stood up with them and signed as witnesses. Margarita Lolani Lantaka became Mrs. Margarita Santini.

Ric and Margarita called her parents. Margarita introduced them to her husband and then explained they were going to have a child. Although it was a shock to her folks, it was also a bit of glowing light. Her father had been ill and housebound for months. The thought of a new life coming into the world was a happy feeling they had not had for some time.

Ric explained his plan on finishing school, getting a good job, and taking care of his new family. Later, Margarita's mother told her she liked Ric and was convinced he would take good care of her.

They moved into their new apartment in December. It was scantily furnished, but it worked for them. A few days after they moved in, Gini brought over Margarita's mail. There was a letter from her parents:

> Margarita and Ric,
>
> Enclosed is a check for $5,000. This is the amount we had saved for Margarita's wedding. We know it's not much, but hopefully, it will help to pay for some of your expenses. We love you and miss you terribly."
>
> Love, Mom and Dad

Ric appreciated the help, but he was determined to take care of his family on his own.

On January 12 in the early morning, Ric woke up hearing Margarita crying and groaning in pain.

"Something isn't right with the baby," she sobbed.

He jumped out of bed, dressed, wrapped Margarita up in a blanket, and carried her out to his SUV. An hour after they got to Massachusetts General Emergency, Margarita miscarried.

They had given her a sedative to calm her and something for the pain. She slept, and Ric sat next to the bed, holding her small hand in his. He spread her fingers out over his large palm. There on her finger was the plastic wedding band. He laid his head down on the bed and cried out loud. She slowly turned her head toward him and gently combed his hair with her fingers.

"It will be okay, Ric," she said, quietly. "I love you."

He continued crying.

After the spring semester was over, Margarita decided she should quit school and go to work. Ric disagreed, but she convinced him she could work until he finished his law degree, and then she promised she would go back and finish her schooling.

She took a full-time position in housekeeping and more hours as a nurse's aide at the hospital that had treated her so well.

The last year and a half of law school was grueling for Ric. With Margarita working many hours, Ric studying, attending extra classes and working, it seemed they never saw each other. When they had time off together, they locked themselves in their apartment, turned off their phones, and had an intimate, loving time together.

For two summers, Franco had worked for an engineering company. Before he started his master's program, they asked him to go to China on a business trip and work on one of the water treatment projects they were doing there. He was excited about the three-week trip.

When he walked down a hill in a remote area in the south of China along a small stream, he saw something shiny in the clear water. It was a beautiful, dark green stone with veins of silver and black streaking through the green color. The stone was perfectly smooth and delicate. He stuck it in his pocket and made his way down to the vehicles. That night at dinner with the eight other men, he pulled the rock out of his pocket and placed it on the table.

"Oh, you vely rucky man, Mr. Regot," one of the Chinese men said.

"Why so?"

"You find loseky lock in rorring stream, that vely rucky. Old saying, give a loseky lock from rorring water to the one you rove and you be vely happy and prosperous rife. You do have someone you rove?"

"Oh, yes, I'm in love with a very special woman."

"You must give her stone."

Franco wasn't so sure about the saying, but the stone was nice. When they got back to the city, he went to a jewelry store right next to the hotel. He took the stone in and asked if he could have it set in a woman's ring. A Chinese woman told him she would set the stone beautifully for his loved one. Franco knew Gini's ring size because he had given her a promise ring when they graduated from high school.

The night before he left to go back to the States, he picked up the beautifully crafted ring with the stone cradled in a white platinum setting. Two thin pieces of the platinum were strung across the top. The strings made an X with a knot in the middle of the X. The jeweler explained the X symbolized a kiss and the knot, intertwining love. Franco loved it.

When Franco got home, the four of them went out to dinner at the seafood restaurant by the aquarium. While they were waiting for their dessert to be served, Franco started to pull items out of the bag he had carried in. First, he handed Margarita a blue-and-green silk scarf. She took it and put it up to her face to feel the softness.

"Oh, Franco, this is so beautiful. I just love it!"

"I thought the colors looked like Hawaii," Franco said as he pulled out a hand-carved pipe and handed it to Ric.

"Wow, what great workmanship. So, you see me as a pipe man?"

"Yep. I see you sitting behind your big desk in your mahogany paneled office, wearing a sweater with leather patches on the sleeves, smoking a pipe." Franco had a mischievous smile on his face.

"This is great, man, thanks." He patted Franco on the shoulder.

Then he took out the small jewelry pouch and placed it on the table. He unsnapped and unzipped the bag, pulled out a white silk fabric, took the ring out, and placed it on Gini's left ring finger.

"What an unusual ring."

He told her what the X symbolized. Then he told the story of finding the stone and the old saying. They all laughed as Franco spoke just like the Chinese man had.

"Oh," Gini said still laughing, "I will cherish this always." She leaned over and gave him a passionate kiss. She had been lonely without him and hoped they would never be separated that long again.

The following June, Ric, Gini, and Franco all graduated with accelerated program advanced degrees; Franco, with a BA in mechanical engineering, received a master's in political science. He went to work full time for The Gaspen Engineering Company in their China project division; Gini, with a BA in political science, received an MBA. She took a job at the State House in the research area, and Ric, Harvard Law. After passing the bar, he accepted a position at the prestigious Lory and Lawson Law Firm in downtown Boston.

Before they all started their new lives, they went out to a fancy dinner. Margarita announced she was pregnant again. Ric was delighted. He knew he could provide a good life for his beautiful wife and all their children.

Within the next year, Franco and Gini married at the office of the justice of the peace with Ric and Margarita standing with them. The Legottis were eager to start a family so their children could grow up together with the Santinis. But as they often do, plans changed: Franco and Gini were transferred to China, Margarita lost their second child, and with their busy lives, the close relationships were stretched, pulled, and splintered.

Chapter 2 – Gala Night

This was the night of the grandest gala Greystone Entertainment Incorporated put on each year. Ric loved the event. It was when he was most certain that giving up the law for a career that made people happy had been the right choice. People had questioned him. All those years studying, all that investment. Maybe he should have spent more time weighing the decision, but once it was in front of him, it had been so easy. Law tomes, law briefs, boardrooms, courtrooms—or this: good food, good wine, friends. Hard work, sure, but now in the service of joy. How could he be luckier?

One advantage of his previous career was knowing men like Victor, who still ribbed him about walking away from the law, but gave him more business because of it. It would have been much harder owning a company like this without entrée to the worlds of laws and politics, and for that alone, Ric was glad he'd taken the path he did. But mostly, he admitted, he liked the company of smart guys like Victor—men who would make a difference in the world. He'd always had smart friends.

I guess I thought I had to prove I was smart, too, he thought. *And I am— smart enough to know what I really want to do with my life.*

He thought briefly of Margarita. The pain was subsiding. The sense of failure was harder to shake off, but goddamn it! This was a party. He let himself imagine the night as it would play out: the lights, the jewels, the pretty dresses, the gleam of silver, the scents of flowers, perfume, good food, human warmth. Conversations, music, laughter. There was always loss and sadness in the world. That's why it was so important to celebrate.

Tonight, he hosted his good friend Victor Westcott. Victor and his wife, Maria, had become family to him in the past few years. Victor was once again running for the US Senate, representing the state of Massachusetts. His yearly gala always filled his campaign chests with generous donations from friends and supporters.

Two smart and beautiful women, Gini and Catherine, were getting ready for the party a few blocks away in Gini's high-rise condo overlooking Boston Harbor.

They were just about to leave when Gini's PET (personal electronic tablet) sitting on the high breakfast bar alerted her of a new email.

"Oh, my gosh!" Gini said with great surprise. "It's Franco. You go on, Catherine. I want to read this. I can just walk over to the hotel."

"There's no hurry. I can wait."

"No, no, go on. Now that I have contact with him, I hope we can have a conversation. It's been months since I've seen him. You wouldn't believe me if I told you exactly how many. And maybe two or three texts or messages from him via someone else!"

"Okay, be easy on him."

"Why should I? You'd think he could find a way to contact me even if he is in the wilds of China."

Catherine wrapped her neck fur tight up under her chin, looking at her friend with compassion. "I'll see you there. Don't be too late and miss the auction. I tell you, there are absolutely the best things in the whole of Massachusetts to bid on."

Surprise! was the first word of the email:

> My darling Gini, you probably thought I had fallen off the face of the earth. I just got back to a place that has contact with the outside world. I took a satellite phone down to the site and guess what? The next morning, when I got up, it was nowhere to be found. You cannot trust anybody here, not even your so-called friends. So I have been out of touch with the world and reality for I don't even know how long.

Gini made herself comfortable on the bar chair and read what appeared to be a lengthy message:

> I just wanted to say I love you. And tell you about the wonderful work we are doing in this remote village that up until now had no, and I mean no, clean water anywhere. We drilled wells, and I invented another device to get the water up, out, and through a filtering system we built from the rock and coal we found while drilling the wells. Working with just the locals and their tools, and I use the term 'tools' lightly, made the work challenging, but rewarding. Especially the end result for the children. The little ones having clean water to drink made all the time away and out of touch so worth it. I have such a soft spot for those little guys. The people are fast learners, and working together, we put in an effective system. Of course, it took us a while to find the water in the first place. I'm attaching a link to the report that was on the "World of Engineering" website last month.

Oh right, the report can find civilization, but not his personal writing. That man! Will he ever change? she thought as she gritted her teeth.

More later, babe. Love, Franco.

Following the personal message were several paragraphs with all the details about his company and his many inventions that were either patented or patent pending.

Not even a how are you, what are you doing, when can I call you or see you? Or how about, I miss you, Gini, so much. *I'm done,* she thought, *just done.* "I'm not even going to respond, or maybe I will next year or the year after that," she said out loud as she turned off her PET screen.

She walked back into her bedroom to make sure she was still put together nicely. When she had approved her appearance in the mirror and started toward the coat closet, she noticed the ring with the green stone on her makeup table. Even though she thought she shouldn't—she went over to the table, picked up the ring, and slipped it on her left ring finger. She twisted it around, admiring the shiny stone. Mixed feelings rose up in her—sweet memories, vulnerability— anger. She almost took it off, but after one last look at her hand, she left it on. Why couldn't he find just a few minutes to contact her more often? He was in the driver's seat since she never knew how to contact him.

That's the way he likes it, she thought. *Well, I don't like it at all. Why did I ever think this would work?*

What if I were hurt or ill? How would he even know? Maybe I'll just change my name and move to Europe. What would he do then? Would he try to find me, or just go on digging his stupid wells?

She needed to leave and stop thinking about her and Franco. All it did was frustrate her and, lately, make her mad. But she still loved him—always.

The hotel on Long Wharf was just a short walk. The cold, damp wind blew up against her face. She wasn't worried about her hair, for the dark brown curls were pulled back into a fancy French twist fastened with jeweled combs. Her long bangs were straightened and swept behind each ear, tucked tightly in place.

She arrived at the front door of the hotel at the same time as Michael Fredrick, her old friend from the campaign offices when they were in college.

Michael leaned down and kissed her on the cheek. "Perfect timing. You should have called me. I would have picked you up."

"Oh, thanks. I had a ride but passed it up to read an email. I enjoyed the walk even in the cold."

He took her arm in his, and they walked in the turning door after the valet gave him his ticket. "You'll be my date tonight."

24

She knew that he'd had a crush on her for years, but he was a happily married man with two darling daughters. She thought he was a nice guy and a good friend. They had frequently talked the past few months about him running for a city council seat in the election in about twelve months. He had asked Gini to consult, or even better, be his campaign manager. She hadn't given him an answer either way.

She had been invited to the Westcott Gala every year for the past few years but had never been able to make it, mainly because she didn't want to go alone. The year before, she had planned to go with Catherine, who was staying with Gini and just raved about what a great night out it was. But the day before, she had come down with the flu, and Catherine went by herself.

The two walked into the lavishly decorated hall full of chatting people. As she took her coat off, she caught Ric's eye. He was up on the balcony overlooking the room, about to speak to the guests. When he saw Michael helping her, Ric wondered why she was with him. Where was his wife, Brenda? He was sure her name was on the list. When he had checked the guest list—delighted to see Gini's name—he had had Carol, his event coordinator, seat both Gini and the Fredricks at his table.

Gini was dressed in a dark wine-red gown with long sleeves that came to a point over the back of her delicate hands. The dress flowed beautifully over her full breasts, hugged her shapely hips, and reached all the way to the floor, just covering the four-inch stilettos. Even with the high heels, she didn't quite reach Michael's shoulder. He put his hand on her back and led her into the room to mingle with the crowd.

She was just as beautiful as Ric remembered. *Gee*, he thought to himself, *how long has it been?*

"Hey, Santini, you're on," Ric heard from behind him.

"Thanks, James."

He walked over to the microphone, peering down on the guests, and in a strong, welcoming voice said, "Good evening, ladies and gentlemen."

Gini quickly turned when she heard the voice, immediately recognizing it. She looked at Catherine. "Ric Santini?"

"Yeah, do you know him?"

She nodded as Ric continued speaking. "I trust you are all having a good time. I must say you're looking lovely and handsome on this fabulous night. Please, enjoy your cocktails while you look over all the wonderful items we have up for auction. I know each of you has your eye on the one thing you just have to have, and for that reason, you must keep bidding until you have conquered the treasured item." He spoke with a dramatic tone and waved his hands and arms about.

"Seriously, I just wanted to welcome you all and tell you a little before nine you will be alerted the bidding will close. At nine o'clock, you'll be escorted into our dining room, where you will dine like kings and queens. Enjoy yourselves and have a good chat. You will be hearing from me again later."

Everyone began to talk again after a brief applause. Ric, trying to get Gini's attention, saw she was immediately acknowledged by Clifford Jones, a reporter for the *Boston Globe*. Clifford had stepped into Gini's view of Ric as he spoke. She thought he looked especially good in his black tux.

The evening passed quickly, and Ric kept his eye on Gini. He wanted to talk to her but was constantly detained by people he knew in the crowd and meeting potential new clients. They would have time to talk when they all sat down to eat. He chuckled every time he found Gini and saw Michael stuck to her like glue—a schoolboy with a mad crush.

Not that he didn't understand. Gini was one of those women any man would be happy to spend time with—lovely, feminine, kind—he'd always thought so, even though she'd been with another guy since the day he met her. He'd always felt happy that he could appreciate her as a woman as well as a friend without it being a problem.

Carol stepped up to the microphone and announced there were only five minutes left in the silent auction, and invited everyone to please make their way to the dining room behind the auction items. At those words, the heavy velvet drapes hanging from the ceiling gracefully parted, and the elegant doors of the dining room opened to welcome the guests. Everyone started to walk slowly toward the back.

Ric watched Gini as she stopped at a small cloisonné box on the auction table. She wrote in a number, signed her name, and proceeded to the dining area.

Michael had found the seating chart and saw that Ric, Catherine, Gini, and he were all seated at table one. When he found the table, the name cards had Ric sitting between Catherine and Gini. Michael was next to Catherine. He quickly took his name card before any of the others at the table had arrived, and put it next to Gini's, moving the card to that seat over next to Catherine. He hurried to Gini's side and whispered in her ear he had found their table and she should follow him. She excused herself from the person she was talking to and went with him.

Ric almost laughed out loud when he saw the name cards had been switched. This had split Randall Cooper and his wife, Betty. Ric knew they wouldn't care.

The former mayor and his wife would be more than glad to visit with anyone. And he knew Randall was a big fan of Catherine White, so he would appreciate talking to her. Also at the table were the honored guests, Senator and Mrs. Westcott. Carol had had Michael's wife's place setting removed so there wouldn't be an empty spot at the table. Ric once again marveled at how efficient and organized his team was.

Gini was escorted to the table on Michael's arm.

Catherine approached her seat. "Where's your lovely wife?" she asked.

"Our trusty babysitter became ill today and canceled. Brenda didn't feel she could have a good time tonight worrying about a new babysitter. So she opted to stay home."

"That's too bad. It would have been great to see her again. Please, say hello to her from me."

"I will." Michael nodded as he answered, and pulled out a chair for Gini and one for Catherine.

Ric was the last to join the table. He shook each man's hand and placed a kiss on the cheek of each lady as he greeted her by name. Gini was the last. As he approached, she rose from her chair, and he wrapped his arms completely around her, and they embraced. After a few long seconds, he pulled back and kissed her on the cheek. Their eyes met, and Ric smiled.

"Wow!" Randall said in his loud voice. "That was a meaningful hug there."

Ric laughed as he held Gini's chair for her to be seated again. "Randall, Gini and I go way back. Believe it or not, we went to high school together in Sacramento."

"No kidding! Couldn't have been too way back. Miss…" He paused to look at the name cards. "You look to be just out of school."

Gini blushed a little and looked down at her plate for a minute.

Randall recognized her name on the seating card. "Ms. Anderson, of course, sorry for the snide remark. And Catherine, how are you both doing?"

They both indicated they were fine.

"High school classmates, huh?" he went on. "In Sacramento—that's a long way from here."

"It is." Ric settled in his chair. "And we both went to college in the Boston area, so we have been friends for a long time. This is the first time I've seen you, Gini, in I'd guess two years and a half, maybe three years."

"More like four."

"So I think that justifies a good hug, don't you think, Randall?"

"Well, sure," he said with a jovial laugh. "I'd think you could justify a good hug anytime with that pretty little lady."

27

Randall sat back, and his big rounded belly jumped as he chuckled. He stretched back and put his arms on the back of the chairs of the two ladies sitting on either side of him. "Really, I could hug all the pretty ladies at this table tonight, including my lovely wife sitting way over there."

"Now, Randy, hush up a bit," Betty said. "This is a formal affair. Use your inside voice and manners, please." She kissed her fingertips and blew the kiss over to him.

Randall sat back properly in his chair. "Sorry, darlin'. Didn't mean to make a scene. I'll behave."

Michael realized he had split the husband and wife team. He looked over at Ric. Ric smiled and raised one eyebrow as if saying: I know what you did. Michael mouthed to him, "Sorry."

There was no need to formally introduce anyone at the table. Gini knew everyone from past meetings or gatherings. It amazed her that Ric knew so many politicians; they were in the same political circles. Why hadn't their paths crossed before now? It was all very curious to her.

Gini, indeed, felt like royalty. The room was filled with soft, beautiful music provided by a five-piece string orchestra, set up in a small area in the front of the room. The windows were draped with a plush dark red velvet fabric that stretched from floor to ceiling. A huge crystal chandelier hung from the ceiling in the middle of the large room. It reflected tiny spots of light around as the muted ceiling lights and the room candles hit each crystal. All the tables were elaborately decorated with candles, low arrangements of flowers, and delicate, ornate fine china. Surrounding the plates were arrays of forks, knives, and spoons, all sterling silver; and three different sizes of leaded, crystal-stemmed glasses; and one champagne flute.

As many courses were served, Gini quietly listened to the conversations around the table. One major topic was the polls for Victor's re-election. The pundits were trying to predict the winners of the upcoming election. Most polls were showing great numbers. Another topic was the excellent work Catherine and Gini were doing through Catherine's lobbying firm. They were fighting hard for children's rights to equal health care, especially underprivileged children. They were lobbying both on the Hill in Massachusetts, Gini's territory, and in Washington, DC. All at the table could see the pride in Catherine's face as she talked about how she bent the ears of anyone and everyone for the cause. Often during the discussion, she looked to Gini for approval of a statement, or to acknowledge the endless hours Gini spent on the issues.

Michael chimed in about wanting to run for city government. All gave him encouragement and told him he would be a good addition because he was young, energetic, and smart. They were judging his abilities by what they had read or seen on the news about his big wins in the courtroom. He was at the top of his profession in legal skills, and as a speaker, he was both convincing and interesting. They all wished him luck and offered assistance if he needed it. Michael was almost gleeful as he counted the potential endorsements around the table. Several times during the lengthy chat on the subject, he lightly tapped Gini on the arm with his thumb as his arm was constantly on the back of her chair. Maybe with all the assurance, she would seriously consider being his campaign manager.

Every once in a while, Ric would move toward Gini and lightly rub against her shoulder. He was a physically affectionate person, always had been, with both men and women, so he didn't think it was a big deal. And yet… Each time, they would look at each other. It was so good to see her again. They had been so close for so many years and then, with life's challenges after school, they had slowly lost contact with each other. Michael was aware of the glances.

Gini was happy to see her old friend. She might have made more of an attempt to attend had she known Ric was to be the MC of the fancy gala. And Catherine didn't know they knew each other, so she never mentioned him.

Ric didn't always sit among the guests at the events he organized. In fact, he usually worked along with the service people behind the scenes to see that the evening ran smoothly. But Victor always insisted he join the party and sit at the head table. It wasn't only an honor for Ric, but a great treat to be a guest. He knew Carol and James would have the whole affair running like a well-oiled machine.

The dinner plates cleared from the table was Ric's cue to go to the podium and speak to the crowd again. "Ladies and gentlemen, may I have your attention. Once again, I'd like to welcome you and thank you all for coming. Your generous donations to our honored guest are greatly appreciated. Without your continued support, his job would be a lot more difficult. I hope you have enjoyed the meal so far and will stay, as the bar will be open until two.

"If you won the bid on an item in the auction, you'll be notified by phone or email. Arrangements will be made to collect your contribution, and for the delivery of the item.

"So with all the business taken care of, I would like you to give recognition to our great senator from the state of Massachusetts, Victor Westcott."

The room filled with applause as Victor approached the podium. He grabbed Ric by the shoulder, and the two shared a hearty handshake.

Victor pulled him back to the mic. "I just want to say Greystone Entertainment can throw a great party thanks to its owner, Riccardo Santini. Don't you all agree?"

Again, the clapping filled the room.

"Thank you, Ric," he said as the room calmed, "for making this such a great event."

Gini thought about the comment. Ric owned a company?

The two shook hands again, and Ric made his way back to his table as Victor started speaking.

"I wouldn't be here tonight enjoying this great evening without all of your help and support." He pointed his fingers, sweeping the room in front of him.

"We have a few distinguished guests sitting at my table. The beautiful and convincing Ms. Catherine White, and her equally able assistant, Ms. Virginia Anderson... Michael Fredrick, the exciting new lawyer on the scene. Don't be too surprised if he's standing at a podium at an event just like this in the near future... The always entertaining former mayor, Randall Cooper, and his lovely wife, Betty... And, of course, my lifelong partner, best friend, and the most beautiful woman in my world, my wife, Maria."

As they were introduced, each stood, and there was applause. Maria threw Victor a kiss as she teared up at the special introduction. Gini was glad Victor introduced Catherine first, so she knew to stand. And Michael was thrilled at the notoriety and the mention of his entry into the political arena. Michael was the last to sit, taking full advantage of the opportunity to get his face seen and recognized.

Ric held the chair for Gini as each took their seats.

Gini leaned over to him. "That was unexpected. You should have warned me."

He smiled and put his hand on top of hers. "I didn't know he was going to introduce the table," he whispered. "You did fine!"

He was surprised at her shyness. She had always been so outgoing when she was young. And he knew she spoke in front of hundreds of people in her campaign for children. He looked at her curiously. His hand remained on top of hers as he squeezed it a bit. But then Victor made a profound statement, and everyone clapped, and the hands parted.

As Victor continued, Ric noticed she was wearing the beautiful green stone ring. He remembered the story of how Franco had found the stone somewhere in China, and that there was some amusingly worded statement made when he presented the ring to Gini.

"I guess Franco isn't here in the States," he whispered.

She shook her head.

"In China?"

She looked at him like he shouldn't be talking and nodded as she puckered her lips—"shh."

He smiled, put his hand on top of hers again, patting it, and looked at Victor. She gently pulled her hand out and laid it in her lap.

As soon as Victor finished speaking, the people got up and started mingling. Ric rose from his chair when Mr. Agado came up behind him and introduced himself.

Gini and Catherine made their way to the door, stopping to say good night to others. Gini turned to find Ric engaged with the same man. She put her hand to her ear and mouthed "call me" when she caught his attention. He acknowledged with a positive nod.

The morning after every big event, Ric, James, and Carol met for brunch to go over the event and decide if there was any further action they needed to take. Greystone had so many parties at the hotel that the hotel offered the brunch to them for free.

As Carol went through the auction list, Ric noticed Gini had won the bid on the small cloisonné box. He told Carol to let him take care of collecting the donation and delivering the item to her. She put the box and paperwork in a gift bag the hotel provided and handed it to him.

Chapter 3 – Catching Up

Tuesday afternoon, the caller ID showed R Santini on Gini's landline.

"Hey, Gini." He was upbeat.

"No one calls me at this number except Howard, our concierge. What's up?"

He was excited to finally get hold of her. "This is the only number I had for you. I looked through all my archived files and finally found this one. I have two things. First, you won the bid on the small cloisonné box."

"Fantastic! That little box drew my attention right away."

"However, to get it you have to pay a tidy little sum."

"I know. I will gladly pay."

"And that brings me to the second thing. I would like to bring the beautiful little box to you, collect the money, and then take you out to dinner."

His invitation caught her by surprise. "Okay… Sounds like fun." There was hesitation in her voice.

"When is a good time for you?"

"Let me get my calendar."

"Let's see, tonight I'm meeting with Michael… Wednesday a conference call… Thursday…" She went on for each day, pausing and stating what was on her schedule.

"Okay, it looks like Friday, Saturday, or Sunday I'm open. Do any of those days work for you?"

"Let me see." He then imitated her by saying each day and mumbling something for each.

"Yes, that works for me, too."

"Which day?"

"All of them. Friday, we go to dinner. Saturday, we'll drive up the coast and have lunch at Gloucester House. And Sunday I host our weekly neighborhood football game party for the Patriots at my house."

"I'd say, why don't we just start with the Friday night dinner. What time?"

"How about I come by about six-thirty? We take care of our dirty little money business, and I'll make a reservation for seven-thirty. Does that work for you?"

"That sounds perfect—fancy or casual?" She was suddenly uplifted in her mood—excited.

"I'm thinking McCormack and Smits in Quincy Market."

"I'll see you at six-thirty Friday night. Remember you can park out front. Howard will show you up."

"I remember the routine. I'm looking forward to seeing you."

As soon as Ric hung up, he thought maybe he was a little too eager throwing out all those get-together ideas. And what about Franco? He needed to find out if he was in town for the dinner count.

"Hello, Ric." There was amusement in her voice.

"Hey, Gini." He sounded breathless. "I don't know where my head is. I just need to know if Franco is in town for the reservation. It would be great to see the ole guy."

Gini let out a sigh. "No worry. He's not here, and I don't expect him anytime soon. It'll be just the three of us with Margarita."

"Ah, Margarita, oh no, no she won't be joining us." He was caught off guard by the mention of her name. "I guess we have some catching up to do."

"I guess so."

Gini put the phone back in the cradle slowly and started to think about Margarita. She had figured Margarita wasn't at the Gala since Ric was working. Or maybe she was with her mom. Gini knew Margs took frequent trips to California to help her mother after her dad had died.

Maybe now they could clear up what must be a misunderstanding between them, although Gini never had figured out just what happened to distance them.

She tapped the cell bracelet on her arm and spoke the number he had just called her from into her phone.

"Save contact. Ric Santini," she commanded the electronic device.

Then she dictated a text message into the round face. "Start text. Now you have my cell number. Period. Looking forward to Friday. Period. Stop. Send."

The week went fast for both of them, as they were busy with their jobs. Ric had a short day Friday, so he went back to his place, put on comfortable clothes, poured himself a beer, and sat in his living room to chill. As the thoughts of his busy week left his head, he started to think about his evening out with his good friend.

He never had known what came between Gini and Riti. He knew the Legottis' long residence in China had made Riti upset because she couldn't be with her friend—as if she were jealous. Ric had just thought she angered easily because she was working so hard in school and at the hospital… she had taken on too much. And the babies, yes, their loss had weighed heavily on her. As the years passed, they both had worked too many hours; their personal lives were put aside.

He was looking forward to dinner with Gini and rekindling the friendship. Hopefully, his two best friends were back in his life. He was in a moment of pure happiness.

Gini looked down at her electronic bracelet and saw it was after five. The meeting that was scheduled at 10 a.m. had been pushed to eleven o'clock, then one and had finally started at three. It looked like it was going to go late, and she didn't feel like she could just get up and walk out since she had requested to attend. She had asked Senator Goodman's staff if she could be at the meeting as a fact-finding mission for his agenda on health care for children, and then she'd report back to Catherine with her findings. She was just about to discreetly text Ric and cancel their dinner date when Pat Goodman stood up.

"Okay, people, it's after five o'clock on a Friday night, and I think we have discussed the issue and come to an understanding. Do you all agree? I say let's adjourn this meeting and go home, and have a great weekend."

"Did you get what you needed, Ms. Anderson?"

"Yes, Senator. Thank you so much for letting me sit in on the meeting."

She stopped long enough from packing her business bag to shake his hand.

"Anytime. You just let my staff know if you need any other information. Okay, everyone, have a good one."

Gini figured by the time she got home she would have an hour to get ready. As she stepped inside her place, she flung her bag on the breakfast bar and grabbed her PET. She hadn't had a chance to check her personal messages all day. She turned the device on and went into her bedroom to debate whether she could wear what she had on or not. She was in a business suit and decided she needed to soften her look for dinner. And then thought how a hot shower would feel good, and, oh, some white wine. She went back to the kitchen and clicked on her email, then poured herself a half glass of chardonnay. Back to look at her email. The first three were from Franco. *Oh, my gosh,* she thought, *this guy's timing is impeccable.* She decided to get ready first and then concentrate on the messages.

After her shower—while sipping her wine—she decided to wear the light gold silk blouse with the low square-cut neck. It was full fitting, so she belted it with a navy-blue belt that had green and rust stripes near the big silver buckle. She pulled on her favorite navy-blue silk pants that were tight fitting across the hips and thighs and flared out to a full leg. Then she slipped on her navy-blue wedge heels, again with a green fabric stripe across the toe.

She had a couple more sips of wine, then, while brushing her hair, she opened her email. All three of Franco's messages had attachments. She clicked on the first one:

> I just downloaded my pictures, finally. I'm attaching three I think
> will tell the story of what we are doing here. You should be here,

babe. You would love all the sweet children. I don't have any way to downsize the pictures, so I'll send them in three different emails.

Gini, my love, I haven't gotten a response for the email I sent you last week. I hope you're receiving these messages. Tell me a good time to call if you want to talk. I can't guarantee good reception. I'll be leaving for the site tomorrow, and I would like to hear from you. I plan to take another satellite phone with me, this time protecting it with my life, but who knows if I'll be able to get a signal out. Please, tell me that you are okay and receiving this. Love, Franco.

Again, there were several paragraphs about his company at the end.

The first picture was of a Chinese child she guessed was about four years old. His nose was running, and his face and clothes were dirty. He looked at the camera with his big eyes. She guessed it was a boy, but there was no real way to tell. He was so cute. The next picture showed the same child leaning over to pick up a large ball, this time smiling. His clothes and face were clean. She figured Franco was playing ball with him and had snapped the picture. The last picture was of a young Chinese woman with a baby in her arms. She held a clear baby bottle out as if to show the clean, clear water in the bottle. From her smile, she was very pleased.

Oh, Franco, you have such a good heart. But I don't have time to write you back. Not now.

She looked at her bracelet again. It was six-twenty. She closed the PET screen and went to mess with her hair until it looked good, then started putting on her makeup.

The landline phone rang—Howard. "Ms. Anderson, there's a Mr. Santini here to see you."

"Yes." Her voice was a bit frantic. "Maybe you could delay him, or, oh, no, it's okay, um, send him up. Thanks."

Howard looked at Ric. "It appears Ms. Anderson is running a bit late, and I see the elevator is stuck up on the tenth floor so we'll just have to wait." He winked.

"Okay, not a problem."

"It has been a while, Mr. Santini, since we've seen you around here." Howard kept working on something behind the counter.

"Yes, it has. The place hasn't changed much."

"No, you know some things never change, and then there are others that are forever changing." He looked down at his watch. "I see the elevator has been released. This way, please." They walked over to the elevator.

Ric had both hands full. In one hand, he held a small bouquet of four yellow roses, and in the other, the bag with the small box.

Howard put the programmed key in the slot, and the elevator door opened. "Have a great evening, Mr. Santini."

"Thank you."

Gini was just finishing putting on her lipstick, and without thinking, she picked up the green stone ring and slipped it on her finger. Just then, she heard the doorbell. She walked to the door, stood in front of it for a second, took a deep breath, let it out, and then turned the knob.

Ric was standing there with his hands full.

"Come on in."

He leaned over, kissed her on the cheek, and handed her the bouquet.

"Yellow roses, my favorite." She took them and walked into the kitchen to find a vase.

"How are you doing?"

"Much better now that it's Friday night and I've had a hot shower and a glass of wine. Would you like a drink?"

"Sure, what do you have?"

"Look behind the bar, just about everything."

"Nice bar." He took a bottle of scotch off the shelf after he had set the bag down. "I'll take some scotch on ice."

"There's ice in the small refrigerator under the counter, and the glasses are there at the bar."

She finally found the vase she was looking for and put the roses in with water and set the vase next to her PET on the breakfast bar. She took her wine and walked to Ric sitting on a barstool. "Thank you for the roses."

"You're very welcome. I like what you have done with the place. Same space, but a lot of work done since I was here last."

"When we first moved in here, we didn't have a lot of money." She settled on the barstool. "We decided to do it piecemeal. And, of course, we started in the master suite since that's where we spent most of our time. One thing I have to say for Franco is he's a great lover."

There was a silence. "Oh, I'm sorry. I think that was too much information." She turned to face him with a solemn look on her face.

In the past, that statement would have Gini full of spirit. There would have been a cute giggle at the end, sparkles in her eyes, and her dimples digging deep into her cheeks. Her serious demeanor was strange to him. What had happened to the spunky, excitable personality that had made everyone around her so happy? He was concerned maybe something was terribly wrong in her life.

"Yes, TMI." Ric winked at her.

"It's amazing how little money we had in college. Even with good jobs, it took us a while to accumulate the cash to remodel."

Ric shook his head. "Poor as church mice. As it turns out, I struggled for no reason."

"What do you mean?"

"You remember when Riti and I went to the West Coast the end of summer after graduation?"

She nodded.

"My mom had called and said she needed me to come see her."

Gini looked puzzled. "I thought you guys went out there after Margs' second miscarriage so she could be with her mom."

"We did that too. We first went to the Bay Area, and I stayed a couple of days. Then I drove to Sacramento.

"I went to visit my mom. The first thing she told me was that my great aunt had passed away years before. I was shocked. I asked her how long she'd been living alone and she seemed confused, talking about neighbors George and Amy across the street who helped out. I was worried about how she was paying for things and asked to see her checkbook. She had more than that—a whole box of envelopes, statements from the Whitmore Investment Company where my dad worked. The first envelope I opened was a recent broker's statement: an account in my mom's name with over six-hundred thousand dollars in it. To say I was stunned would be an understatement! 'Mom, where did you get all of this money?' I asked. It seems my dad had an insurance policy. The people across the street started looking out for my mom after my aunt died in July that year. Mom inherited the house.

"She hadn't changed, always looking like she was half awake, and just kind of wandered around the room as she talked. We were never close after my dad died. It was impossible to communicate with her most of the time, especially on the phone. She got everything so confused. I was surprised I didn't know about my aunt, but not really after thinking about it. I remember her voice, whispery, a little dazed, 'Ricci, I'm going to make some tea. Do you want some?'

"Then she made a fuss over something she wanted to show me. She finally found it—an envelope from the bottom of the box.

"It looked like all of the other envelopes. There was the same return address, but my name was typed on the front. But it was a letter telling about the trust fund my dad had set up for me. It said something like:

"Riccardo Anthony Santini: On September eighth, your twenty-third birthday, the amount of $500,000 plus any interest accrued will be released to you from the Anthony James Santini trust fund to use at your discretion… and if I had valid reasons to use the fund earlier, *like for education*, then I could petition to get the funds. I mean, I could have had a lot of money in college to cover what the scholarship didn't."

"*Really?*" Gini said with her eyes opened wide.

"The trust documents were also in the envelope. The letter was signed by Roger Whitmore, CEO and president, dated August fifth, five months after my dad died.

"Mom told me Mr. Davies took care of everything. I went to see him in San Francisco two days later.

"So Mr. Davies goes, 'I'm glad you came. I have been trying to get your mother to call you for a while. She never could find your phone number. I guess you have seen the letter for your inheritance to be released to you next week.'

"I didn't bother to tell him he could have found my number himself—it's not like I was unlisted. Surely he knew where I was at school. But I let it go. It turns out, John went up to see my mom four times a year just to make sure she was doing okay. I guess a lawyer was also assigned to my mother when my dad died. I tried to talk her into moving here to Boston and living with Riti and me, but she wouldn't hear of it. I found a nice young couple to move in with Mom and take care of her."

"Is your mom still living?"

"No, she died—let's see—when you guys were in China."

"I'm sorry, Ric." She patted his arm.

"Thanks, but it was a godsend. She was so sad for all of those years. The young couple bought the house, so I didn't have to do much to take care of all of Mom's affairs after her death."

Gini had only gone to Ric's house in Sacramento once. He had been embarrassed at his mother's condition and constantly told her how lucky she was to have such a loving mother. After the visit, Gini had felt bad for his mother, and had found his aunt was scary and stern.

"So, that is how you and Margs could afford to buy that brownstone on Beacon Hill!"

"It was already in the works before I went to Sacramento. The law firm had given me a housing bonus when I was hired on. Once the bank found out I had the money from the trust as well, that sealed the deal. Riti had a real knack for decorating. We turned that drafty house into a nice, cozy home."

"You still own it, right?"

"Yes."

"I can't wait to see it and Ma—" Gini was interrupted.

"Oh," he said as he knocked over the bag with his arm, "here is your little treasure."

He handed the bag to Gini. She looked at him and then spread the top of the bag open and pulled out an envelope with two copies of an invoice. She wrote a check for $750, signed it Virginia E. Anderson, and handed it to him. He split the invoices and handed her one. "It's all yours."

She took the white cardboard box out and pulled the cloisonné box from within, rubbing it softly with her hand. "Such a delicate and beautiful box." Inside was a satin lining; she ran her finger over the fabric.

"I know just the place for this." She closed the box and walked over to the fireplace, placing it perfectly centered under an original painting hanging over the mantel.

"There!" She turned around and smiled at him. "It has a home."

Ric loved her dimples when she smiled. "The funny thing is, Franco can probably get you that same box in China for fifty bucks or less." He laughed.

She softly hit his arm as he approached her. "Now, don't ruin my little find. This is a very special little box to me."

"Hey, Gini, we need to be going."

They walked to the front door of the building.

"Let's just walk," Gini said, "it's so nice out tonight."

Ric agreed, so they went out of the building and headed to the Rose Kennedy Greenway.

"How is it you and Franco found your place?"

"Some guy at Franco's work said he had a friend who was trying to get rid of a condo in the Towers at Boston Harbor. We contacted the friend. Turns out the place had belonged to his grandparents. They had lived in it since it was built. When they died, his parents would come and stay there a few times a year when they were in Boston. The brothers tried to do something with the place after their parents passed but found it would cost too much to update. So we got it dirt cheap. Other than the initial remodel to join the units, I don't think anything had been done to the place ever except maybe the carpet was replaced."

Gini lived in Building 1, the taller of the two high-rises known as the Harbor Towers, each forty stories. They had been built back in the early 1970s as affordable rental apartments. At that time, the harbor had been a less than desirable area to live. The warehouses were old and dusty, and the area had been considered seedy and rough. There had been much talk about the design of the buildings; some described them as brutalist. The isolated modern buildings were not at all in harmony with Boston's historic look.

The area had been separated from the city by a two-story elevated highway, known as the Central Artery. It was old and decayed with rust and black streaks. The artery had also cut off the North End, an Italian neighborhood with its preservation of 17th- and 18th-century architecture.

I.M. Pei and Henry N. Cobb had been the well-known architect and building designers. They had envisioned their project would bring new life to Boston's waterfront. The project became a cornerstone for future progress in the area.

In the 1980s, the area had become a desired area to live. The buildings had fabulous views of the harbor and city skyline. Many people had bought several units and tore out walls to make one large home. Gini's condo was a combination of three units with views around three sides of the building.

And in the 1990s, a project called the Big Dig had been started to put the highway underground. The Central Artery would be torn down, and the harbor area would be opened up to the city. Other complexes, like Rowes Wharf, were built, and the gardens popped up along the water and Rose Kennedy Greenway.

The area became an expensive, much sought-after place to live. On Long Wharf, hotels and restaurants brought business to the beautiful harbor. Other tourist attractions, like the aquarium, allowed visitors to see the city at its best.

Once they had arrived at the restaurant and were drinking their cocktails, Ric asked, "Why didn't you and Franco have a proper wedding? You could have afforded one."

"I know. But we loved your and Margarita's wedding. It was so special standing up for our best friends, and we decided we wanted to do the same, just the four of us. Margs and I went to Downtown Crossing just like we did for her and bought my dress. Those were such great times. Life was so simple, and I was so naive and innocent. Margarita too. Remember the time I drove your SUV up to Portland to deliver some papers from the State Department?"

He laughed. "I think you had to sit on a pillow to see over the steering wheel."

"Well, not quite. I thought I was such big stuff. I used that lever to lift the seat as high as it would go. I was the queen of the road. I felt so liberated that day. All by myself, taking care of business and no one had to help me. How did you get that truck, anyway?"

"I came home from school one day the first part of our senior year, and my aunt said, 'Your dad's company delivered your car today,' and gave me the keys.

I didn't know any better and gladly accepted them. I should have figured out there was some money right then, but I was just a kid."

"We were all just kids. However, I think Margs grew up in a hurry when she found out she was pregnant."

"No kidding. Me too. I have never been so scared in my life as that day she told me we were going to have a baby, scared to death!"

"Franco and I wanted to start a family right away too. You guys were pregnant, and we thought it would be fun to have our kids the same age. But even though we tried, nothing was happening. As you may recall, I never have periods. I don't ovulate regularly." She was taking a bite of bread and looked up. "TMI?"

He shook his head and smiled.

"Sorry. Anyway, I found a fertility doctor in New Haven, a community a few miles west of here, at their medical center. I love her. Her name is Dr. Linda Nelson. She started me on fertility pills. It seems I took those things forever. Then Franco announced we were going to China. Dr. Nelson told me to keep taking the pills, and if I got pregnant, I should come back to the States immediately.

"I hated China. We were only supposed to be there for four months, but it stretched into over a year. I remember how angry Margarita was that we could never talk to each other or email or anything. It seemed she disowned me, like I wasn't a good friend, even though I had no control over the situation. It was kind of like when I moved out here for school. My family didn't care about my life anymore. She didn't seem to care about my life overseas.

"But I can tell you, there was nothing there for me to do. If she thought I was living a glamorous life there, she was so wrong.

"We were way out in the middle of nowhere; it was dirty, and all we ever ate was rice. But every once in a while, we would get a shipment of nutrition shakes for the sick ones. I got to really liking that stuff, strawberry vanilla." She made a little face. "Franco, on the other hand, was having the time of his life. He loved his work. And if they ran into a problem, he would invent a gizmo or develop a new process, and the project would go on. He's brilliant, you know!"

Ric agreed.

She stopped to take a sip of her drink. "I guess Franco saw how miserable I was, so we came home. We decided to go with the in vitro method. We went through all the testing and cultivating and then implanted several. Right after that, Franco told me he was going to return to China. I didn't have to go. He had set it up so he came home every two or three months and would stay for a while, working out of Boston when he was here. He explained he had started his own company. He would work directly with the Chinese. That way he could reap the benefit of his inventions instead of letting the company he was working for take all the credit and money. He had worked out a deal with the Chinese government, and they were funding him. He set up an account with an accountant that I work with to keep his money growing, and, believe me, Franco is a very wealthy man. I think he has a legal team, and I don't know what all." She took another sip.

"At first, he called or emailed every day, mostly wanting to know if I was pregnant. Of course, the calls were in the middle of the night. Then it was a few times a week, then sometimes once a month, and now, it has been a long time. Until last week."

"I remember when that all was happening," Ric said as he thought back to that time. "I didn't realize he had started his own company. It seemed once you went to China, we never saw much of each other after that. If I remember right, he did come back at least once."

"You're right; he did come back after the first three months. By then I had gone to work for Catherine, and I was busy running around. Really, if I didn't see the money come in every month, I wouldn't know that he is still alive! I guess Margs is visiting her mom."

"I assume she's with her mom. After Riti's dad died, her mother was unhappy in California and wanted to go back to Hawaii. Did you know Riti finished her degree then went on and got her master's in critical care nursing?"

"Good for her." Gini was eating her crab cake.

"Anyway, she went to California and helped her mother move to Hawaii. She set her up in one of those senior complexes in an independent living apartment. But her mother hated it there, wanted to move out of the 'hotel' as she put it." Ric started on his oysters.

"You said you assume she's with her mother. What do you mean?"

He put his fork down and sat back in his chair. There was silence for a moment. He had been dreading the moment he told Gini. It was painful just thinking about it, and now he had to tell one of his best friends. Then he leaned forward and put his forearms on the table. "Gini, Riti and I got divorced over a year ago."

She dropped her fork and sat back hard on her chair. Tears instantly filled her eyes and then started running down her cheeks. She quickly grabbed her purse, took a tissue out, and dabbed at her eyes.

"Ric, no, you guys were so much in love." The tears were still flowing.

"Why didn't Margarita or you call me? Oh man, this is awful, Ric. I can't believe no one told us. What happened?"

"I don't know. It was probably a lot of things—losing the babies, her dad dying, and all the problems getting her mother settled. I think she just lost interest in our life together. She went back to Hawaii to see what she could do for her mom, and she just stayed. I kept telling her she needed to come home. She finally did, and that day she opened up my hand and put her two wedding rings on my palm, the plastic one and the diamond one I bought after I started at the firm. She said she didn't want to be married anymore. I pleaded with her to go to counseling with me, but she refused. It broke my heart. She packed up and went back to Hawaii. I sat with the lawyers and went through all the paperwork. She never showed up for any of it. I bought her half of the house and made sure she got a good settlement so she wouldn't have to worry about money. She just walked out of my life. I haven't heard from her or seen her since."

"I'm such a bad friend. I should have been there for you guys." Gini blew her nose. "I can't believe it. I just can't believe it."

"No, we should have let you know. We've all been bad friends. You and Riti not speaking, my work hours going crazy, and the both of you gone all the time. Our friendship surely got the brunt of all of that. We shouldn't have let it get between us. I can't believe it's been four years."

"And *I can't believe* Margarita left you." She felt a stab of indignation. Ric had turned out to be such a good and loyal guy.

"I know. I was so scared of getting married, and then I was so happy I did."

"Ric…"

"No, no, it's okay. I mean, it will be okay. I am mending. I'm not just saying that, either. You think your heart is broken forever, but I guess the will to live is stronger than that. Better now than after twenty years, right? But it's just strange how things work out."

"Very strange," she said softly, and he knew she wasn't thinking about him.

The main course was served, and they both started to eat.

"I see you're wearing the green stone ring instead of your wedding ring. You guys are still married?"

"Yes, although most of the time I feel like I'm his mistress, or girlfriend in a faraway land. He's married to his work. Remember the old saying that went with the ring: Give it to someone you love, and you will have prosperous and happy 'rife'?" They both said "rife" at the same time. He laughed.

"The saying must be about the giver, not the receiver." She had a serious look.

"Well, Franco is prosperous and happy, right?"

"Both."

"By law, the money he makes is yours too."

"I know, but I don't do so bad myself, so I take care of all the bills. I just keep his money in his account."

She took a few more bites. "How did you get into the entertainment business? Didn't you want to be a lawyer since you were like three years old?"

"Interesting how things happen. It all took place about the same time my marriage was falling apart. My first and only client at the firm was Albert Greystone. I did his legal and even looked at some of his books. He invited me to a couple of his events, and I just loved it. I loved the energy, the people, the whole thing. I guess at that point the idea of fighting—which is really all the law is—did not appeal to me anymore. He asked me to come to work for him, so I did."

Ric ate a little more. "Then he said he wanted to retire, and his son didn't want to have anything to do with the business, so I bought it from him."

"Really?"

"Yep. I just wrote him a check, and I became Greystone Entertainment. It was good for me, kept my mind off Riti and how much I missed her. And here I am today, still loving what I do, still meeting great people and making them happy. Life is funny, isn't it?"

When they finished dinner, they walked back to the Towers.

"I can't believe the weather," Gini said. "Last Saturday night at the gala it was so cold. I thought for sure winter was here to stay. And look at tonight—it's almost warm out."

When they got to the front door, she thanked him for the evening. "I guess it was a great night. I'm still upset about you and Margarita."

"I didn't mean to upset you. It *was* a great evening. I think we have caught up on each other's lives."

"We have."

He bent down and kissed her on the cheek. She started for the door and turned back to him. "Are we still on for that drive up to Gloucester tomorrow?"

"Well, sure. I have some stuff I need to do in the morning. How about I pick you up about one o'clock? We can have a late lunch up there."

"See you then."

She put her programmed key in the door and went inside. He watched her until she got to the elevator. She turned, and they both waved.

He thought about the many trips they had taken up the coast when they were in college. Often the four of them had shared a sandwich, bag of chips, and drink to save money. He remembered the girls pinching their noses around the shrimp boats, and one time Franco had grabbed Gini up in his arms and run up the steep hill in Gloucester when she had dared him. It had been such a great college life with his friends.

In her condo, she went to the roses and smelled their sweet scent, then picked up her PET and saw the picture of the Chinese woman. She smiled, turning off the tablet. She walked over to the little box, looked at it, opened the lid, slipped the green stone ring off, and put it inside. When she closed the lid, she stood with her hand on the top for a minute. She felt a pang of emotion again thinking about Ric and Margarita splitting up. The ring reminded her of such happy times. And what about her and Franco? They too had once had a great love. Was he just going to walk out of her life as Margarita had Ric's? She shivered at the thought. They *had* a good marriage.

Marriage? Yes, they did have a marriage, and yes, they were in love with each other. She could easily imagine his arms around her, his lips on hers, and feeling excitement, longing—all the same feelings she'd ever had. None of that had disappeared. It was just that there was something else there too—anger.

Anger wasn't an emotion she knew how to deal with, not in her personal life. She pushed it slowly away, like a heavy piece of furniture on tiny rollers, until it was deep in shadow.

And how long can I keep it up?

She was just going through some rough times. He'd soon be coming home to her.

Chapter 4 – Getting Reacquainted

About twelve-fifty the next morning, Gini got a text from Ric:

I'm running a bit late. It will be more like 1:30.

She replied:

> Contact me when you are close, and I'll meet you
> in front of the building.

About a half hour later:

I'm just around the corner.

She went downstairs and saw a black Mercedes S-Class in front of the building. As she approached the front door to go outside, Ric popped up out of the driver's side.

He opened the passenger side door and bowed as he swept his left hand in front of him. "Madam."

"Wow, what a great car!"

She got in and flung her coat and scarf into the back seat. When Ric got in, he saw her running her fingers along the dashboard. "This is nice." Her hand traced the door, down the rich wood paneling, and over all the buttons of the tufted leather. "I'm *impressed.*"

He smiled. "You know I deal with the rich and famous, and they like to be treated right. So, when I meet with them or take them out, I aim to please so they will reach deep into their pockets and pay me the big bucks. I just put on my chauffeur's hat." He stopped to think a second, then reached behind Gini's seat, pulled out a Red Sox baseball cap, and put it on. "And treat them like royalty."

She looked at him strangely. "I hope you don't put on that hat."

"Hey!" He took the hat off and put it back. "What's wrong with my Sox hat?" He looked in the rearview mirror and smoothed his hair.

As he pulled away, she sank deep into the plush, cream-colored seat and ran both hands down the soft, detailed leather.

"Oh, Ric, I love this car."

They drove out of Boston on 1A, the scenic route. He remembered their college days once again; Gini had always insisted they get out somewhere near the water so she could watch the waves.

He stopped in Lynn and parked near the cement outpost that looked out over the water. They went to the farthest end and looked down at the waves dancing up over the rocks below.

After a while, she turned to him. "I haven't been up here for so long."

She hadn't put on her coat, thinking it was warm enough, but a freshening wind gust hit them, and she shivered. She folded her arms up close to the front of her body and pulled her shoulders up to her ears. "It's beautiful!"

He stood up close behind her to block the wind, took off his jacket, and put it around her shoulders. Since she wasn't wearing high heels, she hit him about mid-chest. Ric put his hands on her shoulders. She felt another big chill and shivered.

He leaned over and got close to her ear. "We'd better get back in the car before you get too cold."

Gini was reluctant, but turned around and headed back to the car with him.

They drove on up to Gloucester via Marble Head, through Salem and Manchester. According to Gini, Gloucester House restaurant had the best lobster rolls in New England. It was about three o'clock and the place was nearly empty. They had missed the lunch crowd and were way too early for dinner. The waitress seated them in a booth at the big picture window that looked out over the dock. The fish and shrimp boats were just delivering the day's catch to the fishery warehouse next to the restaurant. The merchants and others were buying what they needed. Seagulls were flying low overhead, making their loud squawking noise. Gini stared out the window with her chin cupped in her hand; her arm rested on the table. When their lunch was served, she didn't notice.

"It's so peaceful and wonderful here. I could sell my place—yes—sell and move up here. I do most of my work out of the house when I'm in Boston. There's no problem jumping on the super-commuter to get into town, and if I need to go to DC, just take the super-train."

"Are you talking to me?" he asked.

Gini, still not completely out of her thoughts, suddenly looked at him. "I'm just dreaming and talking to myself."

She cut a bite of lobster roll. "Life just seems so slow and laid-back here, no stress, no pressure. How perfect."

After lunch, they walked around the shops and through the streets, ending up back at the docks. She once again stopped to watch the seagulls as they dipped down into the water to get the pieces of fish the fishermen had thrown overboard.

On the road again, he took her up to Rockport, another one of her favorite places. He stopped and parked, and she wrapped her scarf up over her head and down tight around her neck. They walked down the stairs and stood on the small flat rock surface with a guardrail. The overhang was on a cliff looking straight down at the waves crashing onto the large rocks below, sending sea spray high into the air. The seas were churning in advance of a storm system approaching. He leaned forward on the guardrail, looking at the water. Gini closed her eyes, put her head back, and took a deep breath of the crisp sea air. She felt the cool dampness on her face and listened to the thunderous waves pound the rocks below. Occasionally, she could hear a seagull squawk. She opened her eyes as he stood up and looked at her. Another loud wave crashed into the rocks, leaving only a white foam as the water receded.

She looked at him. "Mother Nature paints a beautiful picture."

Just then, a big gust of wind swept by them, and it started to rain lightly. They headed back to the car.

Inside, Gini unwrapped her scarf and threw it in the back seat. Suddenly she felt a warming against her back and under her thighs.

"Heated seats!"

Ric grinned, proud of himself.

"Did I tell you I love this car?" She snuggled into the seat.

He wished she would show her beautiful smile. It was as if the warm blaze of her youthful enthusiasm had dimmed and turned to a cold flame. What had taken her happiness—her playful personality? Yes, they had grown older and experienced more of life, but this change was more than maturity—more like a dousing of ice water freezing her spirit.

On their way home, they went through light sprinkles, sleet, and then heavy rain. Once they got through Everett, the precipitation had dwindled to a drizzle.

"Pull into the parking garage and go up to the sixth level," she said when they approached her building.

"See the elevator sign? Go over there and park in space four."

As Ric pulled in, he could see "Owners Only" painted on the wall. "Are you sure it's okay for me to park here?"

"These are our two parking spots." She pointed to the one they were in and the one next to them where a red convertible Audi was parked.

Ric opened the door for her. "Is this your car?"

"That's Red Bessie," she said with some pride. "I let my hair down, drop her top, and we fly around the city like we own the place."

"Well, that's not such a bad ride either."

Gini took him to the back elevator and then up to the eighth floor to her place.

"I'm not a coffee drinker, but I do have coffee if you want some." She took his coat.

"No thanks. I saw some beer in your bar refrigerator."

"Oh sure, help yourself." She put water in the kettle to make some tea. "It sure got cold fast."

"And look at it now."

He walked over to the big floor to ceiling windows overlooking the harbor. Gini walked up next to him holding her mug of tea. It was once again raining.

"I had forgotten what a great view this is," he said.

"Yeah, every time I think about moving out of here, all I have to do is come to these windows and look out. I love watching the ships and boats and seeing the planes taking off and landing at Logan Airport, especially at night when you can see the lights. Come see what we've done."

She showed him the balcony they had enclosed. There were views of Rowes Wharf and Fort Independence. But it was cold, and they quickly went back inside.

Gini turned on the gas fireplace and flicked on the TV to a college football game.

Ric laughed. "What woman turns on a football game?"

"I like football." She looked intense and put her hand on her hip.

"I know. You as a cheerleader in high school didn't even know what a first and ten was or even who had the ball most of the time." They sat down on the couch.

"I've grown up, and you know I love the Patriots; they're my boys." She was sitting on the front edge of the cushion looking rather anxious.

He put his hand gently on her shoulder. "Gini, you're so cute."

"Cute? I'm not sure I want to be *cute*."

"Too bad! You are."

She pushed herself back on the couch. He reached over and put his arm around her, and gave her a big hug. He felt like a kid again, sitting there with his childhood friend. How many times at her house had he and Franco wrestled from the couch to the floor with Gini first cheering for Franco and then for Ric when Franco was about to take him down? He had often given her a hug for cheering him on when Franco allowed him to win. They were the only two friends he'd had then. And now they were together again. It made him feel comfortable—an at-home feeling. He was with family.

After a second, he could tell that she was uncomfortable with the move, and he moved his arm to the top of the back of the couch.

She got up and went into the kitchen to pour some more hot water into her cup, and came back with a plate full of snacks and put them on the coffee table in front of Ric. This time, she sat in the chair catty-cornered to the couch. She curled up into a ball, holding her mug between her pulled-up legs and her stomach.

It seemed odd to be sitting there talking to one of her best friends in the whole world. She hadn't seen him for so long. Part of her felt warm and relaxed, and part of her uneasy—wanting to pull into her shell and wait for him to go away. Had she forgotten how to act around a friend? She'd had so many friends when she was young, and now her only friend was Catherine—her life all work and no play. She needed to try to relax.

"Today was fun," he said.

"It was. Remember all the good times we had in college?" A happy memory entered her mind.

"I can see you and Riti now, trying to be brave and go into the cold Atlantic Ocean," Ric said.

"It was always so inviting, but oh my gosh, so dang cold. Strange now, isn't it?"

"What?"

"Sitting here after not seeing each other for so long. You, no longer married. You're not even a lawyer anymore." She shook her head as she looked down. "And me, well, married, but thousands of miles away from my husband. So busy with work I don't have a life anymore." She looked him in the eyes. "What happened, Ric? What happened to our great friendships, our marriages?"

He was silent a minute. "Life isn't always rosy. You can't just stop living. You must keep going and push through the rough times. We're still friends, right? Just because we haven't seen each other for a while doesn't mean we're no longer friends."

Even though she had brought it up, she wanted to change the subject. The idea of something different in her life scared her. "Yes, still friends." She forced a smile. A betraying thought flickered through her mind, and she felt a twinge of guilt. Was it okay to be with him alone? It had always been her, Franco, and Ric. She had never been alone with him. But they were friends, and it should be okay to be alone with a friend. She shook it off. No one—Franco—would ever know. It was just the two of them.

An uncomfortable silence lay heavy in the room. A loud cheer came from the college game on the TV.

"I think the Patriots might have a chance to go all the way this year," he said.

"Me too. They were doing really well until they lost the last two games."

After talking and watching the game for a while, Ric said he needed to go. On his way home, he would stop at the grocery store and buy supplies for the party.

"You're coming to my place tomorrow for the game?" he asked.

"Well…"

"I'm going to make my famous chili."

"Oh, I love your chili."

"Then the answer is yes."

"What can I bring?"

He thought for a minute. "Bring your brownies."

"Brownies, you like my brownies?"

"Yes, why do you act so surprised?"

"Because you guys used to make fun of them."

"We were just playing with you; you made good brownies, just like Mama Elizabeth."

"It's been a while, but I can make a batch."

She took Ric down to the garage.

"The game starts at four o'clock. Everyone gathers about three-thirty to three forty-five. I'll come and pick you up about three-fifteen."

"You don't have to pick me up. I can walk."

"Gini."

"No, I can take the Blue Line and get off at Park Street, then just walk up the hill. You're the first street off Beacon Street, right? I'm sure I'll recognize the house."

"Okay, text me when you get off the T, and I'll meet you at the corner of my street."

"Thanks again for today. It was wonderful seeing all those places again."

"It was a nice break."

For the first time in a long time, she felt happy. He was easy to be with. How she longed to have that life again—the four of them all having such a good time together. Why did they have to grow up? Why did life have to get in the way?

The next morning, she went through the deep bottom drawer in her hall desk looking for the brownie recipe. She had asked her mama to send it to her when she was in college. She had made them so many times in Ric and Margarita's apartment those last few years of college that she had known the recipe by heart. She could remember everything now except how much sugar, how much baking powder—or was it baking soda?

As she dug further in the drawer, she found some poetry she had written after they moved into the condo. She had loved reading and writing verses in high school and college. Her life had become so busy she didn't have time to concentrate on writing, but she had just written one about all the lonely children.

This one, however, she had saved in a computer file. She guessed she had been inspired by Franco's email talking about the children where he worked.

With that thought, Gini stood straight up. What had happened to their great love? He had always protected her, loved her, and cherished their relationship. She had felt safe, certain they'd be together forever. Had she somehow let him down by not going back to China with him? She felt a moment of anxiety, a twist in her chest, a shadow over her thoughts. Was she really committed? Was she too concerned about her own comfort? She had never thought so... *but we can't see ourselves clearly, can we?* In school and her career, she was always moving ahead, proud of herself—was she too ambitious? She felt exposed for a moment as a shallow, selfish person, and shivered. But wait. That was insecurity speaking. Her ambitions mattered too. She wasn't just his wife; she was a person with her own path to success. It was Franco who wasn't sensitive to her needs and what she wanted to accomplish in life, not the other way around... But hadn't he once been sensitive? Hadn't they been a great couple? Why couldn't they still make it work? *Franco*, she thought, *where are you? Why don't you come to me and love me as you once did?* She *missed* him... This wasn't a marriage.

After a few minutes, she once again dug through the drawer and then there it was, a piece of paper, obviously well used, with batter-remnant stains on the edges. "Yes!" She grabbed the paper and took it into the kitchen.

It was a dark, cold, and misty day. Gini put on blue jeans, a bulky sweater, and fur-lined boots with a small heel. She loved those boots, so warm, waterproof, and with a good grip sole that kept her steady on her feet in any weather. She pulled her hair straight back and put it into a high ponytail. Her curly hair made it easy to twirl the hanging hair into one big spiral curl.

It was about two-thirty; she had some time to kill. She picked up her PET to check messages. She looked up, and the cloisonné box caught her eye. She turned on her tablet and went to her email.

There was one from Catherine:

> Hey, thanks for all the notes from the meeting with Senator Goodman. I have gathered more data and am attaching it to this message. I think we need to put our heads together next week and get a good plan together, then surge the Hill. Let me know when you can come down to DC. Love, Catherine.

Gini responded:

I will look at your information tonight. I'm off to
a football party at Ric's and will be late. If I don't
get back to you tonight, I'll email first thing in the
morning. This coming week is clear so we can
finalize when I go to DC.

GO PATRIOTS!!!

Catherine replied:

Oh, missy, it's all about the REDSKINS.

Gini smiled and typed:

In your dreams!

She laid the computer down, went to the fireplace, and ran her hand over the
inlay porcelain box. The ring was dainty and shiny on the silky fabric inside. She
slowly slipped it on, then clutched her hands at her chest and put her lips on her
fingers. How she loved that beautiful ring and what it symbolized.

At three-ten, she left to go to Ric's with a six-pack of beer, the kind he and
Franco always bought, and a plastic container of brownies in her big bag. She
grabbed her heavy wool peacoat and fashionable woman's small-billed hat. On
the way to the subway, she pulled her ponytail up inside and out through the hole
in the back of the cap.

Ric had his double batch of chili simmering in the Crock-pot. He took the last
pan of cornbread out of the oven and "hot potatoed" each piece out of the pan
and onto the plate without an oven mitt. Everything was in its place for the party.
He had hosted the Sunday football party many times in the past, but he felt a bit
anxious today.

Neighbors started showing up about three-thirty.

"Come on in," he said as he greeted each one arriving.

He kept looking at his watch. When was she going to text?

At three forty-two his phone vibrated:

Just out of the station heading your way.

David and Pam knocked on the door.

"Here you go, old boy," David said as he handed Ric a full bottle of bourbon
and Pam lifted up a bag full of chips.

"Get in here," Ric said, "and get game-ready."

David and Ric fist-bumped, and he kissed Pam on the cheek, then took their coats and glanced out the window.

"Listen," he said to everyone, "I'll be right back. Please make yourselves comfortable, get a drink, and dive into the food."

He grabbed his jacket as he ran out the door and flew down the six stairs off his front porch, putting his jacket on as he went. There she was, just rounding the corner.

Pam walked over to the bay window in the living room where everyone was gathering. "Where's he going?"

"Maybe he forgot the hot sauce for the chili," David said facetiously.

"It's a woman," Pam said slowly. "Ric has a girlfriend!"

Lindsey, Misty, and Ginger all joined Pam at the window.

"Come on," David said, "give the guy a break."

"No really, David, he's running to meet a woman coming down the street." Pam put her hand under her chin.

David walked to the window to see. "So he has a woman! What's the big deal?"

"I hope so," Lindsey said. "He's such a great guy. I don't know what happened with Margarita, but he needs a good woman in his life."

"Geez, girls, give it up. He's a single man; he probably has lots of women." David headed back to sit in a chair in the living room.

When Gini and Ric returned, he introduced his friends.

"You look familiar," David blurted out. "I think I know you from somewhere. No, no, don't tell me. I'm going to figure it out."

Gini felt like everyone in the room was looking at her and sizing her up.

"And here we go," the announcer on the TV said. The Patriots received the ball on the 20-yard line, ran to the 30, and then ran along the sidelines all the way to the Washington 40-yard line. "What a great runback," the sports anchor said.

As the play calls progressed, Gini stepped around to see the big-screen TV in Ric's living room. Everyone in the room yelled and cheered as the runback took shape. She was relieved the attention was off her. The next few minutes were intense while the Patriots took the ball down the field, stalling at the 1-yard line. Gini was completely immersed in the game, forgetting the room full of people. "You have to go for it, you have to go for it," she called out.

Ric—behind her—was close enough to feel her leaning to the right or left as the play panned out. After each play, her body reacted to the play that was over and readied for the play to come.

"Come on, *go!*" She put her face in her hands and let out a big sigh.

He smiled to himself at her emotion. She was much more of a football fan than he was. The third down was a running play. It looked like they got into the end zone, and everyone in the room cheered with delight. Gini jumped up and down. But the officials said the play was downed six inches to the goal. The room fell quiet.

"This is the big play," the announcer broke the silence.

Gini had her fingers up to her mouth. The ball was snapped, and the quarterback stepped back and floated one into the end zone. It was caught, and the Patriots scored.

Gini turned to Ric. "Oh my gosh, oh my gosh!"

Everyone else was cheering.

The next series of plays, the Redskins came right back and scored. At halftime, everyone went into the dining room and filled up on the chili, snacks, and cornbread.

The game went back and forth for three and a half hours. Ric was constantly amused with Gini's interaction with all the plays. She sat next to him on the couch, right at the edge of the cushion most of the evening. Occasionally, she would turn and look at him, but most of the time her focus was on the TV action. Her ponytail would flip and swing with her every move. That was the Gini he remembered, full of life.

With only thirty seconds left in the game, the score was tied 28 to 28, and the Redskins had the ball on the Patriots' 45-yard line. The quarterback reached back to pass; the Patriots intercepted and ran it in for a touchdown, leaving only five seconds on the clock.

"Oh, yes! Oh yes, that's what I'm talking about," Tim yelled. "That's what I *am* talking about."

"We are going all the way to the Super Bowl," Gini shouted.

Everyone cheered. Final score: 35 Patriots, 28 Redskins.

After the game, they all gathered in the dining room again and ate Gini's brownies and other sweets on the table.

"Ric, your friend is quite the cheerleader," Tim said.

"Those are my boys, the Patriots." Gini immediately felt shy when the attention was on her again.

David stood forward. "You're Virginia Anderson!"

"Yes—"

"I knew I knew you. You're Virginia Anderson."

No one else in the room seemed impressed and continued with their chitchat.

An hour went by, and slowly everyone started to leave. Gini helped Ric clean up.

"Ric, this was fun. Thanks for asking me. It put a whole new perspective on watching the game."

"You're very welcome. Someone in the neighborhood has a party every weekend of the season. I'm sure you're welcome to go to any of them."

She went to get her coat. "That's sweet of you to share your friends. You can keep the rest of the brownies. I need to get going. Catherine sent me an email right before I came here. I need to get back and get started on putting a report together."

He walked over and grabbed his coat.

"It sounds like I'm off to DC this week. Why are you putting on your coat?"

"I'm going to drive you home."

"No, I can walk. I like walking."

He finished buttoning his jacket. "But Gini, it's pretty cold out there, and I have heated seats." He sang the word "seats."

"Okay," she said turning toward the door. "The heated seats won me over."

"How long will you be in DC?" he asked, driving out of the driveway.

"I imagine I'll be going back and forth until the Congress winter break. This is a busy time for us, trying to have as much influence on the voting as possible before everyone goes home. The nice thing is all I have to do is pack a small bag and jump on the train. Catherine keeps a room for me at her place, and I keep one for her here. It makes the trips back and forth easy."

"Yeah, this is the busiest time of the year for me too, with all the holiday parties. And I'm sure there will be some celebrating of election victories. This is when I earn a large part of my company revenue."

Gini felt the warmth and snuggled down into the seat. "Sounds like fun, but a lot of work."

"I have the greatest team working for me, and, fortunately, we get to participate in some of the bigger holiday parties, which is fun. You should go with me. When Franco's in town, you'd both have a great time and meet some interesting people." Ric smiled as he talked, glancing out of the corner of his eye to watch her take pleasure in the heated seats.

"We'll see if my schedule will allow it." She looked up and saw he was smiling in fun at her. "What?"

"Nothing. Here we are."

"I have had a wonderful weekend, Ric. Thank you so much for everything. I'm so glad I won the bid on the wonderful little box so we could reconnect."

"Me too." He walked her to the front door. "Give me a call or text when you are back in town. We'll do dinner or something."

"I will, I will." She nodded.

56

"You have a good time in DC and say hello to Catherine for me."

"Okay." She turned and went into the building.

Ric waited until she reached the elevator. As she stepped in, she turned around, and they waved at each other as the elevator doors closed.

Walking back to his car, he thought about the great weekend. He laughed to himself. Funny how in high school and college, his only friends were Franco, Gini, and Margarita.

Tonight, it seemed Gini came alive when she was around happy people, he thought. I have many friends and am more than happy to introduce her to them. If all she needed is to be in a crowd having a good time, I can certainly give her that by taking her to my parties. That's what had saved him through his desperate times. Other people's warmth, other people's laughter. It would help her too. His job now was to heat up that cold flame in his old friend and start a fire in her once again.

Gini opened her messages to read all of Catherine's emails. Her eye went right to Franco's message. She opened it and replied:

> I love the pictures. You're doing such great work for humanity. I'm fine, keeping busy with Catherine. I ran into Ric Santini last week at an event. It was good to see him, brought back so many happy memories. Take care. Love, Gini.

She looked at the green stone ring. A vision of Franco giving Ric a hand-carved pipe from China appeared. Ric was the best friend Franco had ever had. She knew he would be happy to be with Ric again when he returned.

The X symbolized a kiss and the knot, intertwining love. She ran her finger over the knot-covered stone on her way to the bedroom, then took the ring off and put it on her dressing table.

Chapter 5 – Back to Work

While in college, Gini had worked for the Massachusetts State House as a file clerk. Her supervisor's sister had had a difficult pregnancy, and the little boy was born with many health issues affecting his heart, lungs, and stomach. Angela had described to Gini how her sister and husband were middleclass, making a comfortable living, but the minute the baby was born, neither of their companies would insure him because their son had had a pre-existing condition. His health care was going to run into the hundreds of thousands of dollars. Angela had taken time off to help her sister try to find a solution so the baby could get good health care. She helped her sister find programs and agencies to help with the cost. Once they got insured, one of the baby's doctors had not been able to get the medicine he needed approved because it wasn't indicated for that particular treatment. Angela had seemed comfortable talking to Gini about all the issues. It had saddened Gini that an already difficult situation was being made a lot worse because of insurance.

Catherine White had given a presentation at the State House on the lack of good insurance for children who were gravely ill, outlining her agenda to remedy the problem. Gini had been immediately willing to help. After a few conversations with Catherine, Catherine had asked Gini to join her lobbying firm in Washington, DC, assigning New England as her territory. Gini had given her full attention to the cause since she hired on. Over the three years of her employment, she and Catherine had become close friends.

The next two weeks in October were hectic for both Gini and Ric. Gini and Catherine arranged to have meetings and conversations with as many congresspeople and committees as possible. Every night they were wined and dined, or they took people out to further discuss the issues and topics of the day.

"Man, my feet are killing me." Catherine rubbed her right foot.

Gini slipped off her shoes. "Why do we cram our feet in these pointed, uncomfortable high heels? We're gluttons for punishment. I think we have changed some minds. How do you feel, Catherine?"

"We've got to get this health care for kids in the system on the floor. Today I saw a lot of interest, but no commitment for introduction. We can't let the ball drop with winter break coming. So *you* go back to Boston and concentrate on the representatives from New Hampshire, Connecticut, and Maine. They have seen the Massachusetts health care work, and are showing interest; let's not let them get away. If we can get it on the floor, hopefully, it will go into committee with a quick vote. I'll work on the people here. I think we've had two good weeks. Now, we need to go in for the score."

"I'm looking forward to getting back to Boston for a few days. Your bed is comfortable, but I long for my own."

"I understand. Have you talked to Ric at all?"

"We did a quick text the other day, but he's very busy planning parties. I would have never figured Ric Santini as a party planner. He was so serious in high school, and so much in the lawyer mode the last time I saw him."

"I have known Ric for a couple of years. I had no idea you and he had gone to high school together. He's a nice guy, so good-looking and charming. Watch out; he may sweep you away."

"Catherine," Gini said with a sharpness to her voice. "Ric and I are just good friends. Don't forget I'm a married woman."

"Hahaha, married, what a marriage. You haven't seen your so-called husband for months. What kind of marriage is that? I don't know why you put up with it. You should tell Franco to get lost."

"Catherine!" There was a long silence. "Yeah, I need to have a long talk with him. Obviously, we are going in completely different directions in our lives, but that discussion is for another day. Right now, I just want to go to bed."

On Friday, Gini packed her bag and headed to the train station. "Okay, I'll turn on the pressure, bombard them with these reports, sit on the phone until they hear me out. We'll make this work. Let's video call on Tuesday and see where we are."

Catherine hugged Gini. "Good. Try to get some rest, honey, because we have a long row to hoe. See you in the next week or so."

She waved as the cab pulled away.

Gini walked into her flat when she got home and threw her bag on the chair. She quickly went through the mail Howard had put on her counter. He was so attentive to all the people living in the building. They all loved him and did what they could to show their appreciation.

She took a long hot bath and then crawled into her comfortable bed. Without hesitation, she picked up her phone to text Ric:

In Boston, need sleep.

He was at a function when he felt his PET vibrate. He pulled it out and read the message.

Will call u tomorrow, sweet dreams.

She didn't hear the vibration sound on her nightstand. She was in a deep sleep.

About 10 a.m. Gini heard her phone. "Hello, Ric."

"I didn't want to call too early in case you wanted to sleep in."

"I've been up for a while. Saturday is my run-around day: grocery shopping, which I'm doing now, dry cleaners, laundry, hair, nails, get the picture?"

"Got it." He laughed. "I'd like to see you, but I have a party tonight and a brunch business meeting in the morning I have to go to."

"Wow, you're busy."

"How about lunch? Can you go to lunch with me today?"

"Sure."

"Let's meet at Gary's Bar and Grill over by the park, say twelvish."

"Our old college hangout, that sounds good. I'll see you there at noon."

Gini finished her shopping, called her beautician, changed her hair and nail appointments, and walked to the Bar and Grill. Ric was sitting at a table reading something on his PET. As soon as he saw her, he jumped up and walked her back to the table.

"I haven't been here for a while. It hasn't changed a bit. They used to have the best hamburgers here; they even beat Burger King."

Ric laughed out loud. He remembered how Gini always wanted to go to Burger King when they were in college. The rest of them were tired of eating there all the time.

"You and your hamburgers."

Her eyes were wide and bright. The blueness was startling. Her full plump lips parted over her white teeth, and the dimples that went deep into her cheeks somehow made him want to grab her up into his arms and never let her go. He noticed she wasn't wearing the green stone ring.

"How was Washington?"

"It was great but busy."

She pulled closer to the table. "You know, many people see lobbyists, or politics as a whole, as a dirty business involving paying forward in order to get 'payoffs.' But we have such a great country and government, allowing every citizen a chance to be heard, to sit across the desk from our federal or state representative or senator and speak their mind whether they are a paid lobbyist or not. But to do that effectively, you have to be well prepared and documented with facts and figures that support your position. It can be a twenty-four-seven job with very intense periods. It's difficult emotionally. You never know how it will go. There could be sudden lulls in the action with recesses, elections, and other uncontrollables. I can't tell you how many times Catherine and I have spent days on a report, and then we have to sit and wait for a month to present it.

"But it's important to honor the position of elected office, so we play by their rules. It can be exhausting putting a lot of pressure on officials with phone calls, writing letters, making sure we get to the right folks. Wooing individuals who can get us time with those right people. And sometimes not succeeding, feeling like the time was lost… The key is to believe passionately in the cause for which you are an advocate. That's the only way you can sustain the energy to get a bill pushed through Congress. And I'm very committed to our cause. Plus there's such a great vibe in DC, I never get tired of it. I love the energy of the city and working with the different levels of government. I can't see myself doing anything else."

She was always able to state her case when something was important to her. He was convinced Catherine had hired the perfect person, Gini, for the job.

"How about you?"

"Let's see; I have been picking up all kinds of work. You remember the guy that came up to me after the Westcott Gala?"

She nodded.

"He was there representing a man by the name of Valentino Vasquez. He's from Fort Lauderdale, Florida. Gini, this guy is loaded. He is building a resort in Lauderdale-by-the-Sea and wants me to help him promote the sales. And he's also building a huge resort on a private island in the Bahamas. He wants me to help him with that one, too."

"Ric!" Her eyes opened wide. "That's fantastic. Are you going to take the job?"

"Absolutely! I went down to Florida last week. Val lives in this beautiful mansion on the intercoastal canal. You would love the place. It has a nice guesthouse right by the pool. And he has a yacht bigger than my house. Like I said, he's loaded. I told him I need to deal with all the holiday parties and events until the end of the year. Then I could really dig in and give him a lot of my time. He agreed on the time frame."

"Will you be moving to Florida?"

"No, I'll just be taking business trips down there. You and Franco must go with me sometime. It's nice there, *warm* and sunny. Wow, I never thought my life could be so good." He sat back in his chair as he realized what a great opportunity he had been handed.

She could see how pleased he was. "I've never been to Florida. A nice warm day on the water sounds great to me."

"I had never been there either. I mean, I thought I was so worldly rubbing elbows with the rich and famous here in Boston, but this guy makes them all look like paupers. And, Gini." He leaned forward and closer to her. "He's the nicest man. A bachelor, I guess. There are young women and occasionally young men there around the pool all the time."

"Like Hugh Hefner. Now I know why you think it's such a great place." She was surprised she felt a twinge of jealousy.

"Oh, no, those girls are pretty, but certainly not my type. Besides, they are there living off Val; I'm just a small fish. It's kind of nice on the eyes, though, I'll have to admit."

Gini was feeling protective of him. She didn't want her friend to be taken advantage of by some bikini-clad beauty. He was vulnerable now that he was single—so good-looking, women probably constantly hit on him. She laughed silently to herself; that was so much Mama Elizabeth's way of thinking. Should she be concerned? He seemed to take all of Val's extravagance in stride. Ric always had a good sense of reality. But he was still hurting—he'd admitted that. Could he resist someone showing him affection? Men were generally weaker at resisting such advances. He was her friend, and she cared about his well-being. That was all it was, just caring for her friend.

They ate and continued talking about their work. She was having a good time and wasn't ready for him to leave when he announced he had a meeting in twenty minutes across the street.

"Lunch has been great. Thanks for inviting me. It was good to see you again."

Ric leaned down as he started to leave and kissed her on the cheek. "I'm so glad we reconnected." He smiled his handsome smile. "I have a brunch tomorrow, but I think I'll be done in time for the football party at Tim's. Do you want to go?"

With no hesitation, Gini answered yes.

"I'll call you as soon as I finish brunch." He laid the money on the table to pay the bill and pulled on his suit jacket.

After putting on his coat, he ran his long fingers through his wavy brown hair, which immediately shifted back in place once the fingers had passed through. The light in the sun-filled room gave his tanned skin a silky glow.

She could see why everyone was drawn to him. She saw it at the gala, people wanting his attention and time. They wanted to be close to him, just as she did. With the passing of the years, his charm—which had been hidden for the first eight years she knew him—was easily flowing from his body. The softness of his chocolate-brown eyes and the gentleness in his smile were inviting her to be more involved with him, to be closer to her old friend. This was Ric, but also a new man she wanted to learn more about. She had missed him and was now enjoying his company once again—if truth be told, enjoying it even more than before.

She went home and continued with her Saturday chores. She kept thinking about Ric. As she put her freshly laundered clothes away, the green stone ring almost jumped off the dressing table at her. She went over and picked it up. Tears filled her eyes as she thought about her love for Franco—his strong hands swallowing up her face, the kind encouraging words he said to her when she had doubt, the intense lovemaking that never seemed to end. He was always a very private man, but his strength and power turned the heads of both men and women when he entered a room. The flirty female looks never took him away. He was committed to Gini, and she knew it; even with the many months that had slipped by without seeing him, she still felt his love. And *she* loved him. He had always been her hero and protector. She had learned from him what it meant to be committed to one's work—that was hard to admit sometimes, when she was so upset about his absences, but it was true. They would talk when he returned and get their lives back on track together. She would talk to him. He would listen. She could not and would not let herself become too attached to Ric. He was just a good friend, and they could enjoy each other's company on occasion. That and no more. She would never break her marriage vows. When Gini Anderson committed to something, she committed all the way.

It calmed her to reaffirm that to herself. If you knew where you stood, you could handle things like attractive old friends. It was just a question of reconnecting with herself, remembering her values. She spent all Saturday night working on reports and sending emails to Catherine. At midnight, she fell into bed once again exhausted.

Sunday morning, she woke up and was excited about going to the football party. She'd had such a good time the last time. Playing with the green stone ring on her finger, she sat in the chair and pulled her legs up close to her. Then she realized she must tell him she couldn't go today. It wasn't a good idea to spend so much time with him. Suddenly, she didn't feel strong; she felt defenseless.

Ric called at one-thirty. She looked at her phone and didn't touch it. It rang again and again. *How rude I'm being,* she thought. She answered.

"I'm heading home to change my clothes, and then I'll come and pick you up."

"Listen, Ric, I don't think I'm going to go."

"Why not?" He was clearly disappointed. "Come on, Gini, you love football, and it's fun being with the group, right? Everyone wanted to know when you were coming again. You're not sick, are you?"

"No. I just, well, I… I don't know." She couldn't admit the real reason. It would be dangerous… And she'd just feel silly. What grown woman couldn't control her emotions and keep a friend a friend?

"Don't know what? You sound tired. I think you've been working too hard, staring at a computer screen. You need a break. If you don't want to go to the football party, we can watch the game at your house or mine. Gini, you need to unwind a bit. Say yes."

There was silence while she fought back the tears, her emotions bubbling up inside of her. She was lonely. She wanted to be with him, and it wasn't fair… Why should she have to be alone all the time?

"Gini, are you still there?"

"You're right. What's better than watching the Patriots win with a bunch of friends?"

"That's the ticket. I'll be at your place about three."

"Okay."

She quickly wiped the tears from her cheeks and started to take the ring off, but decided to keep it on to remind her she must be careful. She could do this. She could handle herself and keep his friendship and enjoy whatever else she felt—but not let it go any further. It wasn't like he had made a move. He was Franco's friend too.

There were a lot more people at the party. Gini completely relaxed after they got to Tim's. She was introduced to the neighbors she hadn't met and was glad to see the ones she had been with before.

David immediately came up to her. "If it isn't Ms. Anderson back from Washington." He had a big grin on his face. "And I see you have your football ponytail all ready for the game."

"Yes," she said shyly. "I've got the ponytail working."

He put his hand on her shoulder. "You're a good sport. And we need to put a fire under this team!" he yelled out to the whole group.

"Yeah," several people yelled back.

The game was exciting as usual, and Gini was glad she had decided to go. The Patriots won, and everyone laughed and talked until nine o'clock.

Ric stayed close to her all night. He could tell she was emotional about something but didn't want to pry. If she wanted to talk about it with him, he would gladly listen. He once again was amused at how involved she got in the game; she was a serious Patriots fan. At the end of the evening, they walked back to his place.

"Do you want to come in for a while?"

"No, I need to get home. I have some more work I need to do in preparation for a video call with Catherine on Tuesday, but thanks for asking."

"What does your week look like? Are you going back to DC?"

"I'm not sure when I'll go back. I guess that will be determined on Tuesday when we talk."

"You know what Tuesday is? Election Day."

"Oh, yes, I think Victor's a shoo-in. He's looking very strong. And Michael called me Saturday to say Donald Griggs is stepping down from the city council."

"Really?"

"He had a second heart attack in August, a serious one, I guess, and he wants to uncomplicate his life. Michael wants me to help him get a campaign together so he can run for the office. I think he said there will be a special election in February."

"Are you going to do it?"

"I think so. Michael will be a good councilman. He'll be good for the city. He has so much energy and charisma. He can charm anyone, similar to you."

"You flatter me."

They got in the car.

Ric laughed. "I remember when Michael walked into Mitt Romney's campaign center. He was two years behind us in school, so we had to knock him down a peg or two. He never did like being called the newbie."

She half smiled in her prim and proper manner. "You guys were so mean to him, making him carry all those boxes. I always felt sorry for him. Remember when the bottom fell out of the box and the buttons went everywhere? We found buttons until the day we closed up shop."

"You'll get him headed in the right direction. He's always had a crush on you."

"I know. He's a nice guy."

Ric got a gleam in his eyes. "Gini, you and Michael?"

She fidgeted. "No, absolutely not. Ric… he's… well… he's not my type *at all.* He's disorganized and… well… not my type." She was flustered.

"Have you met his wife?" she asked, wanting to move on with the conversation.

"No." Ric was amused at her trying to get out of a tight spot. Amused, but a bit ashamed he had challenged her.

"Me neither. But he has shown me pictures of his beautiful family. He has the cutest little girls. And the way he looks when he talks about Brenda, I know he has a loving relationship.

"His firm's office is right down the hill from the State House. We run into each other all the time and do lunch a lot. He's always asking me questions about politics, so I'm not surprised he wants to run for office. We sometimes have discussions and other times heated debates. I'll have to admit, he has changed my opinion on some topics. But we are just *interested* in the same political issues." She glared at him.

"You should join us for lunch sometime and see how he's matured."

Ric gave her an unbelieving look.

"Really, he's mature and serious about winning in court, and now running for office."

"I think he's actually older than you."

"You think so?"

"Yes, because you are such a genius, but you're really just a baby." Ric wrinkled his nose and tickled her under her chin.

"Oh great, first I'm *cute*, and now I'm a baby. Thanks, Ric, thanks a lot."

"Anytime! Anytime I can make you feel good about yourself."

"I like being with you. You make me feel good." She quickly looked down to her lap when she realized what she had said. It was too easy to flirt—just by being honest.

After Ric had walked her to the condo, he thought about their lives. He had seen her recently in a local TV interview. She was poised and intelligent. Her message was eloquent and committed. She had also been shown at a rally to help disabled children. The foundation had been set up by a family whose daughter died from her disabilities because they couldn't get proper medical treatment. He had seen Gini's willingness to help others and the passion in her heart for the movement to help those children. He was proud of her and her success. She had made quite a name for herself, not only in Boston but in the politics of the nation.

He had done a search for Franco online and read the many articles about his accomplishments in engineering. His best friend was internationally known in his field. Ric had always been impressed with Franco's knowledge, and his way of making things work even if the situation wasn't ideal. He missed him; they'd had such a close bond.

Ric smiled at the thought of his and Gini's renewed friendship. He had never been so happy. This time of year was his favorite, with all the parties. And the new adventure with Val was exciting and challenging. It was nice to have someone to talk to about his work. Gini hung on his every word, genuinely interested in what he was saying. It was flattering, he admitted. And she was so attractive…

But married, he said to himself. To a very successful man. And more importantly, to his friend.

Well, there was nothing wrong with being friends. He knew people of his parents' generation who didn't think a man and woman could be friends—especially not if they were the same age and attractive and alone—but his generation was different. Everyone had friends of both sexes. It was normal, and if he was attracted to her—which he was—so what?

What mattered was the friendship. With *both* Gini and Franco.

He looked forward to seeing Franco and talking about their lives—the ups and downs of being business owners.

We should be *proud* of ourselves, he thought. The three of them had come a long way from being children of lower-middle-class families in their small neighborhood. Now, all could boast their talents. Their hard work and persistence had paid off.

Chapter 6 – End of the Year Push

Michael called Gini Monday morning and proposed they get together that evening. He said a working dinner would work best for him, and he knew a small cafe near the State House that had a good lunch crowd, but not much of a crowd for dinner. Five-thirty to seven-thirty would be good; that way he could get home in time to put his girls to bed.

Gini smiled as he talked about his family. "Okay, I'll meet you there at five-thirty. Bring all your ideas, and we'll start putting your campaign together. I have to tell you, though, after tonight I'm in Washington until Thursday. I don't know about after that because Catherine and I are pushing hard to get the child health protection in motion, and hopefully voted on before winter break."

"I understand. I appreciate you helping me, Gini. I know you're busy, but you are the best on the political scene, and I need your expertise. I think if we have this initial meeting, you can get me started, and then we can work using emails and phone calls."

"Sounds good to me. See you tonight."

Gini got to the cafe early and continued to text with Catherine.

> *Good work, Gini. Now stop working. We have it covered for tomorrow. Go out and have a nice dinner with Ric before you leave town.*

> Thanks. I feel like I'm starting a marathon race.
> I'm going out to dinner tonight, but not with Ric,
> with Michael Fredrick.

> *Michael! Gini, it's raining men in your world. Why with Michael?*

> Lol, I'll tell you all about it tomorrow.

"Gini," Michael said as he leaned over and kissed her on the cheek.

"I didn't see you come in." She gave him a light hug.

"You were flying those fingers all over that tablet."

"Just wrapping up with Catherine."

He sat down across the table from her. "Good, now you're all mine."

Michael was an attractive man in his own way, tall and scrappy, a little like an unmade bed. He was in a suit, but in Gini's opinion, the look wasn't the right one for a polished politician.

"Okay, first we have to do something with your appearance."

He laughed as he pulled piles of paper out of his briefcase bag and laid them on the table in an untidy stack.

"I'm serious, Michael, you need a haircut, and we need to spiff up your wardrobe."

"You don't like my hair? I wash it every day. And my suit, what's wrong with it? A suit is a suit, right?"

"Wrong! A suit has to be worn well to look good. A little tailoring, some crisp ironed white shirts, and a more fashionable tie will help the look tremendously."

"Okay, I'll iron my shirt. Here we are. Here's what I'm looking for. I have jotted down some notes." He stuffed the rest of the papers back in his briefcase.

"Stop! Do you want my help or not?"

"You're serious about this fashion stuff?"

"Yes, I'm serious. You need a new look, a clean ambitious look to go with your personality. I'm sure you can promote your platform with your words, but this isn't a courtroom. People are going to be voting for you. I'm not saying a makeover, just some subtle changes. I'll take you to my gal, and she can style your hair."

"*Oh no!* You are not taking me to a beauty shop," he said sternly. "And you're not making me get a buzz cut."

"Who said anything about a buzz cut? You have a good barber?"

"Yes! My mirror, my comb, and my scissors."

"Oh, my gosh, you cut your own hair?" She slipped her hand up to her mouth to hide her giggle.

"Somehow I didn't think this was how this meeting was going to go," Michael said, disappointed.

"Okay, okay." She patted his hand. "We'll find you a good barber, and we'll get a budget going to get your suits tailored and shirts professionally laundered and ironed. I promise you, you'll like the new you."

The rest of the evening, they got into the issues and business of starting his campaign and getting his name on the ballot.

At seven-fifteen, Gini's PET alerted her she had a text from Ric:

Where r u, can you talk?

"Excuse me, Michael." She looked down.

I'm in a meeting. We'll be done in the next half hour.

Call me when u r done.

She lifted her head and continued the conversation.

"So how does that all sound to you, Michael?"

"Great, I'll start the process of getting on the ballot. And you made some good points about my ideas and campaign promises. Gini, I trust you. If you want me to get my hair cut, I will."

"Just tell the barber you want a trim; he'll know what to do. You have a nice head of hair. You could look real distinguished and even more handsome."

"If it's more handsome you want." He winked. "When can we meet again?"

They decided to meet again Thursday night at the same place, same time.

As Gini walked home, she called Ric.

"Gini, are you done with your meeting?"

"Yes, I'm heading to my place. I still have to make sure I have everything ready for tomorrow. How about you, what are you up to?"

"I'm at a break from the meeting with the hotel on a few of our parties. It looks like all of this is going to run late. I wanted to see you tonight."

"I'll be back at the end of the week." She wasn't sure she wanted to commit to a late-night meet up.

"Okay, Thursday!"

"I have another dinner meeting with Michael Thursday night—"

Ric interrupted, "Oh, Gini, I have to go back into the conference room. I'll text you."

"Good night."

"Have a good trip."

Tuesday and Wednesday, Catherine and Gini talked to anyone who would listen. They were trying to get a bill introduced for state and federal governments to adopt programs that simplified the enrollment process of their government-provided insurance for low-income families, the disabled, and children in the foster system. Many of these people weren't aware of the programs, or the health aid plans were too complicated to understand. And now with national insurance coverage for all citizens being proposed, it was even harder to define what the care was under the programs that seemed to be always changing, as each state had its own interpretation of the laws. Uninsured kids were slipping through the cracks, even for families that could afford insurance, especially the ones with pre-existing conditions. The two of them were lobbying to get something on the floor to provide all children with the opportunity to have good medical care and health insurance.

70

Unfortunately, there were many health-related issues being discussed and others pushing to get their bill through the House. The competition was fierce, so it was taking long, hard hours to try to find the right people who agreed with their point of view—that person who would be specific about provisions for children in a health-care bill.

After the two grueling days, they returned to Catherine's place. Catherine tossed her briefcase down on the couch and flopped down next to it without taking her coat off.

"Well, Gini, all we can do now is wait. Hopefully, Congressman Davis will come through for us."

Gini sat in the chair. "He helped us get the immunization issue on the table, let's hope he will get this one on too. I hate the wait."

"Come on, girl, let's have a drink." Catherine got up and hung up her coat. She opened the liquor cabinet in the kitchen and pulled out a bottle of bourbon. "Do you want a shot?"

"No, I *don't* want a shot!"

"Okay, I'll splash a little bit of coke in it."

"If you have some wine open, I'll have that."

Catherine poured a glass of pinot grigio for Gini. Then she filled a shot glass with bourbon and held it up. "Here's to our children, all of our children in the United States of America. May they all be healthy and happy, the way every child should be." She clicked her glass to Gini's and drank the shot.

"What about our veterans? What's going to happen to Medicare in the years to come?" Gini was serious.

"Whoa, we can only fight on one battlefront at a time."

Catherine filled the shot glass again and drank it down. Gini was amazed at her friend. When the takeout food arrived, Catherine took it and the bottle of bourbon to the living room.

"Now let's hear it; we haven't had a minute to talk. Tell me all about your men. The dashing Ric, and now Michael. What's up with that?" She drank another shot and then started eating.

"Ooh, do you have your eye on Ric?" Gini asked mischievously.

"No." Catherine fluttered her eyelashes. "I think he's taken." She leaned toward Gini. "By *you*."

"We're just good friends. Remember, I'm a married woman. Ric's an attractive, eligible bachelor for the taking."

"Oh, honey, I'm way too old for him."

Gini laughed out loud. "You're such an old lady. What, thirty? Maybe thirty-one?"

71

"Just thirty-one."

"You'd better eat up before you pass out."

"I don't know what possessed me to drink those so fast." Catherine held her forehead. "I'll be okay once I get some food in me."

"How old are you, Gini, twenty-seven, twenty-eight?"

There was no answer.

"I know you aren't older than twenty-eight."

Quietly, Gini said, "I'll be twenty-five next week."

"Twenty-five!" Catherine shouted. "You mean you're only *twenty-four*, and when I met you, you were only twenty-two, maybe twenty-one. Holy crap, you're just a baby! I know I didn't hire you right out of college—how can that be?"

"Why is everyone so concerned about my age and calling me a baby?" Gini said, angry at first, and then concerned for her friend as she was definitely acting drunk. "Let's just say I skipped a couple of grades along the way."

"I *guess* so!" Catherine picked up a glass of water.

"And then Ric, Franco, and I all went to summer school so we could get our degrees faster. There's nothing wrong with being twenty-five, or thirty-one, for that matter."

"And I suppose now you're going to tell me Ric's just turning twenty-five. Honey, he is way too young for me."

"I think Ric's twenty-seven, maybe twenty-eight."

"Still too young. And what are you doing going to dinner with Michael? I know he's married."

"He's very married. He's running for a council seat that was vacated, and I'm helping get his campaign started. See, it's all innocent."

They continued eating and drinking as the night went on, then started laughing at everything they talked about. Catherine was chuckling so hard she was having trouble finishing her story. "…and when she gets up to give her big speech, the electricity goes off, and everything goes silent and dark. She never had a chance. Oooh—" she said trying to slow down the laughing. "She never had a chance. Honey, this has been fun, venting all the stress with booze and laughter."

"Yeah, I don't think I have laughed so hard for years."

"You are a bit serious, Gini."

"I am?"

"Very shy, very quiet, and very serious. Maybe Ric can break you out of your shell." Catherine yawned.

"Why do you keep talking about Ric?"

"Because, honey, you don't know it yet, but you're in love with the guy."

"I'm *not* in love with Ric. He's my friend, and that's all."

"I see the way your eyes light up every time you talk about him. How about that fun weekend you two had together? I've heard the stories more than once. Yeah, you're falling—" Catherine stood up and fell right back to the couch.

Gini grabbed on to her arm when she succeeded on her second attempt to stand, and they both stepped sideways and started laughing. They finally got to Catherine's bedroom, and she went into the bathroom. Gini decided to wait and make sure she got into bed okay. After a few minutes, Catherine came out of the bathroom ready for bed.

"You didn't have to wait for me, little miss *twenty-four-year-old*."

"I just came to remind you my train is at eleven o'clock tomorrow morning, so I'll need to leave about nine-thirty. That's all." Gini pulled the covers up over Catherine, and Catherine immediately fell asleep.

The next morning Gini was surprised to see her in the kitchen, dressed and fixing breakfast. "I thought you would be sleeping in with a hangover."

"Me? A hangover? Never. How about you, honey, how is your head?"

"Fine. I didn't drink nearly as much as you."

"I hope I didn't say anything to offend you last night. Sometimes I just need to blow it all out. Gini, you are a beautiful and an intelligent woman. I don't know how I would do what I'm doing without you. You're the best."

She went over and gave Catherine a hug. "You didn't say anything to offend me. You're my best friend, and I enjoy working and socializing with you. It was fun to just be a little crazy, in private, of course."

"Of course," Catherine said smiling. "I want you to go back to Boston and get some rest. I plan to take some time off and get ready for the next fight when our bill goes to committee."

"A few days off would be great. What are you doing for Thanksgiving?"

"I'm going to North Carolina to my mom and dad's place. There's always a lot of food, drinking, and good times. How about you, honey?"

"I'll be going home to Sacramento."

Gini got back to her place about four o'clock. She checked all her mail, emails, and messages, nothing from Ric. *Strange, why am I looking for something from him?* she thought. After unpacking and going through all her notes from Michael, she sat down with a cup of tea and relaxed. Then she headed for the cafe.

When she entered, Michael was talking on the phone and turned toward the wall, leaning on his arm on the back of the chair. As she sat down, he reached over without turning and put his hand on her arm. She could hear him saying, "Okay, Brenda, Gini has just arrived. Give the girls a kiss for me. I hope they're feeling better. I'll call you when I'm on my way home... Nothing, she hasn't seen it yet. I love you."

Michael turned to face Gini. She was getting all the papers out of her business bag, and she looked up at him.

"Oh my gosh! Oh my gosh, Michael, you look *fantastic!*"

He had a haircut that perfectly framed his face. The style had taken the focus off his hair and put it on his deep-set, light brown eyes, and chiseled cheekbones. He looked sexy and somewhat mysterious. He was wearing a dark gray suit with a pinstriped vest. Underneath was a pale gray shirt with a stiffly starched collar and a gray tie with thin, dark red diagonal stripes.

"Stand up," she said. "I want to see it all."

Michael rose from his chair and turned from side to side.

"New shoes, too! Michael Fredrick, I think you just *won* the election."

He sat down. "Do you like it?"

"Like it! *Yes...* How about you?"

He leaned forward and put her face into both of his hands, pulled her to him, and laid a big kiss on her lips.

She pulled back abruptly. "Michael!"

"Come on, Gini, that was a thank-you kiss. You were right, now I feel like a winner. I feel like a million bucks."

"What does Brenda think?"

"Oh... I think she went out today and bought a fancy stick to beat off all the women. And look." He opened his briefcase. Inside was a fan file, and all the papers were neatly categorized and stacked in the different folds. "She got this all organized for me. What would I do without all of my women?" He smiled broadly.

As they ate, they got down to business. Michael had submitted the enrollment certificate to verify he was a registered voter, and nomination papers to the Secretary of the Commonwealth to get on the ballot. They went through his agenda step by step. Pensions for city employees were the hot topic, especially how they were affecting the city budget. He had started a comprehensive reform plan to discuss with union leaders how to keep unfunded benefits low—a tall order. Public safety was less of a concern, but there were still neighborhoods that had crime and corruption, and those citizens were yelling loudest for help from the city to clear it off their streets. Education was always an issue. Michael jotted down his ideas, and they pondered and worked each angle. The time was passing fast, but Gini wanted to keep going. They didn't have much time before the election.

He looked at his watch. "Gini, can we take a little break so I can call my girls and say good night?"

"Of course."

He got up and went to the other side of the room to make his call.

She leaned back in her chair. How nice it would be to go home to someone waiting with open arms. How she longed to curl up next to a warm, comforting body and fall into a deep, wonderful sleep, knowing someone would be there when she woke up. Although Franco was a wonderful lover and they had amazing sex, he wasn't a cuddly person. Oh, but his kisses could send her reeling. How she missed him!

"I'm done." Her silence and daydreaming were broken by Michael's voice. "We can continue."

They discussed and re-discussed topic after topic. It was nine o'clock and then ten. She sat up and stretched and sighed a little.

"You look tired, Gini."

"I am. It's been a tough week."

"Come on, I'll take you home."

"No, no, I can walk."

"My car is just around the block in the firm's parking lot. You're not walking home."

She didn't want to rely on anyone, especially a man; she could take care of herself. But she was too tired to argue, so she let him drive her home.

When they pulled up to her building, Michael walked her to the door and hugged her tight. She had no fight left in her and fell into his warm body.

"Thank you, really, Gini. You're the best, and I feel comfortable about this election." He pulled her face up toward him. "Now, you need to go up and go to bed. You're dead on your feet."

"I am. We have a good plan. Let's keep the ball rolling."

"I'll call you tomorrow."

She put her key in the slot and walked in the door.

She filled her tub with water, poured a glass of wine, put on some soothing music, and lit a candle. She sunk deep down in the warm water and sipped her drink. When she was done, she put on her favorite heavy cotton pajamas and crawled into her comfy bed. She picked up her electronic tablet and texted to Ric:

I'm home.

Two seconds later her PET lit up.

"Gini."

"Yes," she said very drowsily and slowly.

"Are you just getting home?"

"I've been here for a while. I have been with Michael all night. I'm lying here all cozy and warm in my wonderful nice bed."

"I'm sorry I haven't had a chance to talk to you. Work, you know?"

"I know all about no time for Gini because of *work*," she said again in a sleepy voice.

Ric felt a pang in his heart knowing that statement was all about Franco, and he didn't want her to think the same of him.

"I'm going to hang up now before I fall asleep talking."

"I'll call you in the morning. Sweet dreams."

"Are you up?" Ric asked the next morning on his cell.

"I am. However, I was surprised I slept until nine o'clock."

"Wow, all the way to nine. I hope you have cleared your day because we are going to do something."

"We are?"

"You choose. I'll be at your place in about thirty minutes. Will that give you enough time?"

"I'll be ready."

Howard sent Ric up to her place when he arrived. Her door was open, so he knocked gently and then went in.

"Gini," he called out.

She was just walking out of her bedroom, putting on a heavy sweater. "We're going to Kennebunkport. They have great shops there, so I can pick up some small gifts to take to the family when I go home for Thanksgiving."

"You're going to California for Thanksgiving?"

She nodded.

"That's great!"

"Yes, well, yes." Suddenly her eyes filled with tears.

"Gins, what is it?" With his hands on her shoulders, he started to pull her close. She immediately pulled back and quickly wiped the tears from her eyes.

"Listen, I... well... I'm ready to go. I haven't been to Kennebunkport for a long time." She forced a half smile.

He turned to stand next to her. "Let's go."

Gini sat quietly as they made their way out of Boston.

"The sun is nice," she said finally. "A rare November day in New England."

"Sunny, but not all that warm. Gini, is there something going on in Sacramento?"

"No." She sighed. "Yes… it's just that Mama has had failing health for the last few months. And… it's hard to know what to do."

She turned and looked out the window. He could tell she was fighting back her emotions.

"Sweet Gins, I'm sorry to hear that. Nothing serious, I hope." He reached over and took her hand. He immediately saw she was wearing the green stone ring.

Gini slowly took her hand out of his. "Remember how Mama's garden was so beautiful, her house always immaculate and it smelled of good food?"

"Yes."

"Well, Cindy had been a little concerned about Mama last spring. Then one day she went over there, and she could tell Mama hadn't been eating. She seemed confused and disoriented. Cindy took her to the doctor, and from the tests, they found a small leakage in one of her heart valves, but the doctor said it wasn't a life-threatening condition. He thought she might be in the beginnings of Alzheimer's. Cindy tries to keep an eye on her, but both she and Neil work and it's getting too hard for her to always be there. I went home in August, and I couldn't believe the house. It was so run down, and she hadn't done one thing in the yard.

"Cindy and I decided Mama should move into one of those senior communities, the assisted living one rather than an independent because Mama just forgets to take care of herself. After I had left, they found one in the area they both liked. I told Mama not to worry about the money. If she needed help, I would pay for it. They have all but moved her into her new apartment." Tears started rolling down Gini's cheeks.

Ric pulled over to the side of the road and stopped. "Gini, you're doing the right thing. If your mom needs help, you need to get her some." He took the back of his finger and wiped the water droplets from her cheeks.

"I know. And I *do* feel good about it. Mama wanted to stay in the house until after Thanksgiving so we could have one more big family holiday dinner together." Her lips quivered, and she looked at him with her big blue eyes as the tears continued to flow.

"Oh, Gini." He pulled her close to him.

She tried to control her emotions and finally stopped crying.

"Listen, sweet Gins, if you need me to help you do anything, you tell me. I love your mama. I'd do anything for her."

Gini made a small cry as the lump in her throat got bigger with his obviously heartfelt statement. "Thank you." She put her head down. He rubbed the back of her neck for a moment and then pulled back out onto the highway.

There was silence for some time.

"What are *you* doing for Thanksgiving?" she asked.

"Well, the more I think about it, I think I should go with you to Sacramento and take care of you."

"Oh, Ric! That would raise so many eyebrows and make it so… so, well no, you aren't going with me to Sacramento. You aren't going to be alone, are you?"

"No, my sweets. Victor and Maria always ask me to their house in Rockport for Thanksgiving dinner."

"Rockport! They have a place in Rockport?"

"Yes, and I hoped you could go with me. You would love their place, perched up on the cliffs looking down on the ocean."

"How wonderful. Don't tempt me."

He looked at her and smiled. "Don't worry, we'll go there sometime, I promise."

What if he had asked her to the Westcotts'? Would she have agreed, knowing that she would be seen as his date—a married woman? No, he would just be there with his friend, right? Why was she getting so anxious; she wasn't going with him—at least not this time. And what if he went to Sacramento? They'd all think he was there visiting his hometown and his second mother. Of course, it was just by chance they were both there at the same time. *Stop thinking. We aren't going to be together for Thanksgiving.*

They walked the shops in Kennebunkport, and Gini bought a few things for gifts. They both bought chocolate and penuche at the fudge shop. The air was cool, with just a slight breeze as they walked along the protected small beach area close to town. Gini walked lazily kicking the stones, and occasionally, she leaned down to examine a shell.

Ric was deep in thought about how upset Gini was over her mom. He knew Cindy was involved with Mama Elizabeth, but as far as Ric was concerned, the brothers were all worthless.

"Ric, look! An unbroken shell. Look how delicate it is." She looked him straight in the eyes. "You don't find many of these."

She held the shell up to show him and their eyes locked. Ric felt she could see straight into his soul. He felt suddenly anxious—or was it euphoria, Cupid's arrow piercing his lovesick heart. His feelings for her were starting to control him. He couldn't fight it any longer. She was his first and last thought of each day, and he was constantly trying to strategize ways they could be together. *Look at those eyes…* He almost reached out to grab her and kiss her, but managed to stop before she noticed anything. She wasn't ready to hear of his love for her— *Of course she isn't ready, you jerk; she's married.*

"Look, isn't it beautiful?"

He took her hand and pulled the shell closer so he could take a good look.

"It's beautiful and delicate just like you."

She took his hand and opened his palm. "Here, you keep it. It will remind you of me."

He closed his hand around the shell, took her hand to his lips, and gently kissed it.

"I will treasure it forever." He put the shell up close to his heart, closed his eyes, and swayed back and forth.

"Oh, Ric. You're so funny. I love being with you. I have forgotten all my troubles in this wonderful piece of New England. Thanks for bringing me here."

It was nice to be somewhere beautiful, somewhere timeless, and beyond human problems, thinking of nothing but the sounds of nature, keeping a sharp eye out for the perfect shell. The beach completely cleared her mind and renewed her senses. She felt like her old self again, the Gini she had almost forgotten.

She needed his humor. No one made her feel so at ease—*not ever,* she thought. This dear friend had arrived back in her life just when she needed someone to uplift her.

"Always the chauffeur. Your wish is my command."

They walked to a small restaurant that was open for business. It was off-season, and a lot of places were closed. They went up to the second floor, which had a great view out over the water. The sun was low in the southern sky, and there was just a wisp of cloudiness making the sheen on the water glaring and haunting.

"The daylight is so short this time of year. It makes me feel sleepy." She sighed.

"The water looks pretty, doesn't it?"

After lunch, they walked around a little longer and went back to a shop they had been to so Gini could buy the hat she decided earlier not to buy. On the drive back, they stopped at several places to enjoy the scenery. At the last stop, they sat down on a rock and watched the waves come in and go out.

"I love the water," she said.

"Gini, you have to go to Florida with me. It's so nice there. The beaches are white sand, and the water is so warm. And I know you would love to ride in Val's yacht. It's like a house."

Gini looked at him with wide eyes. "Really?"

"I've never seen anything like it. There was a living room inside and one outside. Of course, he has a captain, so Val fixed us a drink, and we just sat and enjoyed the journey up the canal. We even docked at a fancy restaurant, ate, and then took the boat back to the house. It was like a pretend life, for sure."

He looked back at her. She was leaning back, resting on her elbows. She had her eyes closed, and she was breathing deeply. "Sounds wonderful." She didn't change her position. "If you close your eyes, you can smell the sea air, taste the salt on your lips, and the sounds—you can hear the wonderful sounds of the water, the birds, the breeze. Ah, I could stay here forever."

He sat and watched her. He would never get tired of looking at her.

The sun was about to set as they walked up the rocky slope back to the car. Just as Ric started the engine, Gini's phone rang.

"It's Michael." She stuck her earpiece in her ear.

"Hi, Gini. Sorry I didn't call you earlier. It's such a beautiful day, and the girls have been sick all week. They are much better today, so we took them to the park."

"That's okay. You're right; it's a beautiful day. Ric and I drove up to Kennebunkport."

"Rick? Rick who?"

"Santini," Gini answered, realizing she may have opened a can of worms.

"Ric Santini. Okay… well."

Michael had first met Ric at Harvard. He had seemed to be a nice guy, helpful in many ways. And he had noticed the strong friendship between Ric, Gini, and Franco, although he never really cared for Franco, too macho or something. He remembered the way Ric had looked at her at the gala. Even though Michael and Gini had remained friends over the years, he recalled he hadn't seen Franco for some time.

He found it hard to say the right words without being insulting. "Is Franco with you?"

"No," Gini said slowly and looked at Ric with a "what do I do now?" look on her face. "Franco's still in China. We just thought it would be good to get out of town like we used to do when we were in college together." Her speech began to increase rapidly. "You know, cabin fever from the cold weather." She stopped and took a deep breath.

"A drive along the water sounds nice, too," Michael said, concerned. "So when will Franco be back in town?"

"I'm not sure. He hasn't given me a definite date. He's working on a big project over there."

"Anyway, I guess we won't be doing much work today."

"No," she said, relieved the subject had changed. "Listen, if you want, I can call you when I get home."

"I just have a few questions. I'll email them to you. Enjoy the rest of your day."

"Thank you, you too."

She thought the call ended rather abruptly.

"Michael trying to steal you away from me?" Ric asked in a joking manner.

Gini put her phone in front of her and looked at it, then looked at him. She wasn't sure how she felt about the call. "He's going to email me some questions. Don't laugh at me, Ric, but could we stop on the way home and get Burger King?"

He chuckled. "You crack me up with your Burger King."

"Remember, we used to stop at that one just on the other side of the bridge going into Boston?"

"Yes, yes, I remember." He smiled to himself. "I remember, Gins."

When they pulled into the parking lot, it was full, and young children were running all around. Ric looked at Gini, thinking, *Are you sure you want to do this?*

She looked up at him and smiled with her beautiful glowing smile. "I can smell a Burger King from a mile away."

Chapter 7 – Mixing with the Wealthy

They walked back out to the car.

"Gins, tomorrow the football party is at Ms. Quinley's house. It's the early game. Are we going?"

"Ms. Quinley? Do I know her?"

"She lives in one of the large brownstones on the corner facing Spruce Street. All those mansions, old money."

"I guess that would be fun."

Ric slid in behind the steering wheel. "She has been coming to the football parties for the last couple of years. We didn't know her and her husband until he became ill a few years back. They walked down our block daily; he was using a cane. Then he went to a walker and finally a wheelchair."

"Oh, that's sad."

"After he had died, she was out in her side yard one day, and the water was spraying everywhere. David saw her and went to help. The pipe had broken, and he fixed it for her. He became her friend forever."

"David's a bit strange, but a nice guy, I think," Gini said.

"He is." Ric winked. "One weekend he invited her to the football game party at their house. She came dressed in a nice dress with jewelry, high heels, and her purse. We were all on our best behavior, but you know how it is when the score is close. At moments, we were a bit rowdy. When it was over, she stood up and said, 'Thank you for inviting me. I had a good time.' She was so serious. We thought we had made fools of ourselves. Then she turned and said, 'David, you must come to my home and teach me this game of football. I want to know all the rules, the scoring, and the object of why these men make a point of knocking the other one down.'"

Gini looked at him. "Seriously?"

"Oh, she was very serious. So David taught her the game. She came every week after that until the end of the season. Eventually, she dressed down, to a nice pantsuit, but never lost the jewelry or the purse.

"Her house is so beautiful. It has been in the family for generations. It was never cut up into little condos as so many were. You'll enjoy seeing it."

"I love those beautiful old homes, so much history." Gini settled deep into the warm seat.

Sunday was a dark, cloudy day. Ric and Gini walked from his house to Ms. Quinley's. When Ric went to pick her up, he saw she had set out some dip and chips, and she had made her favorite recipe, dark chocolate cookies with chocolate chips and walnuts. He informed her there would be plenty of food at the mansion, but after she tried to hide her disappointment, he said the cookies would be good to take. They walked up to the big double doors and rang the bell.

An older woman in a maid's uniform answered. "Mr. Santini, please come in. Let me take your coats."

"Eleanor, this is my friend Gini."

"Nice to meet you, ma'am," Eleanor said, making a slight curtsy.

A sweeping imperial staircase caught Gini's eye, its two branches encircling the large foyer.

Eleanor motioned with her right hand. "Please, the group is up in the entertainment room. You know where it is, Mr. Santini?"

"I do. Gini made some cookies." He handed them to the maid.

"I'll add them to the dessert assortment."

Gini was in complete awe of the entrance and didn't absorb any of the conversation between Ric and Eleanor.

At the top of the stairs on the left-hand side was a long wide room. Inside were a large screen TV, couches, chairs, and a walk-in bar at one end. A couple of tables were near the bar with many fancy hors d'oeuvres set out. Gini laughed at herself, thinking how embarrassed she would have been setting her dip and chips on such a beautiful table. She was glad Ric had saved her. His polite and refined demeanor—his superb mastery of social graces—made him even more attractive than his good looks.

"Hey, guys, come on in," Markus said as they entered.

The room was full of neighbors Gini had come to know.

David took the opportunity to give her a bad time after she ordered a light beer on ice. She was getting used to his humor and rather enjoyed his attention.

The game was just getting started, and everyone gathered around the TV. A stately woman entered the room with a distinguished gentleman, his arm lightly draped around her shoulder.

"Oh good, Charles, the game's just starting," Ms. Quinley said.

They were about the same height. She was tall, slim and square-shouldered. Older, but attractive and well dressed. Gini guessed this was their hostess. Somehow she looked familiar.

"Ric," Ms. Quinley said, walking toward them. "You snuck in without me seeing you. Welcome."

"Hello, Ms. Quinley, Mr. Schmitt." Ric leaned forward and kissed her on the cheek, and shook his hand.

"This is my friend, Gini Anderson."

"Ms. Virginia Anderson, I'm glad you could come today."

"Thank you." Gini realized she had met her before.

"You know Gini?" Ric asked.

"She and Ms. White were gracious enough to come and speak at our women's auxiliary group."

There was a loud cheer when the Patriots took off with the ball. The four walked farther in and joined the others.

At the end of the quarter, Gini and Ric refreshed their drinks and went to the food table.

"This is such a beautiful place," Gini said, looking all around. "It's so big."

"Dear," Ms. Quinley said from behind them. "If you want to stay a few minutes after the others leave I will be glad to show you the rest of the house."

"Yes, ma'am, I would like that very much."

Gini had dressed a little nicer than for the other games, but she still wore her hair in the high ponytail. It had become her signature football party hairdo. She found it kind of ironic to be watching a game in such a luxurious place.

Gini couldn't help but see the compassion in Mr. Schmitt's eyes for Ms. Quinley—his arm around her or holding her hand. It was the way Franco had looked at and touched Gini; with him next to her, she had always felt she was in a safe place. Emotion filled her mind. Gini knew Franco would never let anything happen to her. As the game went on, Gini became envious of Ms. Quinley and Mr. Schmitt's relationship. Several times she almost snuggled up close to Ric, but each time caught herself, knowing she mustn't. He wasn't her husband; Franco was, and he loved her... or did he? She had loved him all her life. How was it she now felt she didn't know Franco at all?

The Patriots ran a kickoff back, scored and took the lead. "Hot dog!" Ms. Quinley said jubilantly as she stood up. "That's the way to play, right, David?"

"Right," he said proudly.

At the half, the two tables that had the hors d'oeuvres were now set for dinner. After they ate, a few lingered over coffee, then one by one filtered back into the seating area around the TV.

Ric noticed that Gini's interaction with the game wasn't as intense as before. At the beginning, she had been bouncing around on the couch and cheering, but as time went on, the cheers had diminished, and a somber emotion emerged. He wanted to hug her to him and ease her sadness... no, he couldn't; he was her friend and only a friend. She would confide in him if she wanted him to know, if she wanted help. He had to wait for her move.

He looked around the room at his neighbors. Every single one of them had a partner, someone to share the fun of the party, the ups and downs of life. How he missed that—the love he had shared with Margarita. For a moment, he was caught in the same melancholy Gini was, remembering the early days of his marriage, the dreams talked about late into the night, the familiar warmth of Riti's body, all of it knit into a confidence that he was with his life partner, no matter what.

And then she left him.

But he'd been down that road and knew it led nowhere good. The past was over. He had a good life, and it would get better.

The end of the third quarter, everyone once again walked back to the bar area. The two tables now had a spread of desserts. Gini's cookies were arranged on a beautiful crystal serving plate.

Ms. Quinley was very fond of the cookies Gini had brought and asked for the recipe.

"And the DC lady can cook," David blurted out. "A woman of many talents."

Gini could feel the heat going into her face. She was sure she was bright red, and she wanted to crawl away but smiled graciously. Thankfully, the game restarted and everyone went back to watch it.

Gini had lost all interest in football; she was fixated on Mr. Schmitt's affection toward Ms. Quinley.

At one point, Ric put his hand on her shoulder with concern. "Everything okay?"

She sat forward on the couch. "Yes... I hate the Patriots are losing."

After the game, little by little, the neighbors left.

"Ms. Anderson, are you ready for the tour?" Ms. Quinley asked.

"Elaina, Ric and I will meet you two ladies down in the living room for an aperitif when you are done," Charles said.

As the two women walked out the double doors, Ms. Quinley directed them with her hand.

"To the right." She pointed down the hall past the large room. "There are four guest bedrooms and two full baths to share."

Ms. Quinley led Gini through the whole house, showing each room and telling her about the rich history of her late husband.

"My husband's great-grandfather was a well-known glass blower." She pointed to two tall handblown gas lamps sitting on the mantel.

"He was known for his art. His pieces sold for top dollar back in his day. That's his portrait above the fireplace." She raised her eyes to the picture. "In the 1850s, the bay was filled in, and many homes were being built in Back Bay. That was when he expanded his business into window glass. He commissioned this house to be built after he amassed his fortune in the late 1870s."

Gini noticed two panes in the windows were purple.

In the mid-1800s, many of the brownstones built on Beacon Hill and in the Back Bay had ordered their window glass from France. The glass was crystal clear when it had been installed. But after being exposed to the sun over the months, the glass had started to turn purple—lavender. The homeowners weren't happy about the purple tint. The phenomenon was due to excess manganese oxide in the glass. Some later had equated the color with royalty. It's a part of Boston history still told today.

Gini's favorite rooms were the master dressing areas, all richly decorated in warm colors and heavy fabric, with big floor-to-ceiling mirrors on the walls. She closed her eyes and imagined herself getting ready for a ball. The servants were making sure everything was perfect: her large hooped skirt flowed gracefully to the floor as someone with deft hands arranged the flowers in her hair, and someone else fit the delicate shoes gently on her feet. It was a feeling not only of luxury—though of course there was that—but of being cared for.

And then there was the elegant dining room.

"This has always been my favorite room. Russell, my late husband, and I would have our meals at that table over there overlooking the street." Elaina pointed, and Gini could see it was set for two. "Charles and I have continued to eat there since we started seeing each other. It seems silly to have such a large eating area now that I don't entertain anymore. I should think about selling." She sighed.

"The house has been in your family for so long, isn't there a family member who would like to buy it from you?"

"None of the distant relatives want it. It costs a lot to run, and none of them have the funds or the time. I'm afraid if I gave it to anyone it would go into ruin very quickly. I just can't think of such a demise for this beautiful home." There was a sad note in Ms. Quinley's voice.

Gini suddenly felt the sadness pass to her, and she thought about Mama selling the family house in Sacramento.

She heard Ric's laugh and the sound of the men talking from the interior side of the room. There were two ornate arched openings. One went out into the grand foyer; the other, on the side of the room, went into the living room. Elaina took Gini in there.

"Ms. Anderson and Ms. Quinley, what can I get you to drink?" Charles took Elaina's hand and pulled it under his arm and rested it on his forearm as he led her to the small bar in the room. "Would you like a brandy, love?"

Watching his caring and gentle touch for Elaina, once again that feeling crept into Gini... envy, or was it admiration... or just longing to have someone so in love with her he couldn't let her out of his sight?

"How about you, Ms. Anderson?" Elaina turned toward Gini. "A brandy?"

Ric walked up next to Gini, and they exchanged glances.

"No thank you, I'm not much of a brandy drinker. A Baileys sounds good if you have it."

Elaina agreed.

He poured a small amount into two large wide-bowled, short-stemmed glasses and handed them to the two ladies.

Ric watched Gini take her drink. She was so beautiful, so gracious; her special charm was still there. He wished she would open up and let the world see her as he did—like when they were in school. He gently put his hand on her back to lead her to their seats.

She closed her eyes for a moment at his touch.

Each couple walked back and sat on the two couches adjacent to each other. "Ric and I were just talking about our lawyering days," Charles started the conversation. "Speaking of that, Ms. Anderson, I understand you're helping Mr. Fredrick with his campaign."

"I think he'll be good for the city."

"He's a fine young man. Delbert and Delbert is going to miss him if he leaves the firm. I'm still a partner there, and we handpicked him for the firm when he graduated."

"You work at Delbert and Delbert?" Gini asked.

"I retired some time ago, but I'm still on the board. I remember another young lawyer." He turned and looked at Ric. "His first day in court."

Ric laughed. "And the last time I did any trial lawyering."

"You were against each other in a trial?"

"It was an insurance issue against Greystone. I was the second chair. I had only been out of school for a few months and was convinced it would be good for my credentials to have a case against Delbert and Delbert under my belt, assuming we would win, of course."

"Did you?" Gini looked straight at Ric.

"No way," Charles said with his smooth, toned voice. "Lory and Lawson never won a case against us."

"I don't know about that. If I recall, it was more of a draw. Our client paid two-thirds, and your client paid one-third."

"I call that a win, don't you, love?" Charles looked at Elaina.

"You *are not* pulling me into this." She smiled at him.

"All I know is I never wanted to be a trial lawyer before that, and I was certain after," Ric surmised.

Ric and Gini were sitting separated on the couch; he had his arm on the back, his hand almost touching her. Gini suddenly relaxed. She enjoyed hearing about Ric as a lawyer: his cleverness and success. She turned and looked at him, and they both smiled. Should she move closer? It wouldn't hurt if she sat a bit closer.

"All that being said," Charles went on, "there are a lot of good people over at that firm, and you were one of them."

Gini sat forward to set her empty glass on the table. Just as she was going to sit back under his arm, he brought it down and placed his drink next to hers.

She took a small breath. *It was good he moved.* She needed to stop thinking about all the romance; it was tempting her to let down her defenses. She didn't need it anyway; it was fine to be on her own, not having to worry about interfering with anyone else's plans. She could do as she pleased.

"Refill?" Charles asked.

"No." Ric turned to Gini. "We need to go."

Gini nodded in agreement. "Thank you so much for showing me your lovely home, Ms. Quinley."

"It was my pleasure, dear. As you can see, I'm proud of this house."

Ric shook Charles' hand and kissed Elaina on the cheek. "We'll see you next Sunday?"

Ms. Quinley smiled. "I wouldn't miss it."

When Ric and Gini turned the corner on Ric's street, the skies opened up and poured down rain. They both started running toward his house. Inside, they were out of breath and wet. He took their coats and flung them on the backs of the chairs at the kitchen counter.

"I would have taken my umbrella if I'd known it was going to rain so hard," she said.

Ric ran into the small powder bath off the kitchen and brought back two hand towels and handed one to her. "Who knew?" he said as he dried off his face, head, and hands.

Gini dried up around the edge of her hair. "At least I had my hood. Ric, you're soaked through and through."

"I know, I'm going to go up and change my clothes. I'll be right back." He ran up the stairs, taking them two steps at a time.

Gini's boots were wet on top of her feet, so she took them off. Even her socks seemed a little damp. Her pant legs were soaked at the cuffs; the fabric was less saturated as it went up her legs. She suddenly caught a chill and shivered. Just then Ric came down the stairs.

"There, that's much better. Gini, you're cold."

"I'm fine."

"Take off your pants. I'll throw them in the dryer."

"*I am not* taking off my pants," she said with an indignant tone to her voice.

He pulled the blanket off the back of the chair and put it around her. "Wrap yourself up in this, and give me your pants. Go in the bathroom; I won't look. No hidden cameras, I promise." He raised his hands to show nothing was in them.

"Oh, Ric," she said with a pooh-poohing tone in her voice.

She was going to say no again, but the wet fabric on her legs was uncomfortable. She went into the bathroom and took them off. She wrapped the blanket tightly around her body, so no unclothed part showed. It was so tight around her thighs it was difficult for her to walk.

"Here." She held the covering with one hand and handed the pants to him with the other. He took them into the laundry area on the other side of the kitchen.

She went into the living room, sat on the couch with the blanket tight, and pulled her knees up against her body. Ric had put her boots next to the fireplace, and she could feel the warmth of the blazing fire.

"It shouldn't take too long for your slacks to dry," he said sitting on the other end of the couch.

He was still wiping his hair and the back of his neck with the towel. She sat and looked at him.

"What?" he asked. "What are you looking at?"

"I don't know that I have ever seen you when every hair on your head wasn't perfectly placed. I kind of like the ruffled look."

"Why? What does it look like?" He got up and went into the bathroom.

She smiled a slight smile. *A little vain*, she thought.

When he came back, he had brushed his hair like he normally wore it. She liked the long, soft waves that were pulled straight back from the sides and top. His hair was consistently cut and styled as if he had just walked out of a barbershop. He was clean-shaven and well-groomed always. She remembered him being like that in college as well. He had seemed so much more mature than the rest of them—serious about his future and always responsible with his time and money.

"Better?" he asked.

She gave a half smile. His hair still appeared damp and parted in several places. "Lovely, just lovely. Oh darn, I broke a nail."

"Let me see?"

She lifted her right hand, and he took it to look at her finger. "You need to go to my nail tech, Lucy. She can fix it."

"You have a nail tech?" she asked, amazed.

"Of course, I go every other week to get my haircut and a mani-pedi."

"Your barber does mani-pedis?" She was still surprised.

"I don't go to a barber." He let go of her hand. "I go to a salon."

Gini let out a little laugh. "Which one?"

"Lazy Daze."

She started giggling. "You go to a *spa* every other week?"

"Yes," he said, looking at her with a smile. "They have great massages and facials."

"Hahaha," Gini laughed, losing control. "A facial! Next, you're going to tell me they tweeze your brows." She laughed harder, grabbing at her sides.

"No," he said quietly, enjoying her happiness. "They use thread."

"Oh, my gosh, Ric," she said, still not able to stop her giggling. "No more! You're making my cheeks ache."

Ric reached over and rubbed his hand up and down her blanket-covered leg. "Men go to spas. We should go together sometime. A lot of couples come in on Saturdays."

Gini took some breaths and stopped her hysterical laughter. "I know, I just can't believe the Ric we went to high school with now goes to a beauty spa every other week. Our classmates wouldn't believe it."

"Why wouldn't they believe it?" He was still smiling, enjoying the moment just as much as she was.

"You've changed since then. You were such a… *a nerd*."

"A nerd!" There was silence. "Okay." He rubbed her leg again. "You're right; I was a nerd. If I remember, I carried my chessboard with me everywhere."

He was surprised she let him touch her; she had been so guarded.

"And you were always reading science books or debating with everyone about a new law or policy put into effect. No, no one would believe you ended up being a party planner." Gini got tickled again.

"I'm not a party planner." He loved her laughter. "I'm an entertainment director."

"Okay, okay." She wiped her happy tears from her eyes. "And you are an amazing entertainment director and company owner."

His caressing her leg was soothing. It didn't bother her that he was touching her. Of late, he had a way of relaxing her—he was so amusing. It made her feel at ease.

"You should laugh more often. It looks good on you. I don't think I've seen you laugh since we hooked up again. You're always so serious and quiet."

"That's what Catherine said. Am I really that serious?"

He smiled and moved a little closer to her. "I guess we have both changed since high school. You were always so happy and carefree, jumping or running around giggling. You looked so cute in your short cheerleading skirt."

"There's that word 'cute' again." She gave him a look. "Ric, I just grew up, that's all. When I was in high school, I didn't have a care in the world. Everyone around me loved me and took care of me. Now, it's up to me to pay the bills, make sure I have food, and fight for all the underprivileged children." She looked down. "And Mama— She needs my attention too."

"Gini, everyone around you still loves you."

She shook her head and turned to sit right on the couch, pulling the blanket up tighter.

"Gins, are you still cold?"

"I'm fine."

"How about some hot chocolate, that will warm up your insides."

"That sounds wonderful." She pulled the blanket close around her waist and followed him.

He went into the kitchen area, and she sat on the chair at the counter. He placed a mug in front of her, then walked around and sat on the stool next to her. "How did you like the Quinley place?"

"It's so beautiful. They have kept it up so nicely, modernized it, but it still has the feel of a home from centuries ago. She had such wonderful stories…" Gini paused. "Interesting, the stories were all about her late husband, nothing about herself or her past. Do you think she's having any problem keeping the house?"

"Why do you ask?"

"I don't know; she just mentioned she should probably try to sell it."

"She donates generous amounts of money to several charities every year. I don't think she's hurting for money in any way. She sponsors the big holiday gift party for needy families with children every December."

"That's right," Gini said. "I'm a helper every year. I love to see the smiling faces of those precious children when you hand them their gift."

"You, an elf… an elf, in pointed, curled-toe shoes and green tights." He sat back on the chair with a grin on his face. "Sorry I've missed that."

91

"Oh Ric, stop." She gently swiped his arm with her fingers. "No pointed shoes or green tights. I'm Santa's helper with my red velvet dress trimmed with white fur."

"I'll bet you are adorable." He brushed her face with the inside of his hand as he stood up. "More hot chocolate?"

"Please. You haven't been at the party and seen me?"

"No, I'm sure I would have remembered a cute—oh, excuse me—a beautiful lady in a red dress. I have always had a conflicting event on that Sunday."

Gini started thinking out loud. "Now that you say she's the sponsor, I don't remember working with her. I'm always contacted by and deal with Connie... what is her last name—?"

"Mitchell," he interrupted.

How was it that he knew everyone she knew—or at least it seemed that way? Their lives had paralleled, yet they never connected. She wished they had before now. Maybe then she wouldn't feel so lonely... all alone, having to fend for herself.

"Connie Mitchell, she's the event coordinator. Ms. Quinley puts up the money and her committee puts it all together. I would be surprised if she weren't there, however. She took quite the liking to you today, Gins."

He put the two mugs on the counter and sat back down.

"She's a nice woman," Gini said. "So classy and proper. I think she and Mr. Schmitt make a good couple. You can see that he adores her. She turned and looked him right in the eyes. "He's always making sure she is comfortable, such a gentleman. I love men who treat their ladies like they are the only thing on earth that matters." Her gaze drifted up as she remembered how wonderful it was with Franco when he was so caring and polite—or was it Ric who was crowding her thoughts? Ric was one of the politest men she had ever met. She had fond memories of him hugging and cuddling with Margarita, even in public... and he was gentle. She quickly dashed the thoughts.

"Anyway, I loved watching his tenderness, and I could see how she looked at him. I don't know how long her husband has been gone, for I know she was deeply in love with him, but it has been long enough for her to grieve and move on with her life. The two of them, Charles and Ms. Quinley, will be together for many years to come."

"Do I see a romantic side to my sweet Gins?" Ric watched the many expressions and obvious feelings she conveyed while she talked about the couple. He could tell what she was feeling—up to a point. Longing, the desire for love... But did it include him? That's what he found himself wondering. Damn Franco for being in the way!

Once again, Gini looked straight into his eyes, and he could feel her blue eyes reach deep into his inner being.

She took the last swallow of her hot chocolate and got up, pulling the blanket tight around her, and looking at him to make sure he wasn't watching her lower body. He smiled and supported her elbow as she touched the floor with her feet.

"I just like to see people happy in love."

The buzzer went off on the dryer, and Ric went to get her pants.

After Gini dressed, she told him she needed to get going.

"When are you leaving for Sacramento?"

"My flight's Tuesday morning at eleven-thirty."

Ric took Gini's coat off the chair and helped her put it on. "Wow, your coat is dry." He was surprised. "Look at mine, it's still nearly dripping."

"Mine's weatherproof. That's probably why I wasn't as wet as you."

She walked up close to him without touching, looked up, and smiled a devilish smile. It was as if she were daring him to flirt with her. He playfully flipped the hood of her jacket up onto her head and then grabbed another coat off the hooks by the front door and put it on.

What was she doing? She immediately put up her armor. "Where are you going?"

"Gini, we're not going to have this discussion, are we?"

"I don't know why you don't understand I like to walk." She headed toward the door. "I appreciate your offer, but I don't need your help. I have managed to take care of myself for several years now. And I am doing just fine without a man."

He opened the front door as she talked.

"You know, I ride all by myself on the train down to Washington all the time, and I seem to function and get around without anyone's help."

He opened the passenger door, and she slid in. He got in and started up the car.

"Why do men think women can't take care of themselves?" She looked at him.

"Gini," he said seriously, showing her respect. "I have no doubt in my mind you can take care of yourself, but there's no sense in you walking in the cold and damp when I have a car."

"I have a car," she said, very matter of fact. "I could drive if I wanted to. I can drive, another thing I do quite well without assistance."

"I get it. I get it! You're independent. I find that appealing in a woman. But there's nothing wrong with a friend helping a friend."

There was a long pause as neither of them spoke. She wasn't sure why she was trying to pick a fight. Hadn't she had fun with him tonight? She needed to stop; he *was not a threat*.

He realized she was hurting deeply, and it wasn't just because of her mother's health. The man, his friend—Franco—had scarred her with his lack of commitment, leaving her to manage on her own.

"How are you getting to the airport? I can take you."

"No thanks." Gini leaned down near her feet to pick up her PET, which had fallen out of her purse. "Jimmy's taking me."

"Who's Jimmy?"

"He's my driver."

"Oh, now you have a driver." Ric was annoyed.

Gini picked up on his tone. "Well, he's not only *my* driver. Everyone in the building uses him. And he has lots of other customers. He's honest; he's prompt, and it is much easier to have him just drop me off at the airport or train station rather than go through all the hassle of calling a taxi. I have arranged for him to take me, and pick me up on Saturday when I get back. It's just easier that way," she said, almost apologetic. "You're busy; I know you are. It would take time out of your morning."

He pulled up in front of her building and parked. He ran around to help her out when she opened the car door, and walked her to the building entrance.

"Thanks for the ride." She looked him in the eyes.

He took a bold move, a move he'd been planning—waiting for the right moment. Holding her head in his hands, he kissed her on the lips.

She gently, but quickly, pushed away from him and immediately looked down, digging through her purse to get her key card. "I hope you have a nice Thanksgiving." She was a bit befuddled as she slipped the key into the slot.

Ric pulled the door open to hold it. "You too. I know you are just coming back on Saturday, but there's a fun function that night at the hotel. I'd like you to go with me."

She was still avoiding eye contact. "We'll see how tired I am."

"Okay. I won't call or text you while you're home so it won't be uncomfortable for you."

"I hope the weather will be nice for you at Rockport." Her speech was rapid-fire.

She finally looked up at him. "Good night."

"Good night, Gins. Have a good trip. We really do need to go to the spa together."

She smiled an easy smile—suddenly calm—and walked in the door. He waited until she went into the elevator; she turned and waved. When the elevator doors closed, she rubbed her lips with her fingertips and squeezed her eyes closed. Had the kiss surprised her? Yes—well, no. Inside, she had been begging for it all day, maybe even for weeks. She had watched him talk and smile and laugh all evening. With all that, she should have known his lips, but *there* was the surprise—she had never imagined how warm they would feel pressed to hers, or the smothering heat that went deep down inside her.

Walking back to his car, Ric looked up and smiled, thinking of her laughter, her flirty looks. And the kiss, yes, the kiss was just as he had expected: luscious, enchanting, soft. He was drunk on endorphins—his desire even more heightened to be with her, be with her forever.

Chapter 8 – Thanksgiving Week

On Tuesday, Gini pulled her rental car up in front of the house where she'd grown up. Once again, she was saddened by the appearance of the yard. The grass was different lengths and had brown patches. The flower beds were full of weeds that had died back and lay on the ground. She thought it wouldn't kill Dwayne to mow and weed his mother's yard once in awhile.

When she rang the bell, Gini was surprised she didn't see Cindy's car. No one answered the door. She rang it again and then knocked, still no answer, so she sat in the chair on the porch. She figured they had gone out somewhere.

She hadn't heard from Ric on Monday, which was probably just as well. She was so busy getting ready and tying up loose ends, she didn't have time to contact him, or at least that was her excuse. Her arm rested on the chair. She buried her mouth in her hand, hiding the giggle when she thought about him sitting in a salon chair spreading his eyelids with his hands to get his brows threaded. She laughed again. It was kind of prissy, but he was so much a man that it was okay.

Then she rubbed her lips, thinking of the kiss—*that kiss was so wrong.* Just then a car pulled into the driveway. Only Cindy got out and ran up to the porch.

"You're here!" She hugged Gini tightly. "It's so good to see you, baby sister, so good." The two hugged and kissed. "Why are you waiting out here?"

"I rang the bell, but no one answered."

Cindy turned the door handle and went inside.

Gini laughed. "I didn't think to try the knob."

"Mama, look who's here," Cindy called out. "Mama, where are you?"

Slowly, Elizabeth emerged from the bedroom. "Gini, oh, it's so good you're here."

Gini ran up to her and gave her a big hug. "I rang the bell, Mama."

"I'm sorry, honey, I didn't hear you."

Gini was surprised to see how much her mother slumped, and she seemed slow and elusive.

"I'm just a little tired today." The two still had their arms around each other. "I guess I was going to lie down for a while, but I forgot Cindy was here." Elizabeth shook her head, not knowing for sure what was going on.

"Mama, remember, I went to the store to get your prescription."

Cindy looked at Gini. "I don't know how long it's been since she took her blood pressure medicine."

Gini became concerned. "Mama, when did you run out of these pills? It's important you take them every day."

"I know, honey, I know." She affectionately put her arm around Gini's waist. "It's so good to have you home. I wish you would give up that big city stuff. You and Franco should move back where you belong."

Gini gave her another hug. "I've missed you, but my work is in Boston and DC. That's where I belong."

"And, Franco, where is that handsome son-in-law of mine?"

"He's still in China. He won't be able to come this time."

Gini walked the two of them into the living room with her arm around her. They were about the same height. Cindy was three to four inches taller.

"We baked this morning, your favorites."

"I thought I smelled bear claws."

The three of them spent the rest of the afternoon talking and laughing while eating pastries and drinking tea. As the time went on, Elizabeth became more alive. Gini was glad to see her happy mother emerge.

"I need to get a pen and paper." Mama got up from the kitchen table. "We need to make a list, so we make sure we have everything we need for Thanksgiving." She left the room.

"She's so glad to have you here," Cindy said, "and she's looking forward to the big family dinner. I can see a lightening of her step already."

Gini smiled and nodded her head.

Wednesday morning the three ladies baked pies, made sweet breads, cooked and peeled sweet potatoes, and ironed tablecloths and napkins. All the while, the chatter was constant, with a lot of reminiscing. About two o'clock, Mama wanted to rest. Cindy took her into the bedroom and got her settled in bed.

Gini made some tea and started nibbling on a sweet bread piece in the living room.

"I think we wore her out," Cindy said.

"The water is hot if you want some tea."

"Thanks."

Cindy came back into the room with tea and treats. "This has been fun. Just the three of us, like old times."

"I can remember baking with Mama when I was little for holidays. It was one of my favorite things to do. I miss being with family sometimes."

"Why don't you and Franco move back? I'm sure you could find work here."

"Oh… I love what I'm doing, and Washington DC is a long way from here. And Franco, well, Franco." She stopped and looked down.

"I see you're not wearing your wedding ring."

Gini twirled the green stone ring around on her finger. "Franco gave this to me from China."

"I remember when he gave you that. But that isn't your wedding ring. Is there something going on I don't know about? Everyone will be here for Thanksgiving except Franco. Couldn't he have taken a few days off and come? This is our last big meal in this house."

"How many will there be?" Gini asked, hoping to change the subject.

"Let's see." Cindy started counting. "Thomas and Elsie, their son Troy, his wife, their daughter and husband, Larry, Dwayne, Brit and the two boys, my crew, you, and Mama, that's sixteen.

"Thomas and Larry are going to fix up the house before we put it on the market. They're good handymen. I guess Pop trained them well. Unlike Dwayne—he hasn't lifted a finger to help. Sometimes I wonder where he came from. Did they switch babies at birth?" Both girls giggled.

"I don't know. He's definitely a strange one, and he married a very odd woman. I don't think I have ever seen Brit smile. She's always unhappy about something."

"Yeah, she's weird, but Mama loves those boys, and they love her."

"How old are they now?"

"Five and eight, and little firecrackers both of them, but sweet. So I guess Brit and Dwayne must be good parents."

Gini got up to get more tea.

"You didn't finish telling me about Franco. When will he be coming back? Hopefully in time for Christmas."

Gini came back into the room. "Listen, Cindy, I haven't seen Franco for months or talked to him or had any emails until lately. I have no idea when he plans to come home."

"Gini!" Cindy gasped. "Baby sister, why not? You're not breaking up, are you?"

There was silence for a few minutes.

"Maybe we should. We don't have a marriage. He's married to his work. I figured he'd be gone a few months and come back, but it hasn't worked out that way. I was okay with it at first, but now…" She sighed. A sadness rolled over her, the horrible feeling of loneliness. She didn't want to be a marriage statistic—and Franco hadn't really done anything wrong; nor had she. It was their work that kept them apart. She was sure if they were together, their love would be as strong as ever.

"Franco adores you. He always has. You need to get over there to China and be with your husband!"

"I did go to China. There was nothing for me to do there. He works in remote areas and… and I just hated it, and he knew it. He used to call, but I think he just wanted to know if I was pregnant. When that possibility was over so were the phone calls."

"Isn't it a little difficult to get pregnant if you're not together?" Cindy asked in a snide tone, raising her eyebrows.

Why was Cindy being so mean? She didn't understand the deep hurt Gini was experiencing, the hollow certainty that her husband was more fulfilled by his work than by being with her— She didn't really believe that and yet part of her believed it totally. She needed someone to listen, not judge. "Yes, and it is hard to get pregnant even when we are together. We tried for two years, marking the calendar, in vitro, everything. That's why he was calling—because we had several embryos implanted. Nothing. I know he wants children. And he works a lot with families and kids over there, so maybe that's why he never comes home. I don't know why, Cindy. I really don't know why."

There was a tap on the door. It was Neil, Cindy's husband.

"There she is. There's my special little girl." Gini and Neil hugged.

If Cindy was Gini's second mother, then Neil was her second dad. She loved them both dearly and spent a lot of time with them growing up. And when Todd was born, Gini treated him like a living doll. Even though he was several years younger than she, they became very close.

Thursday morning Gini woke up to the smell of bacon frying and toast. When she opened her eyes, she smiled, thinking about her youth.

It had been a long time since she'd slept in her room. She and Franco had visited a couple of times after they got married, and once when they returned from China. He had insisted they stay at a hotel. He said it was too weird to sleep in her childhood bed. The hotel had been an easy getaway if the family got on his nerves. He had tolerated sitting and talking with the family when they were dating, because he wanted to be with Gini, but he no longer had the patience.

There were some of the family who had been upset when they found out Gini and Franco didn't have a wedding—well, really, only Mama and Cindy.

One of the trips had been when Franco's mother died. His grandmother had died their junior year in high school. Mama had felt she needed to represent the Andersons at the funeral out of respect for Franco. She and Franco's mother had been the only ones at the church; not even Franco was there. When his mom had died, it had been much the same; Elizabeth, Gini, and Franco sat and listened to the priest give a small service. What a lonely life those two women must have had. Franco had sold the house and was done with it. Gini had heard a developer bought up the area to build a new shopping center. She had never checked it out; that part of town had no interest for her. She knew if Mama hadn't come across Franco that day after he was beat up, he would have been in gangs and probably in jail. They would have never met, and she wouldn't know of his love.

Mama had to plead with Thomas and Larry to come see the Legottis when they visited, but they never showed up. Franco had always steered clear of the brothers. He had not liked their disrespect of women. Gini didn't know her older half-brothers at all. When she was real little, they kept demanding she tap like Shirley Temple. She had no idea what that meant until she was older, but what really bothered her was them poking her in her tummy with their fingers as if trying to find the "on" button. They had scared her. Whenever they had visited, she always huddled close to Mama.

"I don't like them," Gini told her mama when she was four.

"I know, honey, they can be mean, but they are your brothers, and you must love them."

And when she was in high school she had snuggled down between Franco and Ric on the couch to keep safe. Now they were just grumpy old men. She didn't care if they came to see her or not.

It made her laugh when she thought about Franco and Dwayne. When they were in middle school, Dwayne had learned that tangling with Franco was never a good idea. Even though Dwayne was a full head taller, Franco could have taken him down with little effort. It hadn't made Dwayne any less willing to taunt, however. But he had known exactly how far to go. If Franco even made a hint that he was getting up, Dwayne darted out of sight. By the end of high school, Gini knew Franco had secretly enjoyed Dwayne's stupid game.

And then there was Ric, who wouldn't purposely hurt anyone. Gini had never seen him angry—sad, for sure, when she first met him—and crushed when Margarita had miscarried their first child. He had been quiet and reserved and basically ignored by the rest of the family, which seemed okay with him. Franco, on the other hand, had been like an adopted child of the Andersons. He'd been at their house so much growing up they saw him as a permanent fixture—that had grinded on Dwayne. Of course, Franco had started coming to the house when he was eight, Ric not until the age of fifteen. It had always amazed Gini how the two could be such close friends when they had such opposite personalities and interests. They had had Mama in common, and Gini guessed they both had wanted to be the best in school or whatever they did. Maybe that had been enough—the recognition of intelligence, drive, and ambition in each other. Lord knows, those traits had been scarce in their community.

Mama had always treated Franco like royalty. She said she had never known a kid, or anyone for that matter, who had picked themselves up by their bootstraps—completely driven to be a better person. She didn't recognize that it had been she who turned Franco around with her love and support. Even if Elizabeth had, she would have never taken the credit.

Suddenly, there was the smell of smoke. Gini jumped out of bed, grabbed her robe, and ran into the kitchen.

"Mama!"

"Oh, that darn toaster, it keeps catching on fire. Your daddy said he would fix it, but he hasn't found the time yet. He's so good at fixing things."

Gini unplugged the toaster, pulled the toast out with a fork, and put it in the sink. "I think you need a new toaster. Mama, don't use this again, okay?"

"No, no, Tom will fix it. Baby girl, what kind of eggs do you want?"

"Let me fix you breakfast."

"Gini, I'm going to fix your breakfast. You have been away at school so long."

Gini hugged her mom. "Did you take your pills this morning?"

Elizabeth pointed at the pill box. Gini went over, picked it up, and handed her mother each pill, which she took with a swallow of water.

It seemed Gini could hardly put one foot in front of the other some mornings, she was so tired. Today was one of those days, but after she had the great breakfast with her mom, she perked right up. It must have been a bit of jet lag.

Gini and Mama put the turkey in the oven at ten o'clock. Everyone started arriving about noon. Cindy and Neil got there first. Gini helped them bring in the chairs and the extra tables the church had lent to them for the day. Neil brought in the coolers. Two of the coolers were for the drinks, and a third had the salads that Cindy had made.

Gini got busy and opened the ice bags and poured the ice into the coolers, then put in the drinks.

"Where's Todd?" Gini asked.

"He and Andrea will be here soon," Cindy said with a broad smile.

Gini figured there was going to be a big announcement coming.

After a while, Dwayne and his family came in.

"Well, if it isn't the big city girl," Dwayne said. "Decided to grace our tables, did yah?" He gave her a quick hug and walked on in.

"Gini," Brit said with a nod as she passed by.

The two young boys raced past Gini and headed right for Mama Elizabeth.

"Grandmama," they both shouted with glee. Each grabbed onto Elizabeth and hugged her tight. Neil was standing close by and took hold of her shoulders to help steady her as the energy passed from the boys to Elizabeth.

"Oh, my little munchkins."

Dwayne yelled, "What have I told you boys about your grandmother?"

He went over, took hold of both of their arms and pulled them away.

"It's okay, Dwayne. Let them love me."

As the hour went by, Larry arrived, and Thomas and his family came soon after; everyone hugged. It was kind of scary to her how much Thomas looked like her dad.

It was close to one when Todd and Andrea got to the house. He was carrying a box full of different drinks.

"Happy Thanksgiving, everyone."

Gini ran over to him and hugged him. "Happy Thanksgiving."

"Aunt Gini, it's so great to see you again." He reached back and pulled Andrea up to his side. "You remember Andrea?"

"Yes, yes of course. Happy Thanksgiving to you."

"Thank you." Andrea fidgeted and then shrugged her shoulders, smiled, and held out her left hand.

"I guess I'll have to get used to calling you Aunt Gini."

"You're engaged! Congratulations. Mama, Mama, come look, they're engaged."

Everyone gathered around the two and admired the ring and gave their congratulations.

"Oh, honey," Elizabeth said. "This is a happy day, a happy day."

The chatter continued as the meal preparations were finished and the food was put on the tables. They gathered and sat down to eat. Everything was delicious. The conversation was upbeat, and everyone was having a good time, including Gini. It was like being home when she was a child. Mama ran around making sure all the family had enough to eat and insisting they eat more, even though they all were full.

It was a tradition for the men to clear the table and do the dishes. The women split the leftovers up and put them into containers for everyone to take home. Gini went out into the backyard to check on the drinks in the coolers. She squatted down to replenish the sodas.

"It's good to see you," Dwayne said, surprising her. She hadn't seen him come out the door.

She stood up. "Thank you. I'm enjoying being with the family again."

"I've missed you and Franco. Where is he?"

"He has a job in China, so he has been over there for a while."

"I remember, he digs water wells, right?"

She smiled, impressed Dwayne kept up on Franco.

"Yes, he digs wells, invents, and makes many people happy. He improves their quality of life."

"And you? You still preaching on the Hill?"

"Yes," Gini answered still smiling. "I still talk a lot."

Dwayne laughed. "You were a little chatterbox for sure, a brat, really."

"*A brat*?" She gave him a face. "I was your cute little sister."

"Right! I just wanted to tell you thanks for coming. I know it means a lot to Mama. And I wanted to tell you…" He paused a moment. "I wanted to tell you, I really do miss you and that I'm very proud of you."

"Well… Dwayne, thanks."

"I guess a university education can take you to better places. Mama and Pop wanted me to go to college. But I thought I was too much of a big shot. I didn't need any more education. You're the smart one, getting a degree and getting the heck out of here. Mama and Pop's money was well spent on you."

"I appreciated Mama letting me leave the state, and I was grateful for the money they had to help me, but most of my schooling was paid for with scholarships. And… I worked the whole time I was in school. You're right, though, a good college education opens doors."

"Yeah, better than saddling yourself with a family that I struggle to support." He looked down at his feet.

"You have a wonderful family. Your little boys are adorable. Franco and I want kids so bad, but we just can't seem to get pregnant."

"I guess I have one up on you." Dwayne walked over and gave her a big hug. "I'm glad you came."

He turned around and went back into the house. Gini stood staring at the door. Dwayne had never been that sweet to her—ever.

Everyone gathered in the living room, and Gini and Cindy dished and served the desserts. There was talk about football, mostly college, and the San Francisco 49ers.

"Do you see the games in Boston?" Dwayne asked.

"What games?"

"The 49ers, our team, of course. Is there any other?"

"I'm a Patriots fan," Gini said proudly with a smile. The room filled with boos.

"Patriots!" Neil shouted. "We have a traitor amongst us."

Everyone laughed and gave her a bad time.

Slowly the family began to leave. Gini could see Mama was completely worn out, but she was happy. Mama kept hugging Dwayne's little boys until they left. It truly had been a joyful Thanksgiving. When Gini went to bed, she thought about Franco. They had had so many great holidays in that house growing up. He should have been there; he should have.

Ric had bought a case of expensive wine for the feast at the Westcotts'.

"Come on in," Maria said, kissing him on the cheek. "You can put the wine in the wine refrigerator. There's someone here I want you to meet."

Maria took his hand, and they walked into the great room where everyone had gathered.

"Ric, I'd like you to meet Julia Morton. She's a lawyer. Julia, this is Ric Santini. He's a lawyer too."

Ric smiled and nodded.

"Ric, ole boy," Victor said putting his arm around Ric's shoulders and giving him a stern hug. "It's good to see you."

"Hey, congrats on the re-election." Ric patted Victor on the arm.

Victor guided Ric into the crowd, leaving the two ladies standing alone.

A football game was on the TV. Everyone shook hands as they greeted each other. Maria took Julia farther into the room.

Dinner was served at a long table in the dining room-kitchen combination.

"Here," Maria said to Ric, "you sit here next to Julia. I'm sure there's a lot you can talk about."

Maria had always been trying to find a girl for him, and she was doing her matchmaking again.

Julia was an attractive enough woman, tall and slender, with blonde hair and hazel-green eyes. She was dressed in a clinging sweater and nice wool pants with high heels.

"Which firm do you work for?" she asked.

"I'm not practicing law, at the moment."

Maria sat at the head of the table on the other side of him. "But he was with Lory and Lawson."

"Oh wow, that's a very prestigious firm."

Ric smiled.

"Julia is a junior partner," Maria said. "Which firm was that?"

"Freed and Associates."

"That's a great firm too. Isn't that right, Ric?"

He agreed.

The conversation continued throughout the meal with Maria's constant interjections. Although Julia was nice, attractive, and seemed smart—his kind of woman—Ric wasn't interested in connecting with her. Through the discussions, he learned she was a serious trial lawyer, passionate about interpreting statutes as they had been intended. He tried to stay engaged in the stories, but he disliked trial lawyering and was having a difficult time paying attention to what she was saying about her cases.

Maria was pleased he seemed to enjoy being with Julia. He was his charming self, showing great interest in her work.

He got up to help clear the dishes.

Maria followed him to the sink with both hands full. "Ric, honey, isn't Julia just about perfect?"

"Maria." He leaned over and kissed her on the cheek. "I don't need a matchmaker."

She smiled as they went back to the table for more dishes. "Yes you do, you need a woman."

Ric and Victor were smoking their cigars out on the enclosed porch.

Julia dried the last dish. "I don't think I impressed him much."

"Oh, don't worry, he likes you. I'm sure you'll hear from him."

"He hasn't asked me for contact information."

"I'll give it to him."

"You're sweet, Maria, but I doubt he has any problem getting women."

"He's a good-looker for sure, but he never seems to have a lady by his side. I think he works way too hard. Leave it to me, Julia."

Everyone left except Ric. The two men were in the great room drinking an after-dinner drink, talking politics.

"Here you go, honey." Maria handed him a piece of paper. "This is Julia's number."

Victor grabbed her onto his lap. "Are you trying your hand at arranging a date for Ric again?"

"He needs a fine lady on his arm."

"Maria, I appreciate your concern, but I have a beautiful woman in my life." He couldn't tell them who it was he was so much in love with. It was too early. He hadn't even told Gini yet how he felt. It was his secret for now.

"No!" Maria said, surprised. "And you haven't mentioned that to us?"

"She's a good friend. We have been going out together. It's nice to have someone to enjoy the good times. Just good friends, for now."

"You have to bring her here. We want to meet her."

Friday morning Gini fixed breakfast for herself and her mom. Cindy came about nine o'clock. They finished packing up the rest of Mama's clothes and then took her to her new home.

They were pleasantly greeted at the reception desk, and Mama introduced the daughters. Mama showed Gini around the facility.

"This is the activity room, and this room is our kitchen." The room was large, with three cooking areas.

Cindy hugged Elizabeth around the shoulders. "I think Mama will spend lots of time in here. All she has to do is tell the kitchen what ingredients she needs, and she can bake her heart away."

Gini was impressed with the luxurious living. The atmosphere was light and cheerful. She was pleased and happy her mother was going to get good care.

After the tour, they went up to Elizabeth's place. It was small, but nicely furnished, and had a balcony that looked out over a lush green, wooded area.

They had a good meal in the dining room, where several people greeted Elizabeth. She introduced her two daughters.

The three of them went back up to Mama's place. At nine, the night nurse came to help Mama get ready for bed.

"Someone will come in to check on Mama every day. They'll make sure she's eating and taking her medication. And at night, they'll help her get to bed."

"This is so nice. I'm glad we are doing this for Mama. She's been good to me. Now, I can repay her by paying for her to stay here." Gini felt much better about Mama selling the family house.

"She's in bed," the aide said. "I'll check on her through the night."

They went to the bedroom to say good night.

"Gini, you have a good trip home," Mama said. "And you give Franco a big hug and kiss from me."

"I will. I love you, Mama."

"I love you too, honey." Elizabeth kissed her.

They walked back to the living room. "I'm going to stay at the hotel out by the airport. I can take you home on the way," Gini said to Cindy.

"No, I think I'll stay here tonight and sleep on the couch. I'll call Neil and have him bring my things. Mama has only stayed here for two nights. I want to make sure she's okay."

Gini gave Cindy a hug and kiss. "You're a good daughter."

"Have a good trip home. It's so good to see you, baby sister." She held Gini away at arm's length. "You go, be with your husband. He loves you, and you love him."

Gini smiled. "Yes, you're right."

She walked into the familiar hotel lobby.

"Mrs. Legotti, welcome home," the man behind the desk greeted.

Once in the room, she got settled and went to bed. She thought about what Cindy had said about her being with Franco. Rubbing her hand across the other side of the bed, she thought about them staying there, making love, talking about the family, and laughing at funny stories about when they were young. Why wasn't he lying there next to her? Why did she have to deal with their lives' ups and downs—Mama's failings—without him? They were partners in a union; they needed to be together. But then she wondered if going to China was the answer. Wasn't that what a *good wife* would do? But she'd be so miserable, and she knew it. He knew it too, that's why he hadn't insisted. She knew one thing, she longed to be back in his arms again, reassured that he loved her, and desired her. That's *all* she wanted. He was her family now, and she needed him.

Chapter 9 – Holidays

Saturday morning Gini sat in first class looking out the window at the line of planes going to the runway. She couldn't get the last thing Cindy said to her out of her mind. Being with the family and having such a good time made her want her husband even more. The memories of the early days kept coming—the days when he'd never been out of this town and so was fully engaged with the people and the situations, when she could talk about Mama and Cindy, and maybe he didn't understand, but he cared. And she'd run out of talk, and they'd look at each other... It used to make them laugh how they'd both at the same moment remember the delights of sex. He'd get that heavy-lidded look and throw an arm around her, or if she were across the room, he'd just look at her and ask, "Gini, why are you over there when you could be on my lap?" It was just such a surprise—that two people could feel so good together.

She couldn't get him out of her head all night.

Once they were in the air, she took out her PET and started writing an email to him:

> Franco, I'm on the plane heading back to Boston after spending a wonderful holiday with my family. They all missed you, as do I, and were wondering when they would see you again. The whole family was there. It was just like when we were kids. All the food, laughter, and Dwayne picking on me. Lol. I hope you celebrated Thanksgiving in some way over there. Please tell me when you'll be home. I love you. Gini.

She sent the message and then started eating the breakfast that was served to her.

In just a few minutes, her PET signaled she had an email. She smiled. *That was fast.*

> I'm unable to respond to my messages at this time. All messages will be forwarded to my assistant. I will contact you as soon as I have an internet connection. Franco Legotti.

Was his assistant going to read her personal mail? Why did she bother? She spread the butter on her breakfast roll over and over furiously. She wished she could delete it. A tear came to her eye.

"Can I get you anything?" the flight attendant asked.

Gini wiped her cheek. "I'll have some orange juice."

Once she finished the meal, she reclined her seat and fell asleep. She was surprised when she woke up, and the loudspeaker was announcing to prepare for landing. Out the window, she could see the airport as the plane made a broad bank over the water.

It was nearly four o'clock when she walked in her door. Right on top of all her mail sitting on the kitchen bar was a note addressed "Gini." She opened it:

> I hope you had a great week in Sacramento. I just wanted to remind you about the party tonight at the hotel. I know you'll enjoy it. It starts at 7. I'll come and get you at 6:15. Text me with your acceptance. Ric.

She set the note aside and went through the rest of the stack. There was nothing of importance. She pulled her PET out of her bag.

"Email Cindy," she commanded. "Start. Cindy, I got home just fine. Period. Thank you for a great time. Period. I absolutely loved being with the family. Period. I love you, sis. Period. Stop. Send."

She checked her emails. There was one from Catherine:

> I hope you're having as much fun with your family as I am with mine. All we have done is eat, drink, and laugh and then eat and drink some more. Happy Thanksgiving, friend.

She smiled. "Respond. Start. Had a great time in Sacramento. Yes, we ate way too much. Happy Thanksgiving to you. Period. Stop. Send."

She picked up the note and went into the living room, sat down in the chair, and pulled her legs up to her chest. She flipped the paper back and forth over her finger. Why not go? She'd just had a great time with her family—so many memories. He had an exciting life; she should go. After all, he was family too. She smiled. A fun night out was just what she needed to forget about Franco and his non-message. She was probably making more of a big deal about it than necessary.

But the kiss. What about the kiss? She shivered at the memory then said to herself—like a teacher who is always right even when she's wrong—*It was just a thank-you kiss like Michael's, to thank me for being his friend, that's all, a thank-you kiss.*

She tapped her electronic bracelet and spoke the message, "Text Ric Santini. I'll see you at six-fifteen. Send."

At six-ten Ric arrived, and Howard sent him up. When Ric got to the door, it was ajar.

He stuck his head inside, tapping gently. "Gini?"

"Come in," she called out.

As he rounded the breakfast bar, she walked out of her bedroom messing with her earring. She was limping, with one high heel on and the other tucked under her arm.

"There," she said lowering her hand from her ear and grabbing her shoe. She leaned on the corner of the bar and put it on. She was wearing a long sweater-knit dress that showed off her slender body and full chest. Ric found himself taking a gasp of air as her look took his breath away.

"Oh, I'll be right back." She turned and went back into her room.

Ric had to concentrate to keep his body from reacting to his desire for her. He had been thinking about his love for her, and each time he felt that rush of euphoria, he was stalled by the thought she was married, and not just married, but married to his friend. He wasn't the type of person who would steal another man's wife; at least he had never thought so. But he truly loved her not just in his heart, but with his whole body—it ached for her. He knew it wasn't right, and he would fight it.

They'd just go out tonight and have a good time. Nothing had to be done or decided. Just two friends having a good time.

"Okay," she said with a beaming smile, carrying a small handbag. "I think I'm ready."

"Gins, you look beautiful, absolutely beautiful."

"Why, thank you, sir." She made a small curtsy.

He hadn't seen her sweet playfulness for years. It was refreshing.

She walked past him to get her coat, looking at her watch. It was six-eighteen.

"Only three minutes late. That's not too bad."

They walked down through the lobby.

Howard looked up. "Ms. Anderson. Mr. Santini. Have a wonderful evening."

They both commented back and left the building. Howard didn't interfere with the patrons of the building or their personal lives, but he knew a budding romance when he saw it. Mr. Legotti hadn't been in the building for some time. Most of the mail was addressed to Ms. Anderson. He wouldn't pry, although he always found the affection between Ms. Anderson and Mr. Legotti quite touching. Mr. Santini and another woman had frequented the building right after the Legottis moved in a few years back. But neither had been there for a long time.

"Where's your car?" Gini asked.

He looked at her and smiled. "We're just going to the hotel. I thought we could walk."

"Perfect!"

He bent his elbow, and she slipped her arm around his.

"What exactly are we going to?"

"The hotel puts on a 'Thank you in advance of the Christmas holidays party' every year for the staff. We, my company and contract workers, take over the services and wait on the hotel workers in the Harbor Bar."

"I love that room, such a great view."

They walked through the rotating doors and down to the bar. A man walked up to them and took their coats.

"What are we going to do?"

He showed her the way. "You, my sweet Gins, are going to sit on the stool and enjoy the festivities. I'm going to take care of the bar duties."

"Oh no, Ric, a bartender. Do you know how to do that?"

"Of course," he said with no concern.

"Uh-oh," the barkeep, Jacques, said as Ric stepped behind the bar. "I'd better take an inventory."

Ric took off his suit jacket and hung it back behind the liquor shelf. "Come on, I only broke two glasses last year."

"And you poured a half a bottle of fine scotch on the floor, if I remember."

Ric laughed. "We covered that expense. Much better than the year before."

"By far."

Jacques walked over to Gini.

"Can I get you a good drink before he takes over?"

"What do you suggest?"

"I have a special holiday tini."

"Sure, I'll try that."

Ric had on nice tailored black pants and a vest to match. He rolled his perfectly ironed white shirtsleeves up just below the elbow. He tied on a sparkling white apron around his slim waist up under the vest. Gini sat and watched him dress for the part.

"Here you go, miss," Jacques said.

"Gini."

Jacques took the martini shaker and gave it a hearty shake, tipped the lid, and poured the pink liquid into a chilled martini glass. He stuck in a short peppermint stick for a garnish.

She took a sip. "Mmm, delicious."

"Okay," Ric said. "Get out of here, Jacques. It's time for you to party."

Jacques patted him on the arm as he walked out from behind the bar. "Have fun."

People dressed in holiday party clothes started filtering into the room; others were in casual dress or still in their hotel uniforms. Across from the bar was a long string of tables with all kinds of food, soft drinks, and water. Not too many people were ordering mixed drinks. Ric was mostly serving wine and beer.

Jacques walked over to Gini about forty-five minutes into the party and put a plate of finger food down in front of her.

"Need another drink?"

She smiled. "Thanks for the food. I think I'll switch to wine. I'm pretty sure the bartender can handle that without difficulty."

"One would hope." Jacques winked.

"Are you having a good time?" she asked.

"Yes, ma'am. We all appreciate our employers. They treat us like family."

She picked up a small puff pastry. "You've always been a bartender?"

"Yes, this is my baby." He rubbed his hand along the bar top. "I give Ric a bad time, but he treats her with respect. I don't trust just anyone inside of her."

Suddenly the room was all busy with laughter and happy conversations. A lot of people had gathered to place their drink orders. A large majority, Gini realized, were young women. Ric smiled and chatted, poured wine, popped tops off beer bottles, held the bottle up high and then swooped back down to the glass, scraping a small amount of foam from the beers, and handed the drinks to two ladies. Each stuck a five-dollar bill in the large fishbowl-shaped dish on the bar.

"And how about you, pretty miss?" he said, walking over to Gini. "Can I get you a refill?"

She smiled. "You're having the time of your life."

"Yes, *I am!*"

"A chardonnay, please, Mr. Bartender."

After she received her wine, she slid down off the stool. The large room was getting crowded. She walked over to the floor-to-ceiling windows and looked out. The night lights were beautiful, a bit of Christmas color here and there. The view was South Boston and planes lined up in the sky, approaching the city, as far as she could see. She loved Boston.

By ten o'clock, the room quieted, and only the hired contract staff filled the room.

Jacques went behind the counter. "Okay, out of my bar."

Ric wiped the counter in front of him with a towel.

"Ahh," Jacques said. "Your dishwashing skills need some work."

There were mugs in the sink, champagne flutes on the lower shelf, and a tray of half-clean glasses sitting near the edge. Jacques walked over and discreetly moved the tray back.

"I'll get them cleaned up. Give me time, ole boy."

He patted Ric on the shoulder. "Your time is up, job well done. Thanks for the break; I appreciate it. Now, go be with your lady."

He nodded his head toward Gini, who was back on the barstool. Ric took off the apron and threw it in the laundry bin. "I didn't break or spill a thing." He put his head up with his chest out—proud of himself.

"Good boy!"

Ric grabbed his suit coat and started to walk out from behind the bar.

"Don't forget your tips," Jacques said.

"Those are yours. Merry Christmas."

He walked up to Gini. "Come with me. I want you to meet my people."

Jacques dipped glasses into clean soapy water in the sink. "Gini, anytime I'm in here, your drinks are on the house."

"Thank you," she said and went with Ric.

Everyone was in white shirts and pants except for a lady in a green pantsuit and a man with nice pants, a long-sleeved button-down shirt, and a bow tie.

"How'd we do?" Ric asked the lady.

"Great. And how about you? How many glasses were broken and liquor lost?"

"None." Ric flashed a smile.

"Carol, this is my friend Gini. Gini, this is Carol, my right-hand lady."

"Nice to meet you."

Ric stood behind Gini and put both of his hands on her shoulders close to her neck.

The man walked out of a door. "We have all the leftover food packed and ready for the homeless shelter."

"James, this is Gini."

"Hello."

"Nice to meet you, James," Gini said with a slight, shy smile. He checked her out with his eyes.

"I couldn't function without these two people," Ric said with pride. "Without Carol and James, Greystone wouldn't be very entertaining."

Carol laughed. "Oh, Ric."

"So now, it's on to tomorrow. Is everything in place for the afternoon tea and the party tomorrow night?"

"Yes, oh master," James said. "All's in order, sir."

Gini could see they all enjoyed their work and working together.

"Go on," Carol said, "be gone. We have this done."

"Are you hungry?" Ric asked Gini.

"Yeah, I guess I am a little."

"Let's go to the Crow's Nest."

"I don't know that restaurant."

He didn't offer Gini her coat. They walked out of the bar and down a corridor into the large open area attached to the hotel. The Long Wharf warehouse from years past had been transformed into an area for small enclosed boutiques. The shops were geared mostly to the tourist trade, but Gini loved walking through them and seeing the interesting, unique items. A large metal screen blocked the entrance to the shopping area since they were all closed for the day. Ric turned Gini to her left, and they walked to a small elevator. Over the door, the sign read "Fly up to the Crow's Nest." The doors opened, and they stepped inside.

"I had no idea this was here," she said.

They went up three floors, and the doors opened into a darkened, seemingly small space. They climbed about eight steps into another room where there was a smattering of tables.

The headwaiter met them at the door. "Mr. Santini, your preferred table?"

"Yes, please."

Gini looked up at him. He smiled and winked, then with his arm around her, he guided her to follow the waiter. They walked up a few more steps to another level of tables and were seated in the corner by two windows.

"A three-finger scotch on the rocks?" the man asked Ric.

"Yes, please."

"And you, miss?"

"I'll have a red wine."

"Bring her the Napa Petite Syrah," Ric suggested.

"And your usual for dinner, Mr. Santini?"

"We'll need to see menus."

"Very well, sir."

Gini looked out the windows. Their view was of where the river met the harbor and the many lights from Charlestown. There was a tanker weaving its way to Chelsea. As the ship moved closer, Gini could see the Tobin Memorial Bridge was closed. The police cars blocking the bridge had bright flashing lights.

"How long has this been here?"

"It used to be a men's club, for seafarers and dockworkers, until about two years ago. I think the city insisted they move to another location. It stood empty for a while and then the restaurant opened. It's a great-kept secret, and the food is out of this world."

"I guess it's a secret. I live a stone's throw away, and I didn't know it was here."

Their drinks were served and a menu handed to each.

He talked her into ordering the crab and cheese casserole.

"I'll have the steak," Ric said.

"Medium rare?" the waiter asked as he wrote.

"Yes."

"Baked sweet potato?"

"Yes."

"Large salad with raspberry balsamic vinegar and olive oil?"

Ric nodded.

"Very good, I'll bring the bread."

"I guess that's the usual," she said, smiling.

"Yes…" He grinned.

"How was your Thanksgiving?" he asked her after taking a sip of his drink.

She sighed. "Oh Ric, it was wonderful. You remember how Mama busied herself making sure everyone had enough to eat and insisting you have more when you were so full you could pop?"

"The food pusher."

"All the family was there, and Dwayne…" She stopped to relish the moment again.

"Even the wicked stepbrothers from the North?"

"Who?" Gini asked, puzzled.

"Your stepbrothers, Larry and Thomas. That's what Franco and I called them. Mean son-of-a-guns."

She laughed. "You really called them that? Yes, they were there, my half-brothers. They are old. And Thomas looks just like Pop." She put her head down and giggled. "The wicked stepbrothers of the North, that's too funny.

"You wouldn't have believed how nice Dwayne was to me. He even told me he was proud of me."

"As well he should be."

Their salads were served.

"So, Mama Elizabeth is doing good." Ric filled his mouth with lettuce after speaking.

"No!" Gini's mood completely changed. "She was her sweet, lovable self at moments, and other times she was confused and distant."

Gini sat back in her chair, put her elbow on the table, and looked out the window again.

"I hate to see her get older." She slowly faced him. "I just hated that was the last time we will be together in the house I grew up in."

Ric was sorry he had brought up the subject. She had been so happy until the question.

"How was your Thanksgiving?" she asked.

"Good, really nice. You know Maria and Victor are like family. So much so, Maria thinks it's her duty to find me a woman."

Gini looked at him with her mouth full. "A woman?" she mumbled.

"Yes, she invited a date for me."

"You do need a woman," she said, after swallowing the salad. "What's her name?"

Ric moved his mouth around a little. "Jackie... or Jewel." He stopped to think. "Julia. That's it, Julia."

"Is she nice?"

"Nice enough. She's a trial lawyer."

"And pretty?" Gini avoided eye contact so kept eating.

"She's attractive enough, tall and slender. Nice blonde hair."

She didn't like that he was attracted to another woman, but why not? He was single and good-looking. She thought about all the young ladies gathering at the bar, knowing they were trying to get his attention. Soon he would find that special person he so much deserved. Maybe Julia was the one. She tried to ignore the jealousy screaming at her—she should be happy for him. But she wasn't; depressed was more the feeling. Once again, she was going to be abandoned.

"Are you going to ask her out?"

Ric looked at her. "What's with all the questions?"

"Well, Maria's right. You need someone."

Ric broke a piece of bread. "We'll see."

"We're pretty pathetic. Kind of down in our love lives. Your wife leaves you, and my husband's miles away. Crazy. Thank goodness we are such good friends so that we can bathe in each other's sorrows."

"Oh, I don't know, I'd like to think we lift each other up." He reached over and brushed a breadcrumb from her cheek with his finger.

By the time they got done eating, it was way past midnight. Gini's long day was catching up with her. Ric helped her on with her coat, and they walked back to the Towers.

"Once again, I have to thank you for another great time."

"I'm glad you enjoyed it."

"You have quite the life, Mr. Santini."

She reached up on her toes and kissed him on the cheek. The door opened with the slide of the card. He watched until she got to the elevator.

After the conversation with Carol and James, Gini knew Ric's Sunday was a full one. She unpacked and did her laundry and other chores. Monday, she didn't hear from him either. About seven o'clock she tapped her bracelet. "Text Ric Santini. Start. I just wanted to thank you again for Saturday night. It was wonderful. Stop."

She pulled in a deep breath. Maybe he was out with *that* Julia, she thought. He seemed taken by her. She knew he needed a good woman to share his life with. He was too loving and affectionate to be alone. And a lawyer, that would be perfect for him; they could talk for hours. He'd probably taken her to the neighborhood football party. She saw them in her mind, Ric and Julia, Julia smiling and confident while Gini sat all alone like a child forgotten at the playground. She took another deep breath. Was she just going to let a woman he didn't even know sweep him away? She needed to meet her and make sure she was good enough for him. Those were all *crazy thoughts*; she had to stop thinking about him. They'd had some good times together, and now they needed to move on with their lives.

"Delete," she said to the bracelet.

She got up from her chair and went to the box on the mantel. She ran her finger along the edge. Finally, she opened the top, took out the ring, and slipped it on. She took her little finger and ran it along the fine platinum ribbon that made the intricate X and the delicate knot. Maybe she should go to China. Yes, maybe it was time to stop thinking about her own professional desires and go be with her husband. But what about Catherine? She couldn't leave now right in the middle of things. She'd wait and go after the bill was introduced. Their marriage could certainly wait for that. Now, she was thinking like Franco, work first, deal with their marriage later. She looked at the ring; somehow, she'd have to figure it out. After all, Franco had never said he didn't love her; in fact, he had said he did in both of his emails. Her job was what made her happy; she'd bury herself in her work and let the world go on spinning.

Gini could tell the holiday weekend was over. Tuesday her electronic signals alerting her of messages or texts started early and went all day. She had several video calls with Catherine plus files transferred through the cloud. Michael messaged her all day asking questions, and she had conversations about the Christmas gift party for the poor families with children.

"I hope you got rested up, honey," Catherine said over the phone.

Gini put her dishes in the kitchen. "I did. I can see it's going to be a busy week."

"Very, we have to get this bill on the floor before the end of the special session and everyone leaves for the holiday break. Come to DC. We'll chase them down and tackle someone if we have to."

Gini laughed out loud.

"Is that laughter I hear?"

"You're funny."

"Have you seen Ric?"

"Now, why would you ask that?"

"Because you're happy?"

"Catherine, Ric and I are just good friends. I think he has found a girl."

"And… her name is Virginia Anderson."

"No, her name is Julia."

"Oh." There was a downturn in Catherine's voice, and the subject dropped.

"When do you want me there?"

"Can you come tomorrow?"

"I can. I'll let you know the train arrival time."

She had just ended her conversation with Catherine when Michael called.

"Gini, can we meet tonight at the cafe? I want to run some ideas by you and, as you can see, I have lots of questions. I think a face-to-face meeting for a couple of hours would be good."

"Sure, I can make that work. I'm off to DC tomorrow, and I have no idea how long I'll be there."

"Good. Five o'clock work for you?"

"See you at five."

"Carol," Ric called from his office.

"Yes," she said stepping up to his door.

"Take my PET, will you, and see why I can't get it to work. How can I do business without my PET?"

She laughed. "Maybe you need to feed it."

He was working on some paperwork Mr. Vasquez had sent him.

"What?" He was puzzled at her comment.

"Never mind." She took the device.

That night Gini and Michael got right down to business. He looked so distinguished and handsome. What a great transformation. About seven-thirty his phone rang.

"It's Brenda."

She nodded that he should take the call.

"I'm sorry, sweetheart. I thought for sure I told you I was meeting with Gini... I know, I know, you're right you two should meet... I don't think we'll be much longer. I have to grab her for advice when she's available... I'm so sorry... I know you worry... Okay, I'll be home soon."

At nine o'clock they wrapped up the meeting.

"Now, I have to go home and explain to my wife why I'm with another woman." He looked at Gini. "Do you need a ride?"

"No, I'm good to walk."

He carefully put his papers in the sectioned compartments in his briefcase. He hugged her, thanked her, and left in a hurry.

As she was walking out of the door, a male voice behind her said, "Excuse me, ma'am."

She turned around to look at him. He had a stupid grin on his face.

"I'm looking for a pretty lady to dine with tonight. Care to join me?"

"No," she said abruptly and quickly walked out the door. Her pace quickened the more she walked, and she constantly turned to see if he was following her, or if she could see a policeman. She started running. After a block, she slowed to a walk; the man wasn't behind her. She was safe.

As she went up in the elevator, she realized she had been overreacting to everything—the man in the restaurant, thinking Ric's kiss was a serious romantic kiss, Franco's office manager reading her personal message. She needed to stop this nonsense and get back to her life. She was good on her own—she needed *no one*.

Gini spent the next four days in Washington, DC. Every day they worked long hours. All they needed to do was get one representative to introduce the bill for special health-care provisions for underprivileged children and children in the foster care system. The health care for the United States had been debated for years. Having government control over the procedures had failed miserably, and the insurance companies fought back hard to keep the government out of the health-care business. The rules and laws had changed so many times and, unfortunately, the poor suffered the most. Many of the children's programs had been cut, and the children in foster care had simply fallen through the cracks.

Various interest groups had pooled their funds and hired Catherine's lobbying firm to help these defenseless children. Both Catherine and Gini had their hearts completely in the fight. Other staffers of Catherine's took care of the other lobbying contracts the company held.

Both walked into Catherine's place.

"Can you believe it," Catherine said joyously. "Finally, finally, we get a commitment."

"Thank goodness. I don't know how long I can keep up this pace. And we didn't even have to tackle anyone to the ground." Both ladies laughed.

"Nearly." Catherine kicked off her shoes. "It was your charm. You know, Senator Jones can't say no to you. That was a great strategy getting him to talk to Representative Mathers. And now we will have a bill on the floor of the house. Yay! Shall we get the bottles out?"

"*Oh no*, I'm going to take a hot shower and crawl into bed. I want to catch the first train back to Boston tomorrow."

"Hot date?"

"Actually, *no*, just want my bed, no offense." There was a bit of disappointment in her voice.

"None taken. So, you and Ric are off?"

"Off? Catherine, how many times do I have to tell you."

"I know, I know, you are just good friends."

"I haven't heard from him for a while. I think he has a new girl. And he's very busy. It will be nice just to have nothing to do for a few days."

Gini was on the train when her earbud announced she had an email. "Read."

"Mrs. Legotti, this is Luca, Franco's assistant. I sent your message down with one of our suppliers. He'll give it to Franco. I'm sure he will contact you as soon as he returns to Shijiazhuang. If there's anything I can do for you, please let me know. Luca."

How many people were going to read her email? Probably the whole village at this point. She shook her head. Why had she sent that stupid message, anyway?

Another announcement came through her earbud. "Text, Ric Santini." "Read text," she said.

"I assume you're busy in DC, that's why you haven't responded to my messages. Let me know when you'll be back."

Messages? Her heart was thumping, and she felt out of breath. She scrolled through her PET for emails and saw nothing, then through her text messages.

Nothing there either. Why was she reacting this way? She took a deep breath and put her hand on her chest. *Let it go*, she thought. But she couldn't, she listened to the message again. He definitely said she hadn't responded to his messages.

"Call Ric Santini," she commanded.

"Hey, Gini," he answered, upbeat. "Where the heck are you?"

"I'm on the train."

"Going which way?"

"Back to Boston. I wanted to catch an earlier one, but ended up sleeping longer than I wanted."

"What time do you get in?"

Ric could hear the jingle of glasses.

"My ticket says three twenty-seven on track sixteen."

"I'll pick you up."

"Okay." Gini realized she had forgotten to call Jimmy.

Ric stood at the end of the platform on Track 16. People began to pour out of the train. He had no idea if Gini was in first or second class. Then he saw her. As she approached the turnstile, he walked toward her. She looked ruffled. Her curls were frayed, and she had no makeup on, not that she needed any. He smiled to himself when he saw she was wearing tennis shoes. He hadn't seen her in tennis shoes since college. When she saw him, she smiled a tired smile and waved. He walked up to her when she passed the crowd coming through, then reached over and took the handle of her roller bag.

"Hey, sweets."

Gini folded her arms up to her chest and fell into Ric's body. She snuggled tight to him. He let go of the roller handle and put his arms around her.

She cocked her head up to see him. "I'm so tired."

"I can see that." He put his hand on the back of her head and leaned down and kissed her on the forehead. He wanted to stay there forever with his arms around her.

"Come on," he said grabbing the bag again and putting his arm around her shoulders. "Let's get you home."

"Park in the garage." She opened her purse and handed him the access key card.

Inside the condo, she asked, "You want something to drink?"

"A cup of coffee if you have it." He sat down on the couch.

A few minutes later she brought coffee for him and tea for her. She set the cups on the table in front of the couch.

"I'll be right back."

She walked back into her bedroom. When she returned, she was barefooted. She turned on the TV to the game at a low volume and then she went over to the couch and sat down next to Ric, and pulled her legs up on the couch. He put his arm up on top of the cushion.

"How long were you in DC?"

"Since Wednesday." She sipped her tea. "Oh, my gosh, I don't think we have ever worked so hard. But it paid off, yes, it paid off."

"How so?"

Gini sat up. She crossed her legs Indian style and moved closer to him, her knee touching his thigh.

"They are going to introduce our bill tomorrow on the House floor."

"That's terrific."

"You have no idea how excited we are." She put her cup on the table. "You said I hadn't responded to your messages."

"I understand, you've been busy."

"No, the only message I got from you is the one on the train."

"My darn PET, I've been having trouble with it all week. I think it's time to update to a new one. I can't run my business if I can't get messages in or out.

"What drives you so hard to make all these trips to DC?"

"I do it for the children, especially the underprivileged and the handicapped. Those kids don't have a chance." She picked up her teacup from the table and stood up. "Someone has to help them." She turned around facing him, still holding the cup.

"The health laws are so confusing. Each state has their ideas on how to interpret them. And then throw in the insurance companies, and all you have is a big mess." Her speech was caring but to the point. "And there are parents who don't think their kids should be vaccinated because of misinformation that indicates the shots do more harm than help. Now, we have diseases that were eradicated at one point and have come back as epidemics because the kids aren't protected.

"What about the poor handicapped child in the system? The institutes are overcrowded and understaffed. And foster families, many of them, are just keeping their heads above water. Trying to get the right insurance takes hours and reams of paper. Bureaucracy has got everything tied up in knots."

Ric had his elbow on the couch arm. He leaned his head on his hand. What she was saying was true. He wanted to hear more.

"And the insurance companies think they know better than the doctors. What's wrong with that picture? What does a family do when a child is dying, and the insurance denies medication and treatment because it isn't indicated for that procedure? Bureaucracy is killing us. Catherine and I are trying to get the legislators to look at all the issues—health issues—and make some sense of them. A simple sign up for insurance, let the doctors treat the patients and help the parents. It doesn't have to be so hard." She put her right hand over her heart. "The politicians need to let go of their pet projects and give the people what they want. The right to have good health care and medical treatment. We need to save our children."

She half smiled and picked up his coffee cup. "Do you want more coffee?"

He stood up and put his arm around her. "Gins, you'll get through to our leaders. You're the right woman for the job. By the way, for not being a coffee drinker, that was a pretty good cup of coffee."

"All I did was put the pod in the hole and pour in the water."

"See, it was good because your fingers did the work."

"Oh, Ric, you make me laugh."

"That's good. Laughter helps the soul. It releases endorphins."

She looked at him and scrunched her eyebrows.

"I'm serious. It helps to release stress. No more coffee, thanks."

She put both cups back on the table, and they sat back down on the couch. "Too bad we missed the game," she said.

A minute later, he turned to talk to her. She was completely relaxed, asleep. Her hand slid down next to his leg. He moved closer to her and carefully took the blanket from the back of the couch and laid it on top of her. He pulled her head over to his shoulder and reached his arm down around her. She snuggled into his body without waking.

He sat quietly listening to the football game on the TV. Her hand rested on his leg. He rubbed his finger gently over the green stone ring on her finger.

At six-thirty, Gini woke up with a jolt.

Ric grabbed her. "It's okay."

She sat up and looked at him. "Ric!"

He smiled. "You fell asleep almost in mid-sentence."

"I did?" She sat for a minute clearing her head.

"Are you hungry?" he asked.

She turned and looked at him. "I am."

"I'll order something in."

"No," she said getting up. "I have something I can fix."

She went to the kitchen. By eight o'clock she was dishing a soup-like dish with big chunks of chicken. The broth was full of curry and chilies. She warmed a frozen half loaf of French bread, steamed some fresh asparagus she had in the refrigerator, and tossed a salad, drizzling it with olive oil and balsamic glaze.

They sat at the breakfast bar.

"Impressive, very impressive," he said.

"Gins, we are doing the Junior League Christmas Ball next Saturday. I want you to go with me."

"Junior League, they have a ball?"

"It's a big blowout. I know you'll have fun."

"They have been trying to get me to join for a couple of years."

"Why haven't you?" He scooped another spoonful of broth.

"I just don't feel I can give them the time they deserve. I would want to be a worthy member."

Ric brushed his hand down her back. "Will you go with me?"

"You sure you don't want to go with Julia?" She was serious.

"No."

"I'm sure she would love to go."

"No," he repeated.

"I thought you liked her."

"Gini." He looked her straight in the eyes. *"No!"*

Their eyes locked. She quickly looked away.

"Sure. Is it like a real ball? Fancy dresses—"

"White tie," he interrupted.

Gini smiled a big smile. "Yes, I want to go to the ball!"

They got up from the bar, and they both carried their dishes to the sink.

"Next weekend is going to be a zinger. I have so many functions at the hotel; I should just move in there. It would save me time instead of running back and forth to my house."

"You can use my place if you want."

"Really?"

"Of course, silly, I'm so close. Yes."

"Boy, Gins, that would save me next Saturday if I could change here before we go, that would be great."

"Absolutely! What are friends for?"

Gini needed to buy two dresses; one for the ball and one for the big party at the Kennedy Library the following Saturday. On Monday, she looked online at the boutiques on Newbury Street to see if there was anything she liked. The one for the ball had to be perfect. She hopped on the subway and went to Pierre Chow's shop. She had always liked his dresses and found just what she wanted.

Ric went by Gini's after work Tuesday evening. They walked over to the seafood restaurant across from the aquarium.

"Ms. Anderson, Mr. Santini," the maitre d' said. "Which table?"

Gini turned to the left and pointed to the one she liked back by the windows.

"My usual," Ric said.

The maitre d' laughed. Gini gave Ric a look.

"I'll tell you what," the maitre d' said. "How about one in our new room?"

He took them to an archway that entered into a private, almost-empty room. It was quiet and away from the rest of the restaurant.

"You like?"

They both nodded yes.

"What are you getting?" Ric asked.

"I always get the same thing."

"Then why are you looking at the menu?"

"I wanted to see if they have any new holiday desserts."

"Ms. Anderson." The waiter looked at her. They ordered.

"Do you remember when we came here in college?" Gini asked. "We could only afford it for a special occasion. Now, I come here all the time. Obviously, you too, since they know you by name."

"A lot."

When they were done with their meal, the waiter put another menu on the table.

She picked it up and flashed a gleaming grin. "They do have a holiday dessert."

Ric loved she was smiling again. He loved her sweet dimples, her shining white teeth, and her excitement. He reached over and took her left hand. There was no ring on her finger.

Gini loved the fact she had nothing to do all week. Ric, on the other hand, was super busy. He called every day at different times to see if he could take a break at her place. She loved him just popping in. It reminded her of home in California, when Ric and Franco were always at her house. No special treatment, just family dropping by.

On Thursday, Gini went for her final fitting. Friday, she picked up her dresses, and that evening, on his way to his hotel event, Ric stopped by Gini's to drop off his clothes for Saturday. She took him back to the small guest room. There was a large armoire with a rod and drawers, a twin bed pushed up against the wall, and a private bathroom.

"This is perfect."

He remembered this side of the condo as stark when Gini and Franco moved in. In fact, the small bedroom was full of boxes then. Now everything was warmly decorated. The room looked comfortable.

"Okay, so, tomorrow I'll be helping set up in the morning. Hopefully, I can get over here early enough to clean up and take a short nap."

"That will be fine. I don't want you to see me after four."

"Why not?"

"Because I want you to see the full presentation all at once. I get my hair done at four. What time do we have to leave?"

"It starts at eight o'clock. I need to be there at seven-thirty."

"I'll meet you here at the breakfast bar precisely at seven-fifteen. And you *cannot* see me before then."

"Okay, sweets." He smiled at her excitement. "Seven-fifteen at the breakfast bar."

"Wait." She quickly walked to her desk. "Here's a key card. It will get you in the front door, the garage, elevator, and my condo door."

He put it in one of the slits in his wallet. "I will guard it with my life. Listen, I've got to get going. I'll see you tomorrow at seven-fifteen."

Around ten o'clock Saturday morning, after Howard told Gini of Ric's arrival, he knocked on the door.

"It's not after four," he clarified.

She laughed.

"I just wanted to drop off my dopp kit."

He was dressed in khaki pants, a long-sleeved rugby shirt, and loafers. He noticed Gini eyeing his clothing.

"These are my work clothes. The president of the league, Melinda, is very exact at how she wants things. It could be a long setup. Don't get me wrong; I like it when they know exactly what they want."

"Are you working tonight?"

"Well, no, not really. James and Carol will be behind the scenes making sure everything is moving smoothly. I'll be out front keeping my eye on the flow there. They don't really need me to help. They run everything beautifully."

"I guess you're just the face of the company."

"Exactly! Yes! I like that, the face of the company."

"You still have your key card, right?"

"Yes," he said patting his back pocket.

"You could have let yourself in."

"I guess I could have. Gotta go."

Chapter 10 – Pretty People

At four-thirty, Ric left the beautifully decorated room.

"See you tonight," James said.

"Yeah, tonight."

Ric used the card to park in the garage. That way they wouldn't have to go out in the weather. He knocked on the condo door before entering. "Gini!" There was only quiet.

The weather had turned bitterly cold, and they were predicting snow overnight. Ric shivered.

After a nice warm shower, he put on a pullover long-sleeved heavy cotton shirt, pull-on pants, and went into the living room to have a beer. If Gini arrived, he'd quickly go into the bedroom. It was relaxing sitting in the quiet, all alone, sipping his drink. At five, he went back into the bedroom and went to bed.

Gini arrived home at five forty-five. "Ric." There was no answer. The beer bottle on the coffee table clued her in that he was there. She tiptoed back to the bedroom and saw him through the small opening of the door, sleeping.

At seven, Ric sat on the bar chair checking his messages as he patiently waited for Gini's grand entrance.

She stood in front of the full-length mirror and looked at herself. The champagne-colored liquid duchess satin gown clung to her. Over the left shoulder was a wide strap and folded fabric draped down across her bustline from left to right. On the right shoulder, a thinner strap pulled the other side up and over. The dress was backless, forming a V at her waist with a straight, formfitting skirt that flowed to the floor just above the four-inch heeled shoe-tops in the front, and into a sweep train in the back. Her heels were a dark champagne satin with a large sparkly piece that was wide at the foot opening and had a swirl tapering to a point at the toe. The clutch bag matched the shoes with the same dramatic sparkly piece widening at the purse closure clip. Gini's hair was pulled back, curls cascading down her back. A fancy rhinestone hairpiece held the curls in place on the right side. Two-inch narrow sparkling earrings hung down, completing the look.

When satisfied with the ensemble, she spread her lips back away from her teeth to make sure there was no lipstick on them. Cinderella herself could not have been more excited about going to the ball. She picked up the matching satin short-cut jacket that was lying on the bed, to be worn only if the ballroom was too cold.

Ric looked up from his PET when the bedroom doors opened. Without taking his eyes off her, he slowly lowered and set the device on the counter. His heart began to race, and there was a tightening of his body.

"How do I look?" She took a step, turning to the right side. Then another step, turning to the left, and all the way around to show the back. He tried to say "gorgeous," but the word got stuck on the lump in his throat. She turned forward and smiled the most beautiful smile he had ever seen.

As she approached him, he said, "Gins, you will steal the show."

She walked past him to the closet to get her soft, full-length white leather-and-fur coat. Seeing him in his black tux with a white bow tie and cummerbund, her first thought was that he looked like a model on the cover of a magazine. "And look *at you*!"

Ric took the valet ticket and stuck it in his pocket, and they entered the ballroom. Only one person was in the room, Melinda, the president. It looked like a winter wonderland. There was a small stage in the center front of the room. A slim black podium was on one side. It almost looked like a music stand. Three white flocked Christmas trees were at the side, all different heights. Muted lights twinkled under the flocking. Under the trees sat a few gifts wrapped in gold metallic paper; all had ribbons wrapped around them in bright Christmas colors—each gift looked different. Silver and gold streamers hung from the ceiling. They twisted and turned in the movement of the air. With the small ceiling lights reflecting down on the ribbons, it appeared something was falling from above, the illusion of snow. The tables had black tablecloths with mounds of white mums in the center. A red poinsettia flower reached out from the middle. All around the centerpiece were tea lights illuminated by tiny fake flames powered by batteries.

Gini turned and looked up at Ric as he took her coat. Her smile let him know how impressed she was with the room.

"Ric," Melinda called out. "Good, you're here." She walked over to them.

"Melinda, this is Gini."

"Oh, yes," Melinda said, acknowledging her. "We have been trying to get Virginia to join us for some time. Listen, Ric, I don't think the wine glasses are set properly on the table."

She turned and walked away. He followed, still carrying their coats. Gini smiled; he just thought he wasn't going to be working tonight.

Carol came out of a door, walked up to Ric and took the coats from him as he intensely listened to Melinda's instructions.

"Gini," Carol said, "you look lovely."

"Thank you."

Carol took the coats to the cloakroom and then returned. "Please, come on in. Let's see, where are you seated?" She thought for a minute and then took Gini to a table.

Carol was brought into the conversation with Ric and Melinda.

Gini sat and looked around the room. It was so quiet; it was hard to believe there was to be a party soon. A nice-looking man came over and sat down next to her.

"Matt Collins."

"Gini Anderson."

"I'm Melinda's husband. I can see she's still working on detail. I knew we shouldn't have gotten here so early."

More people started walking in the door. Melinda concluded the conversation and left to start greeting the guests.

Ric walked over to the table. "Matt." The two men shook hands.

Melinda motioned for him.

"I guess I'm on," Matt said, smiling. He had an easygoing air about him.

"Did you get it settled?"

Ric smiled. "She just needed this thing to get started. Everything's fine."

He gently put his arm around Gini's shoulders. "Shall we mingle?"

Before long the room was humming with conversation. All the young ladies and men were impeccably dressed in modern gowns, lots of bling, and handsome tuxes. Many of the faces were familiar. Gini was surprised when David, Ric's neighbor, walked up to greet her.

"Ms. Virginia Anderson, imagine seeing you here." He took her right hand and playfully bowed.

"David!" There was some shock in her voice.

"I know, I'm probably the last person you thought you would see here. I clean up pretty well, don't you think?" He turned from side to side. "I hate these monkey suits, but anything for the Mrs."

"You look very nice."

"I feel like a fish out of water at these highfalutin affairs, but I promised myself I would be a good husband. Her dad didn't want her to marry a *sorry soul* like me, a blue-collar worker, heaven forbid. But she loves me, and I absolutely adore her. Even though he threatened to cut her out of the will if she married me, he didn't. You know daddies and their baby girls?"

There was the clinking of a wine glass.

"May I have your attention," Melinda said. "It's time to eat."

There was quiet for a moment, and then a rustling of feet, and conversations started back up. Each table had eight people. Ric and Gini were with a great group, and the meal was outstanding. The conversation was about the concert of a popular rock star coming to Boston the next week.

A man started toward the small stage and tripped going up the two steps. He actually put his hand down to catch himself. The clumsiness caught Gini's eye.

There was a muffled statement. "Who put those there?"

He then approached the podium, and the microphone screeched. "Dang!"

The room became dead quiet. When he lifted his head, Gini saw that it was James. She turned and looked at Ric. He had his arm on the back of her chair. At her glance, he slightly gritted his teeth and raised his eyebrows.

"Okay." The mic was working.

"Ah." James, in a tux, patted his front as if looking for a script. His bow tie was tilted, and one corner poked under his chin. Gini's heart started aching. *Poor James,* she thought, *trying to be an MC. Ric should be up there. He was so great at that job.*

"Okay," James said again, clearing his throat.

"I think"—he was still trying to find a script—"I'm supposed to say, now it's time to give the gifts."

His voice was suddenly strong. "And the gifts under these trees are for *ME*!"

There was a small embarrassed laughter from the crowd.

"Isn't that right, Melinda? Isn't that how we rehearsed it?"

"No, NO, NO, James!" She stomped up on stage.

Matt took her elbow and helped her up the steps.

"Ladies and gentlemen, your president," James said in an announcer's voice.

Everyone laughed, applauded, and cheered. Gini looked at Ric as she clapped. He winked.

Melinda went to the podium; Matt stood behind with his hands clasped in front of him.

"Now, James, do you remember what to do?"

"Yes, ma'am, I'm supposed to take the gifts home and open them."

The room filled with laughter again.

"No," she said slowly, trying to find some patience with him. "How long did we rehearse this?"

"Aaahh…" He was looking up with his hand under his chin. "Two days, no, it was three or maybe four." He looked at the crowd. "*She is so picky.*"

Everyone roared with laughter.

"Oh, I remember, I remember."

He went back over to the podium, nudging Melinda aside. She looked at him, disgusted, and stepped back next to Matt.

"Okay, here we go. I've got it now."

Everyone in the room was uplifted by the comedy.

"The Junior League of Boston, Massachusetts, is a wonderful organization dedicated to charity and service. And a lot of *purdy* ladies. You all have had a great year and your president, Melinda Miller, is going to tell you just how great. Melinda."

He turned toward her and took her hand, leading her back to the podium. There was applause again. James went over and stood next to the trees. Gini opened her bag and took out a tissue. James was cracking her up.

"Thank you. Ladies, it has been an especially good year."

She went on to report on the funds raised through their special events, and how the money had been spent on the two city charities they sponsored. Throughout her speech, James stood at attention next to the trees.

"Everyone in this room deserves a big thank you," Melinda said. "For all of your hard work I applaud you."

Everyone clapped. James moved closer to the presents and looked down. He nudged one with his foot.

"James!"

"Yes, ma'am." He looked innocently at her.

"Now, I would like to give special thanks to my chairwomen."

She stood and faced James. Nothing happened. He was looking at his nails.

"James," she said very sweetly. "That's your cue."

"Right," he said, clueless. Everyone laughed.

"The gifts." She pointed to the ones under the tree. He picked one up.

"Now, bring it to me and read the name."

He walked over to the podium, leaned into the microphone, and pulled out a large card and opened it toward the audience.

"James." The card read the same. Everyone was in stitches with laughter. He handed the gift to Melinda and hugged her.

"Ladies and gentlemen," Melinda said clapping her hands. "James the Server."

He ran down the steps and left the room. Everyone applauded and cheered.

"Oh, that was fun. But now I want to get serious. I honestly could not have gotten through my two years as president without my chairwomen."

She read off each of their names, and the ladies went up on stage. Matt picked the gifts from under the trees and handed them to the women.

All the ladies took the pieces of paper from under the ribbons and opened them. With big grins, they held the papers up toward the crowd. In large letters on each one was written "James."

After the laughter quieted, Melinda turned and took Matt's hand, pulling him up next to her.

"I'm not going to pretend this position hasn't been hard. Working a full-time job and filling this office has at times been impossible. I couldn't have done it without my wonderful husband supporting me all the way. And it has given me organization experience for my next big job. Matt and I are expecting our first child in May."

There were gasps, and the room broke into cheers and applause. Tissues came out of purses around the room.

"Thank you, everyone."

Matt kissed her on the cheek.

"Okay," she said, "let's party!"

James, carrying a violin in one hand, walked up and helped Melinda down the steps. Then he walked up on stage and started playing a waltz. The curtain behind him rose, and the Quincy Street Orchestra joined in playing.

"How did you get them?" Gini whispered in Ric's ear.

He pinched his thumb and fingers together and rubbed them back and forth. The dance floor filled up.

"May I?" he asked, taking her hand.

When they joined the crowd, Gini put her left hand on Ric's upper arm. He raised his right arm to a 90-degree angle, pulling his body up—in perfect ballroom dance form. Impressed, she took her position, and they began to sweep around the floor. She felt like she was gliding on air. He was so easy to follow, his steps so effortless.

"Does James really play the violin?"

"Yes, he's quite accomplished."

When the waltz stopped, a fast dance started. Everyone whooped and hollered. Through the night, the dancing went from fast to slow, or to a dance where everyone was doing the same steps. Gini was having the best time she had had in a long time. She danced with Ric, and David, who could also cut a rug pretty well. She danced with Matt and anyone else who asked her. The gentlemen's coats came off, and the ties untied. Women's shoes were kicked off all around the floor. Melinda walked around the room handing out velveteen ballet slippers.

"Having fun?" Ric asked when he came back to the table.

Gini was drinking as much water as she could. "A blast."

Melinda went up to the podium as the lights brightened. "I'm sorry to say, all good things must come to an end. Thank you all again for two wonderful years. I will never forget them, and the wonderful friends I have made through the Junior League. God bless you all. Please, drive safe. If you had too much to drink, let someone else drive. I love you all."

There was applause. The lights dipped low again, and the last slow dance began. Ric pulled Gini up out of her chair. She folded her arms in front of her and fell into his body. He wrapped his arms around her, and they danced.

The lights went back up, and everyone slowly left the room. Ric was back with Carol and James wrapping things up.

"Congratulations," Gini said to Melinda.

"Thank you."

"It was a great party."

"The best; please, consider joining us."

Gini smiled.

"Always the salesman," Matt said as he put his arm around Melinda. "Come on, mama. Let's go home."

Once again, the room was silent. Gini was the only one standing alone. All the happy couples were gone—home to be together. It was a night of mixed emotions. She couldn't remember when she had had so much fun. And the heartfelt sighs when Melinda announced she was going to be a new mother. What an amazing moment: that soft, private joy on her face. Pregnant women didn't exactly glow, as people said, but there was *something*. Would Gini ever have what must be a glorious feeling—telling her husband they were going to have a baby? She could see it in her mind, how she would make him wait (who? The image of the man she was talking to flickered), how she'd let the words ripen on her tongue—the moment he understood—then his joy...

At this point, no, that was probably not going to happen.

She sat down and started to take off the slippers and put on her shoes. Lately, she found herself fantasizing being in Ric's arms. He was always so caring, his touch so gentle. She'd been able to push it out of her mind until tonight when he wrapped his long arms around her and held her tight for the last dance. Just as she had imagined, she melted into his body with a feeling of comfort and security. It took her back to sitting on her Pop's lap, and how it made her feel snug and safe. She envisioned Ric's lips on hers, and then their bodies heated and twisted, making incredible love. She sat back abruptly, holding her shoe, opened her eyes wide, and then closed them. She needed to get that image out of her head, but her body wanted him, really wanted him. Could she do that? Could she step out of her marriage, *maybe* just for one night? *No…* that would be a terrible step.

"Okay, sweets, let's get out of here."

Gini slipped on her shoes. They walked out to the valet arm in arm. When they got outside, big flakes of snow were slowly drifting to the ground. Ric gave his ticket to the valet. She went out from under the cover area, put back her head and opened her mouth. The snowflakes went on her tongue and landed on her nose. He smiled as he watched her.

"Your car, Mr. Santini."

Ric walked out to Gini and swept her up off her feet, then slipped her inside the opened passenger side door.

When they got inside her condo, Ric helped her off with her coat.

"Fix yourself a drink. I'll be just a minute," she said.

"You want something?"

"I'll have an Irish creme."

As she walked back to her room, she thought, *Can I do this?* She felt she was being noticed again as a woman and, yes, she liked it. The night, her feelings for Ric, seemed very separate from her being married, separate from their friendship; it was a different world for just the two of them.

Almost imperceptibly, the other world, the outside world, slipped away.

He took off his overcoat and tux jacket and laid them over the chair. The untied bow tie was pulled out from under his shirt collar and put on top. Then the cummerbund came off and was added to the pile. He took the top two studs out of his shirt and stuck them in his jacket pocket. After pouring her drink and his scotch, he walked over to the windows holding a glass in each hand.

She walked to the bed and looked at it, then she pulled back the covers. Almost in a trance, she took the clip from her hair.

Gini walked back into the room. She still had on her dress, but the shoes and jewelry were gone. Her hair was down, and she was lifting the curls to break them loose. As she did, the long hair fell to her shoulders and down her back. He put his arm around her, bringing the Irish creme in front of her face.

She took it. "Look at the beautiful snow."

He wrapped his arm around the front of her shoulders, and she leaned back on him.

"I just love the first snow of the season," she said in a soft voice. "What an amazing night."

"Amazing."

They both stood quietly sipping their drinks and watching the snowflakes gently blow around in the wind.

Gini took hold of his hand. It was time, time for her to be with him, just the two of them. It all seemed clear to her, for some reason. Why had she been fighting her feelings? She wasn't superwoman to live with loneliness forever. Franco had created this situation as much as she had.

She firmly put Franco out of her mind. She set her glass on the bookshelf next to the window and pulled Ric to go with her. As they passed the walk-in bar, he set his glass down on the counter. When they entered the bedroom, he saw the bed had been turned down. She sat him on the bed and started taking the studs from his shirt.

He put his hands on her hips. He could see her puckered nipples under the fabric of her dress—she was turned on. Pulling her close they kissed, starting slowly, but soon their tongues were dancing, and his hands started up her body from her hips. She put the studs on the nightstand. Half of them fell to the floor when she stepped back away from him.

He took in a long breath and let it out slowly, then started taking the cuff links from his shirt cuffs. Whenever she was ready, he could wait.

She reached up to her right shoulder and unhooked the strap. The fabric went to the back releasing the front. The material folded softly down to her breast but stopped before completely uncovering it. When the other strap was released, the weight of the fabric pulled the entire gown slowly down, revealing her completely naked body.

Ric looked at her and then closed his eyes; his emotions took over. She walked back to him and slipped her hands into his shirt, taking it off, and hung it on the foot bedpost.

He stood up and wrapped his body down around her. She unfastened the button at his waist and unzipped his slacks, letting out a pleasing sigh when she felt his hardness in her hand. He unwrapped his arms, and she slid down his body taking his pants with her. His abs tightened. He reached down and lifted her onto the bed. Then quickly removed his shoes and the rest of his clothes and joined her. He had wanted this for so long. He had wanted to be with her, their naked bodies touching. He had wanted her for his own. They caressed and kissed and then became one, joined by their longing for each other.

Around 4:00 a.m. they fell asleep wrapped in each other's arms. Their bodies had cooled, and their skin was moist under the thick fluffy duvet.

A little after ten, Ric woke up. He needed to get up and go to the brunch meeting at the hotel. He carefully pulled his arm out from under Gini, trying not to disturb her deep sleep.

He went into the small guest room and took a shower. What was he going to wear? He didn't want to wear his dirty work clothes, and the tux wasn't appropriate. The sweatshirt and his pull-on pants would have to work.

When he went back to the living area, Gini was standing at the end of the breakfast bar, drinking some juice.

"What are you doing?" he asked.

Her hair was tossed and her eyes sleepy looking. "Where are you going?"

She was wearing his tux shirt. The open front was showing the inside of her breasts and her beautiful cleavage; the tails reached to just above her knees.

He pulled her into his arms. She snuggled close to his body with her arms tucked between them.

He leaned down and kissed her on the top of her head. "I have to go over to the hotel for our brunch meeting. Do you want to go with me?"

She shook her head against his body.

"You're coming back?"

"I will be. Come on, go back to bed."

He took her hand and led her back into the bedroom. She crawled up on the bed without undressing.

"I love this shirt."

"It's yours. I'll have to admit it looks a lot better on you."

He pulled the comforter up over her body and kissed her.

Ric was late getting into the hotel restaurant. James and Carol were eating their breakfast.

"Were the roads bad?" Carol asked.

James gave Ric a look from head to foot. "Fancy."

Ric slid into the half-circle booth seat. Carol was looking at her electronic tablet and checking a printed sheet in front of her.

James suddenly sat back in the booth seat. "You spent the night with Gini!"

"Coffee, Mr. Santini?" the waitress asked.

"Yes, please."

"And you got some action." James made a definite point of pulling himself back to the table. "You, my friend, got a piece of fine as…"

"James!" Carol exclaimed abruptly cutting him off.

James looked intently at Ric.

"Okay, just so we can go forward here, I did spend the night with Gini. And yes, I got some action. So, now, let's move on with the meeting."

"Lucky you! High five."

Carol gave him a look. "James, show some respect."

They went through the numbers, the check-off list, and all agreed the night had been profitable and a big success.

"We have another busy week coming up," Ric continued. "The big Murray wedding events are all week long, plus the other holiday parties. Do we have it all covered, Carol?"

"We do. Thank goodness we aren't doing the wedding itself."

James and Carol agreed it was a good day to go home and enjoy the day off.

"Are you done with your plate?" the waitress asked.

"Yes, you can bring me the slip."

She poured him another cup of coffee, and he sat back thinking about the night before. *What's wrong with me?* He had made love with the wife of one of the best friends he'd ever had. He'd never imagined in a million years he could do such a thing. He would never have sex with a married woman, he simply was not that kind of man, but Gini, oh Gini. Was the difference in his thinking because he'd had feelings for her in high school, and now those feelings were taking over his good sense? It didn't seem to matter she was married to Franco. No matter how hard he tried to feel guilt, there seemed to be none. That was strange, he thought. He didn't understand himself. Was this what love did? Or was it selfishness? Certainly, his desires were steering the boat.

But what was going to happen when Franco came home? He'd deny anything was going on. Yes, he'd deny if Franco asked, especially if it seemed important to Gini that he didn't know about the affair.

But that would mean the affair was over. That this was just for now, a brief glorious romance, nothing close to what he really wanted. He couldn't stand to think about that, so he didn't.

After signing the voucher for breakfast, Ric went back to Gini's. The house was dark and quiet. She was still in the same position on the bed sound asleep. He gathered his things to go home to change his clothes.

He left her a note on the breakfast bar:

See you soon. Love, Ric.

Gini woke about twelve-thirty. She didn't see or hear him. She walked through the darkened rooms and saw all his clothes were gone from the living room and in the back. Then she saw the note and smiled.

After eating and getting dressed, she started picking up her clothes from around the bedroom. He had laid her dress neatly on the lounging couch in the sitting area near the bed. She picked it up and held it close to her body and started dancing around the room as if she were in his arms. The shirt studs strewn on the floor by the nightstand made her laugh. What a fairy-tale night they had had. What a wonderful, wonderful night. Lovemaking for hours; he loved her, she could tell. Did she love him? Did she have any regrets? She sat on the bed with her dress folded over her arm. The happy, elated feeling was draining out of her body. Did she have regret? No. None. She loved every minute of the night, and she wanted more. It was wrong, and she knew it, and she knew in an instant, many worlds could come crashing down, but she didn't want the incredible feeling of satisfaction, acceptance, and joy to go away. She got up and twirled with the dress one more time. She'd worry about the consequences later. She was too happy now to put a damper on it.

Ric texted her he was on his way back. When he arrived, she greeted him at the door, folded her arms across her body, and hugged tight to him. He wrapped his arms around her and squeezed her.

"Did you get rested?"

"Yes. I was sad when I woke up, and you were gone."

"I needed to get some clothes to wear. You caught me off guard. I usually keep a change of clothes in my car just in case I'm away from the house, and something comes up. But yesterday I brought all my change of clothes up here and wore all of them. It made for an interesting brunch wearing my sweats."

She pulled her head back and looked at him. "You, Riccardo Santini, fashionista, wore sweats to Sunday brunch at the Long Wharf Hotel?" She giggled. "That, I'm sorry I missed."

She took his hand and pulled him into the living room.

He playfully let her drag him. "We can go to the football party. I'm sure Markus won't mind if we're late."

"We could." They sat down on the couch.

The game was on the TV. She leaned up against his body putting her lips to his. He closed his eyes. Her kisses were the sweetest kisses he had ever had. She kissed him again. He put his hand behind her head, let out a loving groan, and began to breathe deeply.

Ric's next week was demanding—parties, contracts, and paperwork Mr. Vasquez was sending for him to review. It seemed he found an excuse to go by Gini's every day.

Every time she thought about Saturday night she smiled. There wasn't much socializing or partying in her life. She had thrown herself into her work—her only friend, Catherine. She knew going to parties alone would be no fun. Now, it was like high school and college, having fun with friends. Yes, her friend Ric. She was looking forward to the next party at the museum and the children's party. She was enjoying life again.

Wednesday Gini had a meeting with Michael. After she was so frightened by the man in the restaurant, he decided to take Brenda's suggestion and meet at their house. Gini met him in the lobby of his office building.

When they walked in the door, his two daughters came running into his arms calling, "Daddy, Daddy."

Gini loved the sweetness.

He introduced her to Brenda and his children, then they worked in the living room while Brenda fixed dinner and got the girls ready for bed. She knew Gini was good for him. She knew Ms. Anderson would send him down the path to success.

About an hour later, the girls once again ran to their daddy. Gini could smell the aroma of clean bodies and the sweet smell of shampoo. Michael gathered the girls into his arms and took the little ones to bed.

Brenda and Gini talked about how Michael and Brenda had met, then about having a family.

"Do you have children?" Brenda asked.

"No, we have tried, but so far my husband and I haven't been successful at getting pregnant."

"You'll love being a mother."

"I'm looking forward to it."

The two women continued talking as they set the dining room table. Brenda appreciated the help Gini was giving Michael to get into office. She was proud of her husband, and both women agreed he'd go further up the political ladder, Brenda thinking all the way to president of the United States.

Michael joined them for dinner.

"Are you going to the soiree over at the Kennedy Library and Museum on Saturday?" Michael asked Gini.

"I am. I'm very excited, my first time. And you?"

"I want Michael to wear a top hat," Brenda interjected.

"That's craziness," Michael said.

"No, it's not. The theme of the evening is the nineteenth century. That's what the noblemen wore in those days, right Ms. Anderson?"

"Please, call me Gini. And I agree with Brenda."

Michael just shook his head and went on eating.

After dinner, Michael and Gini worked to nearly ten o'clock and then he took her home.

Thursday evening Ric walked in the door. Gini was curled up in the living room chair. Her knees were pulled up to her chest, and she was crying.

"Sweets." He quickly walked to her. "What's wrong?"

Gini just looked at him and then closed her eyes, put the side of her face to the chair back and cried some more. Ric sat down on the floor in front of the chair and rubbed up and down her leg.

"Please, Gini, tell me what's wrong."

She didn't respond for a few minutes. Then she looked at him. "I called Mama."

"Oh, Gins." He pulled her up and sat on the couch with her in his lap.

"She didn't know me. She was so distant, so confused. By the end of the conversation she said she knew who I was, but I'm not sure she did. Then I called Cindy. She said Mama has good days and then really bad ones. Today was one of those bad days." Gini took a tissue and blew her nose. "I'm okay, Ric." She got up. "I'm sorry to greet you as a basket case."

She took his hand, going toward the kitchen.

Ric sat on the breakfast bar chair and pulled her close to him and hugged her. "I'm always here for you."

She pulled back and kissed him, then walked into the kitchen to fix dinner.

"Cindy told me when Mama's doing well, she bakes in the community kitchen. I guess people stand in line to grab one of her bear claws. I hope she has a lot of those good days."

"Me too, sweets, me too."

Friday Ric was at Gini's most of the afternoon. He was working at the breakfast bar when James called him. Ric put his PET on the counter on speakerphone. "How's it going?"

"Good, just checking in and making sure everything is a go for tonight on your end," James answered.

"Yes, I'm preparing myself for the bachelorette cocktail hour. Then I'll put them in their limos and send them on their way. How about you, ready for the bachelor party?"

"I guess so. Hopefully, they won't be too rowdy."

"Remember I won't be helping tomorrow night."

"I remember. You're going to be rubbing elbows with the rich and famous. I assume you will be with Gini."

Ric looked at her as she walked to the sink. "Yes, I have you on speaker."

James grinned and didn't go any further with his comments.

"You've got the Gaspen holiday party handled?"

"I can do," James said. "They're just a bunch of nerdy engineers, not a problem."

Gini looked up when she heard Gaspen and engineering. That was the company Franco had gone to work for out of college. She felt a funny feeling inside. The word *cheating* immediately popped in her head. Why was she cheating on her husband? Maybe because she knew Ric loved her, or maybe because she knew Franco *did not*. If he did, he'd be the one sitting at the breakfast bar smiling at her. Or it could be as simple as that she didn't care, because no one loved her, not even herself, and she just wanted someone, anyone, to give her attention and affection, as Ric was doing.

Well, not *anyone*, she thought with a little smile. Ric was pretty special.

Franco sighed when he read the email message Gini had sent him almost two weeks earlier. How he longed to be with her and the family—his family. He missed them all so much.

When he started working in China, he had no idea how difficult it was going to be working with the government. The longer he was there, the more difficult it was. And getting the parts for the project had become a nightmare. They were ordered, confirmed, and then never showed up. He was on the third round to get two crucial parts. The project was continually delayed. He should be home by now. He planned on being in Boston for Christmas, a surprise for Gini. He couldn't tell her because he didn't want to disappoint her if he had to change his plans.

He started to answer her message. When he finished, he would send it back in the morning with the supplier who had brought them food. It would have to be handwritten. Luca would put it in an email. He'd try to call her when he could. Another issue Franco had not anticipated—no internet, no cell phone service, no way to contact the outside world. The area he worked was rural and not yet set up for modern communication. There were plans in the works, but who knew when they would actually be put in place.

He had decided to start his own business, thinking he would have more control over his work hours. He was disappointed, he'd admit, that Gini didn't want to stay with him in China. The work was challenging, and he took great satisfaction in helping people. He knew she had the same desire, but she complained there was nothing there for her to do. She could have nurtured the children or been a teacher. There was so much to do here to help people, to learn and experience. He had thought for sure they could make it work. But he could tell she wanted to leave, though even in her misery, she didn't once ask him to give up his company and go home. He had to respect that and respect her wish to do what she wanted. Partners, they were partners in marriage, and compromise was a big part of that union. But he missed her, missed her sweet smile, the way she looked at him as if he were a god, her hero. And although he knew he did not deserve such praise, he cherished his Gini and adored her love and devotion. His life would be nothing without her.

Once he was done with the project, he would rethink his future. Being away from the woman he loved was wearing on him. If he thought he could leave, he would. But there was too much going on, and he absolutely had to be there or lose a lot of money. Gini understood his work was important.

When Ric left, Gini gathered her PET, wireless monitor, and business bag. She sat on the couch and prepared to start working on organizing her files for Michael.

After working for a while, she laid her head back on the couch. She looked at the small box on the fireplace, walked over and opened it, and took the ring out. Why was she constantly drawn to that unusual stone ring? Maybe it reminded her of the innocence she had when Franco gave it to her. His story of finding the stone and how he felt about her had moved her, and she'd never forgotten. She put the ring on her finger and went back to the couch. The ring needed to go into her bedroom and be put somewhere where she would not be reminded of it. It needed to be put away so she wouldn't think of Franco. She twirled it a few times. He had made his choice not to be active in their marriage, to be the one far away out of sight. The ring must also be placed in a faraway place. Gini sighed. She would put it in her room when she went to bed.

Ric returned after midnight to pick up his business bag and clothes. She was asleep on the couch. Her arm was off the cushion and down to the floor; her PET lay on the rug. He went over and picked up the tablet. The green stone flashed a bright reflection from the overhead light. The ring had special meaning to her. It was more important than her wedding ring. He thought it was her conscience—it was Franco, the barrier between them.

There may be a proverb "All's fair in love and war," but hurting his best friend, breaking his trust, and going behind his back wasn't fair to *Love* itself. Was he willing to ruin three lives, end a deep friendship, end a marriage? Was he okay with any of that?

He didn't know what to think. He wasn't prepared to be in such a situation, had never thought of his life as entering such territory. Maybe whatever was meant to be was meant to be. He loved her like he'd loved no other. Did he have to give that up when Franco was nowhere in sight? Did Franco love her—truly love her? How could he? It was obvious he didn't—not in the way Ric defined love—because of his neglect and her unhappiness. Ric was the right man for her now, he was sure.

Staring at her sleeping, he was trying to come to terms with what was happening.

"Sweets." He gently shook her. "You need to go to bed."

"Ric!" She was startled and suddenly sat up. "What time is it?"

"Twelve-thirty."

She tried to get her eyes open.

"Come on." He took her hand and leaned down to carry her into the bedroom.

"No," she said pushing at his hands. "Give me a minute."

He waited.

"Ric, I want you to stay here tonight. Will you stay?"

He kissed her on the cheek and went to the closet to hang up his coat. "I'll stay."

She quickly took off the ring and put it back in the box and then went into the bedroom. He met her at the bedroom door and put his arm around her.

Ric convinced Gini to go to Lazy Daze Spa with him Saturday morning. They each walked into the salon holding a cup of hot liquid; his coffee, hers hot chocolate from the specialty coffee shop. The manager put them next to each other in pedicure chairs. Each plugged into their music and enjoyed the hand and foot treatment. Next, they had their eyebrows threaded and then a face massage. The whole experience couldn't have been more relaxing. Lastly, Ric had his hair trimmed. She had a hair appointment for later in the afternoon at her salon for a special party style.

When they got back, Ric got ready for the bridesmaids' luncheon at the hotel. He walked out into the living room ready to go.

"An ascot!" Gini exclaimed.

"It's a Scottish family." He was wearing a cutaway coat and gray striped pants.

She threw her arms around him. "I love you," she said happily. "I love how you dress. I love your life."

He hugged her tight. She said she loved him. Did she really mean she was in love with him, as he was with her?

That night they dressed together in her bathroom. She slipped off her robe. He was fastening his black cummerbund and could see her reflection in the mirror. She had on a black lace push-up bra that barely covered the tops of her breasts, and a matching thong. She turned around, unzipped the garment bag protecting her dress, took it out, and put it on the floor. Then stepped into the gown. Her rounded fair-skinned butt cheeks were all he could see. His body began to quiver. Trying to tie his bow tie was nearly impossible; he could only fumble with it.

"Ric," she said pulling the dress up. "Will you please zip me?"

She walked over to him and bent her head forward. He managed to get the zipper up.

Gini took a long chain from the vanity and put it over her head. The necklace had a large antique pendant on it. She picked up another long chain and put it on with the pendant, this time hanging it down her back. It reached to just above her bottom. She went and stood in the middle of the floor.

The dress was a green, crushed-velvet fabric. The tops of the long sleeves were puffed at the shoulders and then fell straight and tight to her arms down to her hands. The bodice was fitted with a high, stand-up collar ringed with lace. At the waist, the dress flared to a full circular skirt to the floor. Gini twirled around, smiling. The bottom lifted, and with a wavy motion, the beautiful fabric floated through the air. The lifting of the skirt showed off her lace-up high-heeled vintage-look shoes.

She stopped and, with a glowing face, said, "Isn't this dress fantastic— *divine?*"

Her hair was piled up curls on the back of her head with soft curls all around her face and one batch of long locks down her back.

Ric's body yearned for hers. When he walked over, she saw the passion in his eyes. He grabbed the side of her face, wrapping his fingers around the back of her head.

"The hair—"

He leaned forward.

"Don't mess up my lip—" she started to say.

He planted a deep, feeling kiss on her lips. She could feel his body trembling.

"Sweets," he whispered. He kissed her again, then quickly stepped back, grabbed his coat on a hanger and moved toward the door.

"I have to get out of here," he said hastily.

Gini stood looking in the mirror. Slowly she walked to it. She opened her evening bag on the vanity and pulled out a lipstick tube. What was she doing? He was getting way too serious. She took her finger across her lips. The feeling of his passion was still there. She rolled the stick out and retouched the shiny dark red color.

After putting a pair of long dangle earrings on her ears, she took her small handbag and went out of the bedroom. Ric was wiping the top of his top hat. He was complete in noble style in his black tux with tails. He folded the top hat back down flat.

"Are you ready?" he asked, avoiding looking at her.

"Yes." She could see he was still a bit flustered.

"Which coat do you want?"

"My fur one."

"Which *one*?"

"I'll get it."

She pulled the coat out of the closet and handed it to him. Their eyes met. She smiled a slight smile. He had that look again. He leaned toward her. She put her finger on his lips.

"No," she said gently. "You'll mess up my lipstick."

He flashed a bright smile. "Are you sure you don't want to just go back to the bedroom?"

"Later."

Chapter 11 – Joy to the World

Ric drove up to valet parking. Others were arriving in limos and cars. As the ladies and gentlemen stepped out of the vehicles dressed in period dress, Gini could imagine being back in the nineteenth century, horse-drawn carriages all lined up to deposit their guests at the fancy affair. When the valet opened the door, Ric stepped out, opened his top hat and properly placed it on his head. He walked around the car to Gini and took her arm. She stuck her hands in her fur muff hand warmer.

They entered the Kennedy Library and Museum Glass Pavilion. The grand hall was massive and impressive. The 115-foot glass structure looked out over the harbor; the lights of the city twinkled all around. Gini loved that room.

The hall was full of people chatting; there were small bar areas stationed around the room, and tables of hot, tasty hors d'oeuvres. After they had checked their coats, they were immediately separated. Gini talked to mostly politicians about politics, and Ric was with the well-known social society of Boston.

She heard ladies laughing. When she turned to look, she saw Ms. Quinley with five other older ladies. Elaina was settling a red Santa's hat with white fur on her head. All of them were having a great time moving the headpiece in different positions. Ms. Quinley saw Gini looking at them and walked over to her.

"What a beautiful Santa hat. Is that real fur?" Gini asked.

"Nope. It's the fake stuff."

Charles walked to Elaina's side. As the three stood talking, more and more people gathered; Victor and Maria, Michael and Brenda, then Ric joined the group. One of the photographers came over and started snapping pictures. Elaina took the hat from her head and gently placed it on Gini's. With the two ladies' cheeks touching and both smiling broadly, the camera flashed off a picture.

As the evening ended, people started to leave. Gini reached up to take the hat off and give it back to Ms. Quinley.

"Ms. Anderson, please, I want you to keep it. It will go well with your costume tomorrow at the children's event."

"Thank you. This has been a wonderful evening. It was good to see you and Mr. Schmitt again."

As Gini and Ric were walking out of the door, he put his arm around her, and she snuggled in close to him. Then he leaned down and kissed her.

"Victor!" Maria said when she saw the action. "Virginia Anderson!"

He looked at her. "What about her?"

"That's Ric's girl." She pointed to the two walking out of the door still arm in arm.

When they got to the condo, Ric hugged her tight, and then led her to the bedroom. "Santa's little helper," he said.

She laid the Santa hat on the breakfast bar.

The next morning Ric was looking at his PET, drinking a cup of coffee. Gini, with sleepy eyes, walked up next to him.

He put his arm around her and gently kissed her on the cheek. "You made the society page big time."

"I did?"

On his screen was a collage of pictures. The most prominent in the front was Gini in the Santa hat and Ms. Quinley, both with big, wide smiles. Another larger one was of their group: the two ladies in the middle, Michael between Gini and Brenda, Victor next to Mr. Schmitt, and Ric on the end by Maria.

The title of the collection was, "Power People of Boston."

"Great," she said. "On the front page."

"Look how adorable your dimples are."

She scrunched her nose and gave him a look, then walked to the stove to put on some water. "What a fun night. Ric, I swear, you know everyone."

"Oh, I don't know, it seems everyone knows Ms. Virginia Anderson." He looked at his watch. "I need to get going to the brunch."

He got up and kissed her. "See you at the arena."

"I'm glad you're going to be there. Those happy little faces, you'll see, they are just precious."

He kissed her again.

After he had left, she looked at her computer. There was an email from Franco's office. *No, not Franco, not now,* she thought. She closed the computer screen and pushed it back out of the way. With one hand on top of the other, she lay her forehead down on top. She wouldn't be attending all these parties if he were here. She was having so much fun, alive again. She sat up—or would she? She had been invited to most of them over the last couple of years but chose not to go alone. She never thought of Franco as a party man; could he dance? She couldn't help but smile when she thought of floating around the dance floor; she never thought Ric was so fun-loving, either. Things were getting too complicated. She needed to stop being with Ric; it was wrong.

She lifted the screen and started to read:

Mrs. Legotti, this is Luca, Franco's assistant. He sent a message back with our food supplier for you. At first, I was going to type it but decided just to take a picture of it and attach. If there is anything I can do for you, please let me know. Luca.

Gini was once again angered by the fact that their personal emails were probably being read by several people. She ran her finger along the edge of the screen for a few seconds and then clicked on the attachment:

Babe, here I am writing another message from far away. When you wrote of your holiday with your family, it warmed my heart. I remembered all the great festivities in the Anderson house. I look forward to being with everyone in the future. Please, give a kiss to Mama from me.

The project just keeps going on and on. I won't bore you with details, but when we are done with this one, things will need to change before we start the next. Stay warm in Boston, and save me some Christmas candy. Love you.

Before the next one. Would he ever come home? She didn't know if she was angry, or sad because she missed him. She closed the computer and went into the bedroom to get ready.

On her way out, she walked to the box on the mantel and took out the ring, slipped it on and then grabbed the hat before going out the door.

The basketball arena was bustling with people. Gini was always impressed with the grandeur of the event: a tall, beautifully decorated tree, colorful presents scattered around underneath, the rocking chair for Mrs. Claus, and a large armchair for Santa himself. It made her feel so good inside, filling her with Christmas spirit. Since she had been alone the past years, she never put up a tree.

She went back to the locker rooms and changed into her red dress and white boots. She carefully pulled the red hat at a perfect tilt on her head. When she walked onto the hardwood floor of the open space, she heard a loud, "Ho, ho, ho, Ms. Anderson, my favorite helper."

Gini had probably known in years past who Santa was, but today she immediately recognized him as Randall Cooper. And then the familiar face of Betty dressed as Mrs. Claus.

Randall walked to her and gave her a strong hug. "Ho, ho, ho, Merry Christmas."

Gini pulled back smiling. "This is my favorite holiday event. Merry Christmas to you… you both."

Within the hour, families started arriving, and the gift-giving began. It was well orchestrated; the families were given numbers. As their numbers were called, they would get in a line. One of the assistants would bring the gift to Gini. Each child was given an opportunity to sit with Santa and talk, then a picture was taken, and she handed them the gift. She smiled brightly when the fourth gift was delivered to her by Ric.

Randall's jovial laugh filled the room with love and laughter. The kids all loved him.

As the line got shorter, another helper came to relieve Gini.

Ric came to her side. "Ms. Quinley has requested for you to go in the back for the special needs children."

He took her hand and felt the ring on her finger. She hadn't worn it for a while. When he lifted her hand to look at it, she quickly took it away and gave him a look he hadn't seen before. Ric got a weird feeling in the pit of his stomach.

In the other room, there were five children in wheelchairs. Ms. Quinley motioned for Gini to come to her.

Ric stood back with his hands clasped in front of him. *She must have heard something from Franco*, he thought. *Is he coming home?* Ric was in love with Gini. He cherished every moment they were together. Franco would mess up everything if he came home. He rubbed his chin. As much as he tried to push the thought out of his mind, he was well aware Franco was her husband, and he shouldn't be stealing his best friend's wife.

Gini knelt next to the first child. He had cerebral palsy. His body constantly moved, and saliva ran from his mouth when he tried to smile.

"What do you want from Santa?" she asked.

The boy mumbled something. Gini softly brushed her hand from his cheek to his ear. "You are so precious. You have been very good this year." The boy tried to smile again.

"Ho, ho, ho." The man in the red suit entered the room. All the children's faces lit up.

Gini picked up each gift and gave it to Santa to give to the patiently waiting recipients. The last little girl was in a pretty red dress. She had spina bifida.

"We're twins," she said to Gini with a cute, squeaky voice. "You're so beautiful."

"Sweetheart, you're the beautiful one."

"I like your hat."

Gini looked at Elaina. She nodded her head with approval. Gini took the hat off and placed it on top of the golden ringlets of the sweet child. "Now, it's yours."

The girl giggled with excitement. With Gini's help, she got out of the chair. Walking with braces on her legs, she leaned forward and hugged Gini.

Gini rubbed her shoulders. "Always remember how beautiful you are."

A camera flash went off. Ms. Quinley walked over and hugged the two. Another flash.

Ric looked over at Betty wiping her eyes and smiled.

After the touching moment, Santa and Mrs. Claus took pictures with the families.

Ric walked up to Gini.

"Aren't they just the greatest kids?" she asked.

"Yes, they are. Listen, Gins, I've got to get going. Another party, you know."

"Okay." She continued looking at the photo shoots.

"I'll be late."

"Ric…" She looked at him and paused. "Maybe you shouldn't stay at my place tonight."

He took in a deep breath. "Okay, sweets." He pulled her close and squeezed her—her body stiffened.

"I'll call you tomorrow. We'll talk," he said.

She pulled back and forced a slight smile.

"Ms. Anderson," Randall bellowed out. "Come get in the picture. We need Santa's helper."

Ric slowly let go of her hand as she walked away from him.

Monday morning when Gini woke up, her body felt strange. Her legs and arms seemed to weigh a ton. A familiar feeling lately. She finally made her way to the bathroom and drank some water. That seemed to help in the past.

Her PET spoke.

"Text, Ric Santini."

She asked it to read.

"Gins, yesterday was great. You're right, those kids' smiles were amazing. I have some time this afternoon. I'd love to see you."

Why did she feel so bad? She hadn't partied. Okay, it was a busy weekend, but she shouldn't be so tired.

She commanded it to answer, "Ah, ish." She had a hard time speaking. "Not today, sorry."

She threw her head back on the pillow, exhausted.

Ric immediately read her message. "a~, s^*."

What? he thought.

"Not today, sorry."

He shook his head. Something had happened. He looked up. *No, please, it cannot be over.*

Gini finally got herself to the kitchen and ate. Slowly she started to feel better, at least not so tired.

Tuesday Gini and Catherine were working on reports and getting ready to follow the voting intent of the House. Ric was busy all day. This was the last week of parties before Christmas.

On Wednesday, he called her. "Sweets, I need to know if I have done something to upset you."

"No, Ric. I…" She let out a breath.

"I don't have anything going on tonight. Let me come over. I won't spend the night. I just want to see you."

"Ric." There was silence.

"I know, sweets, I know. We'll talk."

She agreed. He parked in front and let Howard show him up. When she showed him in, both of their phones lit up. Gini's call was from Cindy, and his, a text from James. They both said almost in unison, "I have to take this." She went into the dining room, and Ric to the living room.

The two sisters had talked frequently. Mama was having a bad day. The doctors thought that she was just fatigued and gave her an IV where she lived.

"Dwayne and I think they should check Mama into the hospital and find out for sure she's okay," Cindy said with concern. "What do you think, Gini?"

"I think the staff at the senior community will take good care of her. I'll call there tomorrow and talk to her nurse and then call her doctor. Don't worry, Cindy, she's in good hands."

"I know. You know me, I worry about everything and…"

"And what?"

"As I told you, Neil is having problems with his knee. Oh, I guess I'm just tired."

"Get some rest."

"I will. Love you, baby sister."

Gini sat on a dining room chair with one of her knees up to her chin. Had she said the right thing? Should they trust the staff at her mom's place?

She could see Ric pacing in the living room. The two rooms were divided by the wide fireplace and short wall. He was running his fingers through his hair over and over.

"We have a contract and have had it for months. They can't take that room away from us. I know… Okay, I'll take care of it… No, you have other things to take care of tomorrow. I'll go and straighten this out."

Gini went into the kitchen and got a drink of water. With her head down, she walked out, then stopped abruptly, almost running into him walking toward her. She set the water on the counter and leaned into his body. She knew she shouldn't, but she was so tired. So tired of the worry and indecision of what to do. He held her close to him; his arms wrapped tight around her. His right hand went under her sweater and rubbed the small of her back. His other hand cupped the back of her head. The backrub felt good. His right hand slowly journeyed down between the gap of her blue jeans waistband and her soft skin, the long piano-player-like fingers reaching to her buttocks. As the fingers went further, one slipped between the cheeks separated by the string of the thong. She gasped. She reached back and grabbed his forearms to stop him from going any further. It was wrong. She was married.

He took both of his hands to her waist. She continued to hold his arms. He reached up to unfasten her bra. At first, she pushed with resistance, and then, let her hands drop to her sides. The bra was released. She lay her head back. He leaned over and started kissing her. Their lips opened, touched and then merged into sexual kisses.

He pulled his hands up, bringing her sweater with them. She raised her arms above her head. The sweater and bra were removed. He caressed her breasts, and they continued the squeezing of their lips, one kiss with his head to the right, the next from the left.

He went to his knees. Her head followed his, now below hers. He unbuttoned the button on her jeans and lowered the zipper. With one hand motion, the jeans and thong went down. He laid her on the floor. Her hands were cupped around her breasts, pushing up and squeezing and then releasing, pushing up again and down, over and over.

He kissed her forehead, her nose, her lips, chin, neck, chest, continuing all the way down her body, her belly button, her abs, in search of her pleasure spot. She couldn't stop him. Her body was so willing for his touch.

She felt a tingling surge rise through her like a slow-moving bolt of lightning. She went to a wonderful place. A place where her whole body was smiling. A place where there was no right or wrong, no worry or fret. A place she wanted to stay forever.

Her body elevated up and dropped down; she was not in control; she just let it all happen.

He carefully caressed her ribs to her abs. She opened her eyes. He was on his knees to the side of her—fully dressed. She reached up and put her arms around his neck, pulling him to her.

Ric once again found himself at her place every day. She hadn't taken off the ring since the children's Christmas party. The green stone loomed large on her finger, reminding both there was someone else in their relationship. Each time Gini looked at the ring, she was reminded of Franco, but the more time passed, the less guilt she felt. He had been a person important to both of them. But it didn't stop their flesh touching or their bodies being joined as one. Their feelings were too strong; neither could deny the love felt for the other.

Over the holiday weekend, they spent time at both of their houses. On Sunday, they went to the football party in Ric's neighborhood. The whole afternoon they clung to each other, cheering on their team.

Christmas morning, they awoke in his bed. The snow was gently falling outside the window. Gini didn't want to get up. She snuggled her naked body up next to his. They would celebrate the holiday later.

They exchanged their gifts; she gave him a stud and cufflink set to replace the ones she had lost, and he gave her a small ruby pin. After the gifts, they fixed a roasted duck with honey and orange marmalade sauce, stuffed with cranberries and apples. They also made wild rice, and green salad with olive oil and vinaigrette. The fireplace blasted out heat; candlelight glowed and soft music played. A nice quiet day they both deserved.

Merry Christmas!

Gini's PET burst out after announcing a text from Catherine:

Call me.

On Tuesday morning, Gini put her phone on the breakfast bar on speaker. "Did you have a good holiday?"

"Absolutely! How about you?"

"Yes, it was quiet and nice. Ric and I stayed in bed until almost noon, then made a nice meal together."

"Ric! Honey, you and Ric are together?"

There was silence for a few seconds. Gini took in a breath. "We are." Silence again.

"I saw all the pictures of you on the Globe website. Gini, you're becoming a rock star."

"Hahaha. I'll have to say the parties have been fun. Mr. Santini is quite the party animal."

"Ohh, you sound happy. I'm glad you're having fun."

Later that day Ric called to tell her about the party at the Westcotts' on Saturday. It was an annual affair to watch the Patriots' last regular season game, celebrate the year coming to an end, and this year Victor's re-election. Just a few close friends.

Saturday, she woke up feeling bad again. She tried as hard as she could to hide it from Ric, but he could see she was pale.

"Are you okay, Gins?"

She hugged him, and they walked to the kitchen. "Just hungry."

They took the morning slow and left for the Westcotts' about two-thirty. As always, she enjoyed the warmth of the heated seats and the beautiful drive to the seaside town. There was a dusting of snow on everything, making the entire area look like a picture postcard.

Gini was excited about going to the Westcotts' home perched up on the cliffs overlooking the sea, but she was also a bit nervous, going as what would be perceived as Ric's "girlfriend." She knew he was close to Victor and Maria. What would they think about him being in a relationship with a married woman?

When they arrived, the cars were parked about halfway down the long driveway that led to the house.

"I'll take you down and drop you off," he said, not looking at her. He was concerned; she seemed to be under the weather but refused to confess that fact to him.

"Ric! I can walk!" She looked at him and smiled. "I want to walk in this beautiful snow. I have on my super-duper weather boots." She pointed to her feet.

Maybe she *was* feeling okay.

He parked, and they walked down holding hands. Every once in a while, she put her head back to collect snowflakes on her tongue. That was the Virginia

Anderson he remembered in high school and college. When they got closer to the house, she started skipping.

Just as they were stepping up to the door, Maria swung it open. "There you are." She walked out and hugged him. "Get in this house."

The three of them stepped inside.

"Maria, you know Virginia Anderson?"

"Yes, of course, Ms. Anderson. Please, let me take your coats."

Gini went in and looked around. "What a great place. I love Rockport. You are so lucky to have a place here."

"Let me show you around," Maria said after hanging up their coats. "Honey, the guys are in the family room watching football."

Ric kissed Gini on the cheek. "You go with Maria. I'll see you after the tour." She could feel herself blushing.

Maria showed her around, ending up in the eating area. "We added on to the deck last summer." There was a large fire pit with furniture scattered around. "We love sitting out there. DC is so intense sometimes." She looked at Gini. "As you know. Coming here, we can completely decompress."

There was a large piece of land beyond the deck.

"Is that all your land?"

"We were lucky back during the downturn in New England and picked up this nice parcel of land."

The two went to where the partygoers were watching a game. To the right, was a large rock fireplace with a glowing fire. On the left, a big-screen TV hung out from the wall with seating in front. And straight across was a wall of windows looking out to the seacoast, today obscured by low clouds. Ric walked to Gini, and Victor to Maria.

Gini immediately offered her hand to shake Victor's. "Congratulations on your re-election. It really was no contest."

"Thank you. I never take anything for granted. I appreciate all my supporters. I'm very interested in your and Ms. White's cause. Please, get in touch with my staff so we can talk."

Gini smiled, feeling good about his interest. Ric put his arm around her and squeezed.

"Come on," someone called from farther in the room. "The game's starting."

The Patriots took charge quickly, with a score of 28 to 0 at the end of the first quarter.

Gini's phone vibrated. She and Ric were standing behind one of the couches. She held it up so he could see it was a text from Cindy.

She walked over to the windows and started typing. He watched her body language.

"Ric, she's such a nice lady," Maria said coming to his side. "You two look good together. I'm so happy you have found someone. Are you going to ask her to marry you?"

He hugged her. "Maria, if I could, I would. There's nothing I'd love more than to have her as my wife."

"So what's the problem?"

"She's married."

"Maria," Victor called from the kitchen. "Come, I need your help, please."

"Married?" she mouthed to Ric and then went to Victor.

Ric walked to Gini. She had put the phone back in her pocket and was leaning on the wall, looking out the window.

"Good news, I hope."

"Yes." She smiled. "Mama is in the residents' kitchen serving the sweet breads she baked this morning. She was just dehydrated. Once they replenished her fluids, she has been fine."

"That's great."

"This is like heaven here." She was still looking out the window. "I would never leave these windows if I lived here."

The game was no problem. The Patriots won the division and would have a week off before the first playoff game. Gini was quiet the rest of the day, staying close to Ric. About nine o'clock they headed back to her place. The snow had stopped, and the sky cleared. The stars shone brightly above them. She wanted to walk slowly up the driveway and take in all the beauty of nature. In only a few minutes, on the drive back, she fell asleep. He reached over and took her hand and twirled the ring with his fingers. God, he loved her more than ever.

Wednesday morning, Ric was fixing breakfast. Gini walked toward the breakfast bar.

"Oh!" She grabbed onto the bar edge and put her other hand to her face.

"Gins!" He quickly grabbed her. She was pale. Her eyes looked dull and then rolled back as her body slid down his. He grabbed up her legs and took her to the couch.

"Gini, what's wrong?"

She opened her eyes and looked at him. "I just felt a little faint." She started to sit up but was too weak. "I think I'm just hungry."

"Don't move; I'll bring you something."

She slowly pulled herself up to a sitting position. He went into the kitchen, grabbed a banana and the glass of juice he had poured earlier.

"Here, drink this."

She drank the OJ and took small bites of the banana. She smiled at him, her eyes brighter.

"I'm okay, Ric. I've just been working a lot of hours and, well, I'll have to admit, not eating right."

"You scared the hell out of me. I want you to go to the doctor."

"I'm fine, really."

"No, you have to promise me you will go to the doctor."

"Okay, Mr. Worrywart. It's about time for my annual well-woman exam. I'll call Dr. Linda Nelson and make an appointment."

He pulled her close to him. "I don't know what I would do without you. Please take care of yourself."

"You're sweet. I'm fine; I promise you."

After a few minutes, she went to the kitchen bar and ate her breakfast. Ric contacted her throughout the day to make sure she was okay.

When Catherine and Gini finished their business talk, she told Catherine about her fainting spell.

"Gini, you aren't pregnant, are you?"

"Pregnant? No; Virginia Anderson does not get pregnant, not even with in vitro. How many times have Franco and I tried? I'm not pregnant. I probably just have a bug or something. I feel fine now and have all day since the episode."

"Did you ever think that maybe your problem was Franco, not you?"

"Oh, no, his little guys are very plentiful and active. The tests all showed it was me. Sporadic ovulation and my uterus won't accept the embryo. It's totally me. I don't think it will change with Ric."

"Well, I'm glad you are going to the doctor."

Chapter 12 – Stormy Weather Ahead

After the call, Gini sat thinking. Could she be pregnant? She and Ric had certainly had a lot of sex lately. She smiled a slight smile and put her hand on her abdomen. A baby would be wonderful. She had wanted one for so long—she and Franco—from day one of their marriage, they wanted to start a family. But sometimes life really stank. If they'd had a child or children by this time, he'd probably be there right by her side. The marriage was in trouble because she couldn't get pregnant. She'd known that for a long time but didn't want to admit it to herself. It was her fault; she couldn't give him what he wanted. She quickly removed her hand and changed her expression. Having Ric's child—oh no, no, no; that would complicate her life to a level so high she didn't even want to think about it. Absolutely no pregnancies now, not with Ric. She had to figure her and Franco out first.

She called Dr. Nelson and made an appointment. She told about the fainting spell and her suspicion she could be pregnant. The doctor asked her to come in the next day without eating so they could take a blood test.

The next morning, Ric had an early meeting and couldn't go with her. She decided to take the train, so if she were weak, it wouldn't affect her driving. She put a nutrition bar and small bottle of apple juice in her bag to eat after the test.

The nurse sat her up on the examining bed in the blood lab room. She stuck the needle into Gini's arm. Gini immediately got dizzy and started to sway.

"Okay, let's lay you down."

"Sorry," Gini mumbled.

"Not a problem, we're almost done."

When all the blood was taken, Gini took the nutrition bar out of her bag. The bite just balled up in her mouth. After drinking some juice to get it down, she immediately felt better.

"You can lie here on the bed until Dr. Nelson is ready for you."

"I'm okay now. I can go to the waiting room."

She texted Ric and told him they had drained all her blood.

Ric could feel his phone vibrate, but couldn't read the message until the meeting was over.

About thirty minutes later, she was called back to the examining room.

"So you think you're pregnant?"

"I don't know. I just feel so light-headed sometimes."

"We're going to check you out."

The doctor checked her heart and lungs and did a complete well-woman exam. Then she helped Gini sit up.

"Honey, everything looks good." Her computer dinged. "Let's see what your blood test tells us."

After looking at the screen, she called over the intercom. "Liddy, can you come in and get another blood test from Ms. Anderson?"

Gini got a lump in her throat. What was wrong? There was something terribly wrong.

The doctor went to her side. "Honey, you aren't pregnant."

Gini put her head down.

She took Gini's hand. "I'm sorry. You still have a few frozen embryos. I can give you a list of potential surrogate mothers if you like."

"No, that isn't going to work for us now."

She ordered two more tests. "Liddy, after you take the blood and Gini is dressed, will you please take her to my office."

Ric texted her:

We're taking a short break. How is it going?

Fine. Taking more blood.

That doesn't sound fine.

It's okay. Have to go. We can talk when we get home.

I'll be there at one. I love you.

He was worried. Drawing more blood meant the doctor was looking for something.

Linda walked into her office and sat across the desk from Gini. "I had them put a rush on the blood work. Honey, you had very low blood sugar when you had your first blood drawn. The condition is called hypoglycemia."

"I have hypoglycemia?"

"Yes. But after you had something to eat your blood levels went back to the normal range. So I think we can control this with diet. You need to keep your blood sugars as even as possible. Always have something you can grab and eat, like some fruit or juice, even a cookie or candy bar. If you feel light-headed, eat something. I also suggest you have a bottle of juice on your bedside table. Drink it before you get out of bed. I don't want you fainting when you stand up."

"Okay, that seems easy enough. Will I always have the blood sugar problem?"

"Probably, but as I said, it's easily controlled with diet. I would like to see you again in a couple of weeks. I want to make sure the diet is working."

"Please, say hello to Franco for me. Whenever you two are ready for a surrogate, just let me know."

"Thank you, Linda. I will eat better, I promise."

Dr. Nelson walked around the table and hugged Gini.

On the way back to her flat, Gini thought about Linda's comment about a surrogate mother. Then her thoughts went to Franco. He was so far away. She should probably be with him. There was a strong pang in her heart. She had loved him all her life. What was happening to them? Their love had always been so strong. Did he still love her? And what was she doing with Ric? She felt another flutter. He made her feel so comfortable. She didn't need anyone to protect her, but she felt safe with him and knew he would never let anything happen to her.

The first thing she saw when she entered her condo was the cloisonné box on the mantel. She took the ring off, held it in her fingers, and looked at it; her eyes filled with tears. She put it in the box and closed the lid. Pulling her legs up to her chest on the couch, she cried. She was sad she wasn't pregnant, she missed Franco, and she wanted to be in Ric's arms right then so he could comfort her.

The door opened, and Ric walked in. She quickly wiped her eyes.

"Gins," he said with sympathy.

He got down on his knees in front of the couch. "Tell me what the doctor said."

He was worried but didn't want her to see his concern.

"I'm not pregnant," she sobbed.

"Pregnant! You thought you were pregnant? Oh, sweets." He reached over and hugged her.

"No, not really. Fainting *is* a symptom, though. I'm hypoglycemic."

"Low blood sugar, Gini, that could be a serious condition." He pulled up on the couch and sat next to her. "What did the doctor say to do?"

"She thinks I can control it with diet. I just need to keep my blood sugar levels from going too low. She said to drink juice before I get out of bed in the morning."

"Good, we'll get plenty of small juice bottles and have them by the bed. That's all? You feel okay now?"

She smiled, put her legs down, and got up. "I feel fine and kind of stupid." She walked into the kitchen and got a glass of water.

"Why stupid?"

"Thinking I was pregnant and then crying because I'm not."

He pulled her around to the chair, sat down, and put his arms around her. "What if I had told you I was pregnant?"

"I would be the happiest man on earth. Having a baby with you would be absolutely terrific." Just saying *baby* filled his heart with love. Since his family had been torn apart by this father's death, he longed for a family again to call his. And as an adult, that family would be his own flesh and blood, someone belonging to him. After the shock of finding out he was going to be an unexpected dad, he couldn't wait. The death of both of Margarita's fetuses had been almost more than he could bear; it was loss after loss. If Gini told him she was going to have his baby, oh… that would make his life complete. Then they'd have a true bond forever connected by a child who was a part of both of them, a testament to their true love.

"What about Franco?"

His happy thoughts dipped. "Sweet Gins, you know I have been in love with you for some time, but you have to figure you and Franco out. I can't interfere, that's your decision to make. Just know I want you and I love you."

She pulled into his body and laid her head on his shoulder. "I'll never be pregnant; it will never happen."

He smoothed her hair with his hand.

Once the new year started, Ric's and Gini's lives became very busy. She immediately went to Washington to work with Catherine, and he went to Florida. Two weeks passed quickly.

Ric was back in Boston. From a phone call, Gini informed him she would be returning in two days. They both were looking forward to seeing each other.

It was January, and Franco was still dealing with problems in China. He decided he needed to go to Shijiazhuang and find out why he was not getting his parts. He was going to be stern with the government agent he was working with. The project should have been completed months ago. Somehow he had to get the issues cleared up. One last water well was all that needed to be done. It was the deepest of the three drilled on the project.

Gini and Catherine finished up work about eleven o'clock. She looked forward to a good night's sleep and then one more day before she could go home to Ric. When she came out of the bathroom after her shower, her phone was blinking. There was a voicemail and an email from Franco.

She held the phone, almost frozen. The screen showed an overseas number. She took in a deep breath and listened to the message.

> "Babe, I know it's late there, but I'm in Shijiazhuang trying to get things straightened out. Oh, by the way, Happy New Year. I hope you had a super holiday. I'll email you. Sleep well, my love."

Tears immediately filled her eyes. She hadn't heard his voice for so long. "Gini, what's wrong?" Catherine ran into the room. "Why are you crying?" She said nothing, just stood looking at Catherine.
"Oh, honey." Catherine hugged her. "Come on, tell me what's going on."
"Franco." Gini held up her phone.
"Oh…"
In the email, he told her he was glad to be back in civilization, at least where he had access to the internet and cell service. He commented on seeing her in pictures on the Globe website and stated how good it was to see Michael and his good friend Ric. He wondered why Margarita wasn't in the picture. He said it made him homesick. At the end:

> I don't know how my time will be spent the next couple of days, but I'll try to call you again, maybe during your day. Love you.

Gini tossed and turned all night. Her head was spinning with thoughts of both Franco and Ric. She wanted to run away—hide, mostly from herself.
They had just started working Friday morning when her phone rang. A chill shuddered through her body. She picked up the phone; it was Michael.
"Gini, are you in Boston?"
"No."
"Oh, okay."
"What's up?"
"I guess I'm just a little nervous about the election. I need you to hold my hand and tell me everything's okay."
Gini let out a laugh. Catherine turned and looked at her. Good, whoever was calling was making her happy, not sad.
"Michael, honestly, no one needs to hold your hand. I've seen your interviews on TV and the internet. You're doing great. Everyone's predicting you as the winner."
"I hope so. Can we meet when you get home?"
"Yes, of course. I'll be home tomorrow."

On the train home, she got an email from Franco. He apologized he hadn't called her again. The story was too long to tell, but he was being taken back to the site by two government officials. He would contact her as soon as he could. Hopefully, the officials would get things right with the missing parts.

She felt a little relieved.

The next week, Massachusetts expected a winter storm by midweek. As the days went by, it was obvious it was going to be a major event. The governor warned everyone to be ready to be homebound for a couple of days. Ric and Gini decided to ride it out at her place. He could park his car in the Towers parking garage, out of the elements, since his garage was too small for a modern vehicle.

Thursday afternoon at one o'clock was the target time for everyone to be sheltered. Gini shopped on Monday and Tuesday for food. She had plenty of candles if the power went off, and the gas fireplace would provide heat. Howard had a plan in place if there were any problems with the building. The great thing about Towers I—all the residents knew each other and were ready to help a neighbor.

Thursday morning Gini and Ric were texting back and forth. He went to his office to make sure all was taken care of there, then to his house.

David ran up to him as he was leaving. "You staying here?"

"No, I'm going to Gini's. I emailed Markus all my contact info."

"Good. I like her."

"I have turned off my water and drained all the pipes."

"We'll keep an eye on everything. Take care, ole boy."

"You too. See you on the other side."

The two fist-bumped.

His last stop was the seafood restaurant to pick up his order of clam chowder, bread, and salad.

Gini had the TV on in the living room and bedroom as she finished the laundry. The low was working up the East Coast. Washington, DC, was already buried with snow. The storm was just edging into the Cape. New York had been hit with heavy wind, rain, and then snow. It was all heading straight to New England.

Ric texted at twelve forty-five.

One more stop.

She smiled. He was going to make it by the lockdown. When her phone rang, it was Cindy, probably calling to make sure she was okay for the storm.

"Hey, Cindy."

"I know you're bracing for a big snow, but I had to call you. I'm sorry, baby sister; they found Mama not breathing when they went to check her this morning. She died peacefully."

Gini dropped to her knees. "No!" She was having trouble catching her breath.

"You're not alone?"

"No," she whimpered.

"Good. We won't make any arrangements until you and Franco can get here. I love you, baby sister."

"… I love you too. Thanks for calling."

She ran into the bedroom and pulled out her suitcase. She tore open drawers and grabbed at clothes. The TV reported the airport was closed to air traffic. It didn't matter; she would drive. Yes, she would drive to California.

Ric walked into the restaurant. "Mr. Santini," the owner said. "Here's your order. One more to go."

"I hope you weren't waiting just for me. You need to get to your home."

"Oh, no. I live upstairs. We're ready for the storm." He pointed outside to stacks of sandbags. "You never know what that crazy water is going to do. Be safe."

"You too." He took his bag and headed to Gini's.

The TV reports were blaring at her about the major thoroughfares being closed west of Boston. The snow was piling up fast. The driving rain in the city would soon be turning to snow, a blizzard. She had to get out of town. Her legs weakened. She fell to her knees near the bed.

"Sweets, I'm here," Ric announced, placing the bag on the breakfast bar and then taking off his coat.

The TV was on, the mayor talking. "Please, heed our warning. We are dealing with a very dangerous storm. There's no need for you to be out on the streets. If you are near the water, go to one of the shelters. We don't want to send our first responders out in the weather and endanger their lives. Take shelter and do it now."

"Gins," he called.

He walked to the bedroom where he could also hear the TV. Then he saw her on her knees near the bed; a suitcase was open with clothes piled on top.

"Sweets, what are you doing?"

She was shaking, crying, and looking at him with desperate eyes.

He knelt next to her. "What's going on?"

164

"Mama," she cried. "Mama. She died."

"Oh no!" He wrapped his arms around her, rocking her. "When?"

"Cin… in… dee called me earlier. She… she died in her sleep. I have to go. I have to drive to Sacramento."

"You aren't going anywhere. Gins, I'm sorry, so sorry."

"Ric, I have to go. It's Mama. Oh, Mama!"

His heart was aching for the loss of the woman he could call Mom.

He continued to hold her, not knowing what else to do. She was shaking and seemed very warm.

She took a deep breath and sat up straight. "Sorry, I'm…" She sniffed. "I'm okay now."

Her face was splotched red from crying. She used the bed to help her stand up, closed the suitcase with the clothes hanging out all around, and put it on the floor next to the lounging couch. He stood watching her, again not knowing what to do to comfort her.

She walked to the kitchen. "I need to eat. No, I need—" She stopped. "I…"

"Sweets, come here." He wrapped his arms around her. "If you're hungry, I picked up clam chowder."

"That's good, yes, that sounds good." She got a glass of water, then went and sat at the dining room table.

He dished up the soup and placed the bowl in front of her. She moved the spoon around and around the bowl. Finally, she took a taste. Her mind was a million miles away. He sat eating, watching her.

"I closed all the shutters except the living room." She got up, walked past the fireplace, and showed him a box next to the shelves. "Here are the controls." Then she shivered.

He put his arm around her. Her body was still warm. "Gins, I think you have a fever."

She collapsed into him.

"Let's get you to bed. Do you have a thermometer?" He helped her to the bedroom.

"In the linen closet in a wicker basket." She was so cold, pulling the duvet all around her when she got in bed.

When he took her temperature, it was 103.4. "Gini, you need a doctor."

"Josh."

"Who is he?"

"He lives on the fourteenth floor." Her words were slow.

"How can I get hold of him?"

She licked her lips and closed her eyes.

"Gins, tell me how I can call him."

"There's a list." She closed her eyes again. He shook her gently. "A list by the landline," she said.

He found the laminated card with all the residents in the building. He took his finger to Dr. Joshua Turner, called him, and explained who he was and that Gini was running a high fever. Within minutes, the doctor came to the door.

"Ric," he said, introducing himself as he approached the doctor. "She's in the bedroom."

There had been a vicious bacterial infection in the Northeast for the past few months. New York City was hit hard in December, with several dying. The first week in January, Connecticut reported over 20 percent of the population sick; since then a hundred people had died.

Dr. Turner told Ric there was an elderly man in the building he was watching over while his sons were away. He had IV bags in his condo; he would bring one to Gini. The most important thing was to not let her get dehydrated. People with compromised immune systems seemed to be the most vulnerable. When Ric told him Gini had been diagnosed with hypoglycemia, the doctor became quite concerned.

"We have to get her temperature down. She needs to be in the tub or shower with tepid water."

"I can do that," Ric said.

"Good. Dress her in something that opens in the front, so I can monitor her vitals. I'm going to call Mass General and see if we can't get some antibiotics. You take care of the bath. I'll do the rest."

Ric undressed both Gini and himself and stood in the shower with her. At first, she fought him, but then gave in to her weakness. Afterward, he put on a pair of front-button pajamas he found in her drawer. She said nothing other than her head hurt. He put on sweats and then got under the covers and lay next to her. The shower had worked; her fever was down to 101.

"Breaking news," the TV anchor announced. "It seems we have two crises. As well as the storm, reports are coming from area hospitals they are getting many calls about people with sudden high fevers. We all know of this illness and the deaths it caused in New York and Connecticut. Mass General is setting up a medical hotline number. It will soon be on the screen. Please, *do not* go out in the storm. If you are sick or have a sick person in your home, call the hotline. Here's the number."

Dr. Turner returned with a rolling stand, an IV bag attached, and his doctor bag. They gave Gini aspirin and juice.

"I called the hospital. They are working with the National Guard to get help to the sick people. I told them to bring the medication here. I can administer it. No need to get her out in the cold."

The storm raged outside the windows. Hard blasts of wind made the walls crack and the storm shutters shake. It was a complete whiteout.

Through the following hours, Gini's temperature spiked again, and Ric took her back in the shower. It was taking a while for the meds. They were using military vehicles and sand trucks to carry medical personnel around the city. The doctor and Ric monitored Gini closely. She mostly slept and complained of a headache.

"Josh, I need to drive to California," she said while he wiped her face with a cool face cloth.

"I don't think you'd get too far. There's a fierce storm brewing outside."

She turned her head to the side and closed her eyes. "I need to go to California," she repeated in a quiet voice.

The two men walked to the kitchen, and Ric made them each a cup of coffee. "She's had a rough day. She found out this morning that her mother died in Sacramento."

"Oh, my! That's why she needs to go to California."

"Her family is waiting for her to hold the service."

"The infection seems to respond to antibiotics quickly if they are strong and administered close to the onset of the fever. She should start feeling better once we get the meds in her. I'm concerned about the hypoglycemia. When was she diagnosed?"

"A couple of weeks ago."

The walls cracked and popped, and the wind and snow blew all night. Ric closed the shutters on the living room window, leaving only a small window in the master sitting area to see out of. But the snow was too intense; all he could see was a sheet of white.

When Josh went to the parking garage to meet the doctor bringing the medication, the wind was so strong they had a hard time opening the door to get out of the storm. The meds included glucose to keep her hypoglycemia in check, a blood-sugar testing kit, and the antibiotics. He or Ric took her temperature every hour. She slept restlessly, constantly rubbing on her head. A little before five o'clock, she broke out into a heavy sweat. The fever had broken. Finally, Ric could get some sleep.

Dr. Turner checked on Gini about six o'clock. He ran his hand all over her face; she felt cool. Ric was lying on the other side of the bed, asleep.

"Josh," Gini said quietly

"How are you feeling?"

"Much better, thanks. Thank you for taking care of me."

"I want you to take it easy the rest of the day. You can't go anywhere for a while. There are probably two to three feet of snow out there, hard to tell with the drifts. I'm sorry to hear about your mother."

She closed her eyes and nodded her head.

He pricked her finger and read the blood sugar level. It was normal.

"I'll be back to check on you later. Is there anything I can get you?"

"No."

"I'm going to leave the IV in for a little longer. It has a glucose solution in it to help with your sugar. You just rest now."

"I will." Her eyes were still closed.

After he left, Ric turned over on his back without waking. She reached over, took his hand, and fell back to sleep.

Ric fixed her breakfast later in the morning; the eggs tasted good. He cupped her face with his hands.

"I'm glad you are feeling better."

"I need to get tickets to Sacramento."

"I looked online. They think they can get the airport open by tomorrow morning. I reserved our tickets for Sunday. They are refundable, so if that doesn't work for you, we can look at others. I just thought the sooner I reserved, the better."

She swallowed a mouthfull of food. "You got *our* tickets? You're going?"

"I'm going with you so I can take care of you."

"Ric. My family... you, me."

"Don't worry, sweets, I'll keep out of sight. They'll have no clue. Besides, the trip is perfect timing. Remember I told you about Michelle Walker? She bought a nightclub in Newport, Rhode Island, and wants me to help her promote the opening. We can drive to Reno sometime after the service so that I can meet with her. It'll be a nice day trip, or we could stay there for a night or two."

Gini got tears in her eyes. "Thank you, Ric, for everything. I love you."

He put his hand back on her face, and she laid hers on top. He leaned over and kissed her.

Chapter 13 – Mama

Gini and Ric checked into the hotel she usually stayed at when she visited. It was just easier that way, rather than put family out; everyone had small houses. He requested two rooms with connecting doors. If anyone came to her room, they wouldn't know he was there. While she was with her family, he would comfortably work in his small suite, which had an eating table and couch.

After arriving, she called Cindy and told her she was going to take a short nap. She had already told her of her illness a few days before. The family gathered at Tony's Italian Restaurant in the old neighborhood that evening. There were tears in the beginning, but then the conversation went to stories of Mama in the past.

Tony the owner, third generation, came to the table. He gave his condolences. He and Elizabeth were classmates and had known each other all their lives. He told of a very bad time in the business when his parents were on the verge of losing the restaurant; he was in his mid-twenties at the time. Mama was still living with her family. She came in every day to make bread and desserts, for no pay.

"That's a true friend," he said with emotion.

The priest arrived, and they discussed the service. They all decided they would carry in one of Mama's favorite flowers and at the end of the service lay their flowers on the casket.

When they asked for the bill, Tony told them it was on the house in memory of Elizabeth.

When she returned to the hotel, Gini told Ric what they had done for the evening.

"Ah, Tony's." Tears came to his eyes.

"Ric." She snuggled close to him.

"I have a fond memory of the place. When I turned eighteen, I was at your house. Mama couldn't believe there wasn't going to be any celebration with my family. She called my mother and asked if she could take her and me to dinner for my birthday. Of course, my mom declined but gave Mama permission to take me. There was a big football game that night that you and Franco went to. It was just her and me at Tony's; one of the best birthdays I'd ever had." He sniffed, wiped his eyes, and hugged Gini. "I loved that woman."

"Are you coming to the service tomorrow?"

"I might try to sneak in so no one will see me. I'd really like to go."

The next day, the family arrived in limos and then gathered just outside the sanctuary doors. How Gini wished Ric was there giving her strength; she was so dreading the day.

"Gini Anderson," a woman called out. The high school friend ran to Gini and hugged her. "I'm so sorry to hear about your mother."

"Thanks for coming. We all appreciate it."

The woman reached over and grabbed Franco's arm. "It's so good to see you again, Franco."

Gini quickly pulled out of the hug when she heard his name. Franco, how… why… what was he doing here? *No, he can't be here; he'll see Ric… no he cannot be here!* she thought.

He gathered her into his arms. "Babe!"

From over his shoulder, Gini saw a man in a ball cap and sunglasses come in and stand off to the side. It was Ric. He looked at her and then quickly slipped through the doors to find a seat. She started to feel panicky.

Gini pulled back, Franco's strong arms still wrapped around her. "What are you doing here?"

"Cindy sent me an email and told me about Mama. I couldn't miss her funeral."

She looked at Cindy; Cindy smiled.

Gini pushed away from him, unsure of what was happening.

"We're ready for the family to enter," a man said.

Franco had his arm around Gini's shoulders, and with the family, they went to their seats. She didn't have the strength to take it off. She just needed to get through the day.

Father Gordon greeted each of them and patted their hand between his. When he got to Gini, he put his hand under her chin. A strong wave of sorrow ran through her. They sat down in the pew; she dropped her head into her hands, crying. Franco wrapped his arms around her and pulled her to him.

Ric could see everything that was happening from the back of the church. *He should be the one* holding and comforting her. He was fidgety in his seat, fighting the urge to get up, go to her and take her in his arms—demand that she be with him. He knew he couldn't do that; he must keep to the shadows. In his mind, Franco was no longer in her life, but in reality, Franco was still her husband. She hadn't said anything to him about ending things, and there was nothing Ric could do about it. He shouldn't look but he couldn't stop; his eyes took in every sign of their intimacy as it raked his heart. Gini seemed so comfortable in Franco's arms, and it reminded him of the early years, how Franco adored her, how Gini seemed to glow with that attention, that protection.

He had always been attracted to her, but he'd thought she needed Franco, that Franco was just right for her. It was all coming back to him.

Of course it was a different time. He knew that Gini loved him now. But it was almost too much to bear, seeing her with him. He was desperate to leave, to go somewhere where he could hit a wall, protest loudly for them to stop, but out of his respect and love for Mama Elizabeth, he wouldn't be rude and walk out.

Father Gordon greeted everyone, prayed, and read scriptures. He talked about how wonderful Mama Elizabeth was, how much she had done for the church and its parishioners. "We are here today to celebrate Elizabeth Anderson's life. We all know God has her now, and she will have eternal life."

Gini once again fell into tears, resting her head on Franco's shoulder. He put his hand on her face and whispered to her.

Ric cringed at the movement, the genuine show of affection by both of them for each other.

The priest walked down to the front pew and gave the family Communion. Then he took Cindy's hand and helped her up to a pulpit.

"Elizabeth was my stepmother, but I can tell you she was the best mother I ever had. I didn't meet her until I was in high school. Those were tough years for me. She was my glimmer of hope, my ray of sunshine that helped me find my way. She taught me how to love and be loved. Even though we weren't blood-related, she was my mama." She took a hanky and wiped her tears. Dwayne met her at the steps to help her down, and then he went to the pulpit.

"My mama." He sighed. "What a woman. Tiny in stature but, believe me, she boxed my ears many times to get my attention. She had two natural children, and a whole neighborhood she called her kids. I'm the lucky one that could claim her as mine."

Franco turned his head to Gini's, still on his shoulder, while Dwayne was talking. "Are you okay?" he whispered.

"I'm fine."

"I'd like to say a little something before you speak. She was my mama, too."

She looked at him and forced a smile. "I know. Yes, please, speak your piece."

When Dwayne was done, he walked to Gini. She and Franco stood up. Dwayne kissed her on the cheek and patted Franco on the shoulder. He took her flower and went to his seat. Franco and Gini went up the steps.

"Elizabeth wasn't my mother; I had a mother and grandmother." He took in a slow breath and squeezed her hand. "And Gini wasn't my sister, but it felt like it. Mama treated me like one of her own. She helped me out of some pretty serious stuff when I thought I was the toughest kid in Sacramento. I would not be the man I am today, running a successful business, without her love and encouragement. She helped me and *my brother*, Ric Santini, find our way."

Ric almost choked on his breath when he quickly took one. They *were* brothers.

"Eventually, she became my mother-in-law." He squeezed around Gini's shoulders. "And Gini is now my wife. I will truly miss Mama Elizabeth. She was my mom."

He leaned over and kissed Gini.

She stepped forward and stood silent. Franco stepped away from her to give her her moment.

"This is so hard for me. I was so loved growing up. I had the best mama and pop in the world. They both taught me to be the best I could be. They showed me the love of a good family. And she encouraged me to be my own person. It has been hard the last few months to see her health failing. She was always so strong, but even in poor health and with a fading memory, she still loved everyone around her. She baked her cookies and famous breads for the people at the home, and they all loved her for it. She did think all the children were hers, hers to take care of and teach and love. Her heart was too big for such a small lady. I love you, Mama. Rest in peace."

Franco pulled her to him and kissed her on the cheek; they walked down the steps hand in hand. Ric stood up in the back. He had removed his cap but was still wearing sunglasses. She looked at him. He stood for a moment staring at her. He could no longer watch the tenderness between them. He *had* to leave and made his way to the door.

She wanted to go to him. As he slipped out the door, Dwayne handed her flower back to her. After a few more words from Father Gordon, the whole family walked to the casket. Each laid their flower on top.

Gini burst into tears and sank her face deep into Franco's chest. There was so much pain in her heart, partly for her mama, mostly for Ric. He should have been with the family. He had just as much right being there as Franco. She had messed it up for him. Her cheating was messing up everyone's life. Franco led her out of the church.

Outside, she composed herself and started to walk to the limo. He wrapped his arm around her neck. "I'll take you to Mama's house."

The house was empty, ready to go on the market. The church took care of the whole reception, supplying the chairs and tables. Friends of the family were providing the food and drink.

There was silence for the five-block drive from the church. Gini tried to compose herself, but there was a huge lump in her throat. When they pulled up in front of the house, and she saw all the people gathering, she leaned over with her face in her hands. She couldn't hold back the tears any longer.

"Babe." He put his arm around her and leaned down to her head. "I'm sorry you're so sad."

After a few minutes, she gained control, and they walked into the house. There were chairs set up all around the living room and dining room. Two long tables had food on them. She walked into the kitchen and went to the sink to look out the window.

"Franco," Dwayne said walking up to him. The two men shook hands and hugged at the same time. "I'm glad you're here. Gini needs you."

"She's taking it hard." Franco looked at her lovingly. "I want to comfort her, but I think she just needs to grieve."

Later they were talking to friends from school. "I think I saw Ric Santini at the church," one of them said. Gini immediately felt a stab at her heart. She had to hide her emotional feelings for him. Franco couldn't know how she felt.

"Yeah," Franco said putting his arm around her. "I was hoping he'd show up here. I haven't seen him for so long. I saw him stand up in the back of the church. He feels the same about Mama as I do."

"Gini. Franco." Patrice hugged Gini with one arm. She was holding her infant son in the other. "Of course, you two are married. Could it be any other way?"

"What a cute baby," Gini said.

The group of friends got bigger as more people arrived. Gini took the little boy from Patrice so she could use the restroom. She sat down in a chair and held the bottle of juice and the little boy sucked on it, looking up to her. He soon fell asleep in her arms.

"That baby looks good on you." Franco sat down in a chair next to her.

She looked at him and smiled. "Isn't he just so cute?"

"How in the world did you two have a blond baby?" another classmate asked, sitting on the other side of Gini.

"He's not ours." Gini gently hugged the little boy. He was so cuddly in her arms, his body so warm next to hers.

The crowd started to leave, and the family decided to get a drink together. They ended up at Tino's Bar and Grill.

"Oh, wow, this place takes me back," Franco said.

"Frankie!" Tino walked from the kitchen, his apron wrapped around his waist. Tino was the only one who got away with calling him anything but Franco.

"Look at you. Just look at you all grown up." He held Franco at arm's length in front of him. "You still live around here?"

"No. Haven't for a long time. Tino, this is my wife, Gini."

"And married! Who would've ever thought that tough street kid would turn out to be such a good man?"

"A lot of that had to do with you." Franco gave him a quick side hug, and then introduced the rest of the family. He told him of Mama's passing, and Tino expressed his sympathy.

As they all settled around a high table in the bar, Franco took off his suit jacket and loosened his tie. Gini could see his large upper arms hard under the shirtsleeves that covered them. She wasn't too fond of the scruffy, unshaved look in general, but it looked good on him—sexy. He pulled his chair as close to hers as he could and sat down.

"Hey, Frankie, is that a bun on the back of your head?" Dwayne asked in a snide way.

"Yeah, what of it?"

"You a girly now?"

Franco reached back, pulled at the wounded hair, and took out the band. The wavy black hair fell around his ears and neck. Gini's body reacted—aroused. She still had strong feelings for him, which surprised her. She felt a tingling of her body and a strong desire to make love with him. She picked up her water and quickly took a swig.

"Hahaha. Look at those locks."

Franco stood up. "You want to go outside?"

"Franco!" She grabbed his arm.

"Sure, why not?" Dwayne was still laughing. "It looks good. I'll have to admit I never thought I'd see the tough Franco with a bun."

Both men laughed together, and Franco sat back down. He pulled the hair back and put the bun back up on the back of his head. "Keeps it out of my face."

Franco always wore his hair longish and greased in high school; he thought it made him look tough. Sometimes he shaved it close on the sides, leaving it long on top and in the back. He was kicked out of school once for wearing a Mohawk. The only time he ever had a buzz cut was when he shaved it off. He was very conscious of his height, wishing he could be as tall as Ric. When he was a young boy, he had been constantly picked on by the bigger kids.

"How do you know Tino?" Cindy asked.

"He saved my butt more than once when I was a kid."

174

One Saturday when Franco was in fourth grade, he was following a gang of boys. Franco desperately wanted to be part of the gang. The four boys, older and much bigger, went into the corner store and then ran out after stealing some beer. Franco ran after them.

"Get out of here, squirt," one called out.

As they continued to run, Franco picked up a rock and threw it, hitting one in the back. The gang member stopped and then went after Franco. He knocked him to the ground and was just about to beat him when he was suddenly lifted up.

"Get off him," Tino said. "Find someone your own size to pick on. Get out of here before I call the police."

Franco was still lying on his back looking up at the man who had probably just saved his life.

"Come on, kid. Come with me."

"I could have taken him."

"Ahh, I'm thinking not." He helped Franco to his feet. "Hungry? I make a pretty mean hamburger."

Tino had seen Franco around the streets and knew someday he was going to get into a lot of trouble if someone didn't get a hold of him and help him out.

Franco followed him into the bar and back to the kitchen. Tino sat him at a small table. Franco watched as he put the hamburger on the grill.

"What's your name?"

"Franco Legotti."

"Wow, awesome name. I'm Tino. This is my joint. Give me your dad's phone number, and I'll call him."

"I don't have an old man." Franco drank the Coke in front of him.

"How about your mom then?"

"Nope, no mom either."

"There has to be someone I can call."

"Nope, I'm my own man."

The two sat in the kitchen and talked while Franco gulped down the hamburger. Tino made him another one. Tino shared his stories about being a street kid until he finally was thrown in juvie. He hated it. Once he got out, he changed his life. After close to two hours, Franco finally told Tino about Mama Elizabeth. Tino knew who she was.

When Elizabeth came to pick him up, Tino told Franco he was always welcome to come get a hamburger and talk.

"I spent a lot of time in this bar until I got into middle school. Tino was a great friend. I don't know what I would have done without him and Mama."

Gini gave a quiet sigh and put her head in her hands.

"Babe?"

"I need sugar," she said quietly.

Cindy immediately got up and went to Tino. He brought Gini a glass of juice.

"Here you go."

She took the glass, her hand shaking.

"What the hell's going on?" Franco asked, helping her with the drink.

After Gini started feeling better, she told Franco about her diagnosis. And Cindy told him about how sick she had been the week before.

He had a sinking feeling. How could this be happening to her all at the same time? No wonder she was so emotional. He wrapped his arm tight around her. He felt helpless. He couldn't fix death, and he couldn't fix her illness. It made him want to yell and throw something.

Ric was sitting in a booth in a darkened area of the hotel bar, reading his emails, and sipping his drink. He suddenly heard a familiar voice.

"Babe, come on, come to San Francisco with me."

"I have things I have to wrap up here."

"Then come when you're done..." The voices trailed off as they walked past.

Ric quickly laid his tablet facedown and put his head down, partially hiding his face in his hands. Gini and Franco sat on two stools at the bar. Ric could see her facing Franco, and he could see Franco's face in the reflection of the mirrored column she was leaning against. He couldn't hear what they were saying, but they both were emotional. He couldn't stop watching.

"I have a nice suite we can stay in for a few days. I've opened an office there, and I'm here to get it set up."

"You have an office in the States, and you didn't even tell me... not only that you have an office, but also that you were in California." She huffed and turned away from him.

He ordered a whiskey for him and a cup of tea for her.

"I was going to call. Then I heard from Cindy about Mama so decided to surprise you there. Gini, we can live together in San Fran. I'll still be going to China, but it will be easier to come home."

"You..." She was so angry she found it hard to speak. "You think I'm just going to pack up and move to California? Franco, my job is in Boston and DC." She faced him and stared him in the eyes. "You do remember I have a job? And a successful one at that. How many times have you been to the States and not let me know?"

"Babe, now, calm down." He put his hands on the sides of her face, slowly pushing back the curls. "I just got in a few days ago. I contacted you every time I could get a signal from China. I would let you know if I'd been here. I love you. And I want to be with you."

"Then open an office in Boston."

He took his thumbs across her eyebrows, leaned over, and kissed her.

"Mmm…" she quietly groaned and fell into the kiss.

He pulled back. "I have to catch my flight." He took a business card out of his pocket and wrote something on it. From his wallet, he laid a twenty-dollar bill on the bar and put the card next to her teacup. "Come to San Francisco. We'll figure this out, I promise. We'll figure what is the best for both of us."

He reached over once again putting his hand on her face. He kissed her, this time leaving his lips on hers after the kiss. "I love you."

Ric saw the look of passion in both pairs of eyes.

Franco stepped away from the bar and turned to leave. He ran his hand down her arm slowly as he left, grabbing her hand briefly. Gini sat, not moving, and watched him leave.

Ric once again hid his face. After Franco had walked by, Ric looked back to Gini. She was crying. She turned her stool back to face the bar, ran her finger around the cup rim, and then picked up the business card. Franco had written his hotel and suite number on the back.

Ric grabbed his tablet and quickly walked out the opposite door from Franco and went to the elevator hall.

Gini opened her purse and took out a tissue. She had to pull herself together before going up to be with Ric. That's where she wanted to be—or was it? In the elevator, she touched her fingers to her lips. She could still feel his kiss, the softness of his lips, the firm Gini kisses, meant just for her. She thought of his strong arms pulling her into his safe zone. Announcing to the world that she was his and no one else's. By the time she got to her room, the tears were flowing again out of control.

Ric heard the connecting door on her side click closed. He walked over to it. "Gins, is that you?" He heard another door close from inside her room. "Gini." He got no answer. Then he thought he could hear water running.

He went to the small refrigerator, took out a small bottle of scotch, and poured it into a glass. He would order up some carrot cake for her. She loved carrot cake.

About an hour later, the connecting door for the rooms opened, and Gini walked through it. She had on pajamas and a robe. Ric stood up and went to her.

She felt she ought to guard herself. She was so confused she didn't know where she wanted to be. But when she saw him, she snuggled close to him. "It's been a long, hard day."

"I know, sweets." He kissed her on the top of her head. "I got you carrot cake."

"Comfort food, just what I need."

They both walked over to the couch and sat down. She leaned forward and took a bite of the cake. "I guess you saw Franco came to the funeral?"

"I saw him." He got up. "I'll make you some tea."

She smiled. "Thanks. He opened an office in San Francisco and is there for a few days. He wants me to move there."

"What? Are you going to?"

"NO! Ric, I can't believe he thinks I'll just pick up on a whim and move. He has never appreciated I have a job—a good job, one that I love." She could feel her anger rise as she spoke.

The last thing Ric wanted to talk about was Franco. The two of them hugging, him kissing her—he wanted that image to go away. "I talked to Michelle. We made our plans to meet. She sounds like a nice person. I think I'll enjoy working for her." He squeezed the water out of the tea bag with a spoon.

"Michelle, who's Michelle?"

"I told you about Michelle Walker in Reno. We're driving there tomorrow, remember?"

She abruptly stood up. "You're moving to Reno. Fine, Ric, go ahead. I don't need you; I don't need anyone." She stomped through the connecting doors and slammed hers closed.

"Gini!" He ran to the door. "Gins, please, we were just going to take a road trip. I'm not moving anywhere. Gini." He put his arm up on the door and laid his forehead on it. He could hear her crying. "Let me in so I can hold you. Sweet Gins, I want to comfort you. Let me in."

"Go away. Leave me alone."

He sat on the couch for a while trying to work, but couldn't concentrate. About midnight he walked over to the door. He couldn't hear her, so he went to bed.

Around three o'clock, he was startled awake when the bed moved. He opened his eyes and saw her crawling under the sheets naked. He moved to her and pulled her into his arms. They kissed, her mouth hot and hungry. It aroused him of course, but also made him feel strong. She needed his love.

She turned over onto her back. "Franco wants to talk." She turned back and looked at him.

"Sweets, you have to decide how you want to do this. I will help in any way I can, but you have to make the decision. Just know how much I love you."

"I know. He just doesn't get it. Do you think he'll realize I don't want to move?"

"I don't know, Gins. I don't know." He pulled her close and held her tight. He didn't want to let her go ever. They fell asleep in each other's arms.

At five o'clock, she carefully got out of bed and went back to her room. After getting dressed, she went into the living area and left a note on the bar. Then she dragged her suitcase out of her room into the hall.

At the airport, she sat across from the ticket counters. What was she going to do, go back to Boston or go to San Francisco? Each time she decided on Boston, she stood up, took a couple of steps, and then sat back down. Franco had so much explaining to do. Did she just say "enough" and walk away from him, or give him a chance? She had loved him all her life. And the kiss certainly showed that her feelings for him were still there. Then she remembered the lovemaking with Ric only a few hours earlier. His gentleness and caring, making her feel wanted.

She finally walked up to the ticket counter. "I need to change my ticket."

Ric woke up and saw she wasn't in the bed. "Sweets, are you in the bathroom?" He went through the open door. "Gini."

When he walked into the living area, he saw the note:

I have to go to him. I have to; he's my husband.

Chapter 14 – Reconciliation

"Okay," the kind lady behind the ticket counter said. "Let's see what you have."

Gini handed her the ticket. "I want to fly to San Francisco with a stayover, and then an open-date ticket from there to Boston."

"We can take care of that for you."

When Gini got to the hotel, she was taken to Franco's room. The man at the reception desk was asked by Franco to call him when she arrived. She put down her purse and went to the window. The view was of the Bay with only a small glimpse of the Golden Gate Bridge. She had so many mixed emotions inside of her. So much so, she had a stomachache.

It seemed like only moments later when the room door opened. "Babe, you're here."

Franco walked over to her and wrapped his arms around her. She laid her head on his shoulder and started to cry.

He pulled her closer. "I know this has been hard for you. She was a terrific lady and we will all miss her."

She nodded her head against his body. Then she stood back and took a tissue out of her purse and wiped her face.

"I want you to forget all of your troubles. We are going to take a cruise around the bay. It's so beautiful out there. It will give you solace." He put his hands on her face, pulled it to him, and kissed her.

The familiar kiss she had so loved. His strong hands swallowing up her face. She started to cry all over again. What was she doing? Her life was so messed up. Her mind so confused. He pulled her close to him again.

His phone rang quietly in his pocket.

"Thanks, Mario. We'll be on our way."

"Our boat is ready," he said cheerfully.

"Our boat?" She stood up straight and pulled down on her jacket.

"My office manager here, Mario, owns a sailboat. It's quite beautiful. You'll love sailing around on it. I promise you'll love it."

Gini suddenly had a feeling of doubt. Franco seemed way too comfortable in San Francisco for it to be his first time there. Had he been to the States often without contacting her? No, she pushed the thought away. He wouldn't do that.

Mario handed them both a fancy life jacket after Franco had helped her step onto the polished deck of the large schooner. He slipped it up over the heavy windbreaker jacket he had bought for her earlier and zipped it up her front, then carried his farther into the boat.

The captain, Mario, had fixed them lunch. It was placed on a table in the front of the large open space. Next to the two plates and a large bowl of seafood salad was a chilled bottle of sparkling wine. Mario popped the cork and poured each flute about half full.

After Gini and Franco got settled, the boat slowly went through the marina using a small motor. Once in the open water, the captain started hoisting the sails. She watched him go through a routine of untying the ropes and pulling down hard on them with his gloved hands. The fabric billowed out in the soft breeze. The rope was then tied tight to hold the sail. She found it quite fascinating.

"Want to try your hand, mate?" he asked looking at her watching him.

She shook her head quickly—looked like hard work to her.

Franco leaned over and kissed her on the cheek, got up, took the gloves from Mario and helped him hoist the second sail. Gini could see his arm muscles harden under his long-sleeved shirt each time he pulled down on the rope.

When they were farther into the bay, the wind popped at the sails. Mario pulled at the mainsheet to maneuver the large mast; once it was in place, he went to the ship's wheel to operate the sailing vessel.

There was a soft, whirring sound as they glided over the water. It was so peaceful. A fine mist floated across their faces occasionally. Franco was right. It was like heaven. They ate while taking in all the beauty of the bay. They went out and around Alcatraz Island. The seagulls were flying all around. The tour went up to Sausalito and then toward the Golden Gate Bridge.

"Gini, just look at that bridge. Isn't it the most beautiful thing you've ever seen?"

The ride underneath was utterly amazing. She had heard of its beauty, and now she had witnessed it herself. They went a little past the bridge and then turned to go back.

"When we go under this time, lie down on the bench. The underside is an engineering marvel." Franco was excited to show her the creation.

She lay faceup. He was on the deck next to her, watching her face and expressions. He loved his wife and was so happy to be with her again. When they went under, he leaned back on his elbows and looked up.

They made their way back to the marina as they ate a delicious creamy dessert.

Back in the room, they went into the bedroom. Franco put her suitcase on the luggage rack by the door. Gini undressed to take a shower. He came up behind her and wrapped his arms around her and started kissing her on the shoulder. She turned around, wanting to push him away, but she couldn't. She loved him. They soon ended up in the bed making love.

Afterward, they took a shower. They both walked toward the bed with their hair wrapped in towels. She quickly got under the covers. He got in from the other side. His strong, naked body pulled close to hers. Draped around his neck was a shiny gold chain. She had noticed the new ink on his neck earlier at the restaurant, a Chinese red-and-black dragon that started behind his ear and went down his neck onto his chest. It was sexy the way it moved with his muscles, the tail partially hidden in his long wavy chest hair. When he reached for her again, she knew he knew every inch of her body, every sensitive spot that would take her deeper into oblivion. His hands searching and then finding her breasts, so sensitive, the touch that sent her over the hill—you know, the feeling of going up a hill, then suddenly down, that crazy swoopy feeling in your stomach. There was no denying she loved him, and she wanted him deep inside her. Her emotions started bubbling up again. She closed her eyes and let him take her.

An hour later, Franco got up. He gathered the two wet towels that had been tossed around on the bed in their fury. Gini was sound asleep. Her curls flowed freely in all directions around her head on the pillow, like a beautiful goddess. He had so missed his gorgeous wife, but now it was as if they had never been apart.

He went into the bathroom. His wavy locks were also messy and unmanageable. He stuck his head under the sink faucet and got his hair wet. Then he took a wide-toothed comb through the strands, combing them all to the back. He used his hands to pull it all tight to his scalp and wrapped a band around, holding the hair in a thin ponytail that reached off his head about halfway between the crown and his neck. After pulling to make it perfect, he braided it, grabbed the end, and wound the tail into a neat, small bun. He wiped his hands on the short whiskers all the way down on his neck.

Gini slept for about another hour. When she woke, she felt weak. "Franco," she called out.

"Yes, babe." He walked into the bedroom.

"Is there any juice in the room refrigerator? I need some sugar."

He quickly went and found the juice and took it to her. It was worrisome to him she had this condition. He wished she had told him when she was diagnosed. He would have come home immediately.

"I have a reservation for seven-thirty at my favorite restaurant."

She drank the juice and looked at the bedside clock. It was six-fifteen.

He could see she was feeling better soon after she started drinking. "Babe, I'm worried about you. You should have told me. Hypoglycemia could be serious. And your illness last week. I hope you're taking care of yourself." He was crouched by the side of the bed with his hand on top of her thigh.

"I'm fine. Dr. Nelson said I can control it with diet, and I have. Don't worry. Nothing has changed in my life." She was offended by his comment. "I'm still very busy. I've taken care of myself for a while now. And I can handle all of it just fine. The antibiotics cleared out the infection. I only have a couple more days of pills."

He reached up and brushed her hair back. "That wasn't fair of me. I know you can take care of yourself. You look healthy. And those clear blue eyes. I had forgotten how beautiful they are. I swear, sometimes I feel like they can see right through me."

"Maybe they can. Have any secrets?"

"Nope, not a one. I'm pretty transparent."

"Been with other women?" *Why did I ask him that? Do I really want to know?*

He laughed a gentle laugh. "No, I promised myself to you a long time ago. I don't even look. Don't want to look, don't need to look." She could hear his phone vibrating on the table in the other room.

She sat up and put her hands up to push the curls back. "Oh, brother, my hair feels like a crazy pile of leafy branches. I need to take another shower."

He didn't seem to hear his phone. "Leave them. Just pull the curls back. I love your curly hair." He went to his knees and pulled up closer to her face. He leaned forward and kissed her.

"Once we move here, we'll implant the embryos and get our family started."

"Dr. Nelson said we need a surrogate. I'm not able to have children. Not now, not ever." She was annoyed he mentioned moving there again.

The phone had stopped.

"Then we'll get a surrogate."

The vibrating sound started again. He gave her another quick kiss and got up to get his phone.

Gini went into the bathroom, looked at her hair in the mirror, and laughed at herself. She looked like a scarecrow. She popped back in the shower. When she got out, she started getting ready for dinner. She peeked out the door before she went to put on her makeup. He was busy typing into his phone with his thumbs; he didn't see her. Just looking at him bare-chested in his underwear made her feel flushed, warmth running through her body. Their lovemaking had always been so special, leaving her with no doubt about how he felt about her. They should be together; they were husband and wife, and she now knew she still loved him, deeply loved him. She let out a breath and continued getting ready.

They walked the four blocks to the restaurant. He seemed to be deep in thought. They walked in silence; he held her hand. He took out his phone and looked at it, then put it back in his pocket. "You look beautiful, Gini." He smiled. "Here we are."

When they got inside, the maitre d' greeted them. "Mr. Legotti, I have your favorite table ready." He guided them to the table. Once again Gini's suspicions were aroused.

They walked down several tiered steps to a lower part of the restaurant. The whole wall was windows looking out over the city and the bay. It almost took her breath away, it was such a magnificent view. They were led to a semicircular booth facing the windows.

"Nice, huh?" He put his arm around her.

"Beautiful!"

He looked at the label on the wine bottle the waiter handed him. "Yes, that's it. Thank you for finding it for me." The waiter put a small amount into his glass, and Franco approved. After pouring some for her, he handed them each a menu.

"You should try the fish special," he suggested. "The fish is out of this world here."

Franco looked at his vibrating phone several times during the ordering process.

"Are you sure this is your first time in San Francisco? Why do the maitre d' and waiter know you so well?"

"This is the first place I came to eat, Mario's recommendation. I've come here every night. The food is especially good, and they have such variety. I've had something different every time. I've been here a little less than a week. And no, this isn't my first time here. Don't you remember Ric and I came for a few days after high school graduation?"

Her body did an impulsive, small jump when he said Ric's name. "Yeah, I guess I remember that. How could you afford to come here?" She squirmed a little.

"His aunt gave us some money and said go have fun. I think she must have been loaded."

"Ric's mom."

"What?"

"Ric's mom was loaded, and so was he from a trust fund his dad left him."

"Who told you that?"

There was silence. What had she said? How would she explain herself?

"I recall him telling the story later in Boston." She looked down.

"Guess that makes sense. I mean he did have that killer truck. He told me his dad's company had delivered it to him. We both were clueless why they would give him a truck."

Such innocent and carefree days those were. They sat without talking, and Franco's thoughts went back to his school days.

He remembered the perky girl he couldn't be without.

"I'm going to be the first woman president," Gini announced in the hamburger joint the three of them always went to after school.

"Hahaha," Franco laughed.

"Why are you laughing? You don't think I'd make a good president?"

"Babe, do you know how much work it takes to run this country? You couldn't do it."

"Why not? I've studied politics. I'd make sure we govern by what the Constitution says. Equal rights for everyone. I'd take care of the underprivileged children, and the sick and disabled ones too. I'd be a good president."

"Talking about the children, that's Mama Elizabeth talking."

"Franco, stop bullying her. She can probably be whatever she wants. She certainly has the brains."

Gini was impressed that Ric stood up for her. He had just gotten the braces off his teeth. After his statement, he flashed a beautiful, white, straight-toothed smile.

"You think I'm a bully?" Franco looked at Ric and put his forearms on the table.

"Sometimes." Ric grinned.

"You want to take me on? Come on, big boy, let's get it going."

Ric sat farther back in his chair. "I only come in peace."

Gini threw her arms around Franco's neck. "You'll see. Someday I'll be a famous person in politics."

"Well, all I can say is you are going to need to grow up." She gave him a big kiss as he said his last word.

Ric put up his fisted hands. Franco looked out of the corner of his eye and laughed, his mouth still in the pucker for the kiss. Ric laughed too.

"So did you stay in a big fancy hotel then?" Gini suddenly asked.

He turned to look at her. She had an almost angry look on her face.

185

"No, we stayed at a hostel. We had a ball, though, toured on a boat in the bay. Going under that bridge, such an amazing bridge. And those crazy seals. Boy, did they stink."

"Seals, what seals?"

"Trust me, you wouldn't like the smell. I can't tell you how many times we rode that trolley. One day we ran the hills and then rode the trolley back and ran them again." He sighed. "Oh, man, those were the days. Brothers. We're brothers rather than friends. I miss him."

There was quiet again.

"You said you ran into him. We'll have to get together with them when I get home." He smiled at the thought. "He's the only real friend I've ever had, except you, of course." He put his arm around her and squeezed. "But you're much more than a friend. I wonder if he and Margarita have any kids."

Gini opened her mouth to answer and then thought better of it. She couldn't tip her hand. She couldn't let him know how much she knew about Ric, that they were friends now—that might lead to questions that she couldn't anticipate.

She should've gone back to Boston alone. She didn't need either one of them. Tears were forming in her eyes.

"Hey!" Franco reached his hand over to her and put it on her leg. "What's wrong? Listen, Gini, we are going to have kids someday. Don't be sad. We're going to have a family."

She choked up but didn't cry.

They had just finished their salads when his phone rang quietly in his pocket. He took it out. "I have to take this call." He quickly got up, tossed his napkin on the seat, and swiftly climbed the elongated steps.

The waiter put their meals down on the table. After about ten minutes, Gini started to eat. Franco hadn't returned. She kept huffing out her breaths. Although the fish was tasty, she just pushed it around her plate. Nothing had changed. Ever since they started their jobs, his priority was his work. Having hot sex did not a marriage make. She could feel the anger pushing pressure from her chest up into her face and head. She pulled a small bite of redfish with white wine and mushroom sauce to the middle of the plate and started to put it in her mouth, but stopped. She looked at her watch; it had been a good half hour. The waiter had long ago taken Franco's plate so his entree could be fixed fresh when he returned to the table.

She slapped her napkin on the seat next to her, grabbed her purse, and slid out of the booth. She took about four steps and came face-to-face with Franco.

"Where are you going?"

"To the hotel." She pushed past him.

"Wait!"

She was almost running up the steps.

"Everything okay, Mr. Legotti?" the waiter asked. "I'll bring you a fresh plate."

Franco took a few bills out of his wallet and handed them to the waiter. "I'll settle up later." He ran after her.

"Gini," he called when he got outside to see her a few feet ahead of him. "Come on, Gini, please, wait for me."

He caught up with her. "I had to take the call. It was very important."

"More important than me? More important than our marriage?" She stopped and looked at him and then huffed off up the small slope.

"Of course not." He kept up with her.

"Franco, our marriage is over. Actually, it never really started. You're married to your work. I'm just a bed partner."

"That's not true. Gini, please, let me make it up to you."

They walked into the hotel lobby. Neither spoke, not in the elevator either. When they got inside the room, his phone rang again. "I'll have to call you back... I know... I'll call you back."

He put his phone in his pocket and grabbed her to keep her from going in the bedroom. "I love you. Oh my gosh, I love you so much. I can see I have done this all wrong. You have to give me a chance, babe. I thought we both were happy with our jobs. I had no idea you felt we had no marriage. Please, let's work on this. I'll work on it... I'll fix it. Just give me a chance." His phone continued to ring and indicate a message left as he talked to her.

She took her arm from his hand and turned toward the bedroom. "Make your call." The door slammed slightly behind her.

He put both hands behind his head and slowly shook it back and forth, then released his hair from the bun and elastic band. It fell down around his ears. He flopped down on the couch, took his phone out of his pocket, and returned the call.

Gini quickly undressed and put on her gown then packed all her things in the bag and laid out her clothes for the next day. She was so upset; she was having a hard time breathing. She needed to settle down. So much had happened the last couple of weeks. She just needed to go home and get back into her old routine.

She climbed into bed, lying on one side and then the other. Her mind raced a hundred miles an hour. First, she thought about running to Ric; he'd make her feel better. He cared about her feelings, unlike Franco.

Then her thoughts went to Franco next to the bed, talking to her in his kind voice, concerned about her health, and soon her memory went to his hands roaming her body.

"AHHH!" she cried into her pillow.

She didn't need any man. Her life was so much easier without one. No one to account for but herself. She rolled to her right side. *How can I be in love with two men? How did that happen? We are all such good friends. Why couldn't it be that way again? Friends, just friends.*

The last time she had looked at the time, it was nearly two o'clock. Franco had been talking on the phone all those hours.

At three-thirty Franco laid his phone on the coffee table. He ruffled his hair with his fingers. Still wearing his suit—only his tie had been loosened—he took off the tie and jacket. Hopefully, things would settle down so that he could be with his wife, the love of his life.

While the two of them were on the sailboat, a contract worker on his project in China had fallen into one of the wells. The harness strap broke, plunging him twenty feet down. The team quickly got him out, his only injury a broken arm, but the worker was scared and angry. His older brother was a foreman on the job and had worked for Franco for several years. Franco hoped his foreman could settle his brother down and keep him from going to the Chinese government. If the government officials got involved, heavy fines could be charged, and Franco himself could be imprisoned. As long as they stayed on the good side of the government, everything was fine. But it wasn't a fair and just regime like the United States. Franco had been so careful to follow all the rules. This was just an accident and, hopefully, it would only be considered that. They had offered the worker a generous compensation for his injury and pay for time off. He prayed that would be enough.

Franco went in the bedroom. Gini was asleep, facing away from his side of the bed. He got undressed and climbed under the covers and moved over next to her. She smelled so good. He was so tired he couldn't think anymore. They would work out their problems in the morning. He needed to sleep.

At six o'clock, Gini was up dressed and heading out of the hotel room door. She didn't look back. She just left him sleeping.

Once on the plane, she tried to relax. She would be home soon. There she could bury herself out of sight so she could figure out her life.

Jimmy was at the airport exit door when she walked out. Howard greeted her when she walked in the Tower's door. "I put your mail on the counter in your kitchen. I hope everything went well on your trip. I know it wasn't a joyous occasion."

"Thank you, Howard. All I need now is some good rest."

"Yes, Ms. Anderson. We don't want you getting sick again."

She had never been so glad to be home. She turned on her PET. Suddenly her PET watch started talking. "Message, Ric Santini. Voice message, Franco. Voice message, Catherine."

"Read Ric Santini."

> "Gini, I don't know where you are. I hope this doesn't put you in an uncomfortable position with Franco. I just need to talk to you. Please. I'll be in Florida for a week. Please contact me."

She sat down on the couch and took off her shoes. It was good he wasn't in town. She needed space so she could think through things. She needed time to figure out how to tell him she couldn't be with him anymore.

"Play Catherine."

> "Oh, honey, have you gone dark? I have sent you so many emails without responses. I hope you're okay. I can't remember when you said you'd be back. Maybe you didn't. I hope you're feeling better, and the loss of your mother hasn't been too hard on you. I understand if you need more time. Let me know. C."

She needed to get back to work just as soon as possible. That is exactly what she needed. She would rest and sleep for a day and then she'd go full speed ahead. Maybe she should go to DC, completely remove herself from both romantic situations. She'd spend some time with her good friend.

"Play—" She stopped. Did she really want to hear from Franco? Oh, God, hopefully, he hadn't followed her to Boston. "Play Franco."

> "Listen, babe, our time together didn't go as I had hoped. I'm so sorry you feel the way you do. But I understand. I have spent all morning thinking about how I have messed things up. I'll find a place where we can live together and work the jobs we love. I owe that to you. I have to go back to China for a few days, but then I will fix us, I promise."

She burst into tears and lay on the couch. Could they be fixed? …She didn't think so.

Chapter 15 – Conflicted

Franco arrived at the airport in Shijiazhuang. He hated he had to leave Gini so unhappy, but if he didn't get a handle on this mess, he might never get home. A thorough explanation when he got back would make her understand. He needed to stop taking her for granted and approach her more strategically.

Luca had set up a meeting with the company's Chinese lawyer, Franco, and himself. The victim of the accident threatened to take a complaint against the company to the government, claiming his harness was faulty, and the company was at fault for his life-threatening injury.

"Life-threatening?" Franco asked. "I thought he had a broken arm."

"He claims he has nerve damage and will never be able to work again. If he can't work, then he and his family will starve to death without an income."

"Come on!" Franco paced the floor, rubbing his forehead. "What do we have to do to make this go away?" He looked at the lawyer.

"I don't think he'll go through with his threat," Luca said. "We can give him more money. If need be, we can pay the government agent under the table."

"Isn't that admitting guilt?"

"Guilty, innocent, doesn't matter here. There will be no trial. You know that!"

"Was the harness faulty?"

"It was one of the parts brought in by the agent, but it appears he hooked the rope to a fabric loop instead of the metal hook. It's pretty ripped up, hard to tell."

Ric took the trip to Reno and met with his client. Then he took a direct flight from there to Fort Lauderdale. Morning and night, doing business or alone, talking, eating, in the shower, paying his hotel bill—whatever he was doing, he thought about Gini. He couldn't get the picture out of his head of her burying her head deep into Franco's shoulder, and his loving reaction to it. How comfortable they looked together even in grief. How was this happening? He should feel terrible he was messing around with his best friend's wife—he tried to feel it—but he didn't. He hadn't seen or talked to Franco for a long time. Maybe it was time to get it all out in the open. Friend or not, he was in love with her, and he wanted her for his own.

Gini went to DC. As far as she was concerned, she could stay there forever. How could Franco just pack up and go back to China knowing how upset she was? Didn't he understand their marriage hung in the balance? Was the love and affection at the funeral just an act, or did he really love her? It all seemed so genuine until he got that call at the restaurant. What could be so important? How was she supposed to feel? But being in his bed wrapped up tightly in his love was something she couldn't easily forget. They had vows to uphold, to honor. He was the only man she had ever been with, the only man's body she had ever explored… until Ric.

Ric, how had she let herself fall for him? She had tried so hard to deny his love. Yes, he loved her. That wasn't supposed to happen. And she wasn't supposed to let her vulnerable heart be taken; she was a stronger woman than that. It all had to stop now. No more Ric, and she would have to think hard and long about staying with Franco. He… he… was not holding up his part of the marriage. Was she? NO! She was having… *an… affair*.

All she told Catherine was Franco had shown up, and she had told both men that she didn't want them in her life anymore. Catherine could see Gini needed to do some deep thinking. She was there for her, but Gini would have to start the conversation.

It had been about a week. Gini was sitting at Catherine's dining room table working on her computer. Catherine was sitting on the couch in the combined living and dining room, working on hers. Her video call signal went off.

"Hello, Ric."

Gini immediately turned and looked at her.

"I hope you don't mind that I'm calling about Gini. Please tell her I need to talk to her. This silence is killing me. I don't even know where she is. Is she with Franco? I just need to know, that's all."

There was a pathetic, sad note in his voice, which was hard for Catherine to hear. He was always so upbeat. She looked at Gini. Gini shook her head.

"Listen, Ric. I'm not sure what's going on in her life. She's not ready to talk about it. I will tell her you called. I agree, she should at least tell you where she is." She leaned down to the screen and in almost a whisper, said, "She's okay."

Ric smiled; he knew she was there with Catherine. "Thanks. I appreciate you telling her."

"Chin up."

He laughed. "I'll get through this. Hope everything is okay with you."

Gini got up and left the room.

"I'm good, thanks for asking."

That evening Ric sat by the pool on the fancy grounds at Valentino's. He was looking up at the sliver moon. He had truly loved Margarita when they were married, but he had never felt the way he felt about Gini. Any spare moment he had, he thought about her. And even when he was busy, she was there, a presence in his mind, like a light behind a screen: beauty, softness, vulnerability, a soul so precious... November, December, and January had been the happiest days of his life—yes, his entire life. She accepted him as he was, no pretense, no trying to impress. He could be himself at all times. She loved him. He knew she loved him. He would just have to wait for her to realize he was the one she wanted in her life.

He took a deep breath and let it out.

Kat walked over and sat on the edge of his chaise lounge. "You need me tonight, Ricky?"

He smiled and put his hand on her long, lean brown arm. "No."

"You sure? I can help you forget all your troubles. I promise you will be satisfied."

He took his hand gently down her arm and put it back in his lap. "Kat, you shouldn't give yourself so easily."

"Come." She took his hand. "I bet I can swim two laps faster than you."

He took a long look at her and then the water. "You're on." He got up and dove into the pool.

His phone vibrated on the table. The caller ID showed Gini.

"That was a short call," Catherine said.

"He didn't answer."

"Did you leave a message?"

"No. I don't know what to say."

"Then let your heart do the talking." Catherine went to her bedroom.

Gini's face call sounded. When she answered it, Ric was wiping his hair with a towel. She could tell he was outside in Florida.

"Sweets, sorry I missed your call. You should be with me. I just had a refreshing swim; it's warm here."

She sat and looked at him without saying anything. His hair parted like it did the day they got caught in the rain. She smiled a half smile. "I will."

"You will?" He wiped the towel down his face. "You will, what?"

"Go to Florida."

Ric could hardly contain his excitement as he waited for her plane to land. On the phone, she told him she wanted to be with him and that she missed him. That's what he wanted to hear. She was going to be his; he was determined. She could only be there for two nights.

Gini and Catherine had gone shopping for warm-weather clothes before she left DC. It had been so cold all winter in the north. Gini looked forward to the warmth.

He jogged up to her when she walked into the baggage area. She reached up and put her arms around his neck, and they kissed.

"Gins, you're going to love it here."

She was in awe when he opened the door of a Rolls-Royce to help her in. She looked at him with a big smile. He raised his eyebrows a couple of times. But the real awe came when she saw the mansion as they drove through the gates. He had described it perfectly. It was a world of make-believe.

He introduced her to Val and some of the staff. Rosa, the head cook, took an instant liking to Gini. On their way to the guesthouse, she saw the young men and women lounging around in the pool area. A tall, lanky, dark-skinned woman in a tiny bikini walked up to Ric on the other side from Gini. In her four-inch spike heel sandals, she was as tall as he.

"Ricky, how about another swim." She wrapped her arms around his.

"Maybe later." He pulled his arm out of hers and brought the two women face-to-face. "Kat, this is my girl, Gini."

"Oh, your girl." Kat was clearly disappointed.

As they made their way through the grounds, Gini couldn't believe it was all real. Did people really live like this? How much money must this man have?

The guesthouse was roomy with a bedroom, luxury bath, and a living room. There was no kitchen, just a wet bar.

The sun was just setting. Ric told Rosa they wouldn't be eating in the big house, to bring their dinner to them.

It took them no time to rekindle their intimacy. They were lying in bed, her head on his shoulder. He had his hand on the back of her head. He let out a soft groan. They were where they were meant to be.

Gini ran her fingers through the soft, fine hair on Ric's arm. The hair added a dark sheen over his flawless olive skin—the same for his legs. She smiled to herself. He had no hair on his rounded pecs. *He must have his chest waxed. He's such a pretty boy,* she thought. *A wonderful, loving, pretty boy.*

There wasn't much conversation. She told him she had walked away from Franco; their lives were taking different paths. She was emphatic she would not move to San Francisco.

The next morning, they had their breakfast on the private patio on the other side of the guesthouse. The view was of the intercoastal canal. Large boats slowly went up and down the waterway. She had her legs pulled up in the softly padded chair, her teacup surrounded by her hands between her body and her legs. She loved the sound of the birds all around her.

He leaned down and kissed her. "I have meetings all day. Enjoy the pool. If you want to go anywhere, just tell Eduardo; he'll arrange transportation. I should be back midafternoon."

"Thank you, Ric. This is exactly what I need, a fairy-tale day."

"You're quite welcome, my princess."

Gini took a long spa bath in the large tub in the bathroom. There were Epsom salt and lavender bath treatments to enhance the enjoyment. She put on one of the two-piece suits she had bought in DC. She couldn't remember the last time she wore a swimsuit. Her skin was fish-belly white. She put on a cover-up, picked up her e-reader, and went out to the pool area around lunchtime.

She sat in a lounge chair near the pool and read her book. Rosa asked what she wanted to drink.

"Oh, I don't know, what do you have?"

The tiny Cuban lady told her she had just the drink, and to please go to the long table with food and get what she wanted.

As Gini sat reading, the young people started to filter in. She recognized Kat right away. Rosa brought her a delicious fruit punch drink. She laid her reader down and went to the table, filling her plate with fruit, meat rolls, chips, and several dips. Then she looked over all the desserts and picked a couple.

"You eat like that you'll get fat," Kat said in passing. "I don't think Ricky will go for fat. If I were you, I'd only eat the fruit."

Gini smiled politely and then went back to her lounge chair. She spent the rest of the afternoon reading and jumping in the pool to cool off. Kat continued to eye her.

About four o'clock, Ric and Val walked out to the patio area. Kat immediately went to Val's side, and he wrapped his arm around her waist; they kissed. In her heels, she was a couple of inches taller than him. Gini was surprised to see the affection between the two. Ric walked to Gini, and they embraced.

"I need to change my clothes," he said.

The two of them went into the guesthouse. Once inside, they kissed and kissed some more. "You smell like lavender and oranges."

"And you," she gave a devilish smile, "you, Mr. Santini, smell like offices."

"Oh no," he said. "We'll have to change that." She undressed him, and he removed her suit. She felt shy and then she didn't. Their lovemaking was intense, invigorating, and what they both wanted and needed.

"I could do this all night," he said.

"Why not?"

Later they went back to the outside eating and pool area. Val was sitting at the table smoking a large Cuban cigar; Kat was sitting on his lap. Gini and Ric sat across the table from them. Rosa brought out a tray of tropical drinks, and the plates full of finger food continued to be served as they drank and the two men talked business.

A little later, Rosa escorted a woman to the door. When Val saw her, he flicked his fingers at Kat, telling her to leave. She quickly jumped up from his lap and joined the other young people across the way. Then he waved to the other lady to join them. Ric stood up when she approached.

Val got up, and he and the woman hugged and kissed. She was older, dressed in a business skirt and jacket.

"Diane," Ric said. "This is Gini." The two ladies acknowledged each other. "Diane's the mayor of Lauderdale-by-the-Sea."

Val held a chair for Diane to sit and then took her hand. "You usual?" he asked in is broken English, kissing the back of her hand.

She smiled. "Oh, Val, I can drink what you're drinking."

"No, *amor de mi vida*, you have martini." He signaled to Rosa.

The dinner was light and delightful. Diane and Ric talked about the permits and property purchase for the new resort.

When they were done eating, Val stood up and took Diane's hand. "To thee boat!"

The four of them walked through the pool area, around the guesthouse, and down a path.

"You're going to love this," Ric whispered in Gini's ear.

They walked to the dock. There it was, a huge yacht waiting for them to board. As they walked closer, lights turned on throughout the boat's rooms.

She looked up at him. "You were right, it's bigger than your house." Her blue eyes were sparkling.

For the next hour or so they slowly cruised down the canal toward Miami Beach. After-dinner drinks were served, and they sat in the outdoor living area.

Early the next morning, Ric took her to the airport. They embraced for a long time before she got out of the car. "I have a trip to the Bahamas, and then I will be back to Boston."

"Good. I'll see you then."

"Thank you for coming here." He kissed her.

"Are you kidding? You won't be able to keep me away now."

The election for the city council seat was the next day. Gini couldn't miss Michael's big event. She did two morning-show interviews. Most of the talk was about the election, but they also talked to her about her role in the health-care bill. Catherine and Gini had made their names well known across the country, especially along the East Coast. With all her visibility over the holidays, she was easily recognized on the streets.

Gini wanted to take Michael and Brenda out to dinner to celebrate his victory. The two of them were together all week as she introduced him to the people of importance in the local and national governments. She met them at the restaurant. They were just finishing their cocktails when Gini got a message. She leaned down and picked up her phone. The three of them were smiling, talking about Michael's road to the White House.

She suddenly looked serious. "I have to take this." She got up and went to the entrance area. She read the message and then walked back to the table.

"Everything okay?"

"I..." She leaned down, got her purse, took out some money, and handed it to Michael. "I have to go. Yes, I need to leave."

He got up and followed her. "Gini, what's wrong?"

She forced a smile. "Nothing, really. Nothing. Enjoy your dinner. I'm sorry, I just have to go."

The next morning, Jimmy helped Ric put his bags in the back of the car at the airport. His trip to the Bahamas had been long and busy. He was ready to be with Gini, just the two of them. The last he had talked to her was just before she went to dinner with Michael and Brenda. She wasn't sure when she was going to DC. Hopefully, they could have one day together. He had left several messages but hadn't heard back from her. He asked Jimmy to please take him to his house.

Michael arrived at Gini's building. He was concerned and wanted to make sure she was all right.

Howard called up to the condo and then led him to the elevator.

"Have a nice day, Mr. Fredrick."

Michael was shocked when Franco opened the door after he knocked.

"Michael Fredrick, as you live and breathe." They fist-bumped.

"I didn't know you were in town." Michael looked around. "Is Gini here?"

"I came in last night to surprise her, and take her to our place in New York City. She told me she was on her way home, but never showed. I didn't think to ask her where she was. I'm a bit worried about her."

"She was with me last night. You must have been the call she received. She left abruptly."

Franco put his hand on his mouth. "Do you think we need to call the police? She isn't answering any of my messages."

"Mine either. Let me see if I can't find her. Give me your phone number." Michael knew she was with Ric.

"Why are you here? And what was Gini doing with you last night?"

Michael didn't want Franco to get the wrong impression and had to think quickly to come up with something. "Ah, we had a meeting this morning for my new job, same as last night. I'll find her."

"Let me know when you do."

Franco knew the visit in San Francisco hadn't turned out well, but was Gini so angry with him she didn't want to see him? After all this time, didn't she want to be with her husband?

When he went back into the living room, the cloisonné box on the fireplace caught his eye. He wondered where she had gotten it; he didn't remember giving it to her. He opened it and saw the ring, took it out, and put it on his little finger, just fitting to his first knuckle. He smiled, remembering the story about the ring.

As Ric settled in the backseat, he got a call from Michael.

"Ric, do you know where Gini is?"

"No, haven't talked to her today. Why?"

"I was just trying to get hold of her. I'll keep trying."

Michael hoped Ric knew not to go to Gini's. Should he tell him? No, that was none of his business.

Ric could see Gini sitting on his porch steps when they turned down his street.

"Just put my stuff on the sidewalk." He ran up to her. "Gins, what are you doing here?"

She looked up at him with dull eyes.

"Have you eaten?"

She slowly shook her head. He reached down to pick her up; she pushed his hands away.

"Okay," he said half exasperated and half concerned. "Please, stand up so we can go inside."

As they went in, Jimmy followed, putting Ric's things just inside the door.

Ric quickly handed her a glass of apple juice, took off her coat, and started fixing her breakfast.

"Michael called and was looking for you."

"Franco." She looked at him; her face seemed almost lifeless.

"No, sweets, it was Michael. How long have you been sitting outside, and why? You have a key."

"Franco's at the condo. I don't want to go there. I don't want to see him."

"Gini, you didn't go home last night?"

"No, I don't want to be with him." She was vague, like a zombie.

"Okay." He sat her on the stool by the kitchen counter. "Let's get some food in you so I can make some sense of all of this."

"He can't just let himself into my place without asking."

"Gini, that's his home too."

"I pay for it; I live there."

"Sweets, here, eat. We'll talk when you feel better."

"I don't want to be with him." She looked Ric in the eyes. The food and juice were working; her shakes were almost gone.

"Tell him I was with Michael. No, I was with Catherine."

He rubbed up and down her back.

"He can't know about us. Tell him I'm not here, I'm in DC."

Her phone rang in her pocket. He pulled it out, the caller ID, Franco.

"It's him."

"I don't want to talk to him."

"Gini, he has to know you're okay. I'll tell him."

She grabbed the phone. "No!" She looked down. "I'll talk to him. Hello."

"Thank God, babe, are you okay? Where are you? I've been worried."

"I'm coming home."

"For sure this time?"

"Yes, I'll be there in a few minutes."

As they were talking, Ric got a call from Michael. "Ric, I don't know where she is. I'm going to call the police. She could have been in an accident."

"She's here with me. She's okay."

"Oh, good, that's so good to hear."

"I'm just back from a business trip. She was at my house when I arrived."

"Franco's home and looking for her."

"I know. She's talking to him now. I think she's going through some rough times."

"I'm glad she's okay."

Michael almost felt sorry for Ric. Franco was a nice enough guy, but Michael wouldn't like to see him angry. He could tell Franco still had some street in him.

Ric was glad he had decided to go to his place from the airport. It would have been more than awkward if he had let himself into her place with all his bags.

She put on her coat. "I have to tell him."

He grabbed his and followed her. "I'll go with you."

"No, *you will not*. I don't need you, and I don't need him. He needs to understand that."

"I'm not letting you walk in this cold. I'm going with you, and that's that."

"No, Ric! This is between him and me. He'll see you drop me off if you take me."

"I'll let you out a couple of blocks away."

Neither spoke while they drove. He pulled the car over to the curb, reached over, and wrapped his hand around her head and kissed her. They pressed their foreheads together.

"Gini, I love you more than anyone or anything I have ever loved." When he started to shake, he let go and sat back. "Please, let me know you're okay. No more staying out all night." He couldn't look at her.

"I'll text." She opened the door. "I stayed at the bed-and-breakfast down from the State House last night."

She got out, and he sat and watched her walk around the corner out of sight, her stride resolute, her dark curls vivid against her pale jacket. He hoped to God she wasn't walking out of his life.

"Ms. Anderson," Howard greeted her when she walked in the door. "Mr. Legotti—"

"I know, Franco's here." She walked, looking straight ahead, not at Howard.

She stormed in the door and set her bag on the breakfast bar. "You should have let me know you were coming."

"Gini," he said with a soft tone. "We need to get through this. We need to sit down and have a good talk."

His suitcase was sitting by the door, his coat rested on top, and his business bag leaned next to it. She walked past into the living room and sat down.

"How can you be out of my life for weeks, and then suddenly you write or call or show up?"

"I know." He couldn't tell her what was happening in China; he just could not bring himself to tell her. In some way, the whole scenario screamed failure. He had failed miserably.

"Okay, so let's talk." She sat with her arms crossed tightly across her chest.

"I have an apartment for us in New York. It's small, but we can find a bigger one to buy."

She closed her eyes; anger had tightened her throat.

He pulled out two train tickets from his pocket. "We have tickets for the one forty-five train."

"Franco, please leave." She turned her head away.

He walked over and stood over her. "Gini, please, come with me. I only have a few days. There was a problem in China; I have to go back one more time, and then I'm done. They are too hard to deal with. I'm closing the office there. We are looking into Central and South America. They need lots of water wells and treatments, and hopefully, they have friendlier governments. An office in New York City is well placed for both of us."

She finally opened her eyes and looked at him. Her arms were still tight across her body. "I live here. I work in Boston."

He didn't know what to do. She looked so distant—and so beautiful, and he wanted her. He reached out his hand. "Come, let's go to the bedroom."

"Franco!" she shouted. "Hot sex is not the answer to everything."

He knelt in front of her. "I love you."

She turned her head away again. "Please, leave."

"How are we going to resolve this if you won't talk to me?"

"I don't think it can be resolved."

He sat down on the couch and rubbed his hand across his eyes and on his forehead. There was silence for a long time. "Is there anything in there but anger? I used to think so. Come on, Gini, we're married. I love you, and you love me. I know me being gone for so long has caused you problems. I realize it's much worse than I thought... I wasn't paying enough attention. I promise you it wasn't my intent to be gone so long, but the Chinese are hard to deal with and... I just have to fix one more thing, and then I'm done over there."

She still wasn't looking at him.

He stood. "Okay. I'm going to go, but when I get back from China, I'm coming here, and we're going to live together and start our family."

"Live here?"

"We'll see. We'll talk about it when you are more willing to talk. The one thing I know is, I love you. And I believe you love me. So we are going to make this work."

He laid her ticket on the breakfast bar next to her purse. "I wrote the address for the apartment on the sleeve. I'll be there until Sunday. Please come and give it a chance."

He walked over to the fireplace, opened the box, and took out the ring. Then he went to her, kissed her on the top of her head, laid the ring on the table next to her, and left.

She pulled her knees up tight to her crossed arms and stared at the ring. The knotted kiss stuck out prominently from the shiny stone. Her body started to jump as the deep crying took her over.

"It was nice to see you again, Mr. Legotti," Howard said when Franco passed through the lobby.

"Howard. Don't worry, I'll be back soon."

Ric waited patiently to hear from her. At midnight, he went to bed, hearing nothing.

The next morning Gini went to the train station and headed to Washington, DC. She told Catherine she needed to get out of town. She needed space to think.

Ric finally broke down and texted her. She didn't answer. Then he called her; still no answer. Was she with Franco? Had they repaired their marriage? Was she wrapped up in his arms making love? It was too much to think about. He could only bury himself in his work. He needed to let her figure it out.

Two days later she texted him:

I'm with Catherine. Franco went back to China. Ric, I'm so messed up in my head. Sorry, just messed up.

I'm going to Val's tomorrow. Come with me. I'll stay in the house, and you can have the guesthouse if that's what you want. Just come. You know how relaxing it is there.

After a good night's sleep and a lot of coaxing from Catherine, she decided she would go to Florida. She needed to talk to Ric. There didn't seem to be anything right in her life. It was probably best if they just remained friends.

When he picked her up at the airport, she told him she wanted to be alone in the guesthouse.

201

"Okay, sweets." He gently brushed down her hair as he took his arm away from around her.

She leaned forward and put her head in her hands. "All I need right now is a friend."

"Gins, no matter what, we are always going to be friends. Come on, relax. You're in paradise."

That night they sat outside on the guesthouse patio and talked for hours. She told him about Franco wanting to go to New York, the apartment he had for them, and his promise that when he came back, they would live together and start a family.

"Is that what you want?"

"I don't know. My gut feel, he won't come back for good. Before long, he'll be gone again. Maybe I'm wrong; he seemed sincere, but I just don't feel like I can trust him anymore. And I don't want to live in New York City. My home is Boston. My life works so well from there." She let out a long breath. "He wants a family. Ric, I'm never going to be able to have a baby. I don't think he gets that. I'm tired, just tired of trying to figure this out."

He reached over and took her hand. He could see her struggle; there was nothing he could do or say to help her.

The next two days Ric and Val worked from dawn to dusk. Gini slept alone with only her thoughts for company. They were dark and confused thoughts. There she was again with Ric. Wasn't she ready to be rid of all men? Why did she keep running back to him? And Franco, she had told him to leave—just get out of her life. Did she mean it? Did she want to give up on their marriage? She felt like two or three different people, and which one was the real Gini? What if they all were? Was this what life was—never knowing if you're making a mistake, and with every choice losing something? Too many questions, and she had no answers.

When she did go out to the pool, she could feel Kat's eyes constantly on her.

The third afternoon Gini was sitting in a chaise lounge, reading. Kat came and sat in the chair on the other side of the small table. "You don't get it, do you?"

"Get what?" Gini asked.

"Only fools walk away from a good thing. Ricky is crazy in love with you, and yet you hold him off. Don't make a big mistake and let him go."

Gini looked back at her book. "You don't know."

"I know two things. One, he is in love with you, and second, you are in love with him. What else is there to know?" She got up and went back with her friends.

That night, the four of them, Diane, Val, Ric, and Gini, had dinner on the yacht while cruising the canal. After dinner, Gini walked to the rail. Ric joined her.

"It's so beautiful here." She looked at him. "I can't believe all the wonderful homes. Who has all this money?"

Diane joined them. She told Gini she should take the water taxi. It was a true taxi, and the driver gave a tour with details about the area and who owned the houses. She suggested she have Eduardo take her to the Hilton Hotel and catch the boat there.

At the end of the canal, they made a wide turn and returned to the mansion. Gini and Ric stayed on the dock, sitting in the lounge chairs, and watched the boats pass for a while longer. When they left, they went arm in arm to the guesthouse. *I know this man so well,* she thought. *It's so easy with him…*

The next days were relaxing and lazy. Gini had no problem falling into the slow pace. She did take the taxi tour and found the information interesting. After the cruise, she asked Eduardo to take her to a shopping area where she could buy more summer clothes. She walked along the streets of the small shops for several hours.

On Friday, Ric and Val got back to the mansion at lunchtime. Their workday was done. They enjoyed the afternoon by the pool. Diane and Val emerged about five o'clock, and Val said they would take his boat, *Dichoso,* down through the Keys on Saturday.

Gini was up and ready early to see the beautiful islands. The ride through the canal during the day was just as magnificent as it was at night. When they got out over the open water the wind blew up on her face, the vessel rocking gently from side to side with a slight chop. Suddenly, her stomach was in her throat. She jumped from her chair, leaned over the side of the boat, and heaved.

Ric took her to one of the bedrooms, and she lay down, but it didn't help. Val said they would dock at one of the islands to let her stomach settle. The gagging stopped, but once they were back at sea, her stomach emptied again. They turned around and went back to the house.

"Ric, I'm so sorry." She was lying on the bed at the guesthouse. "I wanted to see Key West so badly."

He wrapped his arm around her. "We'll fly down sometime. I just want you to be okay."

"I am."

He could tell she wasn't. She was still very pale.

Sunday, she felt better, but not completely well. They took it slow all day. On Monday, she returned to Boston.

The next week, some days she felt okay; others not so much. Maybe it was a stomach bug.

She returned to DC the following week after seeing Ric over the weekend. She and Catherine had a full schedule. They were going to a big committee meeting on Wednesday to present the report they had been working on for several weeks. Tuesday night they went to bed late. Gini was exhausted and still not feeling a hundred percent.

At 7:30 a.m., she leaped out of bed and ran to the bathroom and vomited. Then again at eight o'clock and eight-fifteen. Catherine heard her the last time.

"Gini, are you okay?"

"I will be, just give me a few. This damn stomach bug just won't go away."

She tried to eat, but it just came back up.

"I'm going; you're staying here," Catherine said. "I don't think anyone wants to get sick. You stay here and get well."

"I can do it. I can; I'm feeling better. We have worked so hard on this." Gini put her hand over her mouth and ran to the bathroom.

Catherine wiped Gini's face with a wet cloth. "Just be on standby in case I need you to look something up. Please, rest. You look awful."

"Thank you!" Gini laid her head back on the pillow and closed her eyes. All the trips to the bathroom had worn her out.

Catherine handled the meeting, and Gini started feeling better in the early afternoon. She felt fine on Friday and went home on Saturday. Sunday, the same routine, vomiting all morning—it was getting very old. She hadn't told Ric about any of it. He was busy traveling to Florida and Rhode Island. It seemed when they were together, she felt okay, but she never got rid of the sour stomach.

The weeks passed, and both traveled. They caught a day or two when they could be together, but most of their face-to-face time was on internet calls.

She was meeting with Victor's staff, so she pulled out a business suit, pulled up the skirt, and tried to zip it. When she got near the top, it wouldn't go any farther. She tugged, but it seemed stuck, so she pulled at the waist to button the button. She couldn't get it to reach. Her clothes had been fitting differently lately, but she thought nothing of it. How could she have gained weight? She wasn't eating all that much because if she did, it upset her stomach. She hung the outfit up and found another that fit.

On her way home from the meeting, it hit her. Could she be pregnant? No, that wasn't a possibility. But still… what else could it be? Before she got to the condo, she stopped and bought a pregnancy test. She felt a strange combination of anxiety and elation as she opened the package. She remembered how upset she got before when she wasn't pregnant. Was she going to go through all those feelings again? She loved Ric, but she had to end her marriage first. She had planned to find a lawyer, but then decided she'd wait until Franco came home. They'd work it out amicably, so it was a fair break financially.

No, no, she knew she wasn't pregnant. The doctor had made it pretty clear she would never conceive, naturally or with help. She wasn't surprised when she took the test, and it immediately indicated negative. Maybe that skirt had shrunk at the cleaners.

The next two weeks her clothes got tighter and tighter. It made no sense. She took three more pregnancy tests; two showed negative, and the third showed nothing, no indication either way.

One morning she woke up, stretched, and ran her hands down her body. There it was, she felt it, a hardness in her abdomen. She panicked. Maybe she had a tumor. She immediately called for an appointment with Dr. Nelson.

She explained she had gained weight, but the pregnancy tests showed negative. Dr. Nelson could see the panic in Gini's eyes.

"I think I have a tumor."

While the doctor was examining her, she massaged all around Gini's abdomen and smiled. "Honey, you *are* pregnant. By the size of your uterus, I'd say about twelve to fourteen weeks. Do you remember when you had your last period?"

"Really, pregnant?" She took in a breath. "I did, yes, I did have a slight period the middle of February. Some spotting and then, one day, a little bleeding. That was it."

"That would be about the right timing."

"Why didn't the pregnancy test show positive?"

"Sometimes if your hormones are off a little those tests don't work. They often show false positives, as well. Let's put the due date the first week in December."

Gini was given a prescription for prenatal vitamins and an appointment in a month. She smiled all the way home. *I'm going to have a baby. I'll be a mom.* She couldn't believe it. Her mind raced ahead, seeing herself grow large, feeling the baby move—in the hospital—the newborn in her arms, boy or girl didn't matter… how happy she would be… she would get a rocking chair, a music box that played lullabies, one of those baby slings to go to work in or maybe she'd take a year off; her child would have everything…

And she wouldn't tell anyone until she could tell Ric in person.

Three weeks passed and their paths never crossed. They talked every day, but not in person. He was in the Bahamas trying to work with the government to get that resort started. Gini spent hours on the computer, looking at cradles and strollers, reading about child development, cruising all the mom blogs, which were so detailed, so obsessive… what to eat, what not to eat while pregnant, how to soothe a crying infant, what danger signs to look for, how important her own instincts were; she felt as if a vast new world were opening up…

After working all day with Gini, Catherine closed her computer. "Okay, honey, we're going shopping."

"Shopping for what?"

"I think we'd better get you some professional looking maternity suits before you bust completely out of your clothes."

Gini smiled. "You know?"

"Hahaha, anyone who looks at you knows." She put her hand on Gini's tummy. "Have you told Ric?"

"No, I want to tell him in person. I want to see his true reaction." She threw her arms around Catherine. "Can you believe I'm pregnant? No way in the world did I ever think it could happen. I'm glad you know. It was killing me not to tell anyone."

That night Ric and Gini face-called. "Sweets, you look beautiful. You must have had a wonderful day."

Catherine yelled across the room. "We went shopping." Gini gave her a look.

"Well, shopping must be good for you. I'll be in Boston next Tuesday. Please tell me you will be there."

"Tuesday?" She looked at Catherine, who nodded. "Yes, I'll be there Tuesday. Oh, Ric, I can't wait. It has been so long since we have been together."

"I know, this long-distance romance is for the birds. Never again will we be apart for so long."

Monday morning, Gini was getting ready to take a shower. She looked down at her naked body. The bump that had been down in her abdomen had spread all the way up to her ribs. She rubbed all over it with her hands. She was going to have a baby, Ric's baby.

Tuesday morning, she was just finishing up the laundry when she got a text:

Just landed, see you soon.

She texted back:

> Will you text me when you get in the building?

Why? You aren't alone?

> Yes, I'm alone, silly; I have a surprise for you. I
> just want to make sure it's ready.

Okay, Jimmy's here.

Gini wore a flowing top, which hardly showed the baby bump. She would have towels in her arms when he walked in the door.

I'm here.

They greeted at the door, hugging and kissing with the three folded bath towels between them. He put his hands around her face.

"You're so beautiful."

"Ric, close your eyes."

He smiled and kissed her again.

"I'm serious, close your eyes. I have a surprise for you."

"Ooooh."

He closed his eyes, and she guided him to the breakfast bar and sat him on a bar chair. She put down the towels and took both of his hands in hers and slipped them up under her blouse.

"I love the touch of your soft skin."

"Okay, open your eyes."

He leaned forward and kissed her.

She moved his hands around on her tummy. He just smiled.

"Ric, look down." She pulled her top up.

He slowly went from looking into her eyes down to his hands, with a smile on his face. When he saw her tummy, his expression changed.

"Gins, you're... are you pregnant?" He looked at her.

She nodded her head.

"We're going to have a baby?"

She nodded again; her eyes were filling with tears.

He looked back down. "We're going to have a family?"

He looked up; now his eyes were tearing. He hugged her. "Life is good, so wonderfully good. How long have you known?"

They pulled back; he continued to rub her skin.

"Remember when I got sick on the boat?"

He nodded.

"Morning sickness. I finally figured it out when my clothes were getting tight."

"When? When is it due? Do you know what sex it is?"

"No. Due in December. I have a doctor's appointment tomorrow. Do you want to go?"

"Absolutely! Gini, we are going to be together. No more weeks apart. I can't stand being without you."

"I agree."

The next day they were in the examining room waiting for the doctor. Linda was surprised when she saw Ric standing next to Gini and holding her hand.

"Dr. Nelson, this is Ric Santini, the father."

"Hello, Ric. Congratulations. How are you feeling, Gini?"

"Really good. No more sickness."

"Let's take a look." The doctor did the exam. She moved the stethoscope all around, placing it in several spots, then moved it again as if listening for something special. Gini was getting concerned. Ric squeezed her hand.

"You've grown quickly," Linda finally said with a smile.

Gini relaxed.

"Let's take a look with a sonogram. We may be able to see if it's a boy or girl."

Ric felt a thrill run through his body. Margarita's pregnancies never were far enough along to determine the sex.

Dr. Nelson put the screen so they could all see it. She moved the wand all around, sometimes pushing in deep. Gini looked intently, but couldn't see anything that looked like a baby.

"Come on," the doctor said quietly, "turn around. Yes, it's a boy. See." She pointed to the screen.

"Ric, a boy!"

"I know, sweets, a son." He never looked away from the screen.

"He's big like his daddy." Linda continued moving the wand.

Sometimes the heartbeat was loud. Other times it sounded slushy, almost like there was an echo.

"Aha! Yes, I thought so. There's two. Look, you can see a small part of the head. She again pointed at the screen. Twins!"

"No," Gini said. "Ah... just no."

She looked at Ric in horror.

"Gins, instant family." He leaned down and kissed her and then smiled broadly. "Thank you, Doctor. Thank you."

She smiled. "I've done nothing here."

"We can't have twins. We can't. How will we take care of them?"

"Sweets, we'll hire help if we need to. Don't worry, you'll see, it'll be great."

The doctor never could get a good look at the second one for the gender.

Suddenly her excitement became tinged with dread. Before, she had sloughed off the fetuses, but now there were human beings who would rapidly grow inside her. Could her small body handle the growth and extra weight? Dr. Nelson told her the human body was amazing in how it adapted to drastic changes, especially a woman's body during pregnancy.

Both the doctor and Ric tried to ease her fears. She was a high-risk pregnancy, mostly due to her hypoglycemia—her blood levels had to be constantly checked. But because of the extra attention, if any issues came up they would be detected quickly and resolved. They made it sound like she was better off than the average woman. Nevertheless, she still had concerns.

She now, more than ever, wanted a divorce. It would be more complicated having to explain she was with Ric and they were going to have twins, but it was time. There was a small nagging in her head that she had slept with Franco. But there's no way the babies could be his if she'd conceived after the middle of February.

Chapter 16 – Family

When Franco got on the plane in New York, he was determined to be back in a week. He was going to save his marriage and be with the woman he loved.

When he walked off the plane in Shijiazhuang, he was met by two government agents and a military soldier holding a long rifle.

"What's going on?"

One of the agents took his arm. "Come with me."

Franco took out his phone and turned it on. He had one message from Luca:

There's a problem. I'm working on it.

They took him to a room, sat him in a chair, and took his phone. Franco had learned a lot of Chinese over the past few years, but he didn't understand the words they were spraying at him. What he did pick up was that the injured worker had reported negligence by Franco's company.

He kept asking for his lawyer but was denied. Finally, he convinced them to let his lawyer be a translator, but the two were never left alone.

The next day he was taken from the airport. They took him to a large concrete building in town and put him in a room. There was only a bed, toilet, and sink. It wasn't a jail cell, but Franco knew exactly where he was, the detention center. He had heard stories from other foreign businessmen about people being locked up for years, most of the time for nothing.

A couple of days later, he was allowed to talk to Luca. Luca told him he was working with the consulate to get Franco out of there. The worker had convinced the authorities that Legotti Engineering had cut corners on the equipment, not using the proper parts, and that Franco especially was at fault, always rigging something up.

Ms. White and Ms. Anderson were well known, called "The Sisters of the Children." Catherine's wit and Gini's bright smile and blue eyes made the pair very popular with the talk shows.

Ric and Gini went to Florida together as often as they could, and he followed her when she was invited to speak at various functions. She had concealed her pregnancy as long as possible. It was now apparent to all that she was going to have a baby, and there was no doubt Riccardo Santini, the dashing entertainment manager, was the father. They were seen together everywhere in Boston.

One afternoon in Florida, Gini took her reader and went to the pool. Her two-piece top held her breasts tight and pushed them up; the bottoms slung low below her belly. She sat in the chair, closed her eyes, and enjoyed the warmth of the sun all over her body.

"I told you you'd get fat if you ate so much."

Gini recognized the voice. She turned to Kat and smiled. "Yes, you did warn me."

"I assume you're pregnant."

"Twins."

"And I suppose they are Ricky's."

"Yes, again."

Kat sat looking at Gini for a few minutes. Gini closed her eyes again.

"May I touch them?"

"Touch? My tummy?"

"Yes."

Gini reached over, took Kat's hand and laid it on the baby bump. The slim brown fingers adorned with rings and long shiny nails decorated with vibrant colors slowly moved over the pure white skin.

"Beautiful." She reached over with the other hand and rubbed around and then sat back. "I want to be you. I want a man to look at me like Ricky looks at you. I want a man that would do anything for me, anything. And I want to have a family. You're the lucky one." She got up and walked back to the food table.

Gini grabbed her cover-up and followed her. She picked up a plate and filled it with food, then went and sat at the table with Kat.

"There's no reason you can't have it all. You're beautiful with your long slim body and exotic eyes. Valentino seems happy with the situation. Doesn't he want a family?"

"Oh, no. He made it quite clear, no children." Kat lowered her head. "I've had one abortion; I won't have another."

Gini reached over and put her hand on Kat's shoulder. "Then leave. Go find the life you want."

Kat took hold of Gini's hand. "You're sweet. But I have nowhere to go."

Ric and Val walked out the back door. Kat immediately jumped up and went to him, but stopped almost as quickly when she saw Diane was with them.

When Gini asked Ric about Valentino and Diane, he told her Val had wanted to marry her. She was a widow with children and grandchildren, and not interested in being married, wanting her freedom. They had been together for several years, and Ric knew Val was deeply in love with her.

"And what about Kat?"

"Eye candy, bed partner, that's all. He doesn't, and probably never will, love her."

"That's so sad for Kat."

Dr. Nelson wanted to see Gini weekly. Her hypoglycemia was in check, but Linda had concern because the second child, a girl, was much smaller than the boy. She seemed to be developing okay, and none of the tests showed any problems. Perhaps the two were just going to be built like their parents, one tall, the other petite.

Gini went to her next doctor's appointment alone. Ric was in Rhode Island.

"Gini, I think I'm going to move your due date up. I'm a bit conflicted, but I think you are probably three to four weeks further along than we first calculated. I'm going to say November fifteenth, with conception the last week of January or the first week of February. Were you sexually active then?"

She sat and thought for a moment. She and Ric had been together since November, so yes, she was sexually active. Franco—oh no; she had slept with him right after her mother had died in January.

"Are you sure? I remembered having a period the middle of February."

"Yes, that's why I'm conflicted. You said it wasn't much of one, right?"

"My periods are all different."

"I think you had a small bleed caused by the pregnancy. Your body was trying to slough off the embryo. I'm going to put November fifteenth as the due date."

On the way home, Gini continued to recall when she and Ric had been together. Not before they went to California, because she was sick, and not for some time after because she needed time to figure things out. No, there was no way these babies were Franco's. She wasn't going to let that happen. She and Ric were the parents, and they would be married once Franco signed the divorce papers. Franco had said he was going to try to save their marriage, but once again she had heard nothing from him for a couple of months. Obviously, being together wasn't a priority for him. She just needed to approve the final draft, and then send the papers to him.

The thought of the babies being Franco's continued to nag at her. How cruel that would be—like some fateful punishment for her adultery. No, she didn't believe in that sort of thing. People did this all the time. They fell out of love; they found new love. She wasn't being singled out for anything, and just going by the science, how likely was it? *One night.* She worked at her denial, convincing herself there was no way the babies could be his. When she told Ric about the due date, she didn't voice her concern. He didn't know she had slept with Franco.

She sent a message to Luca:

> I'm sending this directly to you since I know you will read it to send on to Franco. I need to know where the best place to send some papers is. They are important, and Franco needs to see them as soon as possible. I know he has a lawyer here in Boston, should the papers go there? Thank you so much for your help. Virginia Anderson

That night she received an answer:

> Mrs. Legotti, yes, please if you could have the papers delivered there in Boston, that would be best. They could get lost or hung up if you send them here. Luca.

The last thing Franco had told Luca was to be sure and not let Gini know where he was. He didn't want her to worry. There had been no progress on getting Franco released. The fact that Franco confessed he had rigged the motor that drove the hoist to lower the workers into the well hadn't helped. He tried to reassure the Chinese government that the motor was working properly at the time.

His room was kept clean, and he was given three meals each day. But sitting or lying on the bed all the time only gave him more time to worry. At first, his thoughts were of what went wrong. He needed information on what was happening. Why was no one talking to him? He hoped Luca was able to get all of the company's important papers from the job site and back to New York.

He had learned from Mama Elizabeth that being truthful and honest was the best way to live his life. And look where he was now. He had told the truth, and he had only rigged the hoist because the country kept stealing his parts and he needed to finish the job.

He hadn't had a visitor for some time. Was he going to rot in this room? They wouldn't keep him here forever, would they? No, that only happened to political prisoners or maybe people nobody would miss. They were making a point with him—that was all. China was a global nation; they couldn't afford to treat an American businessman too badly.

His thoughts were mostly of Gini as the time went on. He'd lost count of the number of days he'd been there. He'd hoped that Luca had broken the news to her gently and reassured her not to worry. He was getting a bit panicked that he'd never see her again, hold her in his arms or kiss her soft, plump lips. How he longed for her. What a great mistake he had made starting his own company, out of greed, really, wanting more money for himself. And where had it gotten him? In detention with no communication with anyone.

There was a lot of debate on the health-care bill for children. Items and terms were added and then taken away. Gini and Catherine were continually in conversations with politicians, doctors, and hospitals. Gini always looked forward to any time she could spend in Florida. Rosa was like a Mother Hubbard, making sure she was comfortable and well-fed. Kat was constantly reminding her she was fat, but in a funny, caring way, and Val was so happy for both her and Ric. He had become very affectionate, loving her like a daughter.

Ric and Gini together told Maria and Victor about the pregnancy and that Gini had filed for a divorce. They were happy for them and wanted only the best for Ric and his new family.

Ric and Gini decided they would name their children Jason and Jennifer.

It was September. Gini and Catherine were guests on a popular Boston talk show. Ric was waiting for her in the wings. Gini had fully blossomed out in front.

At the break, the show host called to the producer. "Let's get Santini out here."

"He hasn't been in makeup."

Ric looked up from his computer.

"We need him out here. Everyone wants to know about him and Ms. Anderson. Besides, he doesn't need makeup. Look at him!"

Gini looked at Catherine and blushed.

"Okay, Mr. Santini, please."

Ric walked onto the set and was placed between Gini and Catherine.

They were back on the air.

"As you can see, Mr. Riccardo Santini has joined us. We're all dying to hear about you two. Are there wedding bells in your future?"

"Someday," Ric said.

"Right now, we are just preparing for our children," Gini said, looking at Ric with a big smile.

"Are you taking time off?"

"Yes. My boss," she looked at Catherine, "has given me a few weeks off."

"And where will you live, Florida, Washington, DC, or here?"

"We'll split between Florida and Boston," Ric answered.

"We are thrilled for you both. Please, come on the show to announce your wedding."

A few weeks later, the door opened to Franco's room, and Luca and two other men rushed in.

"Come on," Luca demanded. "Let's get out of here before they change their minds."

They all rushed out of the room to a black car with a US insignia on the door.

Luca told him the ambassador had cleared them all to leave the country. The Chinese government had fined the company a hefty fine but decided there had been no criminal act, only neglect. Luca had all the company's important papers in a pouch in the car. Once they were on the plane heading to South Korea, he gave Franco an envelope.

"The last time I was in New York City, I was given this to you from your wife. She said it was important, so I thought you would want to see it right away."

Franco had tried several times to call Gini and let her know he was on his way, but each time the call was cut off before it went through; his phone must have been blocked. He decided to surprise her by knocking at their door. He took a deep breath and smiled. His wife, he was finally going to get to see her. He opened the envelope and saw the divorce papers.

That Saturday, Ric and Gini were cleaning up the breakfast dishes. She was carrying the last of the plates from the dining room table. He was rinsing and putting them in the dishwasher. The landline rang at the same time the front door opened.

Franco rushed in, furious. "Gini, what are these divorce papers?"

"Mr. Santini," Howard announced on the phone to Ric. "Mr. Legotti is on his way up."

"Franco!" Gini said, her rounded belly prominently visible in front of her.

"Oh my gosh, babe, you're pregnant." Franco's voice immediately changed to a caring tone. "Why didn't you tell me you were pregnant?" He walked toward her, putting the envelope with the papers on the breakfast bar.

"Franco, no, these are not your children."

"Children, there's more than one? You used our embryos." He stood in front of her with his hands on her shoulders.

"No, Franco, please," she sobbed. "No." She collapsed to her knees.

Ric ran from the kitchen and knelt next to her. "Enough! You need to leave."

"Ric? What are you doing here?" Then he realized what he was seeing. "You and my wife? What's going on?"

"Gini's pregnant with my children," Ric said, looking Franco squarely in the eye.

There was a split second where nobody moved, then Franco stepped back, his hand jabbing out and his voice rising. "I know those are my kids, and you will not steal them or her."

"No, no, no," Gini was hysterically crying. He had wanted a family for so long. What if they were his children? She cried harder. Could she take them from him? Franco could be the father; Ric could be the father. What a horrible mess she had made of all their lives. She should never have cheated on her husband.

Ric took the plates from her and set them on the floor. "Franco, this is not the time. Please leave. Can't you see you're upsetting her?"

"I can tell you one thing: there will be no divorce. I know those babies are mine; I demand a paternity test." He turned and walked to the door, then faced them again. "Santini, I would have never guessed you'd steal my wife. You were supposed to be a good guy. I can't goddamn believe it. You haven't seen the last of me." He slammed the door behind him as he left.

He swiftly walked through the lobby, not acknowledging Howard's comment. *How could she?* he thought. His fists were clenched. Ric, his best friend ever. Who could you trust in this world? *I thought she loved me.* The stab of pain was unbearable, and he found his thoughts turning back to anger, back to Ric. *He's not going to get away with stealing my wife. He probably thinks because he's some big-shot lawyer at a fancy firm he can scare me with legal papers, but I've learned a few things myself over the past years. I'm not going to be taken again! That son of a bitch is not going to take my wife or my kids. If things have to get rough, so be it.*

When he got back to his car, he yelled and cursed and cried like a baby. How could she disgrace him like this? He was crushed and felt powerless. All that time in prison, so lonely and scared, he'd dreamed of her… of her love and kisses—of starting anew—and all the time she was sleeping with another man, planning a life with him. It was a double betrayal, the classic wife-and-best-friend, the worst, the sort of thing you see in movies. How could it happen to him? He couldn't take it in. It felt like the shock was too big for his system.

And Gini pregnant. The pain rolled over him like a killing wave, and again, he turned to anger. Neither would get away with it. They would pay.

He was going to check into a hotel and then make his plan to do whatever needed to be done to get Ric out of his house and Gini back in his life. But sitting in the car at a stoplight, in a confused state, he decided to go home to New York City. He needed time to think.

"Sweets, come on. You need to calm down."

"They're not his babies." The saliva was pouring from her mouth, and she was shaking. She bent down toward the floor.

"Gini, it's okay. Please, stop crying; I won't let anything happen to you or the babies. Please, stop crying."

He helped her up and took her to the couch. She lay in his arms. Her sobs slowly lessened to a whimper. He caressed her and held her tight. Having never seen anyone so upset, he feared for her and the babies' health.

After a while, she stopped crying. He continued to smooth her hair.

"Ric."

"Yes."

"I slept with Franco in San Francisco. I did." She let out a cry. "I'm married to him." That was her justification.

He closed his eyes and put his head back. He figured they had been intimate, but that was a long time ago. It never crossed his mind that the babies could be Franco's.

"I'm sorry, Ric. I should have told you."

"Shh." He pulled her close to him and put his face close to hers. "We'll figure this out. Please, just calm down."

She eventually fell asleep.

Ric called Dr. Nelson to tell her of his concern since Gini had cried so hard.

"Franco is here," he said.

"I know. I got a call from him demanding a paternity test. I told him he would just have to wait until they are born."

She told him to watch Gini; she would probably be all right, but Ric should call her if they needed anything.

Franco had given Linda an earful about what good friends he and Ric had been in the past, like brothers. And how disappointed he was in both Ric and Gini. She was used to patients' emotions—parents who didn't agree on what to do about a fetus with deformities or were afraid of multiple births, even pregnant women who found out they had cancer and had to choose between treatment and their babies… she was used to talking through those tough issues with people, but this was a new one. She shook her head. She felt for Franco but hoped the babies were Ric's. Custody battles were agonizing.

A few hours had passed. Ric sat on the couch thinking, then paced the room. He felt like a schoolboy who had been caught in a criminal act. He loved Gini with all his heart and had never thought what it would do to Franco when she asked for a divorce. Had deliberately not thought about it, he admitted to himself. Had hoped somehow Franco didn't care that much—that his absences

217

meant his feelings were fading… No, he knew better. He just hadn't wanted to imagine it.

Now he did. He thought of himself in Franco's shoes. How devastated he would be. He should have been a man a long time ago and talked to Franco about his love for Gini. They had both thought there was time… time to be sure (though he'd been sure right away), time to settle into their love and make plans. *But nature doesn't care about plans,* he thought. In any case, the damage was done and now they would all have to work through what seemed to be an impossible task.

Gini's phone on the breakfast bar rang. She was still sleeping soundly in the bedroom. The caller ID showed Franco.

"Hello," Ric answered.

There was silence. Franco thought about hanging up, but he wanted to speak to his wife.

"Ric, I want to talk to Gini."

"You really upset her. I was afraid she was going to hurt the babies or herself. She's sleeping, and I'm not going to wake her."

"How could you, Ric? How could you be with my wife? I thought we had more respect for each other. I thought we were friends."

"Franco, I'm sorry you're hurt. I know that sounds like a lie, or not enough, but it's the plain truth. I don't want you in pain. What happened was that I was lonely, and Gini was lonely. You shouldn't have left her alone for so long. I promise you, neither of us intended to fall in love."

"So it's my fault. She… is… my… wife. And where is yours, where's Margarita?"

"We divorced a couple of years ago. I don't think there's a right place to put blame."

"You're free, so you steal my wife." Franco was furious. "The blame is on you! I blame you, Santini. You stole your best friend's wife. I hope you can live with yourself. Gini will be mine and back with me as soon as I figure this all out. Believe me, I'm going to make your life miserable." He hung up and threw his phone hard at the bed.

Surprising himself, Ric wasn't sorry anymore. Not after that phone call. It wasn't about him and what he had done wrong—it was about Gini. Franco's jealousy, however understandable it might be, made him dangerous to Gini. Ric's only concern was for her. He would protect her from Franco if he had to. He wasn't afraid of him—never had been. He had just always wanted there to be peace.

The next week there were several conversations about who had fathered the babies. Gini was so concerned and constantly upset. She wanted to find out now, and she couldn't bear it that attempting to do that was far too dangerous—trying to get a tissue sample could cause a miscarriage.

"Sweets, this is the last time we are going to talk about this," Ric said. "As far as I'm concerned, those are my kids. It doesn't matter who the birth father is. I love you, and I love them. We'll deal with Franco if we have to now, or wait until after they are born. But now you need to clear your pretty head and stop worrying. I love you, and I'm not going anywhere. I promise."

In the morning, Gini was still lying down. Ric knelt down next to the bed.

"I'm out of here. Sorry, I can't go for a walk with you this morning. Why don't you just rest today?"

"No." She pulled herself up into a sitting position. "I need to walk, and I want to do it before it gets too hot."

He handed her a small bottle of orange juice. "You know I'll just be across the Parkway in the Two International building. I can see the Towers from there."

"I know. I'll be fine. I'll probably just walk to the garden and back."

He leaned over and kissed her on the cheek and put his hand on her bulging belly. "Take good care of the kids."

Just then an elbow or a knee rose up under Gini's skin. "Ow," she said with a giggle in her voice. "Man, that hurts! Say goodbye to Daddy and calm down."

He kissed her tummy and rubbed until the fetal limb moved back away from the skin.

"I'll text you when I start my walk." She took his hand and kissed it. "I love you. Have a good day."

He leaned over and kissed her on the lips. "I love you too. See you probably late afternoon."

"Okay." She slid back down to a horizontal position.

Ric was meeting with the architects for the new resort in Lauderdale-by-the-Sea. He was working with a great team, and everyone seemed on board with all of Ric and Val's ideas. The plans were drawn up and then Ric reviewed them with Val.

Ric hoped he and Gini could go to Florida one more time before Dr. Nelson told her no more air travel. However, he knew her added weight and size were making Gini miserable. It was up to her if she wanted to travel to Florida again before the babies came.

Just getting out of bed and dressing wore her out. It was especially hard to put on her walking shoes. The chore was much easier when Ric was there to put the tennies on her feet and tie them. She didn't mind, though. She was excited about raising their son and daughter together. Her moods shifted back and forth, but today she was certain the babies were Ric's. They just had to wait a little longer, then it would all be fine. Once Franco knew the babies weren't his, they would be divorced, and she and Ric would live happily ever after as a family of four—maybe more. Gini smiled as she rubbed the sweat off her forehead. She needed to eat and walk before the temperature got any higher.

She picked up her PET. There was a text from Catherine:

Call me when you can, Mama.

Gini touched the call icon.

Catherine was cheerful. "How's the little mother doing today?"

"I'm good. I'm not all that little, though. I can't believe how big I'm getting. It seems every day I spread out more and more." Gini rubbed on the large roundness, like a basketball sticking out in front of her. "What's up?"

"Listen, honey, do you think you could come to DC tomorrow? Just for the day. I have a meeting with Senator Jones, and you know how he has an eye for you. You can persuade him much easier than I."

Gini took in a deep breath. "Sure, I can probably come for the day or perhaps overnight. Maybe Ric can come, too. He seems pretty busy, but it would be nice for just the two of us to get away one more time together. I'll talk to him and let you know when we'll be there."

"Good, I want to see that big belly of yours."

"I can honestly say, I won't miss being pregnant."

"I thought every woman felt so special when they were with child."

"Maybe at first, but I'm getting really uncomfortable now."

"Can't wait until tomorrow to see you."

Gini walked to the elevator and went down.

"Ms. Anderson," Howard said. "What a lovely day it is. Are you walking alone this morning?"

"Yes, Ric had to work."

"I saw him earlier. I see your family is growing inside you."

"Bigger and bigger every day." She walked past the counter. "I want to get out and back in before it gets too warm."

"You have water?"

"Yes, have water and juice."

"Don't go too far, and rest if you get tired. You have my phone number?"

Gini laughed. "I have your number, and I promise I'll rest along the way. I love looking at the flowers and the butterflies. I'll be fine, Howard, thank you for your concern."

"Yes, ma'am. Always looking out for my people."

Gini went out the doors and turned toward Long Wharf. She texted Ric:

I'm just leaving.

When she got to Central Street, instead of going straight to Waterfront Park, she turned left to go to the Parkway. The gardens between the two lanes of traffic were always planted beautifully. She hadn't been to those gardens this year. Once she was on the grounds, she strolled along. The flowers were outstanding. She cupped one into her hand, leaned over and took in its wonderful fragrance. There were a few other people around her. The traffic was much lighter now that the freeway was underground. The city was completely opened up without the raised lanes and bridges. Gini lost all track of time. She sat down on a bench and watched two young children running in and out of the spurting water from the fountains; their giggles were music to her ears. *Soon I will be hearing my own kids laugh.* The sound of the water and surrounding foliage drowned out the noise of the city. She closed her eyes and breathed in deep breaths of air.

When she opened her eyes, a couple was sitting next to her. The woman was also pregnant, but not as far along as Gini.

"Beautiful day," the man said.

"Yes, I could stay here all day and watch the birds."

Gini looked at her watch. She had been gone almost an hour. "Enjoy yourselves." She got up and started back to the condo.

She had walked a couple of blocks when her phone rang.

It was Ric. "Just checking up on you."

"It's so nice in the gardens; I've let the time get away from me. I'm about a block from the condo."

"I had a few minutes' break, so I thought I would talk to my beautiful girl."

Gini smiled. "When you get home, I need to talk to you about tomorrow."

"Okay, sweet Gins. I shouldn't be late. Things are moving right along. Love you."

"Love you too."

Gini stepped up to the corner of India Street and Atlantic Avenue and waited for the walk light to change. She could see the Harbor Towers across the way.

Suddenly, there was a screech of tires. An SUV ran straight into a motorcycle, broadsiding the bike. The SUV careened off to the right and ran into the light post, breaking it. The pole bent down and crashed on top of the SUV. The motorcycle flew into the air; the rider went up and then down hard to the pavement. He lay lifeless on the road. The bike came down and went end over end toward the sidewalk, knocking Gini back into the cast-iron bench at the garden's edge. Then it continued further, mowing down an elderly man walking with his daughters. It next went sideways, hitting a couple of more people, and rolled over the couple who had been sitting next to Gini on the bench earlier. It finally came to a stop on top of the other pregnant woman. All of this happened in a split second. No one had time to get out of the way of the motorbike.

Chapter 17 – Life Changer

Two businessmen ran to Gini. She was bleeding from the back of her head.

"She's pregnant," one man said. He took off his jacket and rolled it up, then carefully lifted her head and put it underneath.

"Can you help us," one of the daughters cried out.

The other businessman ran to help them with their father.

The first man called 9-1-1. "There are several hurt, seriously hurt." He could hear cries for help from others in the park.

Gini didn't move; blood slowly trickled down the sidewalk. The man picked up Gini's small bag. Inside he found her cell phone smashed and her ID, Virginia Legotti. Stuck to her driver's license was an appointment card for Dr. Nelson.

A fire EMS truck pulled up next to her. They were at the stoplight going the other direction.

"She's hurt real bad," the man said. "Here's her ID and doctor."

"You know her?" the first responder asked.

"No."

The EMS tech thought Gini looked near full term, and she was bleeding from between her legs.

"Permission to take a pregnant patient with head trauma to New Haven Med Center to her doctor," the EMT said into his radio.

There were sirens everywhere. Several other ambulances came from all directions.

"Permission granted," the radio dispatcher said.

The two EMTs quickly got Gini on the gurney and into the back of the EMS truck and sped off with sirens blazing.

The scene became a mass of activity. Ambulances, fire trucks, policemen, and media started pouring into the location. People were lining the streets to see what was happening.

"Wow, something big is going on down there," one of the architects said.

Ric slowly walked over to the window. "Looks like a car accident."

"I can't believe all the emergency vehicles."

They both walked back to the table and continued working on the plans.

"Dr. Linda Nelson," she said into her phone.

"We have a patient of yours onboard," the EMT said. "Virginia Legotti. We are heading your way, five minutes out."

"Is she in labor?"

"No, ma'am, she has been involved in a vehicle accident."

"I'll meet you in emergency."

"Roger."

"Karen," Dr. Nelson said. "Come with me down to emergency."

The two women left Dr. Nelson's office. Just as they entered the hall to the ER, Dr. Robert Young walked up beside them.

"Robert," Dr. Nelson said.

"Dr. Nelson, you heading to emergency?"

"Yes, one of my patients was in a car accident. They're bringing her in."

"My patient, too."

Linda turned and looked at him. "The patient has a head injury?"

"Severe brain trauma and bleeding."

The three turned the corner and walked into the emergency area. The two doors to the ambulance bay were being held open by two medical personnel; the sound of a siren was getting closer and closer. It was good they were taking her to New Haven. It was renowned for its neurology department.

The truck backed into the bay, and the bed was lifted out of the back.

"She's bleeding from the back of the head," the EMT reported. "There's brain matter on the jacket put under her. We've bagged her. The babies are still alive, but I believe they are severely hurt. We were first to the scene and got away from there quickly. Hopefully, in time to save her life."

Dr. Nelson, Dr. Young, and Karen were all running alongside the gurney as the EMT described Gini's condition.

"Get her into a surgery bay," Robert instructed.

It was determined Gini needed immediate brain surgery to stop the bleeding. As soon as they could stabilize her brain, the babies would be delivered by C-section.

"Karen, contact Ric and Franco. Tell them Gini is in critical condition, and they need to get here as soon as possible, especially Franco. He'll need to sign forms."

"Yes, ma'am."

"Mr. Legotti, you have a call from a Dr. Nelson's office," his assistant announced. "It's parked on line three."

He reached over and picked up the line. "Linda?"

"No, sir, this is Karen, her assistant. Dr. Nelson has asked me to tell you Gini has been involved in a serious accident. She's in surgery, brain surgery, and quite frankly it doesn't look good. You need to come as soon as you can so you can fill out some paperwork."

"What did you say?" He sat up straight. "Gini's having brain surgery?"

"Yes, sir, at New Haven Medical Center. That's New Haven, Massachusetts, about five miles west of the Boston Commons."

"I know where New Haven is. You're sure?"

"Mr. Legotti, I'm very sure. She's in critical condition."

"And the babies? Has she had the babies?"

"No, sir, they were alive last I heard. It was more important to take care of Gini first."

He paced the floor talking to himself. "I'll get a helo; yes, that's what I'll do. I'll fly to New Haven in a helicopter. You have a landing pad there?"

"Yes, sir."

"I'll be there soon."

Ric was surprised when his phone rang and the caller ID showed Dr. Nelson's office. He quickly checked his watch for the date.

"Hello, we didn't miss an appointment, did we?"

"No… Mr. Santini, Dr. Nelson wanted you to know Gini has been involved in an accident."

"What! No, you're mistaken. I just talked to her a little while ago, and she was fine."

"I'm sorry, sir, but she was in a car accident and is in critical condition here at the Medical Center. Dr. Nelson wanted me to inform you."

"How in the world could Gini be in a car accident? And how would she be in New Haven? She wasn't driving today. She went out for a walk, that's all."

"An ambulance brought her here. She's in very bad condition. Dr. Nelson just wanted you to know."

"Okay, I'll, umm, I'll come to the hospital."

"What's going on, Ric?" the lady architect asked.

Ric looked curiously at his PET. "I don't know. I need to take a few minutes and find out."

"Take all the time you need. I think we're done for now."

He called Gini's cell phone. It immediately went to her voicemail.

"Gini, call me."

He quickly went to the elevator and dialed the house phone. After six rings, it went to the message. Then he called Howard.

"Harbor Tower one, Howard speaking."

"Ric Santini. Have you seen Gini?" He was breathless.

"Yes," Howard said smiling. "She went out for her walk. She's blossoming out, in a good way."

"Did you see her come back?"

"Let me think. I've been busy with paperwork this morning; there's always correspondence of some kind to work on. I can't say that I saw her, but she could've come in when I wasn't looking."

"Thank you, I'm heading home."

"Very well, sir."

There was a horrible feeling in Ric's stomach as he ran out of the building. The street was still blocked by all the emergency vehicles. He ran across where he could and then back behind the buildings to the walking path along the water. How could Gini be in a car accident? It just didn't make any sense.

When he got to the condos, he ran through the lobby. Howard wasn't at the counter.

"Gini," he called out when he opened the front door. There was no answer. "Sweets, please be here."

He ran back to the bedroom. The bed was made, but there was no Gini. He put his hand on his forehead. "NO!" he cried out. "Please, no."

Ric ran out of the condo and down to the garage. He raced out onto the street, driving farther on down so he could get on the freeway and out of town. The Parkway was still bottled up.

He went through the emergency room doors.

"Can I help you?" the nurse behind the counter asked.

"I'm here for Gini, Virginia Anderson. Dr. Nelson said she was brought in by ambulance."

The woman looked on the computer. "You said her name is Virginia Anderson?"

"Yes."

"We don't have anyone here by that name."

Ric took in a deep breath. They were wrong; she wasn't there. He relaxed.

"You said Dr. Nelson contacted you."

"Yes, but she must have been mistaken."

"Well, a patient named Virginia Legotti was admitted over an hour ago for Dr. Nelson and Dr. Young."

"Yes, yes, that's her. Virginia Anderson is her professional name. Please, I have to see her."

"I'm sorry, sir, how are you related to Mrs. Legotti?"

"I'm—" He wasn't sure what to say—related? "She's my girlfriend and the babies…" He stopped and looked down. They didn't know if he was the father or not. Calling Gini his girlfriend seemed awkward; she was so much more.

"Okay, what's your name?"

"Ric; my name is Riccardo Santini."

"Thank you. You can wait in the waiting room, Mr. Santini."

"No, I need to know what's going on."

"I'm sorry, sir, but my records show that her next of kin is her husband, Franco Legotti. He's the only one I can talk to about her. You're welcome to wait in the waiting room."

Ric went to a widened hall that was lined with chairs and sat down. Across from him was a small table with thermoses of coffee, cream containers, individual sugar packets, and a stack of paper cups. Above the table was a TV hanging on the wall.

He put his elbows on his spread knees, and he ran his fingers back through his wavy black hair. This couldn't be happening. How could Gini have been in a car accident? The Waterfront Park had no streets, and the walk from the condo was along a street that had very little automobile traffic. It was mostly filled with tourists visiting the aquarium or walking on Long Wharf. She wasn't driving; she was walking. None of this awful nightmare was logical. He sat back in the chair, took a deep breath, put his head back, and closed his eyes.

"It's a mess down here on Atlantic Avenue."

Ric heard a man talking. He opened his eyes and realized it was the news reporter on the TV and recognized the scene. It was the accident he had seen from the office building.

"We unofficially have been told that there are four dead. The motorcyclist who was broadsided by the SUV was pronounced dead at the scene. The driver and passenger of the SUV were also killed, as well as a pregnant lady who was walking in the park. We haven't heard if the baby died or not."

Ric stood up. No, they couldn't be talking about Gini. Oh, my gosh, could she have been walking in the gardens on the Parkway? No, no, they never walked to those gardens. He put his hands on his head and continued to listen to the reporter.

"There are also several injured. All have been taken to local hospitals. The streets have been closed in this part of Boston for an investigation. Again, we have heard a man, the motorcycle driver; the woman driving the SUV and her female passenger; and another woman in the park, who was pregnant, have all been killed. We will continue to get updated information so stay tuned."

It is Gini, he thought. That's the only way any of this madness made sense. Surely they would have told him if she had died. But they would have to notify the next of kin first, Ric remembered from his law days. On record, that wasn't him. He slowly sat back down in the chair.

Two EMTs walked out of the double doors and stopped at the coffee table. "I see there's still a mess there," one EMT said to the other. "I just hope we got the mother here in time to save the babies."

Ric was alerted. The EMTs' radio blurted out a sound. Both men dropped their cups into the trash and ran toward the door. Ric stood up and started after them, but they jumped into their truck and took off. He was certain they were the ones who had brought Gini to New Haven. They would have been able to tell him if she was still alive.

He stopped and then went back to the chairs. He felt so hopeless, so worthless.

It seemed like time had stopped, but also like he had been in that waiting room for hours. He was numb, completely numb. Then he heard a familiar voice behind him. It was Franco.

Franco had called a friend of his who owned a jet-propelled helicopter. He flew up and down the East Coast for the police. Franco just grabbed his briefcase and had Jeff pick him up on the roof of the building where his office was. It only took them about fifty-five minutes to get to the hospital. Jeff knew the right contacts to get okayed to land on the hospital roof.

"I'm here for Virginia Legotti." Franco took his driver's license out of his wallet and placed it on the counter.

"Mr. Legotti, we have been waiting for you. I have some paperwork for you to fill out."

A million things had gone through Franco's head on the trip. They said it was bad—how bad? Once he started reading and filling out the paperwork—guardianship—he knew it was serious. He took a deep breath.

Ric walked up next to him. For a second he felt anger, then it just disappeared. Yesterday he would have killed Ric if he'd had the chance—not literally, but he was very hurt by his *so-called friend's* actions. But now he needed someone close, someone he loved, to help him understand what was happening. *Oh good*, Franco thought. His best friend. He put his hand on Ric's shoulder for a moment and then went back to the paperwork.

"How's she doing?" Franco asked the receptionist.

"She's still in surgery. They have delivered the babies. As soon as they can, the doctors will be out to talk to you."

Ric felt a rush of relief. The news report was wrong; the pregnant lady from the park hadn't died.

"Good, good. I want her and the babies to have the best care." Franco tried to keep calm; they were all going to be okay. He continued to fill out each sheet as the nurse handed him the papers.

When he was finished, the nurse instructed him to wait in the waiting area. The two men sat down.

"I'm glad you're here, Ric." Franco put his face in his hands and wiped down. "It's weird, huh? But I need you. I need my friend." He reached over and put his hand on Ric's leg. "I've been upset with Gini—and you, for that matter— but I certainly didn't anything to happen to her." He turned and looked at Ric. "You are my best friend, for God's sake, and so is she. How can this be happening?"

"I should have been with her," Ric said, his voice shaking. "I always walked with her just for this very reason, so I could protect her. But I had to work this morning." He sat back and looked up. "So she went alone."

Franco realized this was just as difficult for Ric as it was for him; both were in shock, suffering the same sorrow. Franco had the urge to call family, but who? If only Mama Elizabeth were still living. She'd know how to comfort both him and Ric. She'd take care of all three of them, just like the old days. They needed each other. "Honestly, Ric, if Gini was going to be with anyone else but me, I'm glad it's you." Franco patted his leg again. He wasn't good at comforting people; he could see his friend was hurting deeply—feeling responsible. What could he say or do to ease his pain? The words blurted out, "Don't beat yourself up too much. You didn't know. How would you know?"

Dr. Young and Dr. Nelson had finished the surgeries and together were going to talk to Franco. They were notified he had arrived and filled out all the paperwork. He was now Gini's legal guardian since she wasn't capable of making decisions.

Just before the doctors walked through the double doors, Linda held out her hand to stop Robert.

"Before we go out there, I have to give you some information."

Robert was puzzled.

"See those two gentlemen sitting next to each other? The stout one is Franco, her husband. The tall one is Ric." She stopped and thought how she could best explain the situation. "Ric and Gini are living together. We don't know whether he or Franco is the father of the children. It's a complicated situation. Both men love her very much."

Robert looked again through the small window in the doors. "I can only talk to her husband. That's hospital policy."

"I know, but since they are together, I just wanted you to know the situation. Believe it or not, Franco told me they are—were—best friends."

"Well, let's get this over with. I hate this part of the job."

The two doors swung open, and the doctors walked into the waiting room. Ric saw Linda first and stood up. Franco immediately followed.

Robert walked to Franco. "I'm Dr. Young, your wife's neurosurgeon."

Franco shook his hand.

"Let's step into this private waiting room, so we can talk." Robert looked at Ric. "I'm sorry, sir, due to hospital policy, I can only talk to her next of kin."

"No, no," Franco said quickly. There were grim looks on both of the doctors' faces. He couldn't face this alone; he just couldn't handle what was surely more bad news. Besides, he knew Ric loved Gini as he did. They were too close to let anger come between them, especially now. "Anything you have to tell me, you can tell Ric. This is Riccardo Santini, a close family friend."

"You're sure?" Dr. Young asked.

"Yes, I'm positive."

The four walked into a small room with six chairs.

"Please," Robert motioned with his hand, "take a seat."

Ric sat closest to the side wall. Franco sat next to him, and the two doctors sat directly across from the men.

"First," Robert started, "I'm so sorry for what has happened to Mrs. Legotti. She has sustained a serious wound to the back of her head. From what I understand, she was hit, as a pedestrian, by a motorcycle that was propelled into the air when it was broadsided by another vehicle. Unfortunately, your wife was in the wrong place at the wrong time. She was thrown into a heavy metal park bench. Part of the bench impaled her skull and severely damaged the lower brain lobe on her left side. There's also damage to the lower right lobe. Brain matter was lost."

Ric turned toward the wall and started rubbing his mouth with his thumb and forefinger.

"What does all that mean?" Franco moved forward in his chair.

"Mr. Legotti, basically what it means is your wife won't recover from this injury. Her quality of life has been significantly altered. She'll be in bed the rest of her life on life support."

Ric lowered his face into his hand with his fingers on his forehead.

"Does she have a living will?"

"A living will?" Franco repeated the question.

"A request to not be kept alive by artificial means."

"No," Franco said emphatically. "No living will."

"Then you may want to consider—" Robert started to say.

"Are you going to say pull the plug?" Franco said, very animated. "No way am I going to kill my wife. If Gini doesn't want to live any longer, she's going to have to die herself. I'm not going to pull the plug."

"I know this is a difficult decision, and this all happened so suddenly, I'm sure it's hard to get your head around it. You don't have to make the decision right now. But I hope you will give it real consideration. She'll have no meaningful life."

"Listen to me, Doc. I will not kill my wife."

Ric said nothing, his fingers back to his lips. Robert had observed Ric's deep feelings. He could tell he was strongly attached to Virginia. It was hard not to reach out to him, but that wasn't his job. He could only deal with Franco.

Ric turned, facing straight. "Dr. Young, I'd like to be with Gini, if I may." His voice was quiet.

"Yes," Franco said in a louder voice. "I want to be with her."

"Dr. Nelson needs to speak with you. As soon as she's done, I'll give them instructions so you can be with your wife."

He paused for a second. Then he turned to Ric. "I'll tell them you may see her, as well."

"Thank you, Dr. Young, thank you for all that you have done."

The doctor stood up. Ric immediately stood and shook his hand. Franco did the same without getting up.

"Ric," Dr. Nelson instructed, "please, sit down."

He sat back down and looked at Linda. He knew the news she was about to give them wasn't good.

"We delivered the babies." She looked at her watch. "About two hours ago. They're small, two months-plus early. I believe Jason took a direct hit protecting his sister. Jennifer is especially tiny."

She stopped and reached out a hand to both men; Ric immediately took one. She laid her other on Franco's knee. "They aren't going to make it. It's been just too much for them. I have ordered a paternity test. We'll have the results in the morning."

A tear ran from Franco's eye. Ric squeezed Linda's hand and then lowered his head.

"If you want to hold them, you can. They're both still alive, maybe holding on to meet their father."

Franco quickly wiped his eyes.

"Yes," Ric said moving to the front of his chair. "I want to hold them."

Linda led the two men to the neonatal ICU. The two babies were wrapped in blankets, not hooked up to any machines. Ric went over and looked at the two infants lying next to each other. He first picked up Jennifer. She nearly fit in the palm of his hand she was so small. He held her up and kissed her on the forehead.

"Hello, sweet girl."

"You can rock her if you like," the nurse said.

Ric sat in the rocking chair. The nurse pulled the tiny knitted cap from her head. She had dark curly hair. Jennifer made a little squeaking sound and then sucked her lips. The dimples went deep into her cheeks.

"You have dimples, just like your mama. She loves you so much, sweet girl, so much."

The nurse unwrapped Jennifer so he could see her whole body. She was petite and fair-skinned like Gini. Jennifer threw up her arms and legs. He quickly wrapped her back up. The baby started coughing, and he could tell she was having a hard time breathing. He pulled her close to him, stroking her cheek with his finger.

"I love you, Jennifer."

He rocked her for a few minutes, knowing she had stopped breathing.

Franco only stayed in the room for a few minutes and then walked to the hall. Dr. Nelson followed him.

He leaned back up against the wall and slid down to a squatting position. "My whole life is being taken away."

Linda was watching him carefully to make sure he was okay.

Ric handed the baby to the nurse. He went to Jason and picked him up. He was small but not as fragile as Jennifer. The nurse took off the baby's cap after Ric sat back in the chair. His hair, skin, and eyes were dark. Without the cap, Ric immediately saw that Jason looked just like Franco. There was no doubt; these babies had been fathered by him.

He pulled Jason to him and kissed him on the cheek. "I know your mommy would love to hold you. She has wanted a son for so long."

The nurse unwrapped the baby. Ric smiled at Jason's stout body, just like his dad's. He wrapped him back up and held Jason in his arms. "I love you." He kissed him again.

He rocked Jason for a while and then handed him to the nurse. "I can't have another one die in my arms."

"I understand," the nurse said taking the baby. "They are handsome children."

Ric went out into the hall. "Franco, you need to go hold Jason. You need to hold your son and your daughter."

"I can't; it's just too much. Ric," he looked up with tear-drenched cheeks, "we've wanted children for so long. I just can't bear the thought that they will die. I can't hold them. I'm losing everything dear in my life."

"This will be your only chance. They're so sweet, Franco. Don't miss your chance."

Franco put his hand on his head. "I can't."

"I just heard from ICU," Linda said. "You may visit Gini now."

Franco stood up, and they all left the nursery. When they got to the ICU floor, Dr. Young met them and asked them to step into a room surrounded by glass. He looked at Linda. She shook her head, indicating the babies both had passed on.

"You'll need to sign in at the nurse's station," Robert said. "And sign out when you leave. You may both go in and see her for a few minutes one at a time. I'll see about getting you on a schedule tomorrow. You can touch her, just don't interfere with any of the monitors or equipment. And you can talk to her. It will help you feel close to her, and she'll sense your presence. I've had patients tell me after they came out of comas they heard their loved ones and could feel their love. She isn't going to look like herself. Her face is swollen, partly due to the injury, partly due to surgery. She has two cracked ribs and a sprained wrist. We think she might have a fractured hip. We'll check that later. We have stabilized the leg. She's not in pain."

The room was very quiet.

"Mr. Legotti, come with me, please," Dr. Young requested.

Franco stood up, rather hesitant, and followed the doctor to the nurse's station.

After he signed the clipboard, Robert took him to Gini's room. Franco got no farther than the end of the bed and gasped. The male nurse attending Gini turned and looked at him.

"Bruce," Dr. Young said. "Bed pan, please."

The nurse quickly handed Franco the pan; he threw up. The nurse took a wetted towel to him. "Are you okay now?"

Franco handed the nurse the pan. "I can't be in here." He turned to the door.

"It's okay," Dr. Young said.

They both went out when the door automatically opened.

"I'm sorry, I just can't see her like that."

"Thank you for letting me be with the babies," Ric said to Dr. Nelson in the glassed-in room, waiting his turn to see Gini. "They were so sweet. Jennifer tugged at my heart. She looks so much like her mom. I wish Gini could have seen them."

There was no need to tell the doctor Franco was the father. The test results would confirm that in the morning. It didn't matter. Ric had loved them before he knew, and he would always love them as his own.

"You're welcome. I hope it helped you find some solace."

"It did. I just wish Franco could find the same peace."

Dr. Young motioned for a nurse from the nurse's station to take Franco into the restroom.

Robert walked to the waiting room. "Mr. Santini, you may see Mrs. Legotti now."

Ric followed the doctor to the nurse at the station.

"You'll sign in and out here every time you come into the ICU. Tomorrow when you come, go to the main entrance of the hospital. They'll give you a wristband, then come up here and sign in."

After Ric filled in the information, the men went into Gini's room.

Ric walked to the opposite side of the bed from the attending nurse. "Sweet Gins, what have you done?"

He picked up her hand, leaned over, and kissed her on a spot on her cheek that was clear of any tubes, wires, or electronic connection pads. "I love you, Gini."

Robert reached over and moved a rolling stool over to Ric.

"Gins, I held the babies. They're so precious. Jennifer looks just like you. Believe it or not, she has dimples deeper than yours. And Jason, oh, Jason, you wouldn't believe how strong he is. I wish you could have held them. They are really special."

There was a moment of silence. Ric was still holding Gini's hand. He stroked the fingers of his other hand gently down her cheek.

"Sweets, I know you have been through a terrible ordeal. And I know you are hurt really bad. If you want to go with the twins, I understand. But if you want to live, then fight. And if you're willing to fight, I'll be right there with you, all the way."

He lowered his head, and there was silence in the room. Robert felt like Ric was praying, so he said nothing.

Linda met Franco as he came out of the bathroom. "Are you okay?"

He took in a deep breath. "I didn't expect her to look like that."

"I know it's a blow. Tell me what I can do to help."

"I need a place to stay tonight, and I'll need a vehicle tomorrow."

"Let's go down to admin. They keep a night staff. I'm sure they can help you. If not, I'll help you find a room and a car."

Dr. Young and Ric walked out of Gini's room.

"Thank you for letting me see her. I appreciate it."

"There's a small chapel down near the main hospital entrance if you're a spiritual man."

"Thank you," Ric said. He shook the doctor's hand.

When Ric walked into the chapel, he saw Franco in the second pew kneeling with his hands folded in front of him, his head bent down. He walked to the front and sat next to Franco. He closed his eyes and laid his hands one on top of the other in his lap.

Dr. Nelson was sitting in the back. She was very concerned about Franco and wanted to make sure he got safely where he was going that night. Reverend Gilbert walked in the door.

"Dr. Nelson," he whispered.

She smiled. "Thanks for coming."

"I was in the hospital."

Linda explained the situation with Ric and Franco, and how Gini was hurt, how the babies died. "These two men are best friends from what I see. Even though I believe they were at odds over Gini, I can see their friendship is still strong."

"That is fortunate," the reverend said.

"We don't know who fathered the twins. We'll know tomorrow."

Reverend Gilbert walked to the front of the chapel and stood in front of the two men. Franco had pulled himself up on the pew and sat almost in a daze, staring at the cross hanging on the front wall of the chapel.

"Good evening," the reverend said. "Well, I guess it's way past evening. I'm Reverend Gilbert. I'm here to help you find peace through our Lord."

Both men acknowledged the reverend.

"Dr. Nelson has told me of the babies and their mother. I would like to say a prayer."

The men agreed.

"Dear Lord, please take those precious little souls into your hands and lead them into heaven to live an eternal life in your love. They are so innocent yet so full of your spirit. Be with their mother and guide her through her trials and tribulations. Put your healing hand on her heart so she may know you are always with her. And light the path for her to follow. We trust in you, Dear Lord, for all you are. Help these men understand their love for the babies, the mother, and themselves for this will surely comfort them. And hold the bond of their friendship tight and everlasting. Let them seek forgiveness, so they may heal their broken hearts. We ask this in the name of your Son, Jesus Christ, who gave his life for us. Amen."

"Amen," Ric said.

Franco began to shake with grief. Ric reached over and around his friend then gently rubbed up and down his arm. Franco pulled his handkerchief out of his pocket and quickly wiped his face.

"Is there anything I can do for you?" the reverend asked. "Have arrangements for the babies been made?"

"No."

"I would be more than happy to help with that. We have a wonderful funeral parlor here in New Haven. It has been family owned for many years. They are good people. I can set up an appointment for you tomorrow."

It was agreed.

"Give me your contact information, and I'll get back to you with the time."

Ric pulled a business card out of his small case in his pocket. He took a pen and underlined his cell number. Franco put out his hand, open palmed, to Ric for the pen. He took Ric's card, and on the back, he wrote his name and cell number. Then he handed the pen back to Ric and the card to the reverend.

"Thank you for your help, Father," Franco said. He got up, knelt before the cross, and moved his hand to his forehead and across his chest. Then he walked to the back of the chapel to Dr. Nelson.

Ric stood up. "We appreciate your help and thank you for the beautiful prayer, Reverend Gilbert. I think it touched both of our hearts. Please, keep Gini in your prayers. I don't want to lose her. I love her so deeply."

"I'll keep her in my prayers as I will you and Mr. Legotti."

Linda took Franco to the administration office.

"I'd like to stay somewhere close," Franco said.

"There's a nice hotel just across the town square," the woman behind the desk said. "Would you like me to get you a room there?"

"Yes, please."

"They'll arrange a rental car for you as well."

"Do they have a restaurant? I think I need to get some food in my stomach."

The woman turned. "Adam, are there any restaurants open this time of night?"

"I don't think so."

"Not even the bar at the hotel?"

"They close at midnight."

"I'll call down to the cafeteria," she said smiling. "They'll bring something up."

Ric walked up beside Linda.

"Ric, they're bringing food for Franco, do you want something?"

"No, thanks. I'm going back to Boston. I need to sleep."

"Okay, drive carefully."

He walked over to Franco. "Listen, why don't you stay at your condo." His voice was weary.

"They got me a room here in town. Where will you stay?"

"I'm going back to my house." He patted Franco on the shoulder and then left the hospital.

Robert walked out to the nurse's station.

"Are you going to be here all night, Dr. Young?" the nurse asked.

"I'm heading home. I just wanted to make sure Mrs. O'Brien was settled for the night. My two patients seem to be holding their own for now. Please, page me if either of their conditions change."

"I will. I think it's been a long day for you."

"Yes, I can live without days like this."

Ric couldn't sleep. He was up early and out the door. He walked up to the nurse's station in the ICU at seven-ten.

"May I help you?" a nurse from behind the counter asked.

Ric saw her name tag, Debbie Pierce, RN.

"I'm Ric Santini, here to see Gini, ah, Virginia Anderson, please."

Debbie looked at the patient list. "We don't have a Gini Anderson," she said in a clipped tone.

She leaned over and put her purse under the counter in a drawer.

"I'm sorry, I meant Virginia Legotti."

"I don't see your name either."

Another nurse came in and sat down. "Go tend to your patients, Debs; I'll help him."

"Let's start again," she said with a pleasant smile. "My name is Lisa. How can I help you?"

"I'm Ric Santini. I would like to visit Virginia Legotti."

"Yes, sir."

Lisa looked at the list of visitors permitted to see the patients in the unit. She turned to face the small room behind the desk.

"Debbie, is Dr. Young in yet?"

Debbie walked out of the room with a handled box with medical supplies in one hand and folded towels in the other.

"He's in his office. He'll be down in a minute."

"I'm here," Dr. Young said, coming up to the station.

"Good morning, Doctor," Lisa said.

"You're here early, Mr. Santini."

"I couldn't sleep. I'd like to be with Gini."

Debbie walked past, giving a disapproving look toward Ric.

"Go ahead and sign in. Lisa, put Mr. Santini down for visitation fifteen minutes in the a.m. and fifteen minutes in the p.m. Also, add Mr. Legotti for fifteen minutes each."

After Ric signed in, Dr. Young led him to Gini's room. The doctor held his badge to a sensor panel, and the door slid open. Debbie was talking to the night nurse, Bruce, in Gini's room.

"How can you be so cheerful after a twelve-hour shift?" Debbie asked.

"Twelve hours? I've been here for sixteen. Debbie, this is the best time of the day. The sun is rising, the birds are singing, and the air is fresh and clean to start a new day. How could you not be happy? And besides, now I can have a nice hot cup of coffee, and no one will interrupt me."

The two continued to sign over the patient from one to the other.

Ric walked to the side of the bed and took Gini's hand.

"Debbie, let's start with Mr. O'Brien and give Mr. Santini some private minutes with our patient here."

"Let me finish the check-off list, and I'll meet you in Mr. O'Brien's room."

Dr. Young and Bruce left the room together.

Ric took Gini's hand. He leaned over and kissed her cheek and then sat down. "I hope you had a better night's sleep than I did, Gins." He paid no attention to Debbie. "I missed holding you in my arms sleeping."

Debbie took the check-off list with her and left the room. She walked to the station and exchanged the list for the check-off list for Mr. O'Brien.

"Isn't he the most gorgeous man you have ever seen?" Lisa asked. "In his three-piece suit, crisply ironed shirt, and beautiful tie?"

"Oh, Lisa," Debbie said giving her a look.

"He can visit often and stay long," Brian, the other nurse at the station, said. "He must be a model. He looks like he just walked off the cover of one of those Hollywood magazines."

"Stop," Debbie said walking away. "Both of you."

Debbie walked into Mr. O'Brien's room and started the check-off list. Dr. Young was examining his patient.

"I'm sorry to see him in here again," Debbie said.

"I think you had a busy day yesterday." Debbie laid the tablet on the rolling table. "What time did he come in?"

"Midmorning." Robert checked Mr. O'Brien's eyes. "Right eye clear and reactive. Left eye widened pupil."

Debbie wrote the information on the electronic patient record. She picked up Mr. O'Brien's hand.

"And Mrs. Legotti?" Debbie asked.

"She arrived a little before noon. We were in surgery for over six hours."

"Wow, I'm glad I had the day off."

"Lucky you." Robert smiled.

"When did you go home last night?"

"I guess it was around one o'clock when I got to my place."

"Such dedication."

She wrapped Mr. O'Brien's fingers around her hand with her palm up and then straightened his fingers. The elderly man's knuckles were knobby and bent.

"You are aware you could take a day off now and then."

"Who would take care of my patients?"

"I can see why you are still single."

"I don't see you with a family and being a stay-at-home mom."

"Well, at least I'm in a relationship."

Mr. O'Brien groaned and reached up and grabbed Dr. Young's upper arm.

"Good morning," Robert said.

The older man acted frightened and confused. The left side of his face sagged. Robert patted his hand.

"It's okay, Mr. O'Brien," he said in a soothing voice. "Remember, you're in the hospital. We are taking good care of you. Your favorite nurse, Debbie, is here."

The man slowly turned his head and looked at her.

"Mr. O'Brien, can you give me a squeeze?" She leaned close to his face and smiled. "Just a little squeeze," she repeated.

The man closed his eyes.

"It's okay; we'll try again later." She looked at Robert and shook her head.

Ric was softly running his hand over the top of Gini's left hand. Her usually long beautiful nails were chipped and broken. Her knuckles were scraped and bruised, and her thumb was swollen, black and blue.

"I'd give anything if we could go to Lazy Daze Spa today, anything in the world."

Ric heard the door swish open just as his cell phone vibrated. He reached into his pocket and took out his phone.

"You can't use those in the ICU," Debbie said curtly.

He put the phone back into his pocket.

"Your fifteen minutes are up!"

Ric stood up still holding Gini's hand. He leaned over and kissed her on the cheek. "See you this afternoon, sweet Gins." He kissed her hand and laid it on the bed.

"Thank you, Ms. Pierce, for taking care of Gini," he said sincerely. "You just don't know how much I appreciate it."

"That's fine." She didn't look at him.

The door swished again, and Dr. Young walked in.

"I think this isn't such a good time to visit," Ric said to Robert.

"We encourage loved ones to visit when they can. We know you must go on with your lives so we try to be as accommodating as we can. But the 7:00 a.m. shift change tends to be a little busy."

"I'll come later tomorrow."

Dr. Young stepped into the room, and Ric left.

"Debbie, you seem a little hostile toward him."

"He's just a pretty boy." She walked to the bed. "It took him two tries to get her name right. He won't sway me with his charm and good looks. Who is he, anyway?"

"We'll talk about it later, but don't be too quick to judge."

He leaned over and looked at Gini's eyes, lifting each of her eyelids open. "No change." He let out a breath. "I hope I can convince her husband to let her go. This will be her life from now on. Surely, he doesn't want this for her."

Debbie could see the compassion in Robert's eyes and knew what he was talking about. Machines were needed to keep her alive.

Ric went to the nurse's station to sign out. "Is there somewhere I can use my cell phone?"

He was directed to the glassed-in room.

Ric checked his messages. He saw one from Reverend Gilbert telling him the meeting at the funeral home was set later in the morning for nine o'clock. He messaged back that he would be there. He had some time to kill. He needed to make some phone calls since he had told no one what had happened.

After Robert and Debbie had finished examining Gini, they walked out to the nurse's station.

"Has Mr. Legotti come in?" Dr. Young asked.

"No, sir," Lisa said. "Who is Mr. Santini?"

"Just so we can nip the gossip in the bud here," Robert said. "Virginia is married to Mr. Legotti. However, they must be separated because she's living with Mr. Santini. I don't know the particulars. The twins she lost were fathered by one of the two men, presumably, and the paternity test results should be in this morning. I want to make it clear to everyone Mr. Legotti is still her husband and, therefore, he's legally her guardian at this point, and our contact. We do not discuss her condition with anyone else unless otherwise advised. We'll treat this case with discretion and respect and provide privacy just like we do for all of our patients."

"That goes without saying," Lisa said.

"Please page me when Mr. Legotti gets here," Robert asked.

Dr. Young went to finish the rest of his rounds.

Debbie went into the small room behind the station.

"If I had to choose," Lisa said, "I'd choose Mr. Santini."

"Lisa," Debbie said coming out of the room. "You haven't even met her husband." She stopped at the counter. "It's hard to believe that young woman could be a harlot. Mr. Santini's quite charming. Probably gets whatever he wants. He won't sway me."

"Oh, Debs," Lisa said smiling. "You need to lighten up."

Ric's first call was Carol.

"Ric," she answered with a yawn in her voice.

"I didn't wake you, did I?"

"Heavens no. I'm on my way to the office. Are you in this morning?"

"Carol." There was silence.

"Ric, everything okay?"

"No, it's Gini."

"What about Gini? It's too early for her to have the babies. Ric, please, tell me."

"Gini was badly hurt yesterday. She has a serious head wound."

"Oh no, Ric!"

"We lost the babies last night." He rubbed his head, and there was a lump in his throat. "And I think I'm going to lose her too."

"Ric! How did this all happen? You aren't hurt, are you?"

"No, no. She was involved in that accident on Atlantic Avenue."

"Oh, my gosh!" There was silence again. "They did say there was a pregnant lady, but they said she had—" Carol stopped. "Ric, please tell me where you are. I need to be with you."

"I'm okay, Carol. I won't be in today."

"Of course not."

"I have to take care of some things. I have a meeting with the funeral home at nine for the babies' burial."

She couldn't bear it any longer. She started weeping. "Tell me what I can do? *Anything*, Ric, tell me what I can do."

"Just keep the business going. I don't know what I'd do without you and James, all of you there really. They should be delivering the drawings today. Just put them in my office."

"Okay. Do you want me to call Val?"

"No, he thinks a lot of Gini. I want to tell him myself. Will you tell everyone in the office for me?"

"Of course. Ric, please keep in touch. I'm worried about you."

"Thank you, Carol, you're a good friend, but I'm okay. I just want to stay close to Gini. I'll call you again."

"Ric, we all love you. I'm so, so sorry."

He put his phone down on the couch and took in a deep breath as he stared out the window. Next, he called Victor.

"Good morning, Ric. I hope it's just as beautiful a day in Boston as it is in DC."

"Victor, I'm calling with bad news."

"Oh?" He put his phone on speaker and laid it on the table so Maria could also hear. They were eating breakfast.

"Gini was in an accident yesterday. The babies were delivered early, and they passed away last night. She's in critical condition with severe brain damage. I don't think they expect her to live. It's out of my hands. Franco, her husband, is in control of her destiny." Ric stopped to catch his breath.

Maria had her hand over her mouth. "Oh, honey, I'm coming to Boston, so I can be with you. I'll catch the next train or plane."

"Maria, please don't. I'm okay."

"You're not okay. I can hear it in your voice. You're devastated."

"I am, but please don't come. There's nothing you can do right now."

"You take care of what you need to do," Victor said. "And you let us know how we can help."

"I will. I just wanted to tell you before you read it in the newspaper."

"Thank you for calling us," Maria said. "We love you."

"I know, and I love you."

He had to make one more call. He had to call Val.

"Val, this is Ric."

"Reek, I trrrust you meeting with the arkeytects went well."

"Yes, yes, it went well." Ric stopped. Could he tell the story one more time? "Val," he started. "Gini." He stopped. The words were stuck. He cleared his throat and then told Val what had happened.

"No, mi chica. You must brrring her to Fort Lauderdale. I will hire thee best doctors in the world. Brrring her here."

"She can't travel. She has a wonderful team around her here. But thank you for the offer. You might want to hire someone else to help with the project. I'm not sure if I'll have time to work on it for a while."

"Eet eeays ok, Reek. We can poot it aside for now. You take care of mi chica, Geenay."

"Thanks, I will."

He put his phone down. With his face in his hands, he started to cry. Dr. Young returned to the unit and saw Ric in the room. He gently tapped on the door and walked in.

"Rough morning!"

He sat down and put his hand on his shoulder.

Ric nodded his head. "I've been calling friends."

"That's always hard. I'd be glad to help."

"Thank you," Ric said taking his hanky out of his pocket. "I think I've called them all."

"Does Mrs. Legotti have other family in town?"

"No," Ric said, breathing deep. "They're in Sacramento. I suppose someone should tell them."

Robert could see Ric was weary. "Give me their contact information. I'll call them. I also need to have her employer's number so I can find out her insurance coverage."

"Gini works with Catherine White in Washington, DC." He took out his wallet, went through a small stack of cards, and handed the doctor Catherine's.

When Ric arrived at the funeral home, Reverend Gilbert came out to the parking lot to greet him. Once inside, they sat down.

The receptionist walked to them. "Reverend."

"We are waiting for Mr. Legotti. This is Mr. Santini."

"We're ready for you when Mr. Legotti gets here. Please, help yourselves to the coffee and donuts." She turned around and went back to the reception desk.

"Have you heard from Mr. Legotti this morning?" the reverend asked.

"No. I've been at the hospital. I didn't see him there."

The two men sat without conversation. The reverend looked at his watch at nine-fifteen. Ric was aware of the reverend's impatience. About fifteen minutes later, Franco walked in the door talking on his cell phone.

"Okay, good, thanks for the quick work. I'll talk to you later." He walked over to the two men.

The reverend stood and shook Franco's hand. "I'm sorry I'm late. I had to take care of some important business."

"Please wait here for a moment," the reverend said. "I'll let them know we are ready."

"I had to make sure the press didn't get a hold of the news," Franco started. "I don't want anyone to know about Gini or where she is. The paparazzi will have a field day with this, and the hospital will constantly be bombarded with reporters. That won't be good for Gini or Dr. Young."

"You think they'd do that?"

"Yes, Gini is a celebrity in her own right. She's very well revered and respected. What did I read about you two in the *Globe*, the '*Power People* of Boston'? I have my people out there checking it out. So far, they don't even have Gini on the injury list, and they have reported all the victims are in Boston hospitals. Hopefully, it will stay that way. Anyway, she's here under Virginia Legotti, and she isn't known publicly by that name. But I guarantee you, if the press gets a hold of this, they'll find out who she is."

The reverend walked back into the room. "If you will follow me."

He introduced Ric and Franco to the funeral director.

"Please be seated," Mr. Thompson said. "First we need some paperwork signed to release the babies' bodies from the hospital." He put a piece of paper in front of Ric and one in front of Franco.

Ric picked up the release form; Jennifer Virginia Santini. He looked at Franco. Franco's release was for Jason Thomas Legotti.

"I think there has been some mistake," Ric said. "The babies were twins with the same mother. They would have the same last name."

"Oh, dear," the director said taking back the papers. "There must have been some clerical error at the hospital. I'll have my assistant take care of this. But since you're here we can take care of the funeral arrangements, and we'll get the paperwork straightened out if that's okay with both of you?"

"Yes," Franco said, "that will be fine." Ric agreed.

They were told of the different types of services and shown the caskets. Ric and Franco decided the babies should be buried together in one coffin. They picked the top-of-the-line white with brass trims. There would be a small memorial service in the hospital chapel at Ric's request. At least Gini would be in the same building even though she couldn't attend.

"How much?" Franco asked as he pulled his checkbook out of the front pocket of his coat. Ric let Franco take the reins. He seemed insistent on being in charge. And Ric knew, in the end, it would be determined that Franco was the father.

Ric's phone vibrated just as Franco signed the check. It was a voicemail from Dr. Nelson.

"Here you go," Franco said. Then Franco's phone buzzed.

They each had a message that the test results were ready and to please come to Dr. Nelson's office.

"Dr. Nelson," Karen said. "Both Mr. Santini and Mr. Legotti are here to see you."

Linda smiled. Why didn't that surprise her? She went to the waiting room door. "Which one wants to be first?"

"You might as well tell us together," Franco said. He stood up, and Ric followed.

Once they were all in her office, she sat behind her desk. "It's probably best you are both here together. We have a very unusual case here. Ric, you're the father of Jennifer and, Franco, you're Jason's father." She handed each the paperwork for the DNA test.

"The funeral director's papers were right," Ric said quietly.

"You've seen the paperwork?"

"At the funeral home making arrangements this morning."

"I didn't know you had an appointment this morning. I wanted to tell you the results first."

Franco sat, stunned. "How can this be? How could she have both of our children at the same time?"

"The medical term is superfetation. She was already pregnant with Jason when a month later she ovulated and became pregnant with Jennifer. It's a rare occurrence. Gini's ovulation has always been very irregular. I was concerned that Jennifer was so much smaller than Jason. Now, I know why."

"This is unbelievable," Franco said still staring at the paper. "I had a son. Gini and I had a son." He looked at Ric. "I was sure those babies were yours. We tried so many times. I just figured I was the one keeping us from being parents. I just knew they were yours."

Ric felt a wonderful warmth inside. He had felt such a connection with Jennifer when he held her in his arms, *his* daughter. He had kissed her and seen her sweet dimples. He was so glad he had met her; so glad he had the chance to hold her. If only Gini could have held her children. It wasn't fair.

When the two men left Dr. Nelson's office, they went to the coffee shop. They decided they would still bury the two babies together with both of their names on the headstone.

"Ric, is the offer for me to stay at the condo still on the table?"

"Please, go stay there. I couldn't sleep last night, so I went over and took all my things out of your place. I don't think I can go back there again. There are just too many memories, too many."

Ric looked at his watch. It was eleven fifty-eight. "Oh, good, I can go visit Gini. Have you been in to see her today?"

Franco was reading something on his phone. "I haven't made it up there this morning. Listen, Ric, I need to make a call." Franco got up and walked out of the coffee shop.

Chapter 18 – New Haven Medical Center

Debbie put all the supplies together to bathe Gini. She held up Gini's hand. Her nails were jagged and cracked, with soil and blood under and around the edges. She lowered her hand to the bed and carefully unwrapped the bandage from Gini's head. A long section of dark curly hair fell to her shoulder from under the bandage.

"I don't know why if they are going to cut the hair off, why they don't get it all," Debbie said out loud as if in a conversation with her. "I think they must have been in a great hurry to save your life. You're going to get the full Debbie Pierce beauty treatment special today."

She went to the tall rolling table, looked through the drawers until she found a razor. Both the handle and the blade were sealed in sterile packaging. She took out the two pieces and attached the blade. She soaped a cloth and then rubbed the suds all around the section of hair and shaved it off; the long curls lay in her hand.

"You must have had a beautiful head of hair. Don't worry, baby, the hair will grow back." Her voice was soft and caring.

Debbie continued to examine the rest of Gini's head. She looked at the surgery incisions. Everything looked good. She could see where the skull bone had been removed. Probably later, a custom helmet would be placed on Gini's head. She carefully put on new bandages.

Next, she sterilized nail clippers, scissors, and a nail file, then cut and shaped each nail, removing any debris from underneath. Gini's knuckles were bruised and scraped.

"You poor child, you took a real beating. But I don't want you to worry. You're in a good, safe place now. Nothing will hurt you here."

"Do you need any help?" Lisa said coming into the room. "I've been watching you on the monitor doing your beauty program."

She looked at Lisa. "She's so young. I hate it when they are so young and have such horrible things happen to them. She probably had a wonderful life. Now, look at her. It's a real shame."

Debbie stood up after finishing Gini's last nail. "I'm going to bathe her, and then you can help me change the sheets."

"Okay."

If anything ever happened to Lisa and she needed medical care, she wanted Debbie to be the one. She was the best nurse Lisa had ever known. Not only was she very knowledgeable about medical and nursing procedures, she was also kind and gentle and caring to each of her patients.

Suddenly, there was a noise from one of the machines and a gurgling sound. Debbie looked at Lisa. "She's trying to breathe on her own."

Debbie gently put her hand on the side of Gini's head. "Oh, baby, you fight, that's right, you fight for your life."

Robert took the business card Ric had given him for Catherine and laid it on his desk.

"Ms. White, I'm Dr. Robert Young from New Haven Medical Center outside of Boston."

"Dr. Young. Are you one of Virginia Anderson's doctors?"

"Yes."

"Good, let me get my information." There was silence for a few minutes. "I'm looking at Virginia's list of the doctors she's working with in Massachusetts, and I don't seem to find your name. Can you tell me more about your contact with her?"

"Ms. White, I'm afraid I'm calling with some bad news."

"Oh," she said with concern.

"I understand Mrs. Legotti works for you."

"Yes..." she said slowly. "Mrs. Legotti!"

"Virginia was critically injured in an accident yesterday. She sustained a serious brain trauma. I need to know what insurance company you use."

"Gini was hurt?"

"Yes, ma'am. She was hit by a motorcycle and, as a result, has severe brain damage."

"A motorcycle! Gini was on a motorcycle? I'm sorry, sir, but Gini's pregnant. I doubt that she was riding on a motorcycle." Catherine was getting perturbed and wondering if this was a crank call. "Who did you say you were again?"

"My name is Dr. Robert Young," he said slowly. "I am a neurosurgeon at New Haven Medical Center. Mrs. Legotti was brought here by ambulance yesterday after she was hit by the motorcycle. She was standing on a street corner. I know this is hard to hear, but I promise you this is the truth. Mrs. Legotti has severe brain damage. I need to know the name of her insurance company."

There was dead silence for a few minutes. Robert didn't say anything so Catherine could absorb what he'd just told her.

"That's why I can't get a hold of her," she said in a quiet voice. "Does Ric Santini know?"

"Yes. He has been with her here at the hospital, as well as her husband, Franco Legotti."

"Let me get you the information," she said with a shaky voice. "Is she going to be okay?"

"It's too early to tell."

"How about the babies?"

"I'm sorry, Ms. White, they didn't make it."

"No," Catherine said again in a quiet voice, "I'm so sorry for both Ric and Gini. I can't believe it. I just can't believe it."

After Robert gathered all the insurance information and was done talking to Catherine, he called Cindy.

"Oh, that's just terrible," Cindy said. "I know Franco is devastated. They have wanted to have children for so long. Please give my love to both Gini and Franco. I'm sorry I won't be able to fly out and visit her. My husband had a massive heart attack and is in very poor health. And, well… it's just difficult for me to get away."

Doctor Young could tell Cindy was tired and was sure she didn't grasp the full magnitude of Gini's injury. Perhaps it was just as well if she was dealing with a gravely ill husband. She certainly had more than she could handle already.

"Thank you for calling me, Doctor. I'll try to call Gini."

"She's not able to talk, but I'll tell both of them of your love and concern."

Franco went back to the hotel and gathered his things. He had called his office assistant and instructed him to go to his apartment and pack a bag for Franco. He just needed the essentials for now until he went back to New York or could buy what he needed when he had time. He asked him to have the bag couriered to the hotel. It had arrived while he was at the mortuary.

Ric arrived at the ICU a little after noon.

"Mr. Santini," Lisa said.

"Is it okay for me to see Gini now?"

"Yes, Debbie's just finishing up Mrs. Legotti's bath."

Ric signed in and walked toward Gini's room. Debbie closed a linen bag and walked to the door; it opened. She looked at him and then her watch.

"It's in the p.m.," he said, smiling.

Debbie stepped to the side so he could come in the room. She walked back to the station.

"Can you believe he is here for the second time?" Lisa said. "And Mr. Legotti, her husband, not once."

"I don't know; he just rubs me the wrong way. I think it's because he's too nice, like a fake nice or something. I don't know." Debbie shook her head and took the linens to the laundry drop.

"Sweet Gins." He pulled the rolling stool over to the bed then kissed her hand. He could see her nails were cleaned and shaped.

"Gini, we had a daughter. Jennifer was our daughter. It's a crazy story, but your children had different fathers. It doesn't matter, though; Jason will always be my son just like Jennifer was mine. I love you." He sighed and kept rubbing her hand on his lips.

The door swished, and Debbie walked back in the room. She took the electronic tablet and started typing in information.

"Mrs. Legotti tried—" She stopped abruptly, remembering she couldn't discuss Gini's condition with anyone except Franco.

"What?" He looked up at her. "What was that, Ms. Pierce?"

"Please, call me Debbie. I think I'm going to see a lot of you. So please call me Debbie."

"Okay," he said in a pleasant tone. "And me, Ric. You're right you are going to see a lot of me. As much as you will let me be with Gini, I'll be with her. I love her very much. I want to be by her side all the time. We will get through this together. We will." His voice was more stern and serious.

He looked at Debbie with concern when one of the machines made a noise.

She smiled. "Mr. Santini, I mean, Ric, that's Mrs. Legotti fighting for her life."

"Is that noise a good thing?"

"I'm sorry I can't talk to you about her condition, but that's a good noise."

Ric took a deep breath. "Debbie, I think you will get a better response out of her if you address her as Gini. She has never gone by Mrs. Legotti. She never took her husband's name professionally. I don't know that she would even respond if you called her by that name. Call her Gini."

"Good to know. I'll note that on her chart."

At twelve-thirty, Dr. Young arrived at the ICU. "Has Mr. Legotti been here?"

"No, sir, I would have paged you."

Ric looked up and saw the doctor, and then looked at his watch. He'd been there longer than fifteen minutes. He kissed Gini on the cheek and left the room.

"See you in the morning," Ric said as he left.

"I think they should give Mr. Legotti's time to Mr. Santini," Lisa said. "He isn't using his time to see her."

Dr. Young walked into Gini's room. He picked up her chart and started reading what Debbie had written.

She entered the room. "What do you think? Our girl here is trying to breathe."

"Are you sure?"

"Yes, she's done it twice while I was in the room."

The doctor went to Gini and examined her. The machine made the noise. He looked up at a screen and then at Debbie. "Well, I guess I'll put off the tracheotomy for a while." He was visually pleased. "We'll see if she can do it on her own. We just might have a miracle patient here."

He put his hand on Gini's arm and gently rubbed it. "Prove me wrong. I love being proved wrong."

Franco pulled the car up out of the hotel parking. He was looking right at the hospital. He should visit Gini, he thought, but he knew Dr. Young was probably going to press him to end her life. He just couldn't face that decision. First, he would get settled back in the condo and then he would visit. Yes, that's what he'd do. And he would return Dr. Young's calls.

Ric left the ICU floor. Now, what was he going to do? He didn't want to go home and sit alone. He would have to think too much about what had happened. He leaned up against the wall.

Dr. Nelson walked up beside him. "Are you okay?"

"I can't see Gini again until tomorrow. I wish I could be with her all the time."

"I think Dr. Young is being cautious since you and Franco could cause trouble, both of you wanting to be with her. His first concern is his patient. I know you are both civil men, but he doesn't know you."

"I appreciate his concern, but I just want to be with her. Linda, we're having a memorial service for the babies tomorrow at eleven in the chapel downstairs. I would like for you to come. I know Gini thinks a lot of you, as do I, and she would want you to be there."

"Thank you for letting me know. I'll plan to attend. Are you doing okay, really?"

"Yes, I am. I just don't know what to do with myself."

She patted him on the shoulder.

Carol was surprised when she saw Ric walk in the door. "What are you doing here?"

"I have to work. I just can't sit and let my mind think about things, all the things I could have done to prevent this."

She hugged him. "I'm so sorry, Ric. Tell me what I can do to help you."

"Are the drawings here?"

"They're on your desk."

Franco pulled into the parking space next to Gini's car. He walked in the front door and set down his suitcase and computer bag. There were two large boxes leaning up against the wall in the dining room. He went over and looked at them, two cribs. Howard must have brought them up when they were delivered.

Gini had done a lot to the condo. It looked nice. He remembered when they found the walk-in bar at the flea market in Salem. She was so excited, he couldn't say no. She had it refinished, and it looked good in the living room, just like she said it would. He walked over behind the counter and found a bottle of whiskey. He didn't get a glass, just opened the bottle and started drinking.

Carrying the bottle, he went over to the two large windows and looked at the view. He took a swig, then moved over to the fireplace, opened the cloisonné box; the green stone ring lay on the white satin cloth. He shook his head and then walked to the back of the house. His breath was taken away when he walked into the small bedroom Gini had made into the nursery. The walls were painted and decorated. He looked at the two hot-air balloons with the babies' names on them. He leaned up against the wall, laying his forehead on his arm. He took another swig. He wandered toward the master bedroom. He stood in the doorway for a long time. Another man had slept in his bed. Another man had made love with his wife. He tipped the bottle up and drank two long drinks. His best friend in the world had stolen his wife.

He stayed in the doorway and started to cry. What had he done? This was all his doing. He hadn't been a good husband. He had gotten too involved in his work and forgot the most precious thing in his life, his loving and beautiful wife—the only woman he had ever loved. Their sexual bond was extraordinary and passionate. He could never love another. Now he had to decide whether she should live as a helpless invalid or be put out of her misery and allowed to die. Whatever his decision, he had lost his wife forever. He took another long drink, went into the room and fell onto the bed.

Carol stuck her head in Ric's office. "I'm leaving unless you want me to stay."

"No, go."

She walked farther in. "I'll get you some dinner."

"That's not necessary," he said getting up. "I'm going to go home. I'll eat there. Carol, there's a memorial service at the hospital chapel tomorrow at eleven o'clock if you would like to come."

She hugged him. "I'll be there. Please, try and get some sleep."

"I will. Thanks, for being here."

She hugged him tight and then left.

The next morning Ric was up early again. He constantly looked at his watch, not wanting to be too early to the hospital. He didn't want to upset Debbie. Somehow, he felt he annoyed her. At six-thirty he headed to New Haven. He peered through the gift shop windows when he got into the lobby; it was still too early to go up. He would get flowers to take to the memorial service, later. At seven twenty-five he walked up to the ICU.

Debbie was a bit sad that Gini hadn't tried to breathe on her own since the day before. But she had to smile to herself when she saw him coming down the hall.

He signed in. "Is this a good time?" he asked Lisa.

"Yes, Dr. Young's almost done."

Ric waited for the doctor. Robert saw him and motioned for him to come to the room.

"How's she doing?"

"She's hanging in there."

"Dr. Young, there's a small memorial service in the chapel at eleven o'clock for the babies. I'd like you to come."

"I'll try to make it."

Franco had fallen asleep fully clothed. When he woke up, the sun was shining brightly through the window.

He arrived at the hospital about ten o'clock. Debbie was just collecting her things to go to a consultation with Robert and Dr. John Meyer when Franco walked up to the desk and signed in.

"Mr. Legotti."

"I'm here to see my wife." His speech was slow with no expression.

"Of course. Dr. Young wanted us to let him know when you got here, but he's in a meeting."

Lisa came out of the back room. When she saw Franco had signed in, she immediately paged Robert.

Debbie took Franco. Once again, he got no farther than the end of the bed. He gripped the footrail tightly and closed his eyes.

"Would you like to sit next to her?"

He shook his head, then he turned around and walked out of the room. He went back to the nurse's station and signed out.

Lisa looked at the sign-in sheet. "Wow, he stayed a whole three minutes!"

"See you later after my meeting," Debbie said.

Franco stopped farther down the hall. Why was he unable to hide his emotions? He'd always been able to hold them tight. Being emotional showed weakness—that wasn't who Franco Legotti was. He was always strong. He hated being weak. He hated being out of control.

Ric went into the gift shop after eating breakfast and bought a yellow rose to represent Gini and two white ones for the babies. The woman in the shop tied a pink bow around one and a blue one around the other. He took them into the chapel. Reverend Gilbert was already there.

"I got these. The yellow one is for their mother. Yellow roses are her favorite."

"We'll put them on this table." The reverend moved some things around and placed the flowers next to a large Bible.

Franco walked up behind them. He had a framed picture of Gini. Ric had seen it on the hall table in the condo. He always loved that picture of her. Franco took two envelopes out of his jacket pocket and handed one to Ric. Franco opened the other one and took out a picture of each of the babies, which the hospital had taken before they died.

The reverend took all three pictures. "We'll display them all here." He rearranged the Bible and the roses.

Ric tried to hold back the tears, but he couldn't. His breath hopped as he looked at the babies' pictures. Jennifer looked just as he had remembered her in the pink cap and blanket. He could see the small creases in her cheeks.

Franco put his hand on Ric's shoulder and gave a good squeeze. "They're in a good place."

After a few minutes, the two men sat in the front pew next to each other. Ric felt a gentle rubbing on his upper back. When he turned around, he saw that it was Carol. Everyone from his office was there. He got up and gave each a hug. It broke Carol's heart to see him crying. He was always so cheerful, happy and funny. Now, he was broken inside.

When Ric got done greeting everyone, he saw Dr. Young and Dr. Nelson walk into the chapel together and sit behind Franco.

Reverend Gilbert gave a beautiful service for the two children who had died much too young. Afterward, Ric hugged and thanked all his staff for coming and for all their support. He also thanked the doctors and the reverend.

Franco went up to the table and picked up the pictures. "Here, Ric." He handed Gini's framed picture to him. "You can have this."

"Are you sure?"

"Yes, I have one that I always carry in my wallet." Franco lowered his head.

Ric took the three roses and walked up to the ICU. "Do you have a vase I can put these in?" he asked Debbie.

"Flowers aren't allowed in the rooms in this unit," Debbie said shortly.

Lisa walked up next to her and rubbed her arm. "How about we put them here on the counter." She smiled at Debbie. "We can put them so Gini can see them when she opens her eyes."

She took the roses and went to the back room for a vase.

"Thank you, Lisa," Ric said still standing at the station. "Gini loves yellow roses." He laid her picture on the sign-in counter.

"So that's what she looks like," Debbie said slowly, picking up the picture.

"Isn't she beautiful?"

"Very. Classy."

"She's intelligent and can be really sassy. You'll see."

"I'm sorry this has happened to you, Mr. Santini; to her and the babies, to all of you. Sorry."

She set the picture down and went into the small room. Lisa looked at Debbie as she came out. Ric had somehow moved her; she saw the emotion in Debbie's face.

Ric was thankful he still had the love of his life. They would be together every day.

As Dr. Young was leaving the service, he told Franco they needed to talk.

Franco sat in the chapel with his head bowed for a long time. How could he decide whether she lived or died? She was his wife, and he loved her more than anything in the world. He knew he hadn't been attentive to her the last year or so. His work had been so rewarding, and he got way too caught up in it. He thought she would be proud of him for all the good he was doing, especially for the children of the world who needed a better life. And now he was looking at nothing to live for. He had had a son he would never know, and the woman he so dearly loved was just hanging on—machines keeping her alive.

He thought about her lying on the bed with all the tubes and wires, her face so swollen he didn't even recognize her. He didn't want her to live like that.

What kind of life would that be? She was always so full of spirit. The memories flooded his head:

He unzipped the bag, took out the green stone ring, and placed it on Gini's left ring finger.
Her blue eyes were gleaming. "What an unusual ring. I will cherish this always." She leaned over and gave him a passionate kiss.

The memory of the moment was so vivid. She loved the ring he had had specially made for her, and he loved her response—the kiss, as if no one in the world meant more to her than he did. The kiss that he had so loved then and would always miss. He put his hand on his mouth, still feeling her sweet lips on his; he'd never forget them. Putting his head down, he stood to leave. Robert was standing in the back waiting for him.

Franco slowly walked to the door. He had to let her go.

Debbie was putting supplies away next to the bed when the machine made the noise. She picked up Gini's small curled-up hand. "You fight, baby. I'm here to help you. Fight for your life."

Be sure to read *Life Changer - Forever Friends: Book 2* to find out how the friends cope with the tragedy that took the ones they loved.

About the Author

My name is Karleen Staible. I am a child of the 50s and 60s—1950s, that is; I'm not coming to you from the future—Sci-fi is not my genre. I write contemporary women with some romance in the mix. Life was simple in my younger days: no childproof anything, we never locked our doors, and my dad left the keys in the car so he could quickly respond to a fire with the Arvada Volunteer Fire Department.

Our street was a dead-end dirt road with seven houses. We played outside as long as our parents allowed us, and objected when we heard the call to go home at night. In the open fields, we played baseball or hide-and-go-seek throughout the neighborhood. And yes, we did drink out of the garden hose.

I lived in that same house from the age of two until twenty when I married my husband, Fred. After he graduated from college, we didn't stay in the Denver area for very long.

He worked in the oil and gas business as an engineer. A few years after we married, he got involved with Liquefied Natural Gas (LNG) and we were off to Algeria. And there started our expat lives. We lived and traveled all over the world, met many interesting people, and made friends who became family.

I learned to use the computer on one of our assignments overseas. I'm fascinated with the many things you can do on a computer, constantly learning new programs and techniques. I especially like doing special digital art, from video editing to designing my own book covers.

I can honestly say I'm in need of nothing. I have had a terrific life, have two wonderful kids, and great in-law kids who are happy and successful in their careers. Our two granddaughters are definitely the light of our lives. It has been a fabulous life.

My stories reflect situations and people I have met over the years. The characters are personalities of those people I encountered along the way, and the places are cities or towns I found interesting. My childhood upbringing and my heroes are also written into my stories. Each story has a social message: how women, or people in general, can empower themselves to deal with difficult situations.

My goal is not to make millions of dollars, or make my name famous; I just want to write books that everyone will enjoy reading and will want to read more of.

Thank you for reading *Green Stone Ring* from the *Forever Friends* series. If you'd like to read more background stories, go to http://kssnovels.com/adventure-in-writing/ and check out my blog.

I'd appreciate it if you would make a comment on Amazon about what you thought of the novel. Check out the link below.
http://www.amazon.com/dp/B0772G27LJ

Made in the USA
Monee, IL
27 February 2023